TRYSMOON

Book One: Ascension

By
Brian K. Fuller

TRYSMOON
BOOK ONE: ASCENSION

Edited by Jessica Robbins JessiLynRobbins@gmail.com

briankfullerbooks.com
facebook.com/briankfullerbooks

ISBN-13: 978-1502732019
ISBN-10: 1502732017

For Alexandrea and Charlie, my first fans.
Thank you for being a part of my real world
and enjoying my fakes ones.

PROLOGUE

Knight Marshall Voss Ethelion stood on a sandy embankment with his back to the sea. An evening breeze rushed past him, cooling the sweat on the back of his neck. The ocean's gusty breath strengthened and headed inland, dissipating the fog of war just enough for him to see the moon Trys, now but a sliver, hanging low above the tree line with its companion moons, Myn and Duam.

Voss kept one hand on his sword and with the other fingered the three training stones around his neck, stones that had made him a warrior without peer—a warrior with a sacred purpose that had failed. The Church of the One had commissioned him to find and protect the man and woman prophesied to bring god back into the world, but it was too late. The prophecy had failed and the moon was eclipsing, signaling the end of all things. Death had come for the world, and he and his weary men waited for it now.

The humid wind carried the reek of the corpse-strewn battlefield into the dense forest before them. They had sheltered in the trees and held strong against their enemies for nearly a month. But as every fortress and hiding place had before, their defenses did not last. For two weeks, the enemy had driven the Knight Marshall's army through the dense wood until at last there was no land left between advancing death and the restless sea.

Refugees from the countless cities they had passed through on their retreat lined the beach behind them, huddling around fires and comforting each other with empty words. Voss glanced back at his wife, who cradled his five-year-old son in her lap. He had said some of those empty words himself. Months of brutal defeat had extinguished their hope for survival. Voss and his men no longer fought for the cause of victory or under the banner of any country; they fought to visit what revenge they could upon a relentless foe and to die before witnessing the monsters tear through their ranks and kill those they loved.

They had held the beachhead for two days, and if they survived the inevitable evening assault, it would be three.

"I think I hear them," whispered Captain York standing to his left.

Voss squinted and attuned his ears. Uyumaak were hard to see in the daytime, much more so in their hiding places in the creaking, shadowy boles at evening. Voss most often heard the enemy advance before he saw them.

His soldiers shifted nervously, hands on weapons, standing as quietly as men in armor can manage to catch any sign of attackers they could feel but not yet see. To a man they were dirty and bloody, armor dented and mismatched, veterans all. Voss commanded them at their request. Few of the senior officers of Rhugoth had survived the slaughter as the armies of men scattered in every direction, ragged and routed.

The hissing of arrows filled the air.

"Get behind the embankment!" he yelled, but too late to spare at least fifteen men dropped by the keen eyes and heavy longbows of Uyumaak Archers just out of sight in the foliage. Voss's men had killed most of the enemy's archers a week ago in daytime raids just for the purpose of preventing such attacks. Since then only the lanky, athletic

Warriors and squat Bashers had faced them in their daily skirmishes.

The return of the Archers implied a grim reality: the armies of Mikkik were being reinforced. Voss considered the Uyumaak Archers the deadliest of that race's kind. Their master bred them to pull bows no human or elf could draw, and the long, heavy arrows ripped through horses and thick armor with savage efficiency. The Knight Marshall had watched Archers dismantle more than one cavalry charge to a horse before the knights who rode them could advance halfway across the field.

Arrows streaked close overhead to keep them trapped behind the embankment, and as he expected, the sound of thrashing branches rose above the din as the Uyumaak Bashers and Warriors raced out of their cover in the woods. Voss held his hand up, waiting for the rumble of footfalls to approach more closely; he didn't want to order his men over the embankment too prematurely to be butchered by the Archers. Nor did he want to move too late and lose the advantage of their crude fortification. But as abruptly as the charge from the forest had started, it stopped. No arrows. No charging feet.

What trick is this? Perhaps they wish to lure us over to be meat for the bows.

The Uyumaak thumped their chests or the nearby trees in their strange, staccato language. Bewildered, Voss ascended the embankment and peeked over. To a creature, the Uyumaak stood in the clearing between the wood and the beach. Their backs were turned toward their human enemies, and their multi-eyed faces watched the sky. They slapped themselves furiously, heedless of the men behind them. Voss saw an advantage. If they could fall upon them while they were distracted, they might just survive the day. He turned toward his men to order an advance, but they, too, had cast their eyes to the heavens.

Voss followed their gaze to the sky. The moon Trys had

completely eclipsed, the sign given for the end of the world. A deep rumbling and shaking threw Voss backward down the embankment. The ground heaved, and the screaming of his people joined the thumping of their enemies until a deep rending sound drowned out every other noise. The earth on the other side of the embankment tore away, hurtling into space. Blue sky faded, instantly dissolving to reveal a mass of swirling stars and enormous shards of their shattering world careening through the void.

Voss struggled to his hands and knees, trying to crawl to the beach and his family, only to be thrown down by an overpowering vertigo. He could not get his bearing to stand, stomach roiling. The training stones had not prepared him for this.

As the noise of the ground wrenching apart ceased, the moans of pain, cries of terror, and fits of retching swelled into a cacophony of agony. Voss could find strength to do nothing but stare into the ever-changing sky, the stars and shards of the world dancing as if to celebrate the end. Was this his fault? Had he not been diligent enough in his search for the holy mother and father?

Voss waited for death, but the shuddering beneath him ceased. The stars and shards stopped wheeling, and the sun, which had entirely disappeared, rose in the west, soaring backward across the sky. It slowed its course and stopped, resuming its slow pace back toward the western horizon. At once the vertigo ceased.

Voss rose carefully to his feet, his soldiers and their families struggling to stand as they stared around in wonder. Legs churning, he ascended the earthen embankment and stopped in awe at its summit. The Uyumaak, the forest, and the land they defended for three days had vanished. At his feet a chasm dropped an impossible distance into an inky black space filled with stars and chunks of land—some mere rocks, others as large as a country—floating in a loose ring around the sun.

Most of the shards were too far away to be glimpsed in detail, a distant caravan of a broken world. Voss's wife and son came to his side and he pulled them close. The world had ended, but they were not dead and did not sleep. The moon Trys, the seat of their dead God's power, had eclipsed, but something had robbed the anticipated destruction of its total victory.

Those that could brave the vertigo came to the edge, wonder and hope beaming from their dirty faces. The Uyumaak had fallen into the void. Voss's heart pounded, free of the constricting dread that had followed him for months. If he and his army had survived the shattering, then surely others had as well.

His son tugged at his chain mail shirt, eyes wide with wonder. "Can we go home now, father?"

Voss tousled his hair. Their home was floating around in the shards out there somewhere. "We'll see," Voss said.

He tucked the training stones under his shirt. The army would rest for now, but his mission was not over. The world had not ended. The holy mother and father might still be out there or yet to be born. If he couldn't find them before death found him, he would pass the stones to another.

Then, one day, maybe the world would be whole again.

CHAPTER 1 - WHITE STICKS

"I wish you wouldn't play that abominable game, Gen! You can ill afford to break a finger so near the end of your apprenticeship."

Gen smiled at Rafael. His old master's wispy gray hair and skeletal face always evoked a strange mixture of humor and pity in whomever he addressed, but Gen's long association with Rafael lent him an immunity to the bard's pathetic entreaties.

"Have you looked outside? Do you really think I'm going to stay. . ."

"Not to mention," Rafael interrupted, raising his voice, "the misfortune of losing an eye or getting a huge scar on your forehead! I've not known one successful bard with a scarred face or missing body parts. Save what good looks you have, lad! You certainly don't have a surplus to squander on a silly game!"

Gen grabbed his cloak, hurrying to get in as much recreation as possible. Autumn in Tell rarely offered a day as beautiful as the one that beckoned to him now. While Gen knew that Rafael, as his master, had every right to order him to stay indoors, he rarely chose to issue such demands. Gen's own desire to excel at his craft and the affection that existed between him and Rafael obviated any need for rigid strictures. However, even if the old bard did order him to stay inside, Gen thought he might just disobey.

Harvest Festival had ended the day before, and no one had worked harder than he and Rafael. Magistrate Showles demanded they perform and sing so much during the week-long celebration that afterward Gen genuinely felt sick of playing music and telling stories, an exhaustion he had never felt during all his years of apprenticeship.

What he needed now was mindless, brutal fun with young men of half his intelligence, one-fourth his breeding, and one-tenth his vocabulary. The sons of woodsmen provided just such entertainment. While they could certainly break his arms and knees with ease, he could make them look like idiots with equal facility. Half the time they didn't even know they were being sported with.

But Gen did possess two redeeming qualities to aid him in physical games. He was tall and he was fast. Most peasants in the Kingdom of Tolnor were short, stocky, and of a dark complexion. Gen, in contrast, stood a head taller than most of his peers in Tell and had a fair complexion, light-brown hair, and green eyes. Rafael, who was himself from Rhugoth, told Gen that he looked Rhugothian, though in the larger cities of Tolnor there was a greater variety of peoples than were found in the country dukedom of Duke Norshwal of Graytower.

Gen opened the door of the two-story farmhouse that he and his master occupied alone in what the townspeople called "a shameful waste of a big house." Rafael, a freeman, had bought the seven room home from Baron Forthrickeshire and had proceeded to fill it with belongings acquired from a lifetime of travel, brought in on wagons from several origins. Gen dared only once to ask Rafael why a bard of his obvious attainments and property chose a remote town to live out the remainder of his days. The hurt look in Rafael's eyes and his terse reply that it was "none of his concern" held enough emotion to persuade Gen to abandon the subject forever.

With a wave to his frowning master, Gen bounded down the porch's three steps and into the brisk afternoon wind. High clouds moved quickly over the tall trees of the Alewine Forest to the west, hinting at a change in the weather that, thankfully, had remained clear and sunny during the Harvest Festival.

As he walked, Gen tied his shoulder-length brown hair into a ponytail to keep it from interfering with his vision during the game. Rafael's concern for his pupil's health was not unfounded. While White Sticks most often resulted in only minor bruises, Edmunson, the town farrier, lost an eye to the game in his youth, and Gen's friend Gant broke his forearm, an injury that threatened to end his apprenticeship as a woodsman.

While Gant's wound did heal satisfactorily thanks to the ministrations of Pureman Millershim, Gant's master strictly forbade him from playing the game ever again. Of course, the prohibition hadn't stopped Gant at all, and his master knew it. If anything, Gant treated the game with even more reckless abandon than before, and for the last two years whatever Ministrants presided over the game of White Sticks blessed Gant plentifully. Gen thought Gant's run at White Sticks legendary, but he suspected that his friend excelled at it because he had such a high incentive not to get hurt. His master would undoubtedly punish him harshly for another injury, and Gant loved his master's daughter, Yuerile.

Gant waited for Gen where the Green Road intersected with the small lane that ran into the forest. Gant was less stout than his peers, while still possessing the powerful frame, and his brown hair had just a hint of red in it. He stood with his thumbs hooked under the frayed rope that held his pants up, face happy at the sight of his friend and

11

with the anticipation of an afternoon of sport. The country boy's smile jutted up and down like a tortured mountain range, lending his countenance a ridiculousness and innocence.

"Gant," Gen greeted cheerily. "A fine day for White Sticks!"

"Yep," he replied, falling in beside Gen, "though I 'spect the wind'll play tough with the throws. You ready for the Showles' boys?"

"You arranged a game with Jakes and Howen? How did you manage that? Those two won't come within forty feet of a peasant. I believe they think peasantry is a disease they might catch. Jakes actually puts a cloth over his mouth when he has to talk to me."

"You might be the clever one an' all, Gen," Gant answered, "but I know how to place a barb under a saddle. After we won 'gainst Derk and Gover, I let it drop in places I knew it would get 'round that you said it was just as well that Jakes didn't never play 'gainst us since he throws like a girl."

"Wonderful," Gen said. "I don't think they hate me quite enough yet."

"I always like t' help when I can. But not to fear. There'll be plenty others about. I'd wager we'll only have a few rounds to knock 'em around a bit and then we'll let some of the other boys peck at 'em. Just thank Eldaloth that Hubert ain't here. Dumb as an ox, but I hear he can throw like a Gagon."

Hubert Showles, the eldest son of Magistrate Showles, was a lumbering brute of a young man who, despite his violent temper and absurd behavior, was his father's favorite and spoiled accordingly. By some extremely fortuitous arrangement of his father's, the boy managed to secure a position in Duke Norshwal's contingent of foot soldiers. Everyone, his own brothers included, celebrated his departure.

"I bet yer hopin' for a certain young lady to see yer performance today."

"It is not necessary for you to bring her up every time we get together, Gant," Gen returned glumly.

"Oh, c'mon, Gen. You like her. Yer about the marryin' age. Fess up!"

"Of course I like her, you dolt. Doesn't everybody? I suspect you do too, despite whatever feelings you have for Yuerile."

"'Nah," Gant rebutted as he picked at the callouses of his palms. "Regina's too uppity fer me. You two were made fer each other. You're both as pale as birch and use words no mouth within fifty leagues of here has any right sayin'."

"She's a freeman, Gant. It's going to take me years to earn enough money to purchase that status."

"How long'd it take Rafael?"

"Ten years. But he was better than I am and played in Rhugoth where it is more lucrative."

Gen wasn't sure if Gant knew what *lucrative* meant, but a gathering of young folk ahead of them drew their attention back to the impending game. Gen eyed the crowd expectantly, disappointed to find Regina missing but surprised at the number of people there, nonetheless. Jakes and Howen obviously invited everyone they could find. They stood in the center of the throng, a large leather bag propped up against Jakes's leg.

Jakes and Howen, stoop-shouldered twins, appeared to be putting on a little girth. Like their father, shockingly red hair and small eyes punctuated bland, puffy faces. Jakes and Howen had every one of their older brother's deficiencies of character but in addition possessed a sullen meanness cultivated from living with a boorish favorite their entire lives. In the realm of stupidity and brash behavior, they were crowned kings. Gen avoided them as often as possible, though he did take some delight in abusing them to their faces without them knowing it.

"Jakes, Howen, or Howen, Jakes," Gen greeted brightly, "I'm not sure that bag is big enough to hold all your ignominy." From the blank stares all around, Gen knew he was alone in understanding the sentence.

"It is too big enough," Jakes returned crossly. "We didn't want to play with your stupid sticks, so we got our pa to get us a real set with real Uyumaak bones!"

Jakes turned the bag over dramatically and the White Sticks fell out, everyone pressing in for a better look. By the sound of the sticks knocking against one another, Gen knew immediately the set was not fashioned from bones at all, but from some hardwood carved to look like them. Sets of real Uyumaak bones were very hard to come by and extremely expensive. Uyumaak, the principal soldiers sent against the nations during the Mikkikian wars, were considered all but extinct by most.

The game of White Sticks was born from the mind of idle soldiers who had invented it during lulls between battles using the bleached leg and arm bones of Uyumaak Hunters. Over time, the sport spread through the ranks of the human kingdoms, growing in popularity to the point where the rules solidified and soldiers formed leagues within military legions.

The game involved forming a square—called the Box— out of the long leg bones. At a distance of twenty paces from opposite sides of the Box, one arm bone rested in a cradle formed by two sticks pounded into the ground. Each team of two consisted of a Thrower and Goaler, each holding an Uyumaak arm bone.

The Throwers started inside the Box and on "go" ran toward the opposing team's cradled bone. The object was to bat the opposing team's bone as far away from the Box as possible. After batting the opposing team's bone, the Throwers had to run, circling around to retrieve his team's bone, directed by the Goaler.

Once retrieved, the Thrower could score points by

throwing or placing the bone in the Box first and by getting it all the way inside the Box. The Goalers's job was to distract the other team by chucking his bone at them. He could also use a precise throw to knock their already placed bone from the Box.

As he helped set the game up, Gen decided that despite the bogus bones, the Showles's set of pieces outclassed anything they had played with before. The white bones felt smooth and heavy, far superior for throwing in the wind than the lighter, roughly carved pine sticks they normally used. Anyone hit with one of these bones would have a nice bruise to show for it, and the crowd backed away to a safe distance as Gant, Gen, and the Showles brothers finished setting up.

"We've played 'gainst nobles," Jakes bragged, holding a cloth over his mouth as he came close to Gen and Gant.

"Did you win any of the games?" Gen asked. Jakes paused, taken aback by the unexpected question.

"Of course we did!" he protested with enough heat to reveal the obvious lie.

"Congratulations," Gen replied sarcastically. "You should have no problem with a couple peasant louts, should you? I mean, it's hardly fair that we malnourished, dirty peasants should have to face such well-fed, experienced players like yourselves. It bespeaks a horrible inequity that begs attention and redress, and I fully anticipate that if you were Magistrate someday that you would take upon you the manly yoke of righting these injustices."

Jakes squinted, having gotten lost somewhere around "bespeaks."

"Don't listen to 'im, Jakes," Howen growled, grabbing his brother by the arm. "He talks too much. Let's play!"

Gen started as the Thrower, lining up in the Box with Howen. Gen faced Jakes, and on "go" ran forward and knocked the Showles's bone high in the air and to the left before running back toward Gant, who signaled where theirs had fallen in the grass.

Gen retrieved it quickly, waiting to see if Jakes would throw at him, but when he turned around to face the Box, Jakes was yelling at Howen and telling him he had no idea where the bone had gone. Gen, realizing he had all the time he wanted, walked casually back toward the Box at a leisurely pace, Jakes watching him carefully, bone cocked back and ready to throw.

Gen braced himself for Jakes's throw, and when it came, he turned and looked at Gant in shock—Jakes really did throw like a girl. The bone barely went ten feet before skidding to a halt in the dirt. Snickering erupted in the crowd. Gen, having the luxury of placing the bone in the Box rather than throwing it in, situated it in the exact center to get two points for being the first to put it in and three for getting it inside the Box without touching any of the sides.

When he looked up, Howen was still bent over rooting in the grass, butt-crack grinning above the rim of his pants. Not wanting to waste an opportunity, Gant reared back and threw his bone as hard as he could, hitting Howen's ample backside with impressive accuracy. Howen got a bruised tail bone and a face full of dirt and grass.

In the end, Gen helped Howen find the bone. Since Gen had already scored, the rules forced Howen to make his throw from the spot where the bone had fallen. He missed horribly.

The first round robbed the hulking brothers of their bravado, and by the fourth, Gen and Gant succeeded in stripping them of their dignity, self-respect, and whatever maturity they could lay claim to. They whined, threw fits, and hurled poorly supported accusations of cheating, demanding Gen and Gant switch sides of the Box with them twice.

But despite the twins' deep bruises and the mocking of

the crowd, they demanded one last game to decide everything once and for all and that the score (which had risen to eighteen to six in favor of Gen and Gant) be put at zero. Gen and Gant agreed and met to discuss their strategy.

"Can't take no glory in this," Gant grumbled, spitting on the ground. "Never played 'gainst poorer. Played against nobles! Faugh! Bloody liars."

"It might not have been a lie, though. 'Nobles' is probably the surname of a couple blind, lame boys. Jed and Davy Nobles, maybe?"

"Right," Gant smiled. "You wanna do anything special?"

"Do we need to do anything special? Perhaps play blindfolded and throw with our off-hands?"

"Done that last round," Gant said. "The off-hand thing, I mean."

"Really? I didn't notice. Well, if we win, they'll say we cheated and we'll be on the run from a beating. Since I'll be the Goaler, I'll save my throw so I can use it to help us get away, if need be."

Gen placed the arm bone in the saddles of the two sticks and waited as Gant and Jakes lined up in the Box. On "go" Jakes tripped Gant as he started to run, sending him hard to the ground. Gant grimaced and struggled to his feet holding his left arm, which lay limp at his side. Jakes sprinted toward Gen, batting the stick and turning back. If Jakes could get back to the Box before Gant hit their bone, they would win. Gant stumbled forward and hit the bone in time, but it flew low and landed only a few feet away from a grinning Jakes.

Still nursing his arm, Gant ran slowly to find the bone that Jakes had hit. While Gant struggled, Jakes dashed straight to where the bone Gant had hit lay, glee plastered to his face. Gen knew he had one chance to keep Jakes from scoring. Jakes would have plenty of time to get to the Box and put his team's bone in before Gant retrieved theirs. Gen had to slow Jakes down. Gen signaled to Gant, indicating where their bone had fallen and then turned and threw his bone at Jakes just as the boy was standing up from picking up his team's bone from the ground.

As soon as he released the bone, Gen wished he could have pulled it back. Time slowed to a crawl. Gen could pick out each anxious pair of eyes in the crowd as they followed the bone, tumbling end over end, toward its target.

Jakes stood, planted his feet, and turned back toward the Box just as Gen's heavy wooden bone arrived. The rounded end smashed into Jakes's mouth with a sickening crunch, sending his teeth flying out of his head in a shower of red and white. Jakes's head snapped back and he landed flat on his back, dust rising around him from the heavy impact. Everyone winced, and the girls in the crowd gasped, bringing hands to open mouths.

Howen abandoned his post to check on his writhing brother. Gen was glad Jakes was writhing and not dead. A pale Gant jogged slowly to the Box and dropped the bone in. Gen met him there.

"Are you all right, Gant?" Gen asked.

"My arm hurts bad. What happened? What'd you do to Jakes?"

"I'll explain later. We'd best leave. Let's get to town and have the Pureman care for that. He might be able to fix it up well enough to escape your master's notice."

"Hey!" Howen bellowed as they turned to go. "Get back here!"

"You keep going, Gant," Gen said. "I'll take care of this." Gant nodded doubtfully and started toward town, some of the crowd splitting off to follow him, trying to get a look at his arm. The balance stayed to watch the outcome of Jakes's felling.

Gen turned and got his first glimpse of Jakes's new face. Howen had helped him up, and they stood side by side, both seething with rage. In his agony, Jakes had smeared

18

blood all over his face, and his lips had already puffed to twice their normal size, a throbbing purple and black. Color drained from Gen's face.

"My teep! You basppurd!" Jakes yelled, more teeth and blood spraying to the ground. As one, the two brothers lumbered at Gen like angry she-bears. Gen turned and sprinted toward town as the crowd cheered him on.

"Meet me at the Church!" Gen yelled to Gant as he passed him.

Gen didn't have to run very long before Jakes and Howen gave up, poor conditioning hindering their strong urge to pulverize the bard's apprentice. Gen kept a quick pace toward town anyway, not wanting to give his pursuers any chance to catch him unawares; he didn't think he would survive the encounter. The Church was his only sanctuary. Pureman Millershim brooked no fighting anywhere, especially on Church grounds.

Gen jogged into town, greeting the few people still around in the late afternoon. Tell's town center held but one distinction. Some generations back, one of the more thoughtful Magistrates somehow secured funds from the Baron to pave the small square with imported cobblestones. Even after a heavy rain, the square remained pleasant, bearing only the mud tracked onto it from boots and wagon wheels. Four buildings surrounded the square, the Showles's sprawling home, the Church, the Morewold's store, and a run-down inn, the Honey Fly.

Like his master, Gen was well-liked by the townspeople for his good manners and happy disposition. As he opened the oak doors of the whitewashed Church, Pureman Millershim stopped his sweeping and smiled.

"Well met, Gen," he greeted. "How did your game go? I can tell by your face that something is amiss. What is it?"

Gen took a couple of minutes to catch his breath. Pureman Millershim regarded him patiently. The Pureman was tall and bald, and he possessed penetrating blue eyes that could drag the truth from the most recalcitrant liar and yet be comforting in turn. Gen decided that all holy men should have eyes of blue and a strong chin—something about the combination invited reverence and respect.

"Gant hurt his arm."

"Oh no! Not again," Millershim said, frowning. "Is it bad?"

"I don't know."

"I'll prepare the. . ."

"There's more."

"More?" Millershim asked, eyebrows rising.

"Yes," Gen admitted, looking at the floor. "Jakes's mouth is, um, in a sad state of disrepair."

"And I can see by your sheepish look that you are guilty of the infliction?"

"Not on purpose!" Gen burst out hastily, realizing that Pureman Millershim might think he had punched the lad. "One of the bones I threw at him had the misfortune of catching him in the teeth."

"So the bone had the misfortune, then?"

"No, sir. I meant to say. . ."

"Did he lose any teeth?"

"A fair number, yes."

"Fair number?"

"More than three. Less than ten. I think."

"I don't suppose they bothered to gather them? I can fix some of the damage if I have them."

"I didn't see that they did. They were too busy charging at me to worry much about the teeth."

"I see. I will prepare for an injured arm and a broken mouth, then. It would be best if you were not here when Jakes comes. His father will no doubt need several moments to cool down."

It would probably take more than several years. The Showles family hated Gen for the town's good opinion of him and for his good breeding. The Showles placed orphans in with the lowest of social refuse, considering them "double-bastards" for all practical purposes.

It irked the Magistrate that people said Gen could pass for a Lord while passing his own children off as even educated would be like telling someone a chicken was a peacock. The Magistrate and Lady Showles never connected the fact that they indulged their children in everything with their children's poor behavior, and they—and consequently the whole town—suffered for it.

"I suppose I'll go home, if you'll tell Gant to stop by and. . ."

"Oh no, Gen," the Puremen said as he rifled around in a closet. "I mean for you to go and find what you can of Jakes's teeth."

"What?!"

"You heard me. Now off with you! You owe Jakes that much, and it might go some way toward mollifying our good Magistrate's unavoidable explosion of temper when he hears about this."

Gen swallowed his pride and left through the rear of the building, taking the long way back to the clearing to avoid Jakes and Howen and any of the crowd that might still be returning from the game. By the time he arrived at the blood-flecked grass, the sun had dipped behind the line of trees, casting the spot into shadow.

Gen strained his eyes and worked until only the moons Myn and Duam were left to cast their light. Trys, the third moon, was an eclipsed hole in the sky as it had been for hundreds of years. The shards of their broken world sailed through the night sky, edges reflecting the fire of the setting sun as they moved and spun behind a misty veil of thin clouds.

Gen opened his hand to see the fruits of his labor. All his scrabbling in the grass produced five teeth and the pieces of a couple of others before the darkness prevented further search. He started for town, stomach clenched in dread. He walked at a meandering pace, hoping against hope the Showles would have come and gone by the time he arrived, but as he entered the Chapel, his heart sank. There on the back row sat the entire Showles family, Magistrate Bernard, his wife, Sarina, and their sons. They stood as he entered, faces angry.

Jakes remained sitting, holding a compress against his mouth. Howen strode over and shoved Gen roughly. Gen fell backward against a pew, losing his grip on the teeth as he braced himself for the fall. The teeth clicked on the wooden floor as they bounced about.

"Howen!" Millershim thundered. Gen looked up to find the brute towering over him, probably torn between fifty choices of how to hurt him. The Pureman interposed himself between the two boys, and Gen struggled upright, back bruised.

"For that, Howen," the Pureman said calmly, "you will need to find your brother's teeth on the floor."

"Indeed, he shall not!" Bernard bellowed, ample gut shaking in indignation with the rest of him as he strode forward to lock his beady eyes on Millershim. The Pureman regarded him coolly.

"Gen assaulted my boy! Look at him!"

On cue, Jakes moaned pathetically and lifted the compress from his swollen lips, which, while perhaps a trick of light, throbbed as if ready to burst. "Furthermore, I am going to have him arrested!"

"Come now, sir," Millershim said, brow creasing. "White Sticks often causes injuries. Don't forget that Jakes injured Gant in the same round. Will you arrest him?"

"Certainly not, Pureman! Jakes tripping Gant was purely accidental." Jakes agreed with a muffled "uh-huh." "Gen's assault was a deliberate and calculated attack!"

"It was not!" Gen protested.

"Quiet, peasant! Howen, fetch the Warden. Gen will sit in prison until Jakes can eat meat off my table again!"

Howen sneered at Gen before bounding out the door with a celebratory whoop.

"Magistrate," Millershim objected, "don't you think that a bit excessive?" Bernard's face turned the color of his hair, stubby finger starting to rise.

"I will go," Gen interjected before the Magistrate could spit out more vitriol.

Millershim patted Gen on the back and turned away from the Magistrate. "Let's see if we can find those teeth," he said. For the next few minutes, they searched the shadows of the pews. The Showles family muttered amongst themselves, the word *outrage* breaking above the mumbling at regular intervals. Millershim whispered to him that Gant had merely dislocated his shoulder and would recover quickly. Gen thanked Eldaloth for that favor.

"That's five," Millershim said, finding the last.

"Five!" Bernard shouted, coming to his feet again. "But you said there were nine missing!"

"We'll look again tomorrow," Millershim promised soothingly. "I won't be able to do anything until the swelling goes down, anyway."

"*We* won't look. *Gen* will be on his hands and knees tomorrow until he finds every last one!"

Howen banged open the door, Sikes coming behind. Gen winced every time he saw the Warden. Sikes, once a woodsman, had lost an eye and some of his brain when a fellow woodsman had swung at a tree and hit Sikes instead.

From what Gen gathered, Sikes was once a likable sort, but after his injury the man had turned mean. He dressed in black, and a small club hung from his belt. His black hair, perpetually unkempt, shot out at all angles. As a consequence of the injury, he always walked with his head at a tilt. An eye patch covered the hole in his face, the deep furrow of his old wound denting the forehead above it.

"Where is he?" Sikes asked, lifting the club from his belt.

"There," Bernard signaled authoritatively. "Gen."

"The bard's apprentice?"

"The very one! He is to remain in the prison until Jakes can eat meat again. Tomorrow you are to escort him to the field to find the rest of my boy's teeth."

"Meat? Teeth? Sir?" Sikes asked, confused. Jakes lifted the compress from his mouth.

"Mikkik's Breath!" Sikes exclaimed.

"Pray, Sikes, do not use that name in this Chapel!" Millershim admonished. Sikes ignored him.

"The bard walloped ye a good one, eh? Well, assault it is! C'mon boy!" Gen shook his head and walked out the door, Sikes clubbing him on the back on the way out.

"Sikes!" Millershim said, "For the…"

The door closed and Pureman Millershim's complaint was lost. Gen walked as quickly as he could, hoping to avoid another painful blow. The prison sat a scant fifty yards from the town center. Before the Showleses, Tell never had a prison. As soon as Bernard was elevated to the status of Magistrate by the Baron, he ordered one built. It served as Sikes's home as well, and Gen would have the only bed in the building, forcing Sikes to sleep on the floor.

"In you go, lad," Sikes said after lighting the lantern.

The cell had no amenities other than the bed and a chamber pot, which, Gen discovered, Sikes had not emptied for a day or two. Sikes closed the cell door and stared at his keys, trying to determine which to use. Gen wondered what the other keys were for, since the only lock in town was on the cell door. Not even Daven Morewold, the store owner, bothered locking up his wares.

After locating the right key, Sikes stared at it as if trying to determine whether to put the key in the lock or the lock in the key. After some consternation and several different keys, the cell was shut and locked.

"You keep to yerself, boy! I don't want no racket while I sleep."

Not being a reader, Sikes banked the fire and

extinguished the lamp immediately. A few minutes later he forced Gen to relinquish the blanket from the bed. In short order, Sikes set to snoring like a drunk, congested sailor, awaking with a screech from time to time, perhaps reliving the wicked blow to his head.

Gen finally learned to ignore Sikes's discomfited stirring and fell asleep, only to be awakened by the desperate Warden demanding the chamber pot. Unfortunately, it wouldn't fit between the bars, which set Sikes to fumbling with the keys again. Before long, his need became so urgent that Sikes forsook the keys and went outside.

The rest of the night passed in a similar fashion, and, as the fire faded, Gen could hardly sleep for the chill. When the sun rose, he felt out of sorts and was hoping some of the Pureman's treatments would help Jakes's lips heal quickly. Sikes still slept, limbs sticking out of the blanket at wild angles. He twitched as Bernard Showles's shrill voice split the calm morning air.

"Get that thing back where it belongs! By Eldaloth, I will kill whoever has done this!"

Gen poked his head up to peer through the bars of his window. There, sitting just outside the jail, was the Showles's outhouse, the words "Free Gen" scrawled into the side. Gen grinned. Hearing Sikes stirring, he dropped back to the bed and pretended to be asleep.

"Sikes!" Bernard howled, kicking open the door. "Sikes! Get up! They've done it again."

Gen feigned waking and saw the Magistrate in his long johns kicking Sikes in the ribs. At the sight of Bernard in his underwear, Gen couldn't decide whether to laugh or vomit. Bernard scowled at him as Sikes collected himself and stood. Howen poked his head in the door, sticking his tongue out at Gen.

Sikes grabbed his club. "Any idea who done it, sir?"

"How would I have any idea who did it? Howen, help Sikes get this back to the house!"

The three left, voices trailing off. Gen lay back, wondering who his benefactors were, especially since the obvious choice, Gant, had likely been confined to his home by his master besides being injured. Of course, it could be anyone. The people of Tell could do nothing to protest the Showles's childish behavior. Entreaties to the Baron only resulted in petty revenge from the Magistrate, so the townspeople exacted their frustration with the Showles family in the only mode available—pranks.

And pranks there had been aplenty. The favorite target was the Showles's outhouse. The outhouse lowered the Showleses—fancy clothes, fancy house, social standing, and all—to the same level as everyone else in the town.

Pranksters had inflicted just about everything imaginable upon the structure at one time or another. Every animal that could fit had been left in it as a surprise for the unfortunate victim in search of a little midnight relief. It had been knocked down, dragged out to a field, had the roof removed during rain and snowstorms, piled with cow manure, sticks, and leaves. It had been filled, broken, hidden, greased, and painted in so many ways Gen concluded an entire book couldn't hold the tale of them all.

At one point, the pranks became so bad and so frequent that the Showleses set their boys out to guard the structure during the night. But after a few days, their whining, lazy sons gave up. A lock was next, but this idea was abandoned the very next day when someone rendered the lock unopenable by jamming it full of small stones.

Gen could only think of two things that hadn't been done to the outhouse yet. For one, nobody had set it on fire, but why would anybody destroy their one source of revenge? The second thing was something so terrible, so heinous, that no one dared to do it.

The best thing, however, was that Sikes never caught any of the perpetrators and never would. For just as surely as Bernard Showles was ordering Sikes at that very moment to track down the dastards who dared move his toilet seventy-five yards away, Sikes would find that no one had the faintest idea who had done it. The Secret Society of the Outhouse would never give up its members, and Gen took satisfaction in the fact that someone in that society had seen fit to honor him.

The days passed slowly in the cell. Finding the four teeth took nearly an entire day, as at least two of the teeth were in several pieces. Rafael came every morning, and, after a stern lecture that got shorter each time, always brought a book, which Gen hid under the mattress so that Sikes, who couldn't read, wouldn't confiscate it.

Gant talked to Gen through the bars when Sikes was away, and his friend gave him daily reports on the state of Jakes's mouth. After the third moving of the outhouse, Bernard forced Sikes to camp by it, which gave Gen the pleasure of uninterrupted sleep for the rest of his stay. To further the Showles's frustration, the children in town frequently puffed up their lips in an imitation of Jakes's face, and to make matters worse, the two teeth that the Pureman could not repair were the top front two.

"I guess all his *th*'s will be whistled," Gen quipped to Gant one chilly morning.

"Yep. Folks are already makin' fun of that."

"Can he eat meat yet?"

"I dunno," Gant answered. "He'll certainly have to cut it from now on, so I hope that'll count or you'll be in here fer life."

But after a week and a half of imprisonment, Gen received a sudden reprieve.

CHAPTER 2 - REGINA

Hubert Showles was coming home.

Gen yawned and flung the shutters of his room wide to invite the chilly pre-dawn breeze to pry open his eyes the rest of the way. His own efforts had failed. He had slept little that night, finding that an evening of rigorously practicing his repertoire of songs for Hubert's return celebration only set his mind to lively wanderings that chased sleep away, despite finding himself in the comfort of his own bed for the first time in nearly two weeks.

The second-story window of his room overlooked the last of the Green Road and commanded a pleasant view of the dense Alewine forest. Dying night winds that set the forest to sighing and bending wafted the fermented scent of autumn's decay into his room.

A statuette of a hideous Uyumaak on the table caught the weak, pink light of the clouds and shifted its color from night black to the brown of the table. Gen picked it up and regarded it, its color changing to match that of his fingers. Rafael had gifted him the statuette when he had shown a fascination with it as a boy.

The long, powerful legs and the gangly arms terminating in vicious claws marked this Uyumaak as a Hunter. The different breeds of Uyumaak had different bodies designed for different purposes, but all had the same face—a circular mouth ringed with triangular teeth pointed at the center of the hole, slightly protruding so it could suck meat into its maw for the teeth to devour.

A set of three nose holes formed a triangle above the mouth just beneath an inset crevasse in the conical upper skull, which held a row of glassy black eyes. His statuette had nine, though Rafael said that some had as few as three, while stories from the Mikkikian wars talked of some having as many as twenty. The thought of all those eyes moving about sent a shiver down Gen's spine.

The statuette imitated the talent of the Uyumaak's scaly skin—it changed colors to match its environment. Some of the songs he'd prepared the night before told stories of the creatures hiding nearly invisible in the deep grass or woods for a chance to chase down a horse or tear apart an elven scout.

The miniature statue had scared and fascinated him as a boy, and, to overcome his fear, he took to giving it the name of whatever person in town annoyed him at any particular time. The habit stuck.

The statue had borne Hubert's name many times before. Gen considered the snotty, stupid son of the town's Magistrate the worst of the Showles lot. His only redeeming virtue was that he didn't play favorites. He tortured everyone, including his own kin, until loneliness drove him to relent enough for those with short memories to come within earshot of him again. Gen's memory was not short. After Hubert threw him in the well behind the Church when he was ten, Gen had avoided the brute diligently.

He set the statuette back on the book-laden table and shut and latched the shutters in case rain or wind blew in while he was out. Quietly, he took the creaky stairs down to the kitchen, though his stealth was unnecessary. Rafael was already there, slouched over the table with breakfast at the ready. Gen drank the cinnamon tea and ate the barley cakes slowly, hoping they could throw off the grogginess and get him into performing condition.

Rafael looked as tired as Gen felt. The old bard usually slept until the sun was well past full up, and rising early in the morning disagreed with him. He had combed back what little straggly gray hair still clung to his scalp and donned his performing clothes. His pants and shirt were baggy on him. During the successful years of his barding, he had eaten from the larder of lords and ladies and grown plump. The food of his retirement was less rich and less abundant.

If he were telling the truth, Gen wanted the same traveling life as his master, hoping Baron Forthrickeshire would permit him to travel to Khyrum, the capital of Tolnor, or even to other shards such as Tenswater and Rhugoth. Staying in Tell would resign him to a life of inconsequence and boredom. The poor town was good for one thing only—lumber.

Few traveled the long, unkempt Green Road that connected a string of towns set on the southeastern edge of the expansive Alewine forest. The farther north the road went, the smaller and less frequent the towns became until at last one arrived at Tell, after which no permanent settlement could be found all the way to the nearly impassible Rede Steppes and Red Wind Desert.

Despite the constant cutting of branch and tree, the wood still threatened to overrun the towns built with and sustained by it. Tales passed down from the first woodsmen to work the timber told of groves cut down one day and regrown the next. While Gen had never seen a tree grow overnight, the townsfolk waged a constant battle to keep the seedlings out of house, garden, and field. Under the previous Magistrate, every mid-spring the children would be let loose to pull as many suckers and saplings as they could from around the buildings in town, the child who brought in the most winning a rabbit or a bronze piece.

Very little else of importance, however, came from Tell, not in product or person. Few people outside of the nearby towns of Sipton and Hazelwhite knew Tell existed at all, and they were mostly relatives of the townspeople who had worked the forest and the land for several generations.

The folk in Tell, especially the older ones, enjoyed the solitude and separation, while the young did little more than dream of leaving. Some of the apprentices accompanied their masters as far west as Green Wall when the lumber was sold. Their tales of the inns, festivals, and pretty girls set the rest of the young men to longing for adventure and travel and to a great deal of complaining—mostly to unsympathetic parents—about how dreadfully dull Tell was. Gen agreed with them.

Only two things had happened in the last twenty years that people thought amounted to anything worthy of talk, and Gen was one of them. While orphans were not rare in Tell, ones who wandered about naked in the woods with burn-scarred feet were. They said Gen was only three or four years old when a lumbering party found him sitting in a tree. They took him to the woodmaster, who in turn gave him to the care of Tell's young Churchman, Pureman Millershim. The Pureman diligently searched for the boy's parents in the small towns along the road, but with no success.

At first, the strange circumstances of Gen's appearance caused the normally friendly families of Tell—long accustomed to raising orphans—to shun him.   While the forest might provide for their bread, the people believed it a fey and dangerous place. Pureman Millershim ardently preached against entering deep within the shadowy boles, as, he said, worshipers of the dead goddess Owena kept watch over the trees and practiced strange rites. A child found in the wood, therefore, was an ill omen, especially considering the strange condition of his feet, which conjured images of strange rites by firelight. People whispered in low voices that Gen was the kin of cultists, and they waited to see what he would become.

The Pureman gave Gen his name and entrusted the strange boy to the only person who took vocal pity on him: Rafael. The retired bard had just bought the status of freeholder with earnings from the success of his trade and settled into the large, abandoned farmhouse.

After Gen was successfully placed, the town mothers would often cluck and fuss about how the boy should have a proper mother, though none wanted the job personally. To add further controversy, Gen's skin was pale white, his eyes green, and his stature tall—all marks of noble heritage, unlike the short, stocky, and swarthy traits of most Tolnorian peasantry.

For a time, Gen remained a thing of conjecture and gossip, but as the boy grew under the tutelage of the learned bard, his strange history faded in importance and he became a regular part of the town, though not an ordinary one. Rafael was learned in lore and in the ways of court. Before long, Gen stood out for his manners and speech rather than for his mysterious origins. The coarse, rough-and-tumble boys of the rural town had plenty of reasons to despise Gen as their parents continually used the bard's apprentice as a standard of sterling behavior. "Why can't you be more polite, like Gen?" "If you had half the sense Gen had. . ." "You could learn a thing or two from Gen about how to behave. . ."

The ill feelings died off as they grew older and Gen demonstrated that he was neither aloof nor conceited. The fact that few—if any—mothers would allow their daughters to take the orphan bard seriously helped, too. As the boys started their apprenticeships, something Gen had embarked upon years before, Gen became a mentor in finding ways to romance the young ladies of Tell. He felt foolish giving advice about something with which he had no personal experience, although he knew the heart-wrenching tales of his trade.

But experience or no, Gen's reputation as a bard and as a young man grew. His voice was strong and clear, his fingers nimble upon the lute. His easy manner endeared him to the townsfolk (with the notable exception of the Showleses). Only the glint of cunning intelligence in Gen's eye, his refinement of speech, and his appearance marked him as different; in all other ways, he was a boy of the country. Rafael always looked on Gen with a proud glow and had said more than once that the boy would go far— the good Baron permitting.

The second notable thing to happen in Tell was the placement of Hubert Showles into the armies of Duke Norshwal. While the Showleses were technically nobility, they were not the kind that mattered. Somehow, however, Bernard arranged for his son to serve in the Duke's regular army.

At first Hubert seemed mortified at the opportunity, but his father saw to it that the town paid him the proper attention and respect—things the entire Showles family held in short supply—and Hubert soon took to strutting around as if he were a King, lacing the ears of the young ladies with all manner of fabulous tales about the adventures and dangers in which he *might* find himself (and which every boy in town hoped he would find himself). In Tell, the general lack of news made even stupid fiction incredibly interesting, and Hubert enjoyed his own inventions as much as anyone.

When the snow finally broke on Hubert's sixteenth year, he was sent off to Graytower, an arduous journey from the eastern edge of the Dukedom to its capital. Bernard pressed the townspeople into a great production for his departure even though the unusually long and harsh winter had depleted their stores. The Magistrate had even gone so far as to buy new dresses for several of the more attractive young ladies so they could line the road and wave their

33

sashes at his son as he left. The dresses were collected directly afterward, however, and sent to be resold elsewhere.

Hubert was soon and pleasurably forgotten, and life returned to normal until that morning in late autumn when Rafael came with an order from Bernard to collect his apprentice from jail. Hubert would return the next day, and once again the Showleses demanded that a festival be thrown in his honor. Celebrating Hubert's departure, while inconvenient, was at least palatable because he was leaving. Gen thought that working up a festive attitude for Hubert's return would require the type of cheerful disposition only the truly ignorant can possess. Everyone else would need to pursue a drunken stupor and endure his arrival the best they could.

"Well, lad," Rafael mumbled, voice weary, "let's get to it. Bernard said he wanted us to play 'from dawn to dusk and then some' and dawn is nearly broken."

"We will get some breaks, won't we?" Gen asked. He wanted some time to have a little fun himself. Starting the festival so early was as insensitive as it was ridiculous. Everyone knew Hubert would arrive during the late afternoon at the earliest.

"Of course," Rafael answered sarcastically. "The Magistrate is a considerate man." Gen grunted and stood, gathering his cloak and his instrument, which he wrapped in a blanket.

"You'll have to retune that once we. . ." Rafael began.

"I know," Gen cut him off. "I've done this before. We play at All Peace Day in the dead of winter every year."

"No harm in a reminder, especially to the tired, which would be you, or the hungover, which would be me. Let's say the Oblation and get going. If you would do the honors, Gen. My mind is still a little foggy."

Gen nodded, and they both knelt.

In Eldaloth's name and for his sake,
We to his servants oblations make.
To the Ha'Ulrich, our loyalty and our might,
To the Chalaine, our reverence and our life.
The world broken due to sin,
They twain will make whole again.
The moons our witness in the sky,
The soul, the body, the blinded eye.

After finishing, Gen helped Rafael to his feet and they left the house to take the short walk north to the town square. Their breath steamed from their mouths and nostrils, and they pulled the cowls of their cloaks up over their heads. Due to the absence of traffic on the road, Gen thought they might just be the first to arrive, but as they came to the square, he saw that several of the townsfolk had arrived earlier, setting up booths and games. Gen doubted the balance of the populace would arrive until it warmed considerably.

After waving a greeting to several familiar faces, Gen and his master crossed to the permanent platform set on the east side of the Church. Gen sat on a three-legged stool and started tuning his lute absentmindedly, his thoughts again turning to the reason for their early morning performance. Why Eldaloth in his supposedly benevolent wisdom had chosen to curse their small town with a family that could torment a city several times Tell's size escaped the most careful of his reasoning. No matter what Pureman Millershim said about not judging others, Gen knew, as did everyone else, that Eldaloth would never let the Showles family set one foot into the paradise of Erelinda. And if he wouldn't let them into Erelinda, why did he send them to Tell save to make the townspeople suffer?

Bernard Showles lorded the fact that he was Magistrate over everyone with every effort he could muster. He'd managed to get the position some twenty years ago, a favor from his distant cousin, Duke Norshwal. The relationship was so distant, in fact, that if it were a town, Gen calculated it would take a good three months to get there on a fast horse. Magistrates weren't even within sniffing distance of real nobility, but they were above serfs, freemen, and merchants, and Bernard Showles exaggerated the minuscule status gap as much as possible. Despite Tell's glaring insignificance, Bernard acted like he was the Magistrate of the Khyrum itself.

Gen imagined, however, that even Magistrates of more important towns and cities had the good sense to behave civilly toward those they governed, but Bernard treated anyone below his rank with palpable disdain. Every look, every frilly outfit, every word was meant to put the puny people in their place and to remind everyone of his own elevation. Why the man would want to live with and rule over a town full of people he despised puzzled Gen until his studies in history led him to understand the extreme pains men would endure to garner themselves the smallest bud of power, no matter how insignificant it might be in terms of the larger tree.

"My boy," Rafael said, "that look on your face is positively black. I can only hope I'm not the target of whatever darkness you've got swimming around in that head of yours."

Gen broke out of his reverie and smiled at his master. Most had expected the old man to die years ago, though he had proved tougher and more resilient than folks half his age in a town where winters killed the weak.

"Fear not, Master DeBellemain," Gen replied formally. "None of my ire is for you. I think you know the throat my black thoughts are squeezing."

"I think so, but don't tell me anything about it. I'd like to answer—and truthfully— 'I know nothing,' when the time comes. But I beg you not to be too extravagant in any plots you might be hatching. You can be expelled from this town, you know, and forced to face the Baron. I've got a wonderful house and the biggest collection of books in this Dukedom. They're yours when I die, if you can manage a bit of restraint."

Rafael told Gen this often as a deterrent against any rascality his young pupil might engage in. Rafael had no children of his own, none that he knew of, anyway. The old man made it widely known that he had chosen Gen as his heir.

Gen was very thankful. Gen knew the books Rafael collected over a lifetime were worth a fortune in most places, though no one in the town seemed to value them more than a barrel of beans. Since apprenticing with Rafael, Gen had read most of those books. At first it had been a struggle for Rafael to harness the young boy's youthful energy to the task of reading, but eventually Gen had come to love reading so much that Rafael had to try doubly hard to pry him away from books long enough to learn music.

"Well, if I can't manage restraint," Gen said, "I'll do my best to be discreet. But trust me when I say that the victims will be most deserving."

"Please!" Rafael pleaded. "No more! I enjoy a good outhouse prank as much as anyone, but I'm an old man and want no trouble till the snow gets me and I sneak my way into Erelinda. Besides, what need is there of such dark thoughts when fair creatures like that one are about?"

Gen followed Rafael's gaze out into the square. Few people had arrived, but Regina had just left her house to greet a group of young men who had been loitering around her porch. Without reservation, Gen and every other young man in town proclaimed Regina Morewold, daughter of the merchant Jeorge Morewold, the most beautiful creature—besides the Chalaine, of course—to grace Ki'Hal, or at least the towns near Tell. All the young men wanted her, and she knew it.

Unlike most other girls in town, Regina was tall and not

huskily built. Her mother was the third daughter of a baron, and Regina had inherited her finer features from that lineage. While the Chalaine was beauty beyond comprehension and far out of reach, Regina's face was there to be doted upon and dreamed about. She was the closest to what the boys imagined a noblewoman looked like. Everywhere she went, tossing her blonde locks about and flashing her big blue eyes, a hopeful entourage of suitors accompanied her.

Gen was no exception to this worship, finding any excuse he could to be near her, though to find her alone was about as likely as hearing an intelligent word come out of a Showles's mouth. In addition to her many fine qualities, she was also the only young lady in town who had learned to read and write, her mother sending her off each spring to be tutored in Green Wall. Thus, Gen felt his claim upon the girl was better than most, for when he did manage to talk to her, there was a connection of the mind that he doubted she found with any of his competition who could talk of little more than trees, hunting, and livestock.

Though most marriages were arranged, the town boys still bragged, fought, and showed off for her as if it would make any difference. But smart young men, young men such as Gen thought himself to be, knew that one secured the hand of a young woman by acquiring the good opinion of her parents. Some parents—though rare—actually took into account the affections of their children; most, however, looked to pair their offspring with someone that was "good" for them or who would raise the family's social station.

To those in love, however, all this parental bargaining meant less than a tin piece in a gold pile, leaving the countryside strewn with heartbroken, forlorn lovers when it came time for marriages—at least that's what many of the songs were about. Gen hoped he could find a happy ending to the song he sang in his heart every time Regina smiled at him. He'd certainly tried to win her, though she would never speak of anything she felt for any man. She kept her feelings away from scrutiny, and all Gen could ever do was guess and hope.

"It's a pity, though," Rafael continued, "that Regina gathers so much attention when there are an abundance of other eligible young ladies about. Take Laraen Fairweather, for instance. There's nothing wrong with that young lady. Kind, sweet, good cook. . ." Gen put his lute down and blew on his hands to warm them. The Fairweathers had invited him and Rafael to their house a fortnight ago for a dinner prepared by Laraen to impress Gen.

While Gen appreciated the fact that one family in town thought him good enough for their daughter—double-bastard and bard-apprentice notwithstanding—the way her parents looked at him, like one would look at a cart horse before buying it, set Gen's skin to crawling. Remembering the dinner—a rather tasty honey basted ham, sweet bread, and potatoes—prompted a rumble in Gen's stomach despite his breakfast. Marrying Laeren would not make him happy, but it would make him fat.

"All I can say," Gen said, "is that it's hard to think the moons are bright when the sun is in the sky. I'm sure Laraen will garner her fair share of attention once someone puts the sun out of reach, so to speak."

"You have the right of it there," Rafael agreed. "The mystery is, who will drag the sun off into the sunset? How about you, Gen? I've seen her smile at you in that particular way from time to time, and you have gift for words that no other young man within fifty leagues of this place has. I know you've been thinking of her."

Gen smiled weakly. The chance that Regina's parents would let her marry an orphan was slim, though Gen had done his best to get in their good graces. He paid for his goods in a timely fashion. He watched and cleaned the store when they were away. He'd even performed free of charge for a small gathering they had when Jeorge's brother had come to visit from Sipton.

"I think the Morewolds like me well," Gen said, "but Regina? I don't know. She smiles at me, yes. She talks to me. But she does much the same with every young man in the town, near as I can tell."

"A generous, happy heart is a wonderful thing to find in a woman, Gen."

"Yes, but such a heart complicates discerning where a man stands in relation to others. I feel like there is something between us and have told her as much, but she says nothing. It may not end up mattering, anyway. I doubt the Morewolds would let their daughter marry an orphan, much less one who is a bard *and* a serf, no matter how much they may like me. What sane parent would let their daughter marry a bard after all?"

"Hey!" Rafael protested, taking Gen's bait. "There's plenty for a woman to like about living with a bard! While I never quite found the right wo—"

"Why Gen," a soft voice broke through Rafael's retort, "I'm sure a bard would have a lot to offer a young lady."

Gen spun to find that Regina had approached unnoticed while he was conversing with Rafael. She stood wrapped in a light gray woolen cloak, looking up at him on the platform. As always, her eyes were full of confidence and playfulness, and her mouth was turned up in a lovely smirk, the kind of smirk that rendered Gen weak-kneed and almost speechless. Almost.

"Why Regina," Gen greeted her grandly, hoping to deflect the conversation, "welcome to our little festival in honor of mighty Hubert Showles, the greatest slouch ever to play dice on the Tolnorian frontier. And I bid welcome to you, too, Cale, Keegan, and Thad. I see you've wasted no time in finding and following the most lovely young lady in town." Gen took Regina's hand and kissed it dramatically. The three young men scowled when they saw Regina's smile. Rafael nodded in approval.

Regina's eyes brightened. "Why thank you, Gen."

"Uh, Regina?" Cale popped in quickly, trying to recapture Regina's attention. "Wanna come see the pheasant I tracked down and killed? It's real big. My pa hung it up over there and we'll cook it later."

"Quiet, Cale," Regina remonstrated. "I was talking to Gen and it is not polite to interrupt. I'm sure I'll have more than enough time later to hear all about the big birdie you caught."

Gen loved how Regina's tone of voice made it impossible to tell whether she was mocking you or not. Gen couldn't figure out if she did it on purpose and suspected that part of her tutoring involved learning to be devious. While it was frustrating, Gen loved it.

"So Gen," Regina continued, "you sounded ever so rude when you referred to our young hero of the day. I certainly hope those comments don't make it back to our town Magistrate."

By the knowing glances of the three young men behind her, Gen knew they would tattle on him, not that Bernard really cared about anyone else's opinion. If he did, he would certainly have killed himself years ago.

"Well, I'm sure the Magistrate knows that I think just as highly of Hubert as everyone else does."

Regina grinned knowingly and was about to reply when a voice, shrill and grating, broke across the square.

"Hey! Rafael," Bernard yelled, "you and your lay-about apprentice should be playing! The second watch has passed and the sun is up. Now let's hear some music!"

Bernard wore an unbelievable bright red coat and breeches, both trimmed with white rabbit fur. The coat bulged over his belly, though recent expansion of his midsection brought the bottom of the coat up short of the belt. The color of it clashed with what little red hair the man had left. Set against the muted browns, greens, and grays of the town, the Magistrate's outfit involuntarily drew everyone's eye toward him, which Gen supposed was the point.

Gen raised his eyebrows and sighed. "Alas, my lady," he apologized. "I must ply my trade."

Regina pouted in mock disappointment. Or maybe it wasn't. "Then do ply it. I apparently have a date with a deceased fowl. If you can manage it, find me for a dance or two. I believe Master Rafael is more than skilled enough to hold the stage without you."

Rafael bowed and swept the stage with his hat in a gesture of gratitude for her compliment, groaning slightly as his spine cracked and popped while reversing the effort.

"I will make a point of it!" Gen replied. "I wouldn't want you to forget about me, since you find yourself in the company of so many excellent young men this morning."

Regina winked at him and turned to go.

"Where's the music?!" Showles bellowed as Regina walked off, young men in tow. Rafael began a quick beat on the drum and Gen joined in with the lute.

As if lured by the music, people emerged from road and path to fill the empty square. While many of the men and women, especially those who had to set up booths, were obviously angry about being there, the children enjoyed every minute with each other. After greeting friends and family, the adults soon overcame their annoyance, and before mid-day the festival lurched into full swing.

The Showleses only condescended to occasional appearances in the square as the day went on, not wanting to mingle with the common folk too much, save to watch for their son coming down the road and to yell at Gen and Rafael if the music stopped.

Gen wished he could step down and enjoy himself with the townsfolk, though he liked the applause he received after he sang a song. Gen had taken over most of the singing duties of late since Rafael's voice tired quickly and had a scratchy quality. Still, the old man could ring out a good chorus now and again, and the people always applauded, having great affection for the old performer. Few towns could lay claim to such talent.

"Gen," Rafael whispered after concluding a song, "I must say your voice is sounding more and more impressive every time I hear it. I had my doubts about you a few summers ago, but you've come along nicely. And, by the way, there's a certain young lady that's been watching you."

Gen searched the crowd, expecting to see Regina's blue eyes and instead finding the brown ones of Laraen Fairweather. Unlike Regina's looks, Laraen's were a sledgehammer of meaning.

"Gotcha!" Rafael said, cackling as only an old man can. Gen rolled his eyes up into his head.

"Don't you torture my poor heart, old man." Gen tried to be mad but couldn't. "When do you suppose Hubert will drag himself into town?"

"I'd reckon around sundown," Rafael replied. "He was supposed to ride out this morning, provided he didn't stay up late engaging in what little debauchery can be found in Sipton. While I share about as much enthusiasm for the boy as you do, it will be nice to hear what news he has. Aughmere is obviously planning to attack the northern border some time soon. That is clear. It appears it won't happen until next year, since the snows will be here before long."

Gen shook his head. "I still don't see why they would want to attack us at all. The Ha'Ulrich is going to be the ruler of all nations in two years. Even if Aughmere were to win, they would essentially be taking what is already to be theirs."

"Indeed," Rafael agreed. "But you forget that Torbrand Khairn is still the Shadan of Aughmere, not his son. The Ha'Ulrich is only your age. The Shadan is a lusty man, the most feared warrior of our times. He wanted to unite the three kingdoms when he first took the throne, arguing that the united rule should begin as soon as possible.

"If Aughmere's way of life were not so divergent from our kingdom's or from Rhugoth's, it might have happened. He half considered attacking Tolnor then, but our alliance with Rhugoth kept him from it. If he could gain control of the Portal to Rhugoth, he would have probably attacked. The Portal Guild made sure that wouldn't happen, however."

The tales of Torbrand Khairn were indeed awe inspiring and frightening. It was said that no man could so much as tire the Aughmerian leader in single combat, much less lay a mark upon him. The last three Shadans of Aughmere were of the Khairn family, and in a nation where all positions were determined by challenges and deadly combat, having three Shadans of the same family in succession was a rarity.

Gen tried to digest Rafael's information. "So you're saying he's going to get thousands killed because he wants to fight something and our nation just happens to be on the same shard?"

"Not exactly, Gen," his master replied. "No doubt there was some insult or provocation we don't know about. Shadan Khairn and his Blessed Son met with all the nobles from the three human nations this spring to arrange for the transfer of power after the Ha'Ulrich's marriage to the Chalaine. It was after that meeting that rumor of Khairn marshaling his forces first trickled into our little town. Honestly, I suspect that our young King has broken the Fidelium, for that is the only circumstance I could imagine where Rhugoth would not come rushing to our defense, and we have heard nothing of it."

Out of the corner of his eye, Gen noticed the Magistrate coming out the door of his two-story house and knew the conversation was almost over.

"Broke the Fidelium? That would be absurd!" Gen couldn't fathom it.

"It would, but I can think of nothing else that would precipitate a war this close to the marriage."

Gen's mind spun. He barely paid attention to Bernard's red-faced complaints. Every leader of all three nations signed the Fidelium upon the inception of their rule, promising to relinquish their thrones to the Ha'Ulrich upon his marriage to the Chalaine so that the nations would be united against the threat of Mikkik. While the finding of the Ha'Ulrich in the nation of Aughmere was distasteful to Tolnorians and Rhugothians alike, as far as anyone knew, neither the King of Tolnor nor the First Mother of Rhugoth ever conceived of not honoring the holy contract first signed under Pontiff Ethelion the Fourth over two-hundred years before.

Bernard's nettling left Gen little time to consider the import of Rafael's conjecture, and the day passed slowly as they played song after song. Watching everyone have fun while the Magistrate pinned him to the stage soured Gen's mood more. He missed the wrestling contest between Orbrin, a woodsman, and Geoff the Huntsman. He only heard about the footrace won by his friend Gant and was upset—Gen's height and quickness had earned him the footrace crown of Tell for four years running. He missed the apple bobbing, pole climbing, chicken chasing, and the rousing games of White Sticks. Worst of all, he missed the food.

The Magistrate rarely gave them a few moments between songs before he planted his feet on his front porch, put his hands on his hips, and screamed for them to keep at it. Even the good-natured Rafael showed signs of an eroding patience near mid-afternoon. Madlena eventually took pity on them, emerging from her inn with a basket of hot rolls and two mugs of cider. They had to take turns playing to let the other eat, and, while Gen was grateful that the plump Innkeeper had the kindness to bring them a little bread, his stomach pined at the smell of roasting meats—cow, pheasant, and pig—wafting through the square.

He thought of asking Gant to get him a slice of pheasant, but his friend spent his time in the company of Yeurile, Master Owen's bossy daughter. Yeurile and Gant had been very close of late. Since Owen liked Gant almost as much as Rafael liked Gen, Gen had no doubt that Yeurile and Gant would be betrothed come spring and married the next fall.

"Gen," Rafael whispered after a song. "There's Regina. Go to her. Now's your chance. I'll hold up for a song or two without you."

CHAPTER 3 - A HERO'S RETURN

Regina had somehow escaped from the other young men and was leaning against the Church wall, thoughtfully drinking from a wooden mug. She looked a little worn, though beautiful, in her light blue dress. Gen was almost upon her before she noticed him. He bowed and she smiled.

"My master has given me generous license to dance for two songs, if you will," he said. "I hope Thad and Keegan haven't worn you completely out."

"I believe my legs have enough strength in them for another dance. I'm glad you could get free. Magistrate Showles has thoroughly abused the kindness of you and your master today."

Gen extended his hand, and as if that were the cue, Rafael started into his song. It was a lively tune, and Gen and Regina were all smiles as they twisted, clapped, kicked, and spun. By the end, their faces were flushed, their breath coming quickly.

"I'm afraid I'll have to sit for a moment after that," Regina gasped. Gen offered his arm and led her to the steps of her home, enjoying her nearness. They sat side by side, watching the children running amok playing tag or fleeing in terror from those twice their size who carried snakes, bugs, or cold water from the well. Gen stared at her for a while and she smiled back, blushing.

"I can't imagine the Chalaine being more beautiful than you," he said at last.

Regina laughed. "Why Gen, that was most unoriginal. In fact, I think I've heard it once today already. I expect a bit more effort from you, of course."

"I'm sorry to disappoint, but sometimes the truth is unoriginal. I was trying to be honest, not creative."

"Thank you."

Gen thought he saw a flash of affection on her face but couldn't tell for sure. The door banging open behind them ruined the moment. Regina's dad stood behind them, feet apart and face strangely downcast. Jeorge had thinning black hair, a thick strand of it combed over his balding pate. His face was long, oval, and kind, though his brow, scrunched up like a walnut shell, indicated something amiss

"Regina," he said, not meeting her eye, "I—well, your mother and I—need to talk to you for a moment."

His hat was in his hands, and he twisted it absentmindedly in his fingers. Regina's brow matched his.

"I'll be in shortly, Father. I was just talking to Gen since he was finally able to rest after playing all the day long."

"You'd better come in now," Jeorge said. "It's important."

Regina glanced at Gen apologetically and with a little concern. Gen hoped the Morewolds didn't dislike him so much that they objected to him just talking to their daughter.

"It's all right," Gen soothed her. "I'd best be getting back anyway. Rafael's starting to sound like a broken bellows up there." Regina went indoors, and Gen wondered at Jeorge's strange behavior. He had little time to think about it. Rafael had finished his song and was searching for him.

48

By sundown, a brisk autumn wind blew in clouds from the sea over the sighing trees of the Alewine Forest. The wind brought with it a chill and the smell of the autumn's decay, and it whipped leaves and dust in the square, souring the event considerably. Bernard, now with a black cloak over his horrific red garb, came out briefly to scowl at the weather, though even he had the good sense not yell at the wind. Gen donned his brown cloak and wondered if the Magistrate would force the town to wait if it rained.

"He's coming! He's coming!"

A group of boys ran into the square bearing the news. Bernard walked out of his home in a stately fashion, and, for the first time, so did his wife Katrina. In contrast to her husband, Katrina was skinny with a sharp face. She piled her hair on top of her head as Gen imagined noblewomen wore it, and she besmeared her face with paints to make her eyes and lips stand out. The most striking thing about Katrina, however, was her ever-present smile and cheery— mostly faked—disposition. The townspeople often joked that Katrina Showles would look the same before and after being trampled by a herd of cattle.

But anyone who spent time with her, and few did, knew that the calm, cheery voice and clenched-teeth smile was like a coating of honey on a moldy piece of bread, a sweet covering for a rotten mass of rage. Of all the Showleses, Gen pitied her the most. He imagined that once she had been a fairly happy young lady and that the sunny facade she put on now was an attempt the hold on to that good part of herself ravaged by years of living with Bernard.

Bernard removed his cloak. Katrina wore a bright yellow dress that contrasted badly with Bernard's red clothes. Gen thought perhaps they purposefully chose bright clothing to help their stupid son remember who his parents were as he returned. Jakes and Howen stood sullenly behind their parents, Jakes rubbing his still-discolored lips. The town fell silent as Hubert, at long last, rode into the square. Katrina

49

clasped her hands together and smiled in almost maniacal glee. Bernard stood, feet planted apart and arms extended in a proud welcome.

Hubert surveyed the gathering with a questioning expression, his face registering an unpleasant surprise. He was a stocky young man with the start of a belly that he would doubtless cultivate to rival his father's one day. His grease-stained tabard held the symbol of a black hawk on a field of white, the device of Duke Norshwal in whose army he had served, and from his belt hung a broadsword.

The horse upon which Hubert rode Gen recognized as old Billy, a brown gelding plow horse looking for a place to die. Hubert's neglect had brought it closer to the end of its proverbial road. The poor beast's bones poked out and moved under the skin, giving full suggestion of the skeleton underneath. Katrina ran forward and pulled a wreath fashioned of Erstleberry Vine from a pouch in her dress and draped it around the horse's neck. The white flowers of the poisonous, late-blooming vine drooped and fell, only adding to the sickening appearance of the horse.

Gen noticed two things—no one was clapping, and Regina was missing. Bernard noticed the former. With a stern look and loud example, he goaded the townspeople into a hearty applause as his son dismounted to awkwardly receive hugs from his overly enthusiastic parents.

Despite a mounting wind, the rough-hewn table used for such occasions was brought out of the Church and placed on the stand where Gen and Rafael performed. A host of women and men set out the feast. Thanks to Bernard's preoccupation with his son and the food (and it was difficult to tell which he cared for the most), Gen was able to gather a platter of food for himself and quickly get out of sight behind the Church before Bernard could see him and think of music.

And there he found Regina, standing with her hands grasping the stones of the Church well and casting her eyes down into its depths. Yellow leaves from a nearby stand of maple fell about her as the wind stripped them from the branches. She seemed unaware of people or the wind that blew her blonde hair about, the strands catching the weak and uneven lantern light from the square. Oddly, none of her entourage accompanied her, and Gen half-thought of leaving her be, so odd was the scene. His heart prodded him onward anyway.

"Not thinking of jumping in, are you?" he quipped. The look she returned told him she might just be. She regarded him wistfully, face pale and drawn.

"I'm sorry," Gen stammered, understanding that it was not the time for their customary joking or verbal sparring. He watched as she tried to assume an air of happiness and confidence, but she failed, leaving naked sadness on her face. "I'll leave you be. . ."

"Please stay, won't you, Gen?"

"Of course, Regina." Gen stood at her side, setting his platter on the precarious edge. Now that night had nearly fallen, the well was a dark yawning hole of nothingness, unfathomable and frightening. Gen struggled to find words to offer comfort or question her about her distress, but in the silence, Regina found them:

A well can deep waters hold.
A well knows a thousand secrets
No one has told.

A well can run shallow and dry
When dark rivers fail
And rain passes it by.

But a well, whether dry or deep,
Will mute in blackness
All secrets keep.

One of many perhaps may tell,
From faint taste of salt
What tears there fell.

Darkest well, silent soul,
My sorrow keeps,
And none will know.

"*The Silent Soul*, by Sir Mephael," Gen said. "I know it well."

Regina laughed bitterly. "And you are the only one who would know it in this horrible town."

The tears came freely now, and Gen reflexively put his arm around her and drew her near. "Well, Rafael would know it, too."

"I wasn't thinking of *old* men," Regina sobbed. Gen let her cry until she finally gathered herself.

"What is wrong, Regina?" he asked tenderly, hoping that for the first time she would talk to him plainly about how she felt. "What did your parents tell you? Are they sending you west for the winter again?"

With a sad smile, she lifted her hand and touched Gen's face. Her touch was soft and exhilarating. For a moment it seemed as if she would kiss him, but instead she wiped her eyes dry with the sleeves of her cloak and straightened her hair as best she could in the swirling wind. When she faced Gen again, her face was composed and severe.

"I'm sorry to bother you. What ails me, you will soon know."

"Regina. . ." Gen called after her, but she was already rounding the corner of the Church on her way to the square where Rafael was playing. Turning to go, he knocked his plate into the well but was too lost in thought to care.

The feast was well underway when Gen returned to take his place by Rafael on the platform. He watched as Regina threaded through the crowd to stand by her mother, both with sad eyes but resolute expressions. Her father joined her, putting his hands on her shoulders and whispering in her ear. Regina noticed Gen watching her and stared back, face unreadable. Bernard asked for a couple more songs while the feast lasted, Gen painfully aware of Regina's eyes upon him.

"News!" Rafael yelled after finishing his song. "How about a bit of news from the border?"

The crowd joined in the supplication, and Hubert, like a steer with a mouthful of cud, turned to his mom and dad as if to ask if he really had to. They nodded their encouragement, pleased to see their son becoming the center of attention.

"Whaddaya want to know?" he asked.

"Was there any fighting?" someone from the crowd blurted out.

"Well, I saw some people fight over a wench. And another time these guys were drunk and one said, 'You smell like an old potato sack,' and the other said—"

"No!" the man interrupted. Gen could now see that it was Woodsman Hurley, short and thick-chested. "I mean between Aughmere and Tolnor."

"Oh," Hubert replied. "I don't think so."

"Were there a lot of them?" Owen, Gant's master, inserted quickly.

"A lot of what?"

"Aughmerian soldiers. Were there many of them?"

"How much would you think is many?" Hubert asked.

"Never mind!" There was some snickering in the crowd, quickly put down by a bulging stare from Bernard.

"Do you think Aughmere will attack?" Jeorge asked.

"I don't know."

"Did you see any Rhugothian soldiers?" Jeorge pressed.

"Not as far as I know."

Rafael piped in. "Did you find out why Aughmere wants

to fight us? Has the King broken the Fidelium?"

The crowd gasped at the suggestion and shot Rafael dark looks. Hubert shrugged his shoulders.

"Thought I heard of that Fidelium a couple times. I think."

"Were there any good taverns in Elin Fort?" Gen asked.

Despite the grins from the townspeople, Hubert was visibly pleased with the question, face brightening.

"Yep! There's the Duam's Shed, kinda dirty, but with good ale. We went to Hogs Wallop, too. But the best had to be the Ice and Hammer. Good brew, good dice, and the serving wenches were—"

"Well," Bernard interrupted, Hubert obviously put out, "that'll be enough questions this evening. Everyone finish the meal, for I've an important announcement to make soon."

After some dissatisfied grumbling and derisive laughter, the townsfolk went back to their plates and their conversation. Gen felt pleased he could make Hubert both happy and a fool at the same time.

"That was disappointing," Rafael complained, taking a drink of ale. "I'm not sure if I'm more informed or less after Hubert's detailed answers."

"I certainly didn't know about those taverns. Sounds like the Ice and Hammer is the place to go," Gen joked.

Rafael snorted. "I know every one of those 'fine' establishments. Filthy places! I played them all in my younger days and barely made a pittance. What was earned was usually stolen before I could cross the street afterward! If Hubert thinks the Ice and Hammer has good brew, then he doesn't know the difference between river water and horse water!"

"Speaking of horses," Gen laughed, "it appears our best bet for information will come from Old Billy. He at least can tell us that there was a shortage of food."

"Shortage of care, you mean. Who knows what that

horse was forced to eat just to survive. Ever since the poor beast dragged itself into town, I've had a clear vision of it being staked up at the refuse pile by the soldiers' commons. If Bernard hadn't stopped the questioning, I would have asked Hubert about it."

"And Hubert would have said, 'I don't know.'"

Rafael chuckled, and Gen smiled at his own joke. A tug at his cloak directed his eyes downward and his mirth died. Regina stood below him on the ground, face ashen.

"I'm sorry," she said.

"For what?"

"People of Tell," Bernard shouted, cutting off whatever reply Regina meant to offer.

"I must go," she said, leaving a bewildered Gen behind.

The crowd did not quiet immediately, and Bernard was forced to yell several more times before complete silence fell. "People of Tell, I know you are thankful for the honorable service my son rendered in the armies of Duke Norshwal where he proudly stood against the forces of that tyrant Torbrand Khairn. Now I wish to make an announcement. It is with great joy that Katrina and I wish to announce the betrothal of our son Hubert Showles to the lovely Regina Morewold."

Gen felt his knees buckle and would have fallen had Rafael not steadied him. Hubert grinned piggishly at the prize his parents had won for him, and Regina stared back at her fiancé, face pale and wearing a paltry smile no one who knew her would believe. Gen's hands clenched, breaking one of the strings of his lute.

"Steady boy," Rafael whispered. "It is the way of things."

Gen barely heard him, torn somewhere between rage and inexpressible horror. The townspeople took several seconds to work up a polite applause. Gen felt as if he should spring down from the platform and shout for everyone to stop. He turned to Rafael, seeing that despite his master's call for calmness, his face also wrenched in disgust and pity.

"They are to be betrothed tonight and married in the spring!" Bernard continued happily.

Betrothals happened in the spring, marriages in the fall, and Gen wondered at the haste and break from tradition. He turned to Regina's father, who would not meet his eye. Jeorge knew what he had done just for the sake of lifting his family a half-rung up the social ladder, and the full weight of it pressed upon him. Gen did not doubt that Bernard had done other things to force the deal. As Regina walked to the platform to stand by her husband-to-be, Gen could not look at her, though he felt her eyes upon him.

The crowd parted as Regina's little sister Murea led old Billy toward the platform where Hubert and Regina would mount him for their short ride to the Church for the betrothal ceremony. Katrina bawled uncontrollably while Bernard watched with proud satisfaction.

The townspeople split apart to create an avenue around the square that led to the Church. Regina used the platform to mount Billy bare-backed and sidesaddle. Hubert sat behind her, placing his meaty hand around her waist. The horse trotted wearily away and unexpectedly stopped, swaying as it stood. Murea, still leading the horse, pulled at the rein, but the horse didn't budge.

"C'mon, ya old nag!" Hubert shouted, kicking it roughly. In response, Billy collapsed and died. Hubert managed to get free of the falling horse, though in doing so, he pushed Regina backward. Her head hit the stones with a sickening crack. Gen's eyes went wide and he leapt from the platform and sprinted to Regina's side. Rafael came quickly behind.

"The beast somehow ate some of the flowers of the vine around its neck." Rafael surmised, glancing over the horse quickly. "Poisoned itself. Is she all right, Gen?"

Regina lay perfectly still upon the ground, face drained of blood. Gen could tell from the rise and fall of her bosom that she was still breathing, and he lifted her head, feeling blood seeping from a wide gash on the back of her skull. Bernard and Katrina Showles rushed over to check on Hubert, who busied himself by swearing and kicking Billy. Gen lifted Regina and carried her to her parents, who signaled for him to take her to their home.

"Fetch the Pureman!" Bernard bellowed.

Gen waited as Jeorge frantically opened his shop and led him up the stairway to their home. The Morewold's house had more nice things in it than most, and Regina had her own room on the second story. Gen laid her upon her bed and backed away. Blood stained the pillows, and Regina's mother came to her side and started to weep, rubbing her daughter's face with her hand.

"How awful," she cried. "On your betrothal night and all."

Gen couldn't bear to watch anymore and stormed by Jeorge Morewold, who stood in the doorway waiting for the Pureman.

"Gen," he called.

Gen stopped and faced Jeorge. The older man's eyes were sad. In the absence of his hat, he clenched and unclenched his hands nervously. "Gen, I'm sorry. I. . ."

"You should be!" Gen retorted angrily. "And you'll get to keep being sorry for the rest of your life. You'll be sorry every time you see how miserable she is bouncing that buffoon's children on her knee!"

Jeorge's face fell, and Gen charged down the stairs noisily. At the bottom stood the Showles family. He wondered rather than cared how much they had heard of his outburst.

"So how is she, boy?" Bernard inquired with a guarded tone. Gen ignored him and shoved Hubert aside so he could get away, away from the square and away from people. He almost knocked down Pureman Millershim as he ascended the porch stairs. Gen ignored him too, striding

57

into the throng of people talking in low voices to one another. Gen spied Gant, and one glance was all that was needed to set in motion a night of revenge.

CHAPTER 4 - THE CHALAINE

The Chalaine sighed. "She probably told the ship Captain to sail more slowly just to torment me! Will she ever arrive?"

Her complaint fell on unsympathetic ears. She noticed Fenna's attempt to hide the roll of her eyes up into her head. Her handmaiden possessed a bubbly temperament that did not tolerate fretting and frowning—unless Fenna was doing the fretting and frowning. The Chalaine felt quite sure Fenna thought her ridiculous for her darker moods.

"Really, Chalaine, what could your mother possibly say that we don't already know? He is kingly. He is handsome. He is kind. He is overcome with the desire to meet you, to dance and talk and woo."

"But he is Aughmerian, Fenna! Women there are slaves and are given no more notice than dogs. I sent him one of my veils as a token, hoping he might respond and reveal somewhat of his character. What if he doesn't understand it or despises it?"

"What's to despise? And what's to understand, for that matter, other than that you wish him to return the attention?"

"But don't you see, Fenna? How could he understand?

The idea of giving and getting attention is foreign to him. Anyhow, I thought sending the veil was terribly symbolic. He is to be the first man to see me unveiled, after all."

"Come Chalaine," Fenna said. "Surely those in charge of his education taught him the customs and ways of the nations he is to rule. He has agreed, has he not, to be married in the Rhugothian fashion? That shows some understanding, at least. Besides, look at that fine tapestry. Does the proud, handsome man there appear so stupid as to not understand the meaning of a young lady's token?"

The Chalaine no longer needed to look at it. The artistic rendition of her and her husband-to-be hung embroidered into a tapestry above the head of her bed, etched into her mind by hours of staring and dreaming. Woven over a hundred years before her birth, the artist had imagined her bold yet delicate, and him fierce yet handsome, treading hand in hand across a bloody battlefield of fiends, demons, and monsters. She carried the reincarnation of God in her pregnant belly. He carried a sword shining white, and on his brow was the prophetic birthmark, the veiled moon of Trys.

In the tapestry, all three moons shone, sharing the sky with the sun; but that was the future. Eladoth, the God whom Mikkik slew, veiled Trys at his death, eclipsing it to block the magical power that emanated from it. Mikkik weakened as the moon waned, for in Trys was his might and his power. The Puremen and Prelates taught that Mikkik had for years afterward wandered Ki'Hal sowing what seeds of evil and malice he could in his dissolution.

Eldaloth would return and end him with finality. He would return through the Chalaine. At that day, Trys would shine again, for in Trys was Eldaloth's power as well, and the power her husband would wield in protection of the infant and his mother. It was the power that would bind broken Ki'Hal together again.

She studied the tapestry for a moment, fixing the image

in her mind's eye, striving to think of herself as the woman portrayed there—strong, confident, and fully trusting the man at her side. She hoped Chertanne was half the man the tapestry portrayed him to be; she hoped she could be half the woman. His part seemed the most difficult, to rule, to lead, and to fight. Her role was little more than what women had done through all ages of time.

"It is just a tapestry, Fenna. The artist was no prophet. My hair is certainly not black, and if I am that much shorter than he is, he will be a tower of a man indeed!"

"All I am saying," Fenna argued as she weaved a thin braid into her own brown hair, "is that you are the most fortunate of women! You will marry the Ha'Ulrich! What better man could there possibly be than the Savior of Ki'Hal? The rest of your sex must root through the rascals and rakes of this world and hope to sniff out a good one."

"And how does Kimdan smell?" the Chalaine teased. Fenna had doted on the son of Regent Ogbith, High Protector of Rhugoth, ever since the First Mother had called her into service as the Chalaine's handmaiden three years ago.

Fenna blushed. "He is pleasant to the nose, though if his own were not pointed skyward so often, he might chance to notice me. So you see, I envy your position. How can the Ha'Ulrich not spend all his days daydreaming about the most beautiful woman in the world?"

"And how could Kimdan, unless he is uninterested in womankind, not dream of you? I've seen the way men gawk at you. Whatever beauty I have was deliberately bred into me. What you possess is a gift."

"Your beauty would make Kimdan wild with passion, no matter how self-absorbed he is. My 'gift' isn't even enough to elicit a warm greeting from him."

The Chalaine moved to sit by her handmaiden on the bed, commandeering the task of braiding her hair. Fenna's carefree nature in the face of the Chalaine's troubles evaporated at thoughts of her own, and the Chalaine could not stand to see her friend so out of spirits, even if she thought it a little selfish.

"To comfort you, then, I suppose I should confess how I envy you."

"And in what way could 'Divine Beauty Incarnate' envy me?"

"I envy your uncertainty. Don't you see? At least you get to play the game! My beauty may drive men mad, but what use is it? I don't get to do it. My rutted road lies before me thoroughly planned and predicted with no chance to wander or wonder. I will marry Chertanne and have his child. That is all. I may have the assurance of a good husband, but you will have the satisfaction of winning the man you choose. We will surely both find happiness in the men we love, but your journey will be more interesting and satisfying than mine."

"I thank you for your comfort, Chalaine," Fenna said, inspecting the completed braid. "I just hope I can get Kimdan's attention without stooping to throwing myself at him. But throw myself I will, if it comes to it."

"That's better," the Chalaine smiled. "But if it doesn't work out, I assure you there are other eligible men about." The Chalaine pointed to her door, indicating her day Protector, Dason, who was standing guard outside.

"Dason is a gorgeous man," Fenna whispered. "But I am settled upon Kimdan. I cannot keep my mind off of him! Besides, Dason is eight years my senior."

"Eight years is nothing," the Chalaine whispered back. She herself fought mightily not to be infatuated with her dark-haired, gregarious Protector. "He is also intelligent, sensitive, a Prince of Tolnor. . . "

"Do stop or I shall think you have designs on him! But isn't it about time for—" A knock at the door interrupted Fenna's sentence and she swore. "I am trapped again!"

The Chalaine laughed quietly and replaced her veil.

"Come!"

Dason, handsome and smiling, opened the door and greeted them. After letting Prelate Obelard inside, he entered himself and gathered chairs for the plump Churchman and the ladies. While a kind enough man, the Chalaine and Fenna found the Prelate a terrible bore and more than a little fastidious. His black robes, silver moon medallion, and darkly stained walnut staff marked his position. He sat heavily, squeezing a smile from lips not accustomed to much upward movement.

"Chalaine," he said, inclining his head. "And Miss Fairedale! I am so glad you could join us yet again."

The Prelate's voice was a high, nasal monotone that managed to grate on the ears and somehow be inconsequential enough to start the mind to wandering at the same time.

"Welcome, your Grace," Fenna returned, standing and curtsying.

"Very well. We shall begin, as always, with the recital of the prophecy. Chalaine, if you would please."

The Chalaine nodded, hiding her resentment of the duty. Since she could speak, this task had been laid to her every day. "Hear the prophecy given to Pontiff Ethelion the Second upon Bay Mountain by angelic Ministrant, signaling to Eldaloth's children a way to hope and to prepare Ki'Hal for the war to come:

Hearken, for joy sounds in your ears.
A way is prepared for God's return,
To bring health,
To bring happiness,
To bring holiness,

For decreed are their names
And fixed their course
Below the moons,

63

Standing upon Ki'Hal
In the hand of God.

The Ha'Ulrich,
Born with Trys upon his brow,
Shall lead them, Blessed One,
Gatherer of Nations,
Savior of Ki'Hal.

The Chalaine,
Pure, undefiled, and unmarred,
Divine beauty incarnate,
Mother of God,
The Hand of Healing.

In the Hall of Three Moons
They are bound,
And Trys will show her face,
And in its first light,
God again conceived.

And upon the field of death they shall walk,
Hand within hand.
And about them the fire of war shall burn,
And about them the arrows fall,
And around them the blades cut,
And around them demons rage.

But he bears no burn, no wound.
From his heart to her hand is love,
From her heart to his hand is healing,
Without will,
Without spell,
Without sacrifice.
Hand in hand. Strength for strength.

And from her womb His child,
The tabernacle of our God,
And in His hand the power of Trys
To thwart the Dark One,
To bind the nations to battle.

But hearken and ware,
A claw is set against them,
To bring terror,
To rend the Chalaine,
To ruin the Blessed One.

It is the Ilch, Mikkik's hand,
Trys upon his foot,
A killer in the darkness,
A might unseen,
A poison to the heart of nations.

And in his face a horror spoken,
And at his words hearts falter.
What is joined he tears in twain,
Where The Ha'Ulrich stands, he hunts,
Where the Chalaine hides, he waits.

The battlefield becomes birthplace.
Then is foot set against brow,
Blessing against curse,
Beauty against horror,
Heart against hand,
Our God against Mikkik.

She ended, and, as Obelard explicated every point again
and again, she thought of how the prophecy seemed
incomplete in her estimation. While Prelates and Puremen
talked of the day of joy and triumph without hesitation, the
Ministrant's elision of the outcome begged the question of

who would lay hold of the victory.

Most prophecies pronounced everything from the beginning through the end; this one left the end unrevealed. A return to paradise under Eldaloth's hand was nowhere guaranteed, and that lack of surety burdened her with a double sense of duty. She must act her part because prophecy foreordained her to it, but she must also perform her duty strictly and well, lest the grander purpose fail and she unintentionally ruin the hopes of the world.

The burden of her calling, she thought, should rightly weigh her down. She was but sixteen, worshiped and revered, held up and preached as an example by the same people who remonstrated her for any childish or indecent behavior. Great expectations of happiness under Eldaloth followed her name, and when she was permitted to leave the castle to minister to the sick and afflicted, she caught a sense of her own importance. The people cheered after her and knelt as her heavily guarded wagon rolled by. While she thought such worship should instill some sense of confidence and self-worth within her, it instead made her nervous. So many counted on her and she felt so inadequate.

"And thus we see," Obelard plodded on, "that in this perfect union of Ha'Ulrich and Chalaine there will be powers unparalleled to heal and destroy— the Chalaine's healing to counter Mikkik's destruction, the Ha'Ulrich's generative powers to counter Mikkik's malcreative force."

The Prelate paused as if expecting some reaction to his brilliant statement. "Well," he continued after getting none, "I have many other things to share with you from the treatise I am writing, but alas, I must go prepare for the return of the First Mother. We are all anxious for word of your future husband. Extraordinary times indeed."

The Chalaine marveled at how he could be so boring even when excited. She rose. "We thank you humbly, your Grace. Godspeed."

The Prelate did the best bow he could muster and shuffled from the room. Dason left with him.

"Did you hear?!" Fenna exclaimed when the door was shut.

"Hear what?"

"'*And the bliss that the Chalaine and the Ha'Ulrich shall feel upon their wedding night as they engage in the blessed creation of Eldaloth's tabernacle shall foreshadow the joy the world shall feel upon His return.*'" Fenna quoted.

"He said that?"

"Weren't you listening? I was absolutely stunned. I nearly burst out laughing."

"No, I wasn't listening" the Chalaine answered unashamedly. "Ever since he started writing his treatise on the prophecy—as if there weren't treatises enough on the subject—the good Prelate has become even more of a bore than usual. I am disappointed I missed that little scrap of speculative doctrine, though. I wouldn't think a Prelate would dwell on such . . . particulars."

"I wouldn't either," Fenna replied. "But such steamy conversation has put me in mind of Kimdan. I believe he and the Regent are arriving soon. I beg permission to leave you until tonight."

"Of course. Good luck, Fenna. I will expect every detail on your return."

Fenna left, and the Chalaine removed her veil and lay back on the bed. Obelard's instruction was a powerful soporific. Despite her insecurities and doubts, the Chalaine felt she possessed one reason to rejoice, a reason no other Chalaine before her had: she would have a husband and a lover. The Chalaines who had come before her had waited for the Ha'Ulrich to be born and, that failing, had been mated upon their seventeenth birthday to men whose identities they could not know. When the pregnancy was assured, the nameless men were sent away, never to be seen by the Chalaine again.

After the Shattering, the people of Rhugoth chose the Chalaines to rule them as queens, the office later named "First Mother." Every Chalaine for two-hundred years sat upon the throne, powerful, alone, and forbidden to love, lest another child be born that could claim the title Chalaine.

The Chalaine could only partly understand the loneliness of her predecessors, a loneliness fate or Eldaloth had spared her. The year she was born and on the same day, the Ha'Ulrich also came into the world, bearing the mark of the unveiled moon of Trys upon his brow. He was a son of the Shadan of Aughmere, Torbrand Khairn, and an unnamed concubine who was slain soon after she gave birth so that no other child could issue from her womb and upset the surety of prophecy. The Chalaine had never seen the Ha'Ulrich, though she knew his name was Chertanne and that he likely lived as protected a life as she did.

But the most important nobles and aristocracy from the three kingdoms had finally met him during the summer. Her own mother undertook the journey to assess her future son-in-law and to negotiate on behalf of Rhugoth about the wedding and the transfer of power to the Ha'Ulrich at the appointed time. King Filingrail of Tolnor also attended. The Church of the One planned a great festival and presentation for them so they could meet the Ha'Ulrich for the first time.

The Chalaine could not help but think that the Rhugothian aristocracy was nervous that an unknown boy, one rarely seen, would—by prophetic right—take ownership of their lands and command their armies. Her mother would bring them a report. The Chalaine had begged to go on the trip—she was to marry the Ha'Ulrich, after all—but they had forbidden her to do so. They said they could take no chance of exposing her to the danger of a trip through two Portals and the long road through Aughmere. She knew they were right, but she desperately wanted a face to go with the name, an image to dote upon and anchor her desires to.

She loved to daydream about her wedding day, dancing in the Hall of Three Moons, ancient and elegant, with the most powerful man on Ki'Hal. Upon their marriage, he would reign as High King over all, and she would sit at his side, Queen and wife, until she birthed Eldaloth and he again ruled Ki'Hal as he had anciently. The Chalaine knew her handmaiden was right—however the Chalaine might miss the tortured game of love, she would have such bliss as most women would never know.

She reminded herself that even with an arranged marriage, she would still need to woo him, make him feel important, support his decisions, encourage him in his manly endeavors, and comfort him tenderly at his losses. Long years of careful breeding had fashioned her the most beautiful of women. She felt confident Chertanne would want her and love her better than any man had loved any woman. She could hardly wait to see what Chertanne would send as a token in return and what report her mother had for her. She hoped he would at least send a letter.

To distract herself from the wait, the Chalaine decided to use the Walls. Long ago, Magicians created the Walls with which the Chalaines could divert themselves by looking magically on any vista they wished in and around Mikmir, the capital city of Rhugoth. All the rooms in her bedchamber were enchanted to this purpose, and, by concentrating, she could travel to the town square, the castle gardens, or the nearby hunting grounds of the Regents. The people she watched could not see her, and she could not hear or interact with them, but watching the unsuspecting citizenry had taught her to have compassion and love for them, as well as shown her a number of other things she thought her mother might object to.

After watching some performers in the market, she released her concentration. The images faded and she settled on a nap to pass the time. Even this, however, she approached with trepidation. Two reoccurring dreams, one a converse to the other, had started the day her mother left in the spring. Every time she closed her eyes they came, and in those dreams she was always running.

Everyone, it seemed, took her dreams seriously, and when others asked her what she dreamed of—and the Prelate and the Mage Ethris regularly did—they would have her describe what she dreamed with precise detail from start to finish. But she told no one of these latest dreams and wouldn't until she could make better sense of them herself.

For one, she hated the way Ethris stared at her with his engulfing eyes and shook his head or said "mhmm" as if he somehow knew more about her dreams than she could fathom. She feared that he did and hated it. For another, her dreams were her own. She developed a habit of saying nothing of her dreams until she had puzzled over the odd images for herself and arrived at some conclusion, but the two dreams she dreamed now were a paradox that were simple in imagery and symbolism but contradictory enough to thwart any grasping of their meaning. The fact that they had started when her mother left gave her reason to think them special or at least that their meaning was somehow tied to her departure.

As she laid her head upon finely embroidered pillows, safe within the confines of her veiled bed, she sensed the dreams coming in a way she never had before. The images flashed in her mind before she closed her eyes. And when sleep came, she was running.

The first dream started pleasantly enough. Her breath steamed from her as she sprinted down a narrow track through a stand of yellowing aspen. The damp ground smelled sickly sweet with fresh autumn rot. Leaves fell about her hair and shoulders as she moved beneath the thick trees, and at times a soft but chill breeze raised bumps on her skin. Ahead of her the sun sank over tree-draped mountains, weak as it always was when summer ended, but friendly and inviting nonetheless. Since her mentors and masters never let her near any place so remote, wild, and beautiful, she thrilled at everything she saw and smelled. The pleasantness, however, stopped just as she started to immerse herself in it.

All at once a flood of terror drowned her, suffocating her heart and her will as she negotiated the path. She would notice then that she wore a plain gray dress, tattered and stained with blood. She ached as she ran, sore and weary, to flee from someone or something behind her. She would turn her head and only catch fleeting glimpses of her pursuer. He never ran, just walked, and no matter how fast she churned her legs, he stayed effortlessly behind her, face dark within a cowl and unseen eyes boring into her body with unspeakable intentions. His clothing, a darker gray, was also bloody and torn. She could not escape him, and the dream ended with her tripping and falling. She looked up and he stood at her muddy feet looking down, face lost in the abyssal cowl. The whole twisted scene, a convoluted mass of beauty and horror, left her shaking, sweating, and cold.

And then the next dream started. Again, she was running, but through how different a scene! As before, she ran on a narrow path through a stand of aspen. What season it was, however, she could not tell, as a thick shroud of gray ash blanketed tree, meadow, and mountain. Fast moving, roiling clouds dumped the ash in heavy flakes upon the world in a perverted mockery of winter. Ahead of her, she could see a thin strip of sky between the clouds and the horizon, and, as she watched, the sun dipped into that space and cast a fierce red glow across the sky, transforming the path she traveled into a road descending into a great cauldron of blood.

All about the path men lay dead, half-buried in the

downpour. Arrows protruded from backs, and hacked limbs lay short distances from the bodies they had been severed from. The sounds of battle and the screams of the combatants assaulted her from every side, and fell voices howled in victory. Children wept for slain fathers, women for slain husbands, before horrifying creatures of every description slunk from the woods and killed the mourners.

But rather than feeling full of dread or sorrowful as the scene prompted, her heart soared with joy. Not all her steps were to run. Sometimes she skipped or twirled about, kicking up ash that never fell on or stained her beautiful gown of red and gold. She sang to herself as a girl in love does, for before her, somewhere in the distance, *he* waited. There was no face or name to attach the love to, but there didn't need to be. For a certainty, he waited, and while the land about her fell into destruction and despair for reasons and through powers she couldn't fathom, she cared not. Ki'Hal and all the races and creatures that lived upon it be damned—he waited. She would come. Nothing else mattered.

And that last part, the very last part, disturbed her more than the odd imagery, the relentless pursuer, or the unnamed love. Everyone entrusted with raising her had ingrained within her heart and mind an unwavering care for Ki'Hal and its peoples. She knew that but for her and the Blessed One, the workings of Mikkik would destroy the world, perhaps as the last dream depicted. She was bred to be the vessel that would prevent that from happening. The thought that she would throw aside her duty and condemn Ki'Hal to destruction to satisfy her own yearnings disgusted her and set her to trembling.

There was no sense in it. Her love for the Ha'Ulrich was to provide the end to war and bring peace. Her pursuer, she reasoned, was the Ilch, coming to rend her. The unnamed love, she assumed, was the Ha'Ulrich. The results, however, were switched. Her death brought salvation; her life and

72

love, destruction. *Perhaps,* she thought, *the dreams are the work of the Ilch.*

She woke, and the unusual power of the dreams crushed any need she felt to sleep further. She touched the Walls, concentrating on the dock, hoping to find that her mother had at last arrived. Around her, the Kingsblood Lake emerged into view as lifelike as if she were actually there. The early afternoon sun rippled on the waves, reflecting the watery dance on the hulls of many great ships—ships of nobles and merchants—that waited in anticipation of the arrival of the Defender, the First Mother's vessel.

Among the great vessels floated smaller rafts and fishing boats, and the Chalaine smiled. She could see the common folk, carefree and happy, swimming and laughing and lounging around. Floating next to the Thorn—Regent Morgan's behemoth pleasure craft—was a raft packed with tan, shirtless boys in ragged pants playing some game where they tried to throw each other off their rickety rafts into the water. The Chalaine giggled—something she rarely did—at their antics.

She longed to be like them, unconfined and unconcerned, but such longing only awakened a sense of impatience and dissatisfaction within her, feelings she'd tried to crush many times before. She knew she was more like the well-dressed Regent's sons, Alamand and Jorrick, who stood at the rails of the Thorn observing as longingly as she was the rowdy contest below. She imagined that they, too, secretly wished they had the courage to throw aside propriety and plunge headfirst into the mess of life they were protected against.

She had watched for some time when, to her delight, the Defender sailed into view. It tacked forward quickly on the stiff afternoon breeze, and before long her mother, along with several lords and ladies, debarked. Before the First Mother could step off the longboat and onto the pier, she was surrounded by aristocracy and Churchmen alike, the

Prelate himself among the throng. Her mother spoke to them briefly and boarded her carriage.

The Chalaine let the Walls fade. Donning a veil, she opened the door and passed through the maze to the Antechamber of the Chalaines, chatting with Dason for over an hour until her mother and her bodyguard, Cadaen, came in. The Chalaine couldn't help but notice the weariness on her mother's face as they embraced and made small talk about the journey.

"And what is he like, Mother? You must tell me everything."

Mirelle smiled understandingly. "I'm afraid there is not much to tell. We barely saw him, and I have several urgent meetings to attend to."

The Chalaine tried to push aside the disappointment. "And did you give him the veil I sent?"

"Of course I did, dear."

"And. . ."

"And what?"

"Did he send anything in return?" The Chalaine could barely control the desperation in her voice.

"I am afraid not. He was touched, to be sure. But the custom of a woman's token is not practiced in Aughmere."

The Chalaine groaned in frustration. "Can you at least tell me what he looks like?"

"I will, but you must promise not to pester me anymore. As I said, we barely saw the Ha'Ulrich and anything I say about him is conjecture, save his appearance. He is not as tall as depicted in the tapestry. He is the same height as you are. He has blond hair and blue eyes and wears rather expensive and somewhat ostentatious clothing."

"But what about. . ."

"No, Chalaine. No more questions. Come. Give me another hug and be content."

The Chalaine hugged her mother again, not bothering to hide her dispiritedness. Her mother did not seem to notice.

Dason and Cadaen bowed to the First Mother as she left, and the Chalaine stood rooted in her spot in disbelief.

"Not quite enough information for you, your Holiness?" Dason asked, voice not quite concealing a hint of playfulness.

The Chalaine turned to face him. Dason, son of Duke Kildan, Lord Protector of Tolnor, was the most beautiful man she had ever laid eyes on. He was refined, witty, and absolutely pleasant at every occasion. However, the most delightful thing about Dason was that he was thoroughly Tolnorian, and at the heart of every Tolnorian she met was a foundation of honor that supported a solidity of character rarely seen in Rhugothian sophistication. Why Fenna would even consider the snobby Kimdan over Dason baffled her.

Dason had entered the Dark Guard at nineteen, easily the best sword fighter at the Trials. Pureman Abelard, their Court Librarian and Historian, told her that Dason was the youngest Protector a Chalaine had ever had, acquiring the honor at the age of twenty-two. He only recently turned twenty-four.

For a year and a half, Dason had watched over her during the day. His smiles and bright personality lifted her, and whatever flattery he could offer her he did. The Chalaine tried her best not to enjoy it. In the absence of any knowledge about the Ha'Ulrich, the Chalaine often placed Dason in her imagination in his stead. For if the Ha'Ulrich was to be the best of men, then it followed he would be a lot like Dason.

Of course, now she knew that unlike Dason, the Ha'Ulrich was blond. Dason had dark hair, which set off his stunning blue eyes. Blond hair and blue eyes, however, still played well on a man's face. Geoff, a famed bard she'd seen perform twice, rivaled Dason in looks and had long hair the color of wheat stalks at harvest time. The Chalaine shook herself, realizing that thinking about the excellent qualities of men besides the Ha'Ulrich was not appropriate.

She chided herself and turned back toward her quarters.

"I will be content, Dason," the Chalaine replied, finally. "It is quite possible she wished to address me privately on the matter." The Chalaine hoped, rather than thought, that this was true.

"If it is of any consolation," Dason offered, "my sister Melina didn't see her husband at all until she and he stood before the Pureman, betrothed and married on the same day. You will have several months to acquaint yourself with your betrothed before actually wedding him."

"And are they happy?"

"Who can tell? They have as much chance as any to find happiness."

"As much chance as any?" the Chalaine replied, laughing. "I suppose Tolnorian nobility is used to blind marriages for political expediency. Such things went out of fashion here in Rhugoth generations ago. We believe men and women more likely to find happiness if they are afforded the opportunity to know each other and end or continue the courtship based on what they find."

"Sounds dreadfully complicated to me, your Highness," Dason remarked. "Seems such a course of action would lead to a great deal of distraction and wasted time."

"Now you're sounding like an Aughmerian," the Chalaine returned mirthfully.

"Highness!" Dason gasped, horrified. "That is an insult indeed! Aughmerian notions of women and marriage are so benighted that to call them uncivil is grossly understating the case! The Ha'Ulrich, however, is no doubt much different."

"I am sure he is, Dason, and I apologize for my remark. It was in jest. I know you hold women in the highest regard. Whatever woman you give your heart to will be fortunate indeed, whether she has the privilege of knowing you beforehand or not."

"Forgive me, Holiness. I hope I did not respond too

fervently."

"Do not fret, I was teasing you and hoping for a vehement reply."

"To what end, Holiness?" Dason asked as they entered the maze that served as a barrier to protect the Chalaine's apartments. They both knew it so well they didn't need to think about where they were going.

"My own amusement. A bit unladylike by Tolnorian standards, I imagine."

"I should hardly judge against you. You are the most perfect woman I have ever known."

The Chalaine blushed beneath her veil and prayed that the Ha'Ulrich would be so forgiving and complimentary—and cut such a handsome figure in uniform.

"I thank you for your gracious compliment, however undeserved," the Chalaine replied. Dason ran forward in front of her and blocked the way. The Chalaine stopped, startled at the earnest look on his face.

"It is not undeserved, My Lady," his face was pained. "You are beautiful and kind, the two best virtues to find in a woman. How am I supposed to find a woman and be satisfied when I have to compare her to you day after day? No. I am determined I must forgo any thought of women and wooing while I am in your service. You are the Chalaine, the best of women. I will protect you as long as I am able to draw sword."

He took her hand and kissed it. The Chalaine found it hard to breathe.

"Please, Dason," she stammered. "Do not be overcome and do not make too much of me."

She started forward again and he fell in behind her. The resumption of this normalcy helped alleviate the strange knot in her stomach. "I have a title and a work to do. Besides those, I am just as other women and in many respects their inferior. My mother is the more gifted leader, Lady Fairedale more cheerful. No! Do not protest. Once I wed and bear the Holy child, my beauty will fade and I will take my place with other women, and a passerby will hardly notice me as anything out of the ordinary."

As she said it, the Chalaine realized she looked forward to that anonymity a great deal—if she was ever afforded it.

"Say what you will, Holiness," Dason said, voice subdued. "You will never convince me another woman's virtues are greater than yours."

The Chalaine bit her lip, grateful that the door to her room was in view, and standing on the threshold was Eldwena, her night handmaiden. She had already dragged a table and chairs out into the hallway. Unlike Fenna, Lady Eldwena Moores had served as the Chalaine's handmaid since the Chalaine was an infant. She had five children of her own, and some still thought she should give up the post for their sake, but since the Chalaine would be married soon, she begged to remain in service until that day.

"Your Holiness," she bowed. "And Dason. I've the table set up and ready. I so love these card games in the evening, so I apologize if I am a bit presumptuous in my preparations." Eldwena scrunched her eyebrows together. "But are you both quite all right?"

"We are fine, Lady Moores," the Chalaine said, attempting a light tone. "My mother only recently returned and I had hoped she would bear me news of my future husband. Alas, she said she found out little, so I have been a bit disappointed and out of sorts. I am sure a game of cards will help lift my spirits."

"I am sorry, Holiness," Eldwena said soothingly. "But a rousing game of cards is good medicine for getting a man off your mind."

The Chalaine didn't feel much like playing, but she set to it, hoping her mother would exit the maze and take her inside the apartments and tell her everything. But her mother never came. She contented herself with the game, noticing that Dason was letting her win on purpose. This both annoyed and flattered her. After several games, she begged to be excused, wanting nothing more than to sleep and hope for a more informative day on the morrow.

CHAPTER 5 - MERCY AND WEAKNESS

Gen didn't sleep. He sat hands around knees in a stand of golden maple trees to the side of the Church and waited until everyone straggled out of the square and the lamps in nearby buildings winked out.

Gen watched as the Showleses left the Morewold's and went home, where they stayed awake for nearly an hour before going to sleep. He watched as Pureman Millershim and Rafael came out of the same door carrying a basin and a large wooden box of herbs that the Pureman used for the healing of the sick and injured. Still he waited, shivering in the autumn chill. Although the wind had died down, the clouds persisted, covering the moons, shards, and stars, creating perfect darkness.

When the Pureman extinguished the lamps inside the Church, Gen paused a few more minutes and determined it was time to put his plan into motion. Convenient to the back of the Church was a small outbuilding where the Pureman stored various implements used for gardening and interring the dead. The door squeaked wildly as Gen opened it, but he hurriedly picked out two spades he knew leaned against the wall within easy reach.

As stealthily as he could, he sneaked slowly across the benighted Churchyard with spades in hand, trying to remember where everything was. A soft orange glow on the back steps of the Church set his heart to racing, and he threw himself prone, worried that someone had spotted him. The spades clattered loudly when they hit the ground, destroying whatever stealth he had hoped for.

"Get up, lad, and come here," Rafael ordered. "You're going to kill yourself bumbling around like that in this blackness."

Gen stood up sheepishly, swiping the damp leaves off his pants and shirt. As he came closer to the Church, he could make out Rafael and Pureman Millershim quietly sharing a pipe on the rear steps. Gen was glad he couldn't see the Pureman clearly, fearing what those blue eyes might say about what he was doing.

"Good evening, Pureman," Gen said softly, desperately hoping Millershim wouldn't notice the shovels lying on the ground behind him. "How is Regina?"

Millershim inhaled deeply, savoring the smoke before handing the pipe back to Rafael. Pipeweed would not grow in Tell, but the Pureman and Rafael ensured that the Morewolds ordered some from the south every autumn.

"She will live," Pureman Millershim reported. "It took time, Twineweed, and a lot of prayer, but she finally awoke before we left. A bad wound, that one, but she is strong and will be back to herself soon."

"Were it not for you, Pureman," Rafael said, "she likely wouldn't have lived through the night. You do good work."

"I do as Eldaloth wills, that is all." He savored the smoke for a moment, smacking his lips. "The tobacco crop doesn't seem as rich as last year's, master bard. What do you think?"

"It was a dry spring. Let me have another turn at it."

"At least," Gen broke in, "old Billy put the betrothal off

81

for a few more days. Why didn't they wait until spring? That's the tradition."

Neither man spoke for a long time.

"I'm afraid, Gen," Millershim finally admitted, "that the Showleses ordered me to perform the betrothal as soon as she woke up, though I objected. They will be married come spring. As to why, I think as a capstone to the celebration and because Hubert will leave soon after their marriage to go back to the army. You might get pressed into it, too, if Aughmere attacks and things go poorly. I'm sorry it happened this way, Gen. But Bernard is the Magistrate."

Gen felt sadness and anger well up within him anew. "How could you?" he protested. "It's bad enough they're to be wed at all, not to mention the lack of dignity or concern shown by forcing her into the betrothal when she's half-conscious and bleeding all over the place."

The Pureman retrieved the pipe from Rafael. "I agree with you, but make no mistake. Bernard can make plenty of trouble for me, and the two would be betrothed whether I performed the rite tonight or two weeks from now, or in the spring. There is little difference. Perhaps it turned out better this way. Some things are better borne half-conscious."

"I would think," Gen countered, getting angrier at Millershim's cavalier attitude, "that if Regina had the choice of being betrothed to that monster for two weeks fewer, she would take it! What an utter mockery of decency! This is all. . ."

"It appears you have some digging to do Gen," Rafael cut in, voice stern but sympathetic. "You'd best be about it."

Gen expected a rebuke from the Pureman, for undoubtedly he guessed what Gen was about. Instead, Pureman Millershim simply said, "Good luck, Gen. And don't get caught. Be assured that our thoughts go with you, even when our hands cannot."

Gen turned from the two men, gathered the spades, and ran across the square as fast as he could, holding one spade in each hand to keep them from banging together. As quickly as he could safely and quietly manage, he ran up the small incline to the left of the Showles's home and into a thicket. Gant waited for him underneath a tall ash which was pushing up through the center of more diminutive trees. Before them, some twenty feet from the rear of the Showles's house, was the outhouse. It was almost invisible in the darkness, but the stink was unmistakable.

"You sure you want to go through with all this, Gen?" Gant whispered. "This could mean real trouble. I mean real trouble. I know you like the girl and all. . ."

"It has to be done. If you want to leave, then do. I'll manage."

Gant stood silent and still for several moments, and Gen thought that he might just turn and go. Gant was usually the first to cause trouble, but his apprenticeship had mellowed the mischievousness of the young man, and Yeurile brooked no boyishness. Still, Gant hated the Showleses, and Gen wondered whether the hatred or the thought of Yeurile scolding him would win out.

"Let's be quick about it," Gant finally acquiesced. "I got work to do in the morning. You layabout bards don't know what that's like."

Gen patted his friend's back and they approached the outhouse slowly, listening for any sign that the Showleses were awake. After a few minutes of listening to Bernard or perhaps Hubert snore loudly enough to scare away birds, they set about their work.

Although no one had ever done it before, what Gen proposed to do to the outhouse was really a simple alteration. First, he and Gant edged the structure backwards until the waste pit was exposed. Breathing through their mouths to prevent the smell from overcoming them, they dug around the pit, creating a sloped funnel that descended into it. Damp ground made for quiet digging.

That done and the dark dirt piled away behind the thicket, they moved the entryway of the outhouse over the new hole. The next Showles to visit the outhouse would find himself sliding down until he was arm-pit deep in his own filth.

"Thank you for your help, Gant."

"You gonna wait?"

"Yes. I need to see this," Gen replied

"Well, I'm not crazy. If you get caught, you'll find yourself banished from Tell. You be careful, Gen; you stand to lose a lot if Bernard catches you."

"I know, Gant. But how could I stay in this town, season after season, year after year, and watch her with that buffoon? I have to leave here, and whether I'm forced to or choose to, it makes little difference now. But don't worry, Gant. If I'm caught, I'll leave you out of it. You and Yeurile will have a happy life. Take the spades back."

"There will be another girl, Gen. You've got to believe that."

Gen answered nothing, and Gant jogged into the night, leaving him to his crude, cruel vigil.

At first the anger and anticipation kept him awake, but as the night wore on, the rough emotions lost their edge and turned from ardent hate to empty coldness. It rained lightly on and off. While the trees above him protected him from the wetness, the soft pattering of the rain on the leaves and ground soothed and dampened the hurt within him. Gen felt that nature wept with him in the dark, and knowing that someone—or something—shared his pain unclenched his nerves and subdued his nagging headache.

Several times he considered undoing his trap, replacing the dirt, and walking away, but just when he would decide to do it, the image of Regina lying bleeding on the stones of the square returned to his mind, shoring up his resolve. He needed something more than just the comfort of the rain

84

and the trees. Deep inside his heart something demanded justice—and barring that—retribution. Justice in a town controlled by the Showleses was impossible. Justice would be Regina betrothed to someone she could share her heart with, someone like Gen. Justice would have the entire Showles family carted away and left in the Rede Steppes to live or die far from the company of decent folk.

Pureman Millershim taught, however, that in the fallen, shattered world of Ki'Hal, good and right were not always followed or rewarded, and evil was not always shunned and punished. The Church urged the people not to seek their own justice when the men of the world failed but rather to be humble and to pray for deliverance from grudges and hatred. Revenge, it was said, was Mikkik's tool to destroy souls and spread violence and sorrow.

But Gen knew there were limits to how much should be tolerated in the name of humility and faith, for history abounded with stories of those who refused to live with injustice any longer. History counted them heroes.

Ignati, a Prelate of the Church itself, turned against his religious superiors when he saw corruption and vice in them, leading the fighting orders in a five-year-long war against the Church and the nations that would follow it. His action in the face of injustice earned him the adoration of Church leaders in the years afterward. What would have happened if he had sat in his monastery chamber and only prayed for deliverance or hoped that justice would eventually prevail?

While Gen had no delusions that his cause was nearly as grand as that of Ignati, he hoped the same principle applied to his predicament. But the more he thought about it, the more he realized just how rabid and unthinking he let himself become in the hours after hearing of the betrothal. Gen remembered Ignati's letter to the Pontiff announcing his intentions to rid the Church of corruption. The man was deeply sorrowful about what he felt he had to do and his mind was clear, far different from the wild passions that pulsed through Gen earlier that evening, passions that were ebbing as fatigue gained a foothold upon him.

A couple hours before dawn the clouds began to break up and the soft light from the moons Myn and Duam illuminated the small clearing where the rigged outhouse sat. The moon Trys, eclipsed, was an abyss ringed with light. Two moons set against the one, a symbol of the Chalaine and the Ha'Ulrich standing fast against the murdering purposes of Mikkik.

It will be a great war, Father Millershim preached. *Most of us will not stand in battlefields against the enemy. Most of us must win the war only in our hearts and in our homes. While we will wield no sword, we must wield forgiveness; we wear no armor but clothe ourselves in kindness; we spill no blood, but we just as surely strike the heart of evil with every wound we bind, with every tear we shed in sympathy, and with every smile with which we lift the spirit of another.*

With a sigh Gen looked at the Showles's house and then back through the trees where he could barely make out the window where he knew Regina slept. Something broke within him, and tears fell from his eyes and onto the ground. He did not let the feeling engulf him and would not let himself sob or wail. The sadness drained from him in silence, and after a few minutes he wiped his face, cursing Rafael for teaching him introspection. He got up and took a step toward the Church to retrieve a spade. There was little time to undo what they had done, if it could be undone at all.

You are weak. It should not be so.

The voice came from within his own head, but squinting into the moonlight, he could see the figure of a girl, no more than six or seven, standing just outside the line of trees. The light from the moons did not illuminate her, but instead cast her as a black silhouette against a dim

86

backdrop, almost as if his mind projected a shadow untouched by the world around it. Gen wanted to walk forward to see if she were real or a figment of his imagination but found he couldn't move. Something about the voice seemed familiar, but only faintly so. It was not the voice of a child.

You want the woman, so why do you not take her? Why do you defer to idiots and dullards? You should kill the boy and take the woman. You do not yet realize your station. Instead you sit and weep and let things pass as they are, let the world drift by without your mark. I teach you and return to find you wandering ever further from the path set before you! Time grows ever shorter and you are a poor tool, indeed.

What she spoke was not in the common tongue, but Gen somehow understood it. His mind raced. This had happened before, but he couldn't remember it clearly. Every time his mind would find the memory, it slid away. The figure chiding him, half-seen and unknowable, wanted him to do something, to learn something. Gen knew this, but he couldn't retrieve a single lesson or instruction. The apparition demanded obedience, was desperate for him to accomplish something, but with no commandment he could recall, Gen found nothing to obey.

You have resisted me for too long, and it must end! You are without mother. You are without father. What you are, you owe to me. It took three years to find you after they stole you from me! Three years! And the damage done is indeed great. Tell has made you soft and unsuited for your destiny. The world needs to tremble with fear, and you dally. But your time for play has ended. You may not serve as you should, but you will. The power is in you, waiting with Trys to be born. Against that day, I have given you knowledge and instruction, but you do nothing with it. Prepare now, Gen. Tonight I set you on a path to repentance.

The figure dissolved into the night. The force that held him released, and he fell to the ground gasping for air. With effort, he scooted up against a tree and sat for several minutes quite unconscious of anything. A raven landed on the branch above him, startling him from his stupor. He felt dizzy for a moment and closed his eyes.

When he opened them again, he found himself prone on the dirt. With effort, he composed himself. What had happened? Someone talked to him, but the memory slipped away. Startled, he realized the morning sun already paled the night sky and the trap still awaited a victim. Breathing deeply and shaking his head to clear it, Gen stood.

As he took his first step, he caught movement in the corner of his eye and turned to see if he had been discovered. Men moved carefully between the boles to his left, slowly stepping toward the back of the Showles's house. He counted five with swords drawn, blades reflecting the shafts moonlight. They wore cloaks and moved carefully, knees bent for silent walking.

Gen wondered if they might be thieves coming out of the wood to steal supplies for the winter, something that occurred every few years. A dog barked and they stopped, standing as still as the trees, the man at the head raising his hand in a signal to wait. Their unity and weapons made Gen doubt they were mere brigands, though he couldn't imagine who else would take an interest in such a small town. Abruptly the barking ceased with a yelp. As one, the five sprinted forward and with brutal efficiency shattered the Showles's back door, pouring inside.

Gen's chest tightened, heart hammering. Screams erupted from the house and echoed into the night. Throughout the town arose a cacophony of surprise and terror. Women and men yelled in alarm. Children cried. Dogs barked and were silenced. Gen thought quickly. The house where he and Rafael lived was but a short walk from town down the main road. If the men were attacking the center of town, perhaps they had ignored the outlying farms and houses. If he could manage it, he could warn others to flee and press on to Baron Forthrickeshire to get help.

Gen came to a crouch. The noise inside the Showles's house subsided to whimpering and crying. He looked back toward the city center. Someone had lit a lamp in Regina's room, casting a silhouette against the window. His heart took a blow as he thought of what might be happening to her, and, without further consideration of his initial plan, he ran from underneath the ash tree toward the back door of the store. He knew the terrain well, but his feet still tripped on deadfall and rocks he could have avoided easily in the light. Within a few seconds, he leapt up the four back steps and pushed the door open.

The storeroom had no windows, and, while he knew roughly how the Morewolds arranged their goods, he had to walk blindly and slowly, feeling the shelves and sacks of grain as he made his way to the door that led to the storefront. Heavy boots thudded above him, creaking the boards, Regina's father shouting for the men to leave them alone.

Frantically, Gen felt for the door, and at last his fingers grasped the handle, but the sound of footsteps on the floorboards pulled him up short. Rushing headlong into a dark room to face men with swords would certainly gain him nothing and would likely cost him his life.

Moving carefully, Gen put his ear to the door, listening for any signs of what might be happening. Whoever was in the store either wasn't moving or had left. Jeorge stopped yelling. Regina's younger sister wailed loudly, and Regina's mother was crying and begging the unknown attackers not to hurt them. Gen's rage strove with his fear, but a realization of his powerlessness weakened his resolve. While the woodsmen and their axes might put up a crude

89

defense, only three people in Tell had proper training to fight: Sikes the Warden, the huntmaster, and possibly Hubert. Gen cursed. All he knew how to do was talk, sing, and play the lute, none of which would help him against armed men. Footsteps on the stairs turned his attention back to his listening. The crying continued, but there were other voices.

"Shut up, woman. Just get to the Church. If you don't stop that racket, I *will* hurt her! Tarrant! Did you check back there?"

At least they're not just killing everyone, Gen thought, feeling a little comfort. A creak on the boards behind the door made him realize that "back there" was probably where he was standing. He tried to step back, but found that he couldn't move or breathe. While he couldn't see anything, Gen could feel *her*—feel the will and the power—just behind him. Disdain and disapproval emanated from the blackness, flooding Gen with feelings of guilt.

Now you understand your weakness. If you would have but listened to me through these years, you could have saved this town, though it is worth nothing. I told you this attack was coming and you could have saved them all! They would have worshiped you and given you whatever you wanted, including the girl! Now people will die. But not you. You will learn. Remember the pain, boy. Remember you could have prevented it. You could have used this night to rise from obscurity.

Gen wanted to turn, wanted to face his accuser. How could he possibly have prevented this? How could he be accused of not listening when every memory of the encounters meant to teach him faded into nothingness? He struggled to turn, to move his feet and hide. Boards creaked nearer and nearer the door. A hand worked the lock, and still Gen could not move.

The door burst open, slamming Gen backward. With no

power over his limbs he was unable to brace himself for the impact against the shelving. The back of his skull hit something hard, his vision sparking and blurring. Helplessly he slumped to the floor as items from the toppling shelf, and then the shelf itself, fell on top of him. Dimly he was aware of someone leaning over him. He struggled to get up, but his head swooned, and everything faded away.

Chapter 6 - Shadan Khairn

Gen's eyes fluttered open. The sun had just cleared the horizon into a blue and pink sky gashed with fast-moving, ragged clouds. The breeze had enough bite in it to rouse him and he rolled onto an elbow. Rafael leaned against the Church wall nearby, head bandaged and face pale. Despite his obvious discomfort, he managed a smile for his apprentice.

"How do you feel, Gen?"

Gen probed his head. A large lump protruded from the back of his skull, painful to the touch, and his head throbbed. Slowly he became aware of the crying and anxious muttering around him. With Rafael's help, he stood.

Someone had laid him at the steps of the Church along with several others of the wounded. Regina rested nearby, head in her mother's lap. The rest of the town milled about the square under careful watch. Soldiers—too many for Gen to count—surrounded the throng but made no move against them. From time to time, people from more distant homes arrived under guard to join their neighbors.

"Who are they?" Gen asked.

"Aughmerian soldiers, boy," Rafael whispered. "They

wear no device, but they're Aughmerian or I'm a mule's arse." Rafael's tone was angry and resigned. "We've been standing out in the cold and wind for half a watch now while they drag people in. They're waiting for someone— their commander, I presume. They've already carted off some of the people they slaughtered. The Warden and the huntmaster were both killed. A couple of Aughmerians were in the cart, too, so someone put up a fight."

Gen rubbed his eyes. "Aughmerians? How would they get here?"

"Hard to say," Rafael answered. "This makes no sense at all."

"Where's Magistrate Showles?" Gen asked.

"No one's seen the Magistrate, but the rest of his family is around."

Gen rubbed his arms and breathed deeply to clear his head. A steady breeze blew across the square, carrying with it the scents of the night's rain and wood smoke. Gen wrapped his cloak about him and snaked around the wounded to where Regina lay, trying to avoid the attention of nearby soldiers. As he approached, she turned toward him. Her face, which had recovered its healthy hue, revealed her relief at the sight of him. Dark circles ringed her eyes.

"So, what were you doing in our storeroom in the middle of the night, young bard? I see you were injured." Gen crouched down and took her hand.

"I suppose you think that I was ensuring your safety, but, to be honest, I was really checking to see how much wheat you had."

"This is hardly the time for jokes, Gen! How do you feel? Did you fight that soldier? I almost died when I saw him drag you out of the storeroom. You appeared dead."

"I'm afraid there wasn't much fighting to it. I had an unfortunate run-in with one of your shelves and it felled me. I now have a wound nearly identical to yours."

Regina's eyes went wide and she smiled weakly, reaching out to touch his face affectionately. A commotion lifted Gen's eyes back to the crowd. Hubert, a mix of scared and infuriated, pushed his way through the throng to where Gen and Regina were talking.

"Out of the way, Gen!" Hubert grumbled. "She's my betrothed. I'll care for her."

"Unless you think playing dice and hard drinking will lift her spirits or cure her wounds," Gen said, "I suggest you'd best leave the caring to those more suited and able to give it."

Hubert twisted up his face as if conjuring up a retort, but after a moment he abandoned the attempt, choosing instead to shove Gen roughly to the ground. Gen, already weak, fell onto his back and stayed there, head spinning. Nearby soldiers laughed. Rafael spat in Hubert's direction.

"Foolish lad!" he said acidly, taking Gen's arm and helping him sit up. "Can't you see what's going on here? This isn't the time for brats or brawling!"

Gen didn't know if Rafael was addressing him or Hubert.

A scream ended the altercation and hushed the crowd. Rafael helped Gen to his feet, and they both cast their eyes about. The door to the Showles's house had opened, and Bernard, dressed in his bedclothes and covered in dried feces, emerged, flanked by two burly guards.

Behind them came a man Gen knew had to be their leader. He wore a burnished silver breastplate engraved with a golden hammer. Golden greaves, worth more than Gen could fathom, shone on his legs, and under his arm he carried a polished silver helmet with a short red plume. On a studded belt hung a scabbard richly appointed with red and blue gems. He was handsome with a sharp commanding face framed by shoulder length black hair streaked with gray. A stern mouth was accented with a close-cropped goatee, and blue eyes regarded the crowd unconcernedly.

"Mikkik take me!" Rafael whispered, "That's Torbrand Khairn himself!"

"Are you sure?" Gen asked. "The Shadan of Aughmere? Here?"

"It his him, Gen. Be wary. He is by reputation capricious."

"Silence!" Shadan Khairn's voice thundered into the square with unusual power, choking out the murmuring. Even children stopped crying. Bernard grasped the porch railing and trembled in his bedclothes. Gen doubted it was from the cold.

"People of Tell," Khairn began in a deep, pleasant voice as if addressing the crowd at a fair. "I claim this town for Aughmere, in the name of, well, myself!" The Shadan laughed, and in that laugh Gen detected the stain of madness. "Those of you with more than rocks in your heads, of which I suspect there are few, will realize that it is a bit late in the season to start an invasion. That is true. Those of you with the intelligence of an ox, of which I suspect there are none, will have figured out that during this nice little invasion we have burned nothing and killed very few. Those who are truly brilliant, of which I *know* there are none, will have reasoned that this little army of mine intends to winter here.

"Now, those same people will realize something else. With the stores of food you have available, there simply isn't enough to go around to feed all of you and my brave company of soldiers, especially after that silly celebration yesterday. We'll address that problem later. First we must resolve a pressing matter regarding respect.

"Your Magistrate here, in a cowardly attempt to save his own life, climbed out his window and ran to hide in his outhouse. Never mind the gross and blatant stupidity of that particular decision on his part, but you have no doubt noticed that your Magistrate is covered in his own filth and

95

the filth of his wife and offspring. Someone, you see, dug out this man's outhouse in a crude prank, resulting in his rather putrid condition and forcing me to smell him while I negotiated with him the simple terms of the surrender of this town.

"I would like to know, who has done this thing? Who had the audacity to play such a prank upon his superior and cause me such discomfort? I know this a gross violation of Tolnor's silly traditions of propriety and rank, and in my country an underling would get death for a stunt like this. And this is now my country. Step forward and identify yourself, or I'll start the killing now. Oh my, there I've gone and said it."

Murmuring and crying kindled anew in the crowd, and in the brief moment of chaos, Rafael came to stand at Gen's side.

"Say nothing or it's your death."

Gen's limbs froze with fear. Gant had helped him. Gen searched the faces in the gathering, finally finding his friend staring firmly at the ground. Yeurile stood nearby, face ashen and shirt stained with blood. Her father was not near her, and Gen wondered if the woodsmen put up much of a defense.

"Silence!" Khairn's voice cut through the noise with ease, cowing the crowd and restoring order. "Please, to the matter at hand. Who has done this? Come now or I begin killing women and children."

Gen's sense of honor wrestled with his will to survive. He looked at Khairn and the sword at his belt. He looked at Rafael and Regina, both grim-faced. He looked to the townsfolk, mothers and fathers clinging to children and friends consoling one another. Then he looked within himself and somewhere found the courage to do what he must.

"I did it!" Gen shouted, raising his hand. Khairn's gaze shot across the square, and it took a sheer act of will to look the King in the eyes. Nothing in those eyes spoke of friendliness or compassion, only dark will and madness.

"There's a good lad. Come forward."

Gen glanced at Regina, who watched him from the ground, eyes tearful. "Goodbye, Regina." Gen said softly, walking through the path created as the throng split before him.

Some reached out to touch him as he passed. *If I am to die, I will try to have some dignity,* he thought, raising his head and straightening his shoulders as he marched forward. Khairn watched him approach without expression. Bernard stared intensely at Gen, almost snarling. As Gen neared, Khairn signaled for him to ascend to the Showles's porch and stand by him.

Gen, head swimming, bent all his will toward not stumbling or appearing as weak as he felt. Khairn's hand lingered near the hilt of his blade. Oddly, the Shadan smiled and put his arm around Gen's shoulder, pulling him close.

"Courageous indeed. A man of fortitude. It will be a shame to kill you. Tell me and the assembled why you did such a horrible thing. I simply must know, and the crowd is in need of some levity. I warn you now, don't lie to me because I can discern it."

Gen considered telling a story that would leave Regina out of it, but his thoughts felt so jumbled and he was so fearful of Khairn's wrath that he told the tale in full, managing to leave Gant out of it without lying. Khairn listened patiently, showing nothing until the end when he laughed.

"How quaint. You disgrace the Magistrate for the love of the woman, though I have a hard time believing Hubert is as much a boor as you make him out to be. But tell me, what is your name?"

"Gen."

"Tell me, Gen, what is your profession? You speak very well for a commoner from a filthy town."

"I am a bard and will be a journeyman come spring."

At this, Khairn's eyes lit up and his mood quickly changed to feverish magnanimity. He began talking so fast Gen had a hard time keeping up.

"Excellent! I must admit that I was going to kill you, but being a bard covers many sins and I thus forgive you for the moments of stink I had to endure. You shall live, as shall your master. I couldn't bear the thought of passing the winter in this rat hole without entertainment. To keep you on your best behavior, the woman shall live, too. Captain, have them come forward please."

"Hey! Hey!" Hubert struggled forward from the depths of the crowd to shout at the Shadan. Gen winced at his stupidity. "She's my betrothed! We were supposed to be married come spring! She's mine!"

Annoyed at the outburst, Khairn stared at Hubert until the young man's knees knocked together.

"Well, Gen, I see now what you meant," Khairn's eyes pinned Hubert to his spot. "Young man, in my country when there is a dispute over whose property a woman is, we resolve it appropriately through a challenge, not through childish whining. In the future, I may give you the chance to challenge Gen for her, but I've no time for that now. A quick lesson will do. Captain Omar, could you teach this idiot a little respect?"

Captain Omar was the very definition of stocky. A muscular head, complete with hair no longer than the stubble on his cheeks, sat upon a practically nonexistent neck. Though thick of shoulder and thigh, Gen noticed that the man moved with exceptional agility. The Captain was more than happy to oblige the Khairn's demands. With a satisfied smirk, he delivered a sound fist to Hubert's stomach and a hammering knee to his face.

"You'll watch your tongue, whelp, or next time it'll be worse!" the Captain barked while Hubert rolled around in the dirt, covering his face as blood from his nose spurted onto the ground. With the help of the townsfolk, the Captain located Rafael and Regina and signaled for them to come forward. Regina leaned heavily on Rafael, knees unsteady. Gen admired her courage, for despite all the injury and terror, her face was firm.

"She's a rare one for a dirt-water town and looks like she comes from noble stock," Khairn said quietly to Gen, voice lusty. "I can see how her being betrothed to that dolt would offend your bardish sensibilities, though I will have her wear a veil from now on so she won't prove such a distraction."

Rafael shot Gen a glance that said *be careful,* and Regina touched his hand as she came to stand behind him. Khairn turned to face them, whispering so that no one else could hear.

"You three get to live. Count yourselves fortunate, but not free. If any one of you disobeys, I will not punish the disobedient but one of the others. Learn it well. Now get into the house and get it clean while I deal with some unpleasant realities."

Gen gazed at the terrified townspeople for a moment as he helped Regina inside and set her down to rest by one of the windows. A dread silence hung in the air, and some who saw what was to come began to pray and say impassioned farewells. Pureman Millershim moved among the crowd, comforting those that needed it most. Regina cried softly behind him as she regarded the scene. Her mother carried her little sister, and her father worked his hat in his hands.

A knot of fear and sadness swelled in Gen's stomach. To take his mind off it, he closed the door and set to the task that Khairn had given. The soldiers had wrecked the Showles's house during their attack. Chairs, broken and overturned, littered the floor. Bed dressings lay flung about the rooms, and the shards of many little trinkets, vases, and pots the Showleses had hoarded crunched underfoot.

Gen straightened the bedrooms while Rafael cleaned the kitchen and the ample front room. As they worked, shouts and cries rose and fell outside, and—after trying to ignore them—Gen walked back to the front room and the window that overlooked the square.

Regina was there already, face anxious and tear-streaked. Khairn still stood on the porch, hand on hips, watching as his men divided the town in two. On one side most of the youth between ten and seventeen huddled together. On the other side was everyone else.

"What are they doing, Rafael?" Gen asked, half-guessing at the grim answer.

"They will keep the youth to serve them during the winter months. The rest. . ." Rafael's voice trailed off.

"They can't kill them!" Regina shrieked, bolting for the door. Gen restrained her. Khairn's head turned slightly at the scream.

"You can't do anything, lass," Rafael soothed as Regina clung to Gen and wept. Tears ran down Gen's face as Rafael continued to talk. "You must be strong for those who are left! It will be a long winter. You and Gen are among the oldest here and will be counted on for strength. We shall all meet again in Erelinda someday."

Outside, Bernard bellowed, "There will be word of this!"

"I certainly hope so!" Khairn smirked. "And I thank you for reminding me. Gen, come out here please. And Omar, fetch the letters."

Gen swallowed hard and wiped his eyes before walking back out onto the porch. Once again, Khairn put his arm around him.

"It is my intention, good people, to engage in your stupid custom of warning each other that you are about to attack. Really, Gen, you must tell me how anyone got that notion into his head. If an enemy is worth killing, then a knife in the back is just as warranted as a knife in the chest, wouldn't you say? Well?"

It took a while for Gen to realize that the Shadan actually wanted an answer.

"Honor, sir, dictates that . . . well . . ."

"Honor! Oh, yes. If you consider someone honorable, why would you kill them in the first place? Honor has no place in war, only advantage. But, as I said, I shall acquiesce this once. I have here two letters, one to be delivered to your Duke Norshwal of Graytower and the other to the 'honorable' Baron Forthrickeshire. They outline my presence here in the heart of Tolnor and my intentions to give them a solid beating come spring should they choose to fight rather than surrender.

"Surrender would be very disappointing, however, so I made it a point to be as arrogant and insulting as possible to inflame their manly indignation. I would like two messengers for each message, and, as a sign of my goodwill toward you, Gen, I will let you choose who they are. Now, don't be an idiot and say Regina, because she gets to stay to be leverage on you."

Gen's mind raced, but one choice was obvious.

"Gant and Yeurile."

"Come forward, then!" Khairn yelled. Gant took a despondent Yeurile by the hand and led her forward. Gen met his eye, finding gratitude there. "Ahh, a friend and his woman, then. Very well. Where shall they go?"

"To the Duke."

"That is fine, though he might not believe two commoners unless I send further proof. Does the Duke know you, Magistrate?"

Bernard perked up, a glint of hope in his eyes.

"He does!" Bernard said eagerly. "He is my cousin."

"Very good," Khairn replied. "I shall send your head with them. Quartermaster! Give these two a horse and provisions. Omar, see to the head."

Bernard, pale, sunk to the ground and pled for his life.

Despite years of abuse, Gen felt pity for the man as Omar dragged him away behind the house. The Quartermaster, a young Aughmerian with dark hair, signaled Gant and Yeurile forward and waited for the second selection.

"Who shall go to the Baron?" Khairn prodded. Bernard screamed and screeched so pathetically that Gen couldn't focus his mind until the sick thud of his head hitting the ground plunged everything into profound and unnatural silence. Khairn's eyes bulged, and Gen thought of Regina.

"Jeorge and Rena Morewold, and their young daughter, if you will." Strangely, Khairn laughed and slapped Gen on the back.

"You are very predictable. The woman holds great power over you, indeed, and now you secure more of her favor by your magnanimous gesture toward her parents. What a game! Very well. I will permit the daughter to go, for she is too young to be of use anyway. Quartermaster, see to it. Here are the letters."

The Quartermaster took them. Jeorge and Rena looked back sadly as they left. Gen felt exhausted, emotions running high.

The Shadan grabbed his shoulder. "Now get back inside. The rest of this will be difficult."

Gen opened the door and found himself in Regina's grateful embrace. Through the window Gen could see the soldiers leading the men, women, and young children down the road that led to the woods. The sky had cleared and the sun shone down on what otherwise would have been a pleasant morning.

For just a moment, Gen could imagine that those chosen to die were simply out for a morning stroll or perhaps on their way to visit family in Sipton, but the terrified cries of the children and the rough shoving of the guards tore the illusion away. Gen didn't have to think very hard to figure out that most everyone else in the town would walk the same path come spring.

The door banged open loudly as Shadan Khairn and Captain Omar strode inside, agitating already raw nerves. Regina pulled away from Gen and wiped her face. They all stared at the floor as the Shadan circled around in front of them

"Nasty business, that," Khairn said in a tone that made it difficult to tell whether he cared. "But I see that you haven't quite finished the chore to which I set you! The floor is still strewn with the broken belongings of that pig you called Magistrate. As this was clearly the job of young Regina here, and since she decided to spend her time weeping and screaming instead of sweeping and cleaning, I shall punish Gen here as a lesson."

Gen barely had time to widen his eyes with surprise before he found Khairn's sword had entered his belly and come out his back. The inhuman speed with which he had drawn his weapon and thrust it shocked Gen, and what pain he felt came slowly by comparison.

Blood poured out of the wound as the King extracted the sword, and Gen slumped to the ground, everything below his waist numb. The world spun, and he dimly heard Rafael trying to speak to him. Regina was near, too, face blurry and voice warbled. Somewhere behind them, Torbrand Khairn and Captain Omar laughed.

Gradually, everything faded and Gen sensed in a detached way the life slipping out of him. Summers and winters passed before his mind. Hours reading books, playing the lute, and singing songs reeled around him. He saw his brief talk with Regina at the well, her blonde hair moving with the breeze, as if he were a spectator rather than a participant. Then it stopped, and everything went black . . . and then he was awake, Khairn leaning over him, a light sweat on his brow.

"See! I told you. It is my gift. I can bring people back from the brink of death, should I so choose. Only the Chalaine herself is said to be able to heal with greater power, and I doubt not that those tales are exaggerated."

Gen checked himself. He lay in a pool of his own blood, his shirt and breeches soaked, but he could feel his legs again. The bump from his encounter with the shelf was gone, and, lifting up his shirt, he could see that the deadly wound was now nothing more than a scar. Gen stood, realizing that not all the fantastic stories told about Torbrand Khairn were false. In fact, most of them now seemed true.

"Of course, what this means to you is this. . ." the Shadan continued. "I can beat and torture you almost to death and have you up and ready to work and suffer the next day if you do not do exactly as I ask." Torbrand daubed the sweat off his forehead with his sleeve. "Get me a drink, old man. Gen, you and the girl get this place cleaned up. Open some windows. It stills stinks like that befouled Magistrate in here. And Gen, it will, of course, fall to you to get an outhouse in working order as quickly as possible. I would like you to dig a new pit and fill in the old one."

Captain Omar examined Gen for a moment.

"You be careful of this one, My Lord. He thinks he has a brain in his head and he ain't no coward."

"*Isn't* a coward, Omar," Khairn replied in exasperation. "For the sake of all civilized people, Captain, let's try a little harder not to talk like we were in the stockade. But just to show you that I still like you, appoint that Hubert boy to be the leader of the children. That will give you plenty of excuses to beat him when he fouls up."

"Excellent, my Lord. I'll be seeing . . . I shall attend to it immediately."

"Thank you, Captain."

Captain Omar left quickly.

"You'll have to forgive the Captain's language. I took him as a slave and trained him myself when I saw how he was built. Perfect fighter. Strong, fast, and no neck at which

104

the enemy can aim a decapitating blow. He is, however, still a little coarse around the edges, and—if you ask me—he enjoys the killing a little too much. A good fighter enjoys the fight, not the end of it. Notwithstanding, his ability makes him a jewel."

The King's face turned contemplative, and Gen wasn't sure if he was addressing them anymore. "Almost as good as Cormith, the Captain. Cormith liked the killing, too, but he was an unsettling person all around. I could do a better job than I did with both of them, though. Neither one could kill me."

The King went silent, lost in thought for so long that Gen glanced at Rafael questioningly. Rafael mouthed, "Crazy!"

Khairn stood suddenly, eyes fierce. "What are you waiting for?!" he yelled. "Get to it!"

By early afternoon, Gen threw the last shovelful out of the new waste pit and climbed out covered in dirt and mud. A soldier lazed around by a tree, watching him with no concern. Gen hadn't seen the Shadan for some time.

Regina passed by the rear windows several times while she cleaned. Sometimes she chanced a look at him, though Khairn forced her to wear a veil after the tradition of his people. He had apparently brought a supply of veils along for the invasion and was distributing them among all the young women.

Rafael played for Khairn later that morning, but the music stopped near the midday meal, which none of them, apparently, was to enjoy.

Gen leaned on the spade. All he had left to do was fill in the old waste pit and move the outhouse over.

"Get on with it, boy," the soldier growled. "I'm tired of goin' in the woods."

"Yes, sir."

A horn blew, and many of the soldiers emerged from the houses and buildings to congregate in the square. Gen's guard left his post.

"You stay here," the soldier ordered. "I run faster than a deer and can track the wind. You run away, I'll find you quick-like and make you regret it."

Gen went to the thicket where he and Gant had hid the dirt they dug the night before. Gen noticed the assembly in the square, Torbrand standing on the Church steps waiting for his men to arrive. Pureman Millershim stood behind him, and Gen wondered why Khairn let him live. Gen thought only briefly of bolting away into the woods to escape and then gave up the notion. He couldn't leave Regina and Rafael behind. From what little he knew of Khairn, the crazed King would send a party to hunt him down and kill him, anyway.

"You ain't done yet?" the guard strode around the corner of the house after several minutes.

"I was about to get a drink, sir."

"Want a drink from the pretty lady, eh? Well, you get nothin' until I'm sittin' down in that outhouse. You ain't got it done soon, I think Khairn will beat on your lady for punishment. Now get goin'."

The soldier grabbed him roughly by the shirt and threw him headlong into the hole he had just dug, chuckling at the result. The thought of Regina taking a beating at Khairn's hands spurred Gen to greater efforts, and, putting aside his hunger and discomfort, he worked frantically, finishing the task just before Torbrand appeared around the corner of the house.

"Good work, Gen," he said, tone light. "After I personally inspect your handiwork, I want to hear you play. Your master is tolerably good, though a little slow and cracking around the edges. Now get cleaned up. Guard, you are dismissed."

Gen noticed that the soldiers never returned or reflected Khairn's lighter moods, remaining somber and focused. Gen took it as further evidence of their captor's capriciousness. He decided to follow the soldiers' strategy—say as little as possible and take every remark, however flippantly given, as God's law.

CHAPTER 7 - BOREDOM

Gen watched Torbrand Khairn's face and knew the expression: boredom. The Shadan's eyes, normally lively with anger or some private glee, gradually dimmed into vapidity while he watched his captive bards strum, beat, and sing until their voices cracked.

Two weeks had passed since his incursion into Tell, and every day Gen grew more nervous. They had long since come to the end of even Rafael's extensive repertoire, and those people the Shadan thought spent or useless were shoved by rough hands into a line at dawn and marched into the woods, never to return.

The weather had turned bitter and cold since the Shadan's arrival, a light snow falling three days later, and a heavy storm rolling in two days after that. Unfortunately, the weather increasingly confined the unpredictable Shadan to the indoors.

Gen and Rafael found themselves hard-pressed to satisfy the Torbrand's thirst for entertainment. Some days, he would watch them intently, clapping and even singing along; but overnight or even unexpectedly during the day, his feverish, magnanimous self would transform into an agitated, sullen taskmaster. When the Shadan was in his distemper, everyone suffered for it, and Rafael pointed out to Gen that even Khairn's own soldiers knew when to avoid him. On the Shadan's bad days, visits and reports from his men dwindled by nearly half, and the offhanded slaps and punches he used to express his displeasure doubled.

Regina, veiled and desperate to please, fretted and worried over every small task Torbrand set her to, for if a meal was not timely, a potato not cooked to its proper tenderness, or a piece of meat overdone, she could do nothing but watch guiltily as the Shadan found some new way to hurt Gen.

Whether a quick stab with a knife or a swift fist to the nose, Torbrand would always heal his victim and demand thanks for it afterward. In his happier moods, the Shadan could be tolerable if not outright forgiving. But those days had faded, and for the three captives forced to endure his presence even more than his own soldiers, a sense of dread dominated every other feeling.

In this desperation, they whispered half-formulated plots to escape with each other whenever the Shadan went outside on some matter of business. If nothing else, they figured that starving in the cold—choosing their own fate—was better than finding death at the whim of Shadan Khairn.

Regina's distress brought out a protective feeling in Gen, and he did whatever he could to shield her from the worry and violence around her, offering what scant humor could be found in their dreadful circumstances. She clung to him, and they both relied on Rafael for counsel, though as for that, even the practiced performer could not fool his young charges with pretenses of hope. "Just keep your dignity. Be strong," was all he could offer most days.

Today, the 26th of Auber, had started poorly, the Shadan having risen early to fuss them all around after they awoke at dawn to perform the chores and duties set to them. Rafael was to play while Gen helped Regina in the kitchen. Captain Omar entered later, leering at Regina before giving his morning report: eight more youths were now useless and had been removed from the town. Even the massive warrior knew when to keep it short and left quickly.

"I can tell by the smell that you've burned the biscuits again," the Shadan fumed, plopping down into his seat with enough force to nearly break the chair. Regina yelped, and she and Gen, who had been setting the table, ran into the kitchen. Regina pulled the biscuits from the oven hurriedly. While not technically burnt, they were a browner shade than the Shadan preferred. Gen swallowed hard.

"I'm so sorry, Gen," Regina wailed quietly, tears filling her eyes. "I . . . I . . . think the fire must have been too warm. I'm. . ."

"Well, let's see them!" Torbrand yelled. The rest of the meal was set, and Regina tentatively brought the biscuits in and laid them before the Shadan. He nodded his head slowly as if to confirm to himself his own olfactory prowess. For perverse reasons of his own, the Shadan always had them eat at his table, and as Gen, Rafael, and Regina sat, the Shadan stood, mouth turned down in a frown.

Rafael eyed him nervously as he walked around the table. Gen kept his eyes riveted on his plate. The Shadan's heavy boots stopped behind the young bard, and Gen closed his eyes, keeping an ear out for the sound of steel against the scabbard. Instead of swinging his sword, the Shadan stooped, grabbed the underside of Gen's chair, and heaved. Gen crashed into the table face first, biscuits, jam, and tableware exploding in all directions, silverware and plates cracking and clanging on the floor. Regina screamed and Rafael nearly fell out of his chair. Gen struggled to his hands and knees just as the Shadan brought the chair down on his back. Gen grunted in pain, slamming back into the table. The Shadan took what was left of the chair and threw it at the fireplace.

"I hate this place!" he yelled, stomping toward the door. "I want biscuits done to perfection in an hour or Gen dies."

He slammed the door shut behind him. Rafael and Regina sprang to Gen's side.

Rafael stooped low, putting his face even with Gen's. "Are you all right, lad?"

"I'll manage," Gen groaned. "Help me off the table." Rafael and Regina pulled him slowly to the edge, sending more food and crockery to the ground. They let him take his time standing up, and when he did, they braced him from both sides until he could get his balance again.

"I'll get him cleaned up," Regina said, voice subdued and sad.

"No!" Rafael objected. "I'll see to him. You bake those biscuits, Regina, and you poke your nose in that oven every minute!"

Regina nodded and half-ran to the kitchen.

"It's not your fault, Regina," Gen called out to her, wincing. The clatter of pots was all the answer he received.

Rafael started gathering items from the floor, back cracking as he bent over. "You just take it easy a moment, Gen. I got hit with a stool in Tenswater when I was strong enough to take a blow like that. I remember everything before but not a lot for several days after."

"I'll be fine," Gen mumbled unconvincingly, wiping honey that was sticking his arms to the table cloth. "We have got to get out of here, Rafael. He's going to see us dead before long, I know it."

"You've the right of it there, but we've got to contrive some reason to get outside so we can survey where he places his men at night. I've no doubt you know a hundred places to hide in the woods around here, but it will do us no good unless we can get there undetected."

Gen started righting items on the table, sharp pains blazing down his back at the slightest twist or turn. Their plan was simply to wait for a night that heavy snow was falling and steal into the woods. The snow would cover their tracks and muffle the sounds of their movement, but they knew that the Shadan patrolled the woods heavily and placed a guard at the front of the house. Fortunately, he had quartered his three captives in the back, but until they had an idea of where the patrols ran, they feared to attempt the journey. They had, at the least, counted themselves clever for sneaking tiny pieces of meat from the table and wiping the grease on the shutter hinges to silence them.

When the Shadan returned, his pants wet up to the knee, his humor had not improved, and Regina's golden brown offering and a newly cleaned and set table did nothing more than prevent another beating. The Shadan ate in silence, eyes smoldering and focusing on nothing in particular.

"Play!" he commanded once the meal had ended. Rafael and Gen speedily retrieved their instruments from their rooms.

When they returned, the Shadan had his feet on the table and his arms crossed, face slack and unreadable. Gen's back ached horribly, but he hadn't the courage to ask the Shadan to heal it. They played for two hours before Captain Omar interrupted them.

"I have come with the report you asked for, Shadan. The scouts have returned."

"What word?" the Shadan asked dully, staring at the fire.

"We have confirmed that both the Baron Forthrickeshire and Duke Norshwal have received your letters, but there is no evidence of any preparation for war. The people certainly have no idea of it."

Torbrand's fist slammed down on the table.

"But what of the head? I sent the Magistrate's head in a sack to the Duke! How could he ignore that?"

"From what our spies could gather, the head was

unrecognizable by the time it arrived and he simply had the two youths thrown in the dungeon."

"And the Baron?"

"He didn't believe the storekeeper. They took matters to some local Puremen but fared no better there."

Both fists slammed down on the table this time. Gen, Regina, and Rafael despaired anew. They had harbored some hope of rescue, and it now seemed impossible.

"Thickheaded dolts. Take twenty men and go to Sipton. Kill as many people there as you can safely get away with. Leave some tabards and armor behind as tokens. Perhaps then the Baron will take the claim seriously."

"I will do it, Shadan."

"Begone with you."

The Shadan crossed to the door. "Gah! Stupid rural nobility. I'll return after lunch. Eat what you like. If you're lucky, I may actually have to go knock on the Baron's door myself to announce my presence."

The Shadan absented himself for nearly four hours. They talked of their plan and peeked out of windows, trying to get an idea of how the Shadan had placed his men. They managed to see a column of soldiers, bundled against the weather, ride out of town in the deep snow before the door guard roughly pulled the shutters closed.

By the time Torbrand returned, his fuming anger had again settled into dissatisfied irritability, and after dinner he sat, face blank, head propped on his elbow. Regina leaned against the door frame of the kitchen, watching silently. The fire provided the only light, and in that light Gen could sense that the Shadan's uses for them were nearly exhausted. While otherwise expressionless, Gen read in his silence a brewing contempt. Anger at the Shadan welled up within him, and he fought to keep his own manner civil.

Just as Rafael opened his mouth to announce his next story, the Shadan interrupted him. "Why is it that no one ever really wins in your stories?"

"What mean you, Milord?" Rafael asked nervously.

"What do I mean? Why, let's see. Two people fall in love and then one of them tragically dies. Two people dislike each other until one of them dies, then the other one realized he loves the dead one, but alas, she is dead. A King wins a mighty battle, but he is mortally wounded and dies. A man has a great fortune but must give it up to wed the woman he loves. Can no one in your stories kill all his enemies, have the woman he wants, and keep the gold all at the same time? In fact, you come up with a story like that by tomorrow or Regina will be very sorry."

"You leave her alone!" Gen wished he could take the words back as soon as he said them. There was much more he wanted to yell at his captor, but the thin malicious smile turning up at the edges of the Shadan's mouth at his outburst silenced him. Torbrand stood, and Gen knew something awful was about to happen.

"Leave her alone?" Torbrand mocked. "I assume you mean Regina there." He started walking toward her and Gen ran forward, stabbing pain erupting down his back. Torbrand didn't try to stop him as he took up a defensive position in front of the kitchen doorway, pushing Regina behind him.

"Beat me all you want, Torbrand. Leave her alone."

"My, my, how gallant. Rafael, I do believe we have the material for one of your tragic stories, here."

Gen's heart pounded, every sense alive. And somehow, despite the Shadan's speed, he saw it coming. The narrowing of the eyes, the slight twitch signaling the backward movement of the arm, and the setting of the jaw. The Shadan's fist careened with frightening velocity straight for his nose—and Gen dodged it, ducking to the right and swinging his own fist in return.

Torbrand intercepted Gen's right-handed blow with his left hand and pulled Gen away from the door and out into the room. Gen gathered himself, anger pounding through his veins. Dimly, he was aware of Rafael shouting at him to stop. Gen turned, ready to charge, but the Shadan stood stock-still, staring at him in such a way that Gen held up, awaiting the outcome of Torbrand's odd shift in mood.

After an uncomfortably long silence, the Shadan laughed, posture relaxing, and he strode forward to embrace Gen.

"Excellent," he beamed, backing away and regarding him at arm's length like a long lost son. "I should have noticed before. You are not built for power, but there is speed there. And as a bard, you would be dexterous. Well, well, perhaps this winter can be put to some profit after all. We're taking a little trip tomorrow, Gen. We'll be gone for a few days. Bring the warmest clothes you have. I'm going to bed."

Torbrand talked with the guard outside the door briefly before retiring, mumbling instructions excitedly to himself.

Regina and Rafael came to Gen quickly. Regina took his hand and pressed her shoulder against him.

"I'm not sure what he's up to, boy," Rafael whispered after several minutes of quiet speculation. "But you watch yourself. He intends you no good, I am sure."

Gen nodded his head in agreement. "There is one good thing. You'll have several days without the Shadan. You should be able to get about town and get some information."

"Leave it to us," Regina said. "You just worry about yourself. Come back to me."

Squeezing his hand, she lifted her veil and kissed him on the cheek before going to her room. He felt warm inside, and Rafael smiled for the first time in days.

"Off to bed with you, lad. Stay alert. You may learn something on this 'trip' that can help us."

Gen, bewildered and scared, retired and laid awake for many hours. What did the Shadan want with him? A trip with the madman sounded less appealing every hour he thought about it, and his mind conjured up one horrible scenario after another until sleep finally took him.

CHAPTER 8 - A FROZEN MENAGERIE

Torbrand kicked him awake before the sun had pushed itself over the horizon. Gen scrambled to his feet and followed the Shadan out into the kitchen. Regina was there, slump-shouldered and tired, putting the finishing touches on a large breakfast. Gen rubbed his eyes as he sat, trying to clear his vision. Torbrand was dressed for travel and practically bounced at every step.

"Isn't this quite a feast, Gen?" he effused. "I do apologize for rousing your woman so early to prepare it, but our journey today will be long and cold and we need a full belly against the task. Eat! I daresay this will be the best meal you've had in some time. And come sit with us, Regina. Sit close to Gen. Say whatever sweet goodbyes you have! For my part, I can hardly wait to be off!"

Regina happily complied with the request, but neither she nor Gen had it in them to say anything in the presence of the Shadan. Even if they had the desire to speak, they wouldn't have had space to edge in a word. Torbrand talked incessantly about everything, from challenges by other Warlords in his land, to the food he liked, then on to an energetic yet gruesome description of the slaughtering of a band of Uyumaak deep in the immense Lakewood.

"You should have burned the biscuits this morning," Gen whispered as Torbrand laughed over his own story of ramming an Uyumaak basher into a tree with his horse.

"Oh, yes," he said, wiping tears from his eyes. "I do apologize for that fiasco yesterday, Regina. I promise not to throw Gen on the table again unless the biscuits are truly ashes or he looks good enough to eat. Come now, Gen, give her a kiss and let's be off! I'll even remove myself for a moment."

While Gen could never trust Torbrand's magnanimity, for once he had little difficulty complying with the tyrant's orders. Regina lifted her veil and smiled, kissing him deeply.

"I wanted to thank you for risking yourself for me yesterday," she said, holding his eyes. Grasping his hand, she placed a braided lock of hair in his palm. "Remember me. Be safe."

"Enough of that," Torbrand said, entering the room. Gen turned and barely caught a backpack the Shadan had tossed at the back of his head. "If you can't fit it in there, you can't bring it."

Regina squeezed his arm and he ran to his room. He hardly had clothes enough to fill the pack even halfway, but stuffing his heavy woolen blanket inside used up the space. After donning and tying his cloak, he pulled on the pack and returned to the kitchen.

"I hope you left room for food in there," the Shadan said as he stuffed his own pack. "We only need enough for a day and a half."

With some creative shifting and cramming, Gen managed to get in an ample amount of dried meat and fruit. "And here is your waterskin. Wear it close to your body so that it does not freeze. All ready to go then."

"Say goodbye to Rafael for me," Gen instructed Regina as he followed Torbrand to the door. "He never did like

118

mornings."

Once he shut the door behind him, Gen wished for the indoors again. The morning was bitter cold. The sky, just starting to lighten, was clear of clouds. Their breath ejected billows of steam from their mouths, and Gen could feel the hairs of his nose freezing together. The ice-covered stairs of the Showles's front porch creaked and crunched wildly from the cold, and the sound of it sent shivers through Gen's body.

The Shadan set a brisk pace north into the empty plains to the east of the Alewine forest, and Gen's back started to ache from where the Shadan had hit him with the chair. Here the wind blew so chill that it penetrated his cloak with ease, pimpling his skin with its icy touch. As day fully broke, spreading a weak light about them, the Shadan turned west, putting their backs to the wind, and headed into the forest. While the wind lessened, the snow deepened. The Alewine forest was thick with new growth and littered with fallen branches and trees. Skinny pines blown over by the wind slanted across their way, a thin line of snow running down their trunks.

While no path was evident, the Shadan walked forward confidently, angling this way and that without the slightest hesitation. Small puffy birds and snow-white rabbits scattered at their approach, and they crossed the tracks of wolves, deer, and foxes running in thin trails all around them. While grateful that the Shadan was blazing the trail through the knee-deep snow, by the time he called their first halt, Gen could no longer feel his legs or his feet.

Torbrand took a healthy swig. "Drink up, Gen. They call it a waterskin, but that's not what you'll find in it."

Gen unstoppered the leather bag and drunk deeply, coughing as fiery liquor cascaded down his throat. The Shadan chuckled at his sputtering, but Gen felt warmth gradually return to his extremities and he wiggled his toes in his boots to ensure they were still there. "We wouldn't last a mile where we're going without this, so don't drink it all."

"Where are we going?" Gen asked, taking advantage of the Shadan's comment to put forth the question he had pondered through the night.

"To my homeland, of course. I need to retrieve something."

"That will take at least two months on foot!" Gen exclaimed incredulously.

"Calm yourself. You don't think an entire regiment of my soldiers walked to your hometown during the summer, do you? We'll be using a Portal."

"But that's illegal! The Portal Guild would never let you send an army into a land not your own! It's against the law!"

The Shadan laughed and took another swig. "Well, let's reason this out as we walk, shall we, Gen? Maybe it will keep your mind off the cold." They adjusted their waterskins inside their cloaks and started forward again. "I should have thought, Gen, that one who prides himself on being intelligent as you do would have figured this out by now."

"I do not pride myself on any such thing. I have much to learn," Gen contradicted, irritated at the Shadan's assumptions.

"Please, Gen. It's as Captain Omar said. 'This one thinks he has a brain in is his head.' It's in your eyes and the lift of your chin, Gen, and you should not be ashamed of it. But to the matter at hand. Since the formation of the Portal Guild, every nation has paid them handsomely to provide use of the Portals and enforce the laws to prevent them from being abused. Additionally, there are small fees to pass through them. You may not know this, but who do you *think* gets all that money and lives on fine estates with an overabundance of women, wine, and food?"

"The guildmasters."

"Correct. Now, your average Portal Mage lives about as

well as Regina's family did, which certainly is not bad. Consider, though, that if the prophecy proves correct, Ki'Hal will all knit itself together again and there will be no need to pay for Portals, Portal Mages, or Portal guildmasters. Now, the guildmasters have an abundance of wealth and will live quite nicely in the end. Can you piece out the rest of the story?"

It wasn't hard for Gen to understand the gist of Torbrand's train of thought. "The Portal Mages will be destitute."

Gen knew that as soon as anyone showed talent for opening Portals, they were immediately removed from whatever station they were in—no matter how low or high—to be trained. Most Portal Mages had no other skills or profession with which to eke out a living.

"And destitute people are highly susceptible to what?"

"Bribery."

"And so you have it. But it is even a little worse than that, I'm afraid. What your distant little town probably hasn't the slightest notion of is that several Portal Mages have simply left their posts and are clandestinely offering their services to whomever wants to pay for them. This is all kept very quiet by the guild, of course, and the guild hunts their 'traitors' vigorously. I have no doubt that all three kingdoms—and perhaps a few wealthy individuals besides—have their own Portal Mages on retainer by now. I have three. You will meet one soon."

"But there isn't a Portal near Tell. The closest one is near Blood Throne."

"As far as anyone knew, yes. But new Portals are being discovered constantly, and, well, there is one close by which Portal Mages under my control found nearly a year ago. In your view, a most unfortunate occurrence, I'm sure."

The conversation ended and Gen walked glumly in Torbrand's wake. Tell would provide a stronghold for Aughmere in southern Tolnor, a place hard to reach due to a great dividing crack in the Menegothian shard and the uninhabitable Rede Steppes that divided the lands of Duke Sothbranne of Bloodthrone and Duke Norshwal of Graytower from their peers to the north. That Shadan Khairn had found such a direct link of travel illuminated the often wicked face of chance, though chance was not all to blame. The Tolnorian people's general understanding that Shadan Khairn was a stupid, bloodthirsty brute was wrong. He was bloodthirsty, but in his lucid moments he possessed a sharp and calculating mind.

The sun at last hefted itself firmly into the sky, sending slender beams of light to the forest floor, though the shadows of the wood stripped them of any vitality. The throats of winter birds finally thawed enough to enliven the wintry scene with a bit of music, but their cheer was lost on Gen, who found his prospects as bleak as the scene around him.

Gen half-considered attempting to run from his captor, who thought nothing of letting the bard's apprentice walk behind him. Gen was smart enough to realize that this wasn't folly on the Shadan's part. Torbrand had every confidence that he could catch and kill Gen at his convenience—and he was right.

The smell of wood smoke pulled Gen from his dark reverie. At the base of a low wooded hill a fire burned in a small, shadowy clearing. A crude shelter had been excavated into a steep slope of the hill, a curtain of hides covering the entrance. A man huddling close to the fire stood and regarded them unhappily as they approached. His close-cropped black hair was greasy and matted, and stubbly cheeks told the tale of several days living in the rough. He wrapped his arms around his thin frame, gray woolen cloak pulled close about him. Dark circles ringed his brown eyes, highlighting them against his pasty white face.

"Do you have *any* idea how cold it was here last night?"

he asked hoarsely in greeting. "Damn near froze to death!" Torbrand stopped and put his hands on his hips as the man turned his gaze to Gen as if just noticing him. "And this isn't one of your soldiers! I thought you weren't going back until spring!"

Torbrand continued regarding him, face displeased. "Gen, this is Udan. Not his real name, of course. Perhaps you can help him think of a less stupid one on the way. He is the aforementioned Portal Mage in my employ. He is here through the rest of the month as the last of my men and supplies are brought over. And of course, you see he has a problem."

Gen regarded Udan, wondering if the Shadan were referring to the cold, but Gen caught the fire in Torbrand's eyes. Udan didn't have time to blink in the instant it took for the Shadan's fist to travel to his nose. Udan stumbled back and nearly fell into the fire, accidentally kicking several burning sticks into the snow to hiss and steam.

The Shadan extended his hand. "Look! He has a broken nose. That certainly won't make the nights any warmer."

"What was that for?" Udan's voice was stuffy and muted, hands over his mouth and nose.

"I am the Shadan of Aughmere, *Udan,* and I am paying you more than you're worth. But you greet me with complaints and questions about my actions. Part of our deal was that you would ask no questions, and, quite frankly, I didn't like your tone just now. You've only to endure the cold a scant week more and then you can find somewhere warm to spend your money. So shut up."

"Yes, Shadan."

"That's better." Torbrand unlimbered his pack and sat by the fire. "I gauge it about an hour until Udan is scheduled to open the Portal. Let's eat. The next part of the journey will be difficult."

Gen settled onto a stump near the fire, noticing a well-beaten track leading around the hill. Udan regarded Gen for a few moments, clearly wanting to ask questions but just as clearly scared to do so. The rogue Portal Mage settled for crouching by the fire and alternately warming his hands and probing his swollen, bleeding nose.

Gen worked up his courage. "Shadan, you said the next part will be difficult. What do you mean?"

Torbrand finished chewing a piece of dried beef, trying to decide whether to answer the question or not.

"We go through a shard of no worth, save its connection here," he answered. "It's called the Whitewind shard, which you may have heard of. We found a Portal to it from the Ellenais shard. We will travel Whitewind for four or five hours, and it will be a trial. It is chilled beyond anything you likely know. It does have one curiosity that will merit your attention, though I beg you not to bother me while I am eating. You will see it soon enough."

Gen had only heard the name of the Whitewind shard, but tales of Ellenais he knew well. It was the Shadan's home, nicknamed the "Harem shard" by decent folk. There Torbrand kept all his wives, concubines, and children. Speculation in Rhugoth and Tolnor varied widely on the number of women Torbrand housed on the shard. Some said ten, others said a hundred. Some said there were so many that the Shadan himself did not know the tally. By all accounts, it was a crude place, a filthy den of sin and female degradation. Gen couldn't guess why Torbrand would take him there.

"Let's go," the Shadan said some time later. They followed the beaten path as it curved to the north. The trees were thick, though the path was cleared and easy to negotiate even in the snow.

After a quarter of an hour, a glade opened before them, a small pond at the center. Weak winter light provided no warmth, though they squinted as it washed over them when they emerged from the shadows. A platform was constructed out into the center of the water and a ladder descended into its icy depths. A crude semicircle-shaped building constructed of rough-cut timber sat just to the side of the platform, a well-used fire pit brimming with ash in the center. A stack of wood lined the back of the hut.

"I broke the ice this morning," Udan said grumpily. "Looks like I'll need to do it again."

"Get the fire going, Gen," Torbrand commanded. "There should be some embers you can use beneath the ash." And then Gen understood—the Portal was *in* the water. "Yes, there will be a similar blaze on the other side," Torbrand continued, sensing the boy's concern.

Gen gathered pine needles and small sticks while Udan banged away at the ice around the ladder with a heavy hammer. Soon, all three warmed themselves by a high fire, and Gen absorbed all the warmth he could. The prospect of entering the freezing pond set his teeth to chattering.

After warming himself, Udan strode out onto the platform, closing his eyes and incanting. Gen moved away from the fire to get a better look at the Magician's work, his hair standing on end. He couldn't see much, but the water at the base of the ladder turned the faintest shade of blue. Udan stood stock-still, face calm, concentrating. Gen startled as something floated to the surface followed by a shaking hand on the ladder. Ten soldiers in all emerged from the pond, running to the fire and stripping off their wet clothes. They dried themselves with towels they pulled from oilskin bags before changing into dry clothes. Torbrand talked with them quietly for a moment before throwing Gen two of the bags, telling him to secure Udan's belongings in one of them as well as putting a heavy rock in each. Gen took off his cloak and stuffed it inside, figuring he would need to keep it dry.

Torbrand smiled as he strode forward to the edge of the platform. "I am glad you are smart enough realize you should remove your cloak. Udan, once again, has forgotten. I don't suppose you have passed through a Portal before, have you Gen?"

"No, Shadan."

"It will cause you discomfort the first few times. Try not to retch into the fire on the other side. The odor would be most unpleasant. I'll take Udan's sack. Just jump in and let yourself sink to the bottom. Use the ladder to get your bearings if you miss."

Without further explanation the Shadan took a deep breath and dove in feet first. Gen edged forward. He could see the Portal clearly now, shimmering blue at some unknown depth below the surface. The Shadan was a spot on the blue field before disappearing through it.

Gen swallowed hard, trying to work up his resolve. If the soldiers hadn't been there, he realized he would have a chance of escape, but they watched him bemusedly from the fire as he vacillated.

"Go on!" one of them yelled. "Go down quick or it'll freeze your manhood off."

His companions laughed, and in their ridicule Gen found the backbone to shimmy forward and take the plunge. Every last bit of air in his lungs exploded from his mouth as cold fire shocked his body. Eyes wide, he flailed, trying to find the ladder to pull himself out. He lost his grip on the bag he held above him. With effort, he fought off the panic, forcing himself to stillness. Turning his eyes toward his feet, he could see the Portal, but it didn't seem to be getting any closer. He desperately needed to breathe, chest aching. He paddled upward with his hands, forcing himself downward. He could feel his body going numb and he inadvertently sucked water, gagging.

And then blue light filled his vision. He felt motionless and disoriented before dropping through the Portal, which flared blue near the ceiling of a modest room. He fell and slammed hard onto a wooden floor, lying prone.

His vision swam, balance completely skewed. Pond water and his lunch shot from his mouth, ejected from a queasy stomach. To complete his humiliation, his bag fell from the Portal and the rock thumped him on the head. Gen's vision faded in and out. Dimly he was aware of the Shadan, nearly paralyzed by a fit of laughter, ordering someone to remove his clothes.

When he came to himself again, he was wrapped in a blanket and feeling woozy. Udan, completely naked, was nearby, holding his cloak up to the fire to dry it. The Shadan had already donned a fresh set of clothes, all black, as was his custom.

"You should have reminded me about the injury on your back. I have healed it. Take some food and a drink from your waterskin. Then clean up your mess." Gen complied, the fiery drink and food reviving him.

They sat in a plain square room constructed of rough logs, two immense fireplaces set on opposite sides. A ladder on one side rose into the ceiling where the Portal was opened, and in the center of the floor there was a trapdoor. Two Aughmerian soldiers stood at attention, one at each fireplace, while a skinny, ill-favored slave worked at stoking the fires. The room had no windows, and the wind howled outside. He dressed quickly, fetching dry clothes from his bag. He used his wet shirt to corral the vomit into a pile before wondering what to do with it.

A nod from the Shadan sent the slave to Gen's side. He motioned for Gen to come to the trap door with his waste, and when Gen neared, the slave opened it. Bitter cold invaded the room, and Gen shoved everything, including his shirt, out the hole. In that brief moment when the trapdoor was open, he could just make out snow flying by, propelled sideways in the powerful wind. His vomit froze before it got halfway down, and he could hear it shatter as it banged against the rungs of the ladder and then dropped to the ground. They were in a tower of some sort. Gen returned to the fire immediately.

"How long has the wind been like this?" the Shadan

asked his soldiers.

"All night," the one nearest Gen answered. "If it follows the pattern of the last few days, it will let up somewhat as day approaches."

"We've got time," Torbrand said. "Udan has to dry his cloak, and Gen needs to recover some of his fortitude."

Gen concentrated on keeping warm, guessing the Whitewind Shard to be approximately six or seven hours behind the Menegothian shard they had come from.

"At this rate we'll be lucky to get to Ellenais before dinner," the Shadan continued, addressing no one in particular.

How long they waited, Gen couldn't guess, but the wind did lessen in intensity, and the Shadan called for them to prepare despite Udan's complaints that his cloak was still damp.

"Now listen," the Shadan explained. "Take a good deep drink from your waterskin and then take some of the liquid and spread it on your hands and face. That will give you enough warmth to reach the bottom. It is about twenty feet to the ground. There is a building nearby. Go into it immediately. Hold your breath for as long as you can. If you must breathe, try not to breathe the air directly. Breathe through the cloth of your cloak. You will go first, Gen. I don't want you falling on top of me. You should probably remove the rock from your pack lest it attack you again."

After Gen had done as Torbrand instructed, the slave threw the trapdoor open again. When he did, Gen judged the pond the fairer prospect. The icy wooden ladder dropped dizzyingly to the snow-covered ground below, and if it were daybreak, Gen couldn't tell. Everything was a purple-black, and, small, icy snowflakes whooshed through the opening to sting his face.

"Get going, Gen," Torbrand commanded. "The virtue of the liquid does not last long."

With trepidation, Gen hung his legs over the side and

grasped the rungs, trying not to look down. As he inched cautiously down the rungs, he realized his danger: the cold here could kill within minutes. In moments, his eyelids had frozen shut, and the wind numbed his legs almost past feeling before he was halfway down. He could only hold his breath for a short amount of time, and when he did draw in air, it stung. He went down on touch, and he guessed he was six feet from the ground when he fell off, grateful for the powdery snow that broke his fall. Once down, he could not feel to move.

"For pity's sake, Gen," the Shadan complained as he dragged him by his cloak hood inside a building Gen couldn't see, "we really do need to toughen you up."

"Merciful Eldaloth!" Udan swore as he banged the door shut. "There isn't enough money in the world!"

The warmth from a brazier of coals gradually thawed Gen's eyelashes enough for him to see. The three men were in a long, stable-like building that smelled of urine and feces. Ten kennels lined the walls behind them. Three cold soldiers were readying three sleds, each pulled by massive dogs with thick white fur and flat faces. Long hair hung over their faces and was so dense that no eyes, mouth, or snout were visible beneath it, which Gen found disturbing. Piles of furs lay about the walls, as well as unused sleds.

"No doubt you are wondering how we are to survive a trek through this waste when a few seconds nearly did you in," Torbrand said. "Watch. You first, Udan."

Gen sat up. The three soldiers wrapped the Portal Mage in bear fur, shoving thick gloves on his hands, furry socks over his boots, and a fur sack over his head. They laid him prone on the sled, covered him with another fur, and then tied him down. Gen felt sick. How could it get any worse?

"How do you breathe?" Gen exclaimed worriedly. "Do the dogs know where to go?"

"Calm yourself," Torbrand remonstrated. "Breathing inside the fur is not pleasant or easy, but it is better than dying. The dogs, yes, know their way. We found them here while exploring the shard with some magical help. They and some other smaller game they prey on are the only things alive in this place. Now stand over there and get covered."

Gen could not remember feeling more uncomfortable. After having him drink more of the liquid from his waterskin, the Shadan ordered his men to serve Gen strong liquor since it was his "first time." Once he was lashed to his sled, he could not move, see, or breathe easily. Sounds were muffled, and he felt the need to scratch everywhere as the fur tickled and irritated his skin, especially as he started to sweat. His stomach twisted in anxiety and he felt fearful and trapped. Just as he felt he would scream and start thrashing, the liquor dulled his mind and his senses.

He heard the doors open and felt his sled move outside. The furs could not completely mask the terrible cold all around him. The wind flapped the furs as they glided through the snow, but the ropes held them fast. Three mummies entombed in fur moved slowly across a dark frozen landscape, the white dogs trotting forward at a relaxed pace, unmindful of the blowing powdery snow churning all around them. Gen couldn't imagine how Torbrand had transported an entire regiment of soldiers in such an uncomfortable and difficult fashion, or how he had found a Portal to Tolnor thirty feet off the ground on a shard no human could survive on for even a few minutes.

Hours dragged slowly by, and, while he felt drowsy enough to sleep, he could never find the peace of mind to do so. From time to time, the sleds would tilt or bump as the dogs padded over hills and gullies that their human passengers could only imagine. But at length, the wind died and the sounds outside changed.

"Sleds approaching," a gruff voice announced from outside. "Stoke the fire and let's get them out." Gradually, the sleds stopped, and unknown hands worked at the ropes and furs. After several minutes, the three of them were standing in a smoke-filled ice cave, warming themselves by a fire. The two soldiers were shocked at the Shadan's presence, and their master disapprovingly examined the encampment around him. Supplies, sacks, and other equipage were strewn about the cave haphazardly.

"Who is your Blade Leader?" Torbrand asked, tone severe.

"Joran Brake," one of the soldiers replied fearfully.

"I shall have him disciplined," Torbrand stated. "I'm sure he will pass it along. Now feed the dogs and clean this place up. Gen, come with me. You will find this interesting."

Gen slipped the fur mittens onto his hands again before leaving the comfort of the flames. Torbrand grabbed a lantern and led him back toward the cave entrance. They had only gone several paces before Gen noticed lumps on the floor, at first unrecognizable, and then as the light revealed them, perfectly clear. Torbrand led him past an entire company of frozen Uyumaak—Hunters, Bashers, and Warriors—all fallen in grotesque poses on the floor, their skin matching the color of the ice and snow around them. An enormous Gagon was slumped against the wall, half its head and left shoulder trapped in clear ice, magnifying one of its misshapen eyes.

There were dogs covered in black, spidery hair, and each had a ring of yellow eyes around its head and a large eye on top in a recessed cavity in its skull. They had no mouths, but thin, tubular proboscises snaked out onto the ground. Gek, wolves that lived in trees and walked nearly upright, were chained together ten at a time in front of a dead dark elf. Birds of prey, wingspans longer than two horses set end on end, were imprisoned in metal cages on flat wagons which had been pulled by massive hounds, now slumped on top of each other. After more Uyumaak, they came on a fallen regiment of mounted riders in black, spiked armor. Their steeds were a dark, metallic gray, skin a series of large overlapping scales, their hooves cloven and teeth thin sharp spikes, menacing in their rictus. One of the face plates of the helmets was open, a pale human face staring blankly at him.

After nearly a mile, the air grew colder as they neared the entrance, and there they found the most horrifying brigade of the column, a group of fifty or more men— peasants and soldiers—wearing tatters and bearing fatal injuries sustained before they had been reanimated and forced to march again by Mikkik's power. Some were headless, others partially dismembered, and some still carried the spear or arrows that had killed them embedded in their bodies. Torbrand paid them no heed, but Gen scooted along the wall, trying to avoid their mangled bodies clumped about the floor, hands clawed in rigor, reaching out from the piles and ice.

They rounded the corner, the opening to the cave yawning before them fifty yards ahead. The cold here was nearly unbearable, and Torbrand stopped, drinking from his waterskin. Gen followed suit. At their feet was a tangle of black snakes, vipers the length of man's arm. There were so many on top of each other that they formed a long hump six feet wide stretching to the mouth of the cave. In the weak light outside, he could tell that more creatures, now buried beneath the snow, stretched into the distance.

"This column stretches for five miles, as near as we can tell," Torbrand explained. "The cold must have come upon it quickly. It seems very few of the monsters in this caravan had the chance to move but a few feet before they died. This is probably just one of Mikkik's legions that was marching to finish off humans and elves before the Shattering. We haven't quite puzzled out where this place was, yet." The Shadan's eyes flamed with energy. "Can you imagine the fight this would have been? What I wouldn't give to have a chance to meet this horde head-on with the might of Aughmere at my back. That would be war! Then a man could prove himself! There is no battle today that could even compare to this! If black days are coming, then let them come!"

Gen hadn't the words to reply, and the Shadan seemed so lost envisioning the past that none were required.

After several moments of reverie, the Shadan sighed. "I must confess," he said, seeming deflated after his outburst, "that this mass of snakes would be nearly impossible to fight. There must be thousands of them. They could overwhelm an entire regiment and give almost no chance of defense. Come on, then. I have given you quite the story to tell your woman, at least."

"Yes, Shadan," Gen agreed, though he doubted Regina would thank him for relating it. Gen reached inside his pocket and fingered the braid, and it comforted him as they hiked past scores of creatures he never wanted to see again, frozen or fresh. However horrible, Gen was sure Rafael could turn this one day's events into a tale worth hearing.

"Let's go, Udan!" the Shadan ordered, finding him snacking near the fire. They grabbed their gear and went a short way farther into the cave. A small section of the ice had been cleared from the cave wall, and it was here that Udan closed his eyes, the blue Portal shimmering into existence before them. "You go first, Gen," the Shadan said. "And do try to keep your feet this time. I think you'll be pleased at what awaits us on the other side."

CHAPTER 9 - BELOVED

Despite its foreign appearance, the Ellenais shard was the most perfect place Gen had ever seen. After emerging from the Portal and recovering from another fit of retching, Gen gaped in awe.

"Welcome to my home," Torbrand said boastfully as he, Udan, and Gen removed their winter garb and repacked their gear. Gen muttered his thanks to Eldaloth for the instant relief from the cold, and he marveled at the scene around him as they descended a steep hill down a broad path of packed, rich soil.

After hours in the frozen waste, the warmth and humidity were both welcome and uncomfortable at the same time. On the heights of the hill where the Portal exited, tall pines rose majestically into the air, light green moss clinging to branches and limbs. Delicate ferns and small red flowers carpeted the forest floor, a breeze mingling their scents with those of sea air and pine. Elegant white birds whirled and sang overhead, some darting back to nests hidden in cracks and grottoes in the cliff wall to the east.

The shard was small, consisting of a clear green-blue sea and a thin island situated roughly in the middle of the water. It was little more than two miles across at its thickest point and five miles long. Brilliant white sand ringed the entire island save where the hill rose, forming a steep cliff on one side. In the distance, Gen could just make out the sails of small fishing boats on the water.

As they hiked down the switchbacks, Gen caught glimpses of the Shadan's home, a massive complex of buildings that stretched away from a palatial manor house that sat close to the hill. The manor house was perfectly square, its domed roof and walls constructed of a white stone accented with thin grooves of gold and silver. Simple cylindrical pillars ringed the three-story structure, supporting the silver roof and a balcony that went around the entire building. Numerous doors opened onto the balcony, and gauzy white curtains hung in wide, arched windows.

The other buildings, built to the north, were simple, rectangular affairs with red tile roofs. The grandeur of the buildings lessened the farther they were from the manor house, though even the poorest quarter of the island seemed a paradise to Gen. A garden and park stretched down the middle of the island, separating the buildings on either side, and people—tiny specks from their vantage point on the hill—milled about lazily in its beauty.

As they neared the bottom of the hill, the firs intermingled with and then gave way to low deciduous trees with broad leaves and slender branches that stretched away from thick, twisted trunks, providing ample shade. Flowers of every shape, size, and color rocked softly with the breeze, their powerful scents pleading with the passerby to stop, smell, and forget his troubles—and in his wonderment, Gen nearly did.

Torbrand noticed him gawking. "Now you understand the sacrifice I made in planning to stay in your miserable town for the winter. I would gladly let one of my Warlords oversee the operation, but I can't trust any of them to act as they should. Now be honest, have you ever seen a place as magnificent as this one?"

"No, sir." Gen answered truthfully. In his mind's eye he had always pictured Aughmere as gray and miserable, though, he reminded himself, Ellenais was not Aughmere proper. He chanced a look at Udan. The Portal Mage had thrown off his sullen demeanor, a comfortable smile overspreading his face in its stead.

"How long will we be staying, Shadan?" Udan asked with a bit of hope and only the slightest hint of apprehension—Torbrand was in visibly good humor.

"Only a day or two, Udan, so don't get too comfortable. I'll return you to your ice cave before long."

The dirt path joined a broad road paved with a light-colored rock flecked with sparkling quartz twinkling like stars in the sunshine. Two soldiers in deep purple tabards bearing the device of the black hammer came to attention as the travelers neared the gate into the complex proper. Through the silver bars, Gen spied two veiled women, simply attired in formless brown robes. They watched with curiosity for a moment and then scampered away quickly. Somewhere children were playing, their high voices carried by the wind.

Torbrand stopped in front of one of the soldiers who tried to hide his surprise at his liege's unexpected appearance. "Please inform my daughters they need to prepare my room and two rooms for my guests. We will need a hearty meal prepared for this evening. I would like Mena brought to the study immediately."

"At once, Shadan."

The guard opened the gate and ran through, taking the steps into the manor house two at a time. Gen and Udan followed the Shadan through the gate and up the same steps, which terminated in an arched wooden door of a blond wood tooled with the shapes of vines.

"Leave your traveling gear here and it will be taken care

of," Torbrand ordered. Three veiled girls, about the same age as Gen, appeared at a run and each came to a knee before Torbrand.

"Your will, father," they intoned, heads bowed.

"Rise. Essa, take Udan here to his room. Leda, help her carry his things. Ona, take Gen's gear to his room. I am taking him to the study with me. Is Mena there yet?"

"No, father," Ona answered meekly. "She was in the park. The guard went to fetch her immediately."

"Very well. Come, Gen."

The inside of the manor house was light and airy. A broad hallway from the door terminated in a circular room open to all three levels. Late afternoon sunlight from a window at the apex of the dome roof fell aslant onto the balconies and walks, illuminating the colorful and comfortable furniture set about the room in the midst of large planters of flowers and pots of tall, exotic plants. Gen wondered why no one was there, all the time hearing activity all around him on the upper levels. Torbrand led him to a nearby door on the south wall and opened it. They entered a spacious study, Torbrand crossing the room and throwing open the shutters on the other side.

Light flooded in, revealing a single desk in the center of the floor, shelves and books running along the sides, and a red divan set against the wall behind the desk and beneath the window. A deep wooden chest abutted the desk, and Torbrand stooped in front of it. After touching the chest in several places in a confusing pattern, he lifted the lid and rummaged around inside. Gen couldn't see what he removed, but the Shadan stuffed it hurriedly in his pocket and shut the lid.

"Make yourself at home on the divan, Gen. I will wait a little longer with you to introduce you to my daughter, Mena."

Gen's brow wrinkled in confusion. "Forgive me, Shadan," Gen chanced, averting his eyes. "Why have you

137

brought me here? What are you going to do with me? Am I to be a slave in this place?"

"You aren't that lucky. Slaves have more rights than you do. Look at me," Torbrand ordered. Gen complied. "There are no male slaves on this island, though there are some tradesmen. Unfortunately for you, I have a bard of several times your skill in my employ already. I will reveal what is in store for you when I choose. In the meantime, enjoy this place. You and I will be leaving it long before either of us will want to. Now sit."

Gen settled himself on the divan, musing while Torbrand wrote a letter. If Torbrand wasn't to use him as a slave or a bard, then why bring him to the island and why introduce him to his daughter? Was he going to kill him for sport, or perhaps shame him in front of his family as a display of power? Perhaps the Shadan would trade him or gift him to a Warlord.

Three soft knocks at the door interrupted his thoughts. The Shadan dropped his pen and rose immediately, crossing to the door and opening it himself.

A young woman waited on the other side. Gen judged her to be a little older than himself. She was tall, slender, and unveiled, which surprised him. Her long black hair, blue eyes, and comely face marked her as the Shadan's daughter, and—unlike her sisters—she greeted Torbrand with her head held high.

Torbrand embraced her enthusiastically. The Shadan's eyes, so often cruel or sullen or tinged with madness, softened to an emotion that Gen understood and did not fear: affection. This was a beloved daughter. Gen's mind fought with the contradiction. Could this be the same man who had so casually ordered the men, women, and children of Tell slaughtered not three weeks before?

Mena noticed Gen and pulled away from her father. "And who have you brought? This is not the Portal Mage. Is this a Tolnorian noble or a Rhugothian?"

138

"Mena," Torbrand said happily, "I bring you a rarity. This is a peasant I found in Tolnor, and one who isn't a complete idiot."

"But he's so tall," Mena remarked, regarding him thoughtfully. "And pale."

"A rarity, as I said. Gen, this is my daughter, Mena."

Gen stood quickly and bowed.

Mena smiled. "I am not nobility, Gen," she said, crossing to him. She wore a fine robe of blue silk quite different from the plain brown robes of the other women. Her hair fell about her shoulders in waves, and her blue eyes, while hard, still managed to convey an intelligence and kindness Gen did not expect to encounter in an Aughmerian woman. Her countenance showed a self-assurance found in those who know they are favored but have not been spoiled by it.

"A curtsey from me and a nod from you is all that is required of those of equal rank in Tolnor. Is it not so?"

"That is so," he replied

She curtsied and he nodded, Torbrand watching with a self-satisfied smirk.

"I have matters to attend to," Torbrand announced. "Mena, I leave Gen in your charge. I know you've been wanting to meet a real Tolnorian for some time. He might actually have useful information for you. Show him the Tolnor Room. He will probably find it most amusing. I will see you both for supper."

After another quick smile to his daughter, he walked out of the room, leaving the door open behind him. Mena waited until the echo of his footsteps faded away on one of the upper levels.

Once she was sure he was gone, her face grew grave and she whispered, "I am sorry, Gen, for what I can guess my father has done to you and your village. He told me of his plan. But why are you here? He made no plans to come back. Did he say?"

"I don't know. I asked him just prior to your arrival and he refused to tell me."

Mena frowned, crossing to the door and shutting it. She motioned for him to sit at the desk chair while she sat on the divan.

"I am fearful of what he might intend. Be on your guard. While slaves have rights of challenge in Aughmere, prisoners of war do not. Do not be carried away by the comfort and finery around you. Aughmere can be a cruel place, though I must admit my exposure to the wider world is limited. My father protects me a great deal."

"He allows you to go unveiled?"

"He has ordered me to go unveiled, though I would feel more comfortable with one. I wear one while he is away, and I am glad I had forewarning of his return. He would be displeased if he knew I disobeyed him. I'm sure you know that my father is of two minds."

"Yes."

"Then remember this, for there is one thing every member of his household knows: Torbrand Khairn, Shadan of Aughmere, despises three things above all others— disobedience, stupidity, and incompetence. He has said you are intelligent. . ."

"He actually said that I wasn't 'a complete idiot,'" Gen corrected.

"For him, that is saying you are intelligent. But listen. You stand the best chance of survival if you obey his every whim and do your best at the tasks he sets you to. If you falter . . . well, I imagine I am telling you things you know well." Her face clouded over and she leaned back. "Torbrand cares nothing for ceremony. He respects nothing and loves nothing."

"Except you."

She frowned. "I do not know why I have his favor, though I am not sure I would call it love. It has been so since I was a child. I am not even a daughter of his first wife. I am the third child of his fifth wife, and, as such, I should walk these halls as lowly as any, but here I am dressed exquisitely and forbidden to wear the veil. I sleep alone in a room larger and finer than that of his first wife—for which she hates me—and I am never permitted to do any sort of work or be useful."

"I am sure your other sisters are jealous."

"It is true. I have no friends among my sisters. But come, that is enough. I must take you to the Tolnor room. I have a hundred questions to ask you, though I'm sure I'll forget every one. Tolnor is a hobby of mine of late."

The Tolnor Room was on the top floor up two flights of long stairs. They took them in silence, Gen engrossed in the finery all around him. Tapestries depicting wars, animals, and landscapes hung everywhere, and treasures of all varieties were on display on tables or in recessed spaces in the walls. Two young boys—no more than eight—tore past them, laughing and yelling, engaged in a raucous game of chase.

"Brand! Dolan! Father is home," Mena warned. Both boys stopped immediately, eyes widening.

"Has he won the war already?" Brand asked.

"No," Mena explained. "He is here for a visit, and I think he will want it more peaceful than you are making it."

Gen took it as a sign of Torbrand's severe discipline that two such energetic youths could change mood so quickly. Both tiptoed off as if a Gagon was sleeping on the floor below. Mena smiled at them and resumed the climb upward. A few other young ladies loitered in the hall, all veiled and attired in the same drab brown cloth. They whispered as they passed, gawking at him.

The third floor felt much warmer than the others. Mena led Gen down a broad hallway to the north and pushed open a set of double doors.

"This is the Tolnor Room," she explained. "It has been here since the building was constructed one hundred years ago." Gen stepped inside. To his astonishment, a complete replica of the southern half of the Menegothian shard from the Emerald Lake southward had been fashioned from clay on an immense wooden table. The Wardwall Mountains jutted up realistically, and even the Alewine forest was meticulously recreated with small trees. Every major geological feature was reproduced, along with cities large and small.

"You are from here, correct?" Mena said, pointing to a small cabin representing Tell, the name spelled out beside it in black paint.

"Yes."

"Then you owe fealty to Baron Forthrickeshire and to Duke Norshwal. Have you seen them?"

Gen was impressed with her knowledge. "I haven't."

"Then come and look. Your King is here, as well."

She directed his gaze to the walls, and Gen turned, taking in the entire room. There were small portraits of every one of the Dukes, their sons, and the barons hanging about the walls, sectioned according to Duchy. They had escaped his notice when he first entered due to his fascination with the map. Gen examined the pictures, finding the artwork exquisite, the faces almost alive.

Duke Norshwal had a fat, clean-shaven face and beady eyes that reminded him of Bernard. Baron Forthrickeshire was his opposite, his thin, angular head terminating in a long, sharp goatee. Gen went to the King, who had the largest portrait, finding him thin with long, blond hair. His beautiful queen, the black-haired Kerenne, was framed at his side.

"That is a wig," Mena revealed. "Your King is quite bald."

"How did the Shadan get these pictures?" Gen asked incredulously.

"It is quite clever," Mena explained. "Something Kaimas—a Mage in my father's service—thought up.

142

Here." She removed a picture of Duke Sothbranne of Bloodthrone. "Touch the canvas lightly."

As Gen did so, the colors of the picture swirled and coalesced into Gen's resemblance.

"Impressive," Gen commented, examining his own face. The only mirror in Tell belonged to Bernard Showles's wife, Katrina, and she didn't share. The best reflection of himself he had ever seen was in the dark water of forest pools.

A question came to his mind. "Surely you didn't convince all the Dukes of Tolnor and their families to touch all these canvases?"

"No," Mena replied, crossing the room to a set of drawers. "I do not know if my father would approve of me telling you this, but the canvases only need be touched by a personal item. Even letters and parchment will do, which account for many of the pictures, as my father has personally corresponded with your Dukes concerning the trip they made to meet the Ha'Ulrich this last summer."

She rifled through a drawer, retrieving a letter and touching it to the canvas. Duke Sothbranne's face appeared in the frame again. She put the letter back and returned the picture to the wall.

"Does the Ha'Ulrich come here often?" Gen asked. Gen thought that if he could chance to meet him and could gain his favor, he might find mercy and a way out of his predicament. Mena's eyes widened.

"No!" she exclaimed fervently. "He has never been here, save when he was born. I beg you not to broach this subject with my father! It infuriates him that he couldn't train the Ha'Ulrich—not in the sword, not in leadership, not in the customs of my people. We don't even say Chertanne's name for fear. '*How can a man lead Aughmere or any nation without knowing the sword?*' he complains."

Gen was perplexed. "Chertanne doesn't know the sword?" Every tale of the prophecy painted the Ha'Ulrich

143

as a man-at-arms.

"No. The Church of the One forbid him to be near blades or weapons of any kind, for his safety. He is to win by force of magic, not the blade. At least that was the argument they gave Father. In any case, it doesn't help that Chertanne will take over this estate in two years. I do not know that there is another place large enough for Torbrand's family. For your safety, do not mention this, either."

"I understand."

"But tell me. . . I must confess that I expected a Tolnorian peasant to be less keen of speech and mind than you appear to be. You are, I assume, apprenticed after the tradition of your people?"

"Yes. I am apprenticed to be a bard."

Mena smiled. "Wonderful! That explains much. You know how to read, then. And you are of the age to be betrothed come spring?"

"Yes."

"Do you have someone special, then?" She motioned for Gen to come to the balcony and sit with her on comfortable chairs.

"No and yes," he said, summarizing Regina's betrothal to Hubert. Her eyes were riveted on his, and she absorbed every detail.

"You discourage me, Gen," Mena commented after Gen finished. "I understood that marriages in Tolnor were of a kinder nature than ours. Most young women in my country are herded into a room where those our fathers deem worthy can choose whom they like, often in exchange for something. I thought that in Tolnor there was more consideration for the feelings of the couple."

"It is more likely among peasants than nobility, but you can see that Regina's parents hoped to elevate her, which is done as often as possible, however wrong I may see their choices to be. But why should our customs discourage you?"

"I am to marry one of your Princes."

"Really? Who?" Arranged marriages were customary when alliances were sought between nations, but Aughmere and Tolnor had not exchanged sons and daughters in marriage for ages. Perhaps, he thought, the coming of the Ha'Ulrich would change that.

"Come," she invited, and they returned inside, crossing to the wall where the portraits of the Kildan family hung. Duke and Lady Kildan were placed side by side, their male children beneath. Dason, one of the Chalaine's personal Protectors, was to the side of his brother, Gerand. The difference in their demeanors was striking.

She pointed to Gerand. "It is him."

Both Gerand and Dason were handsome men with blue eyes and dark hair. Dason's face was rounder, jovial, and inviting, while Gerand's long hair, sharper features, and thin goatee gave him a more serious aspect. Gen congratulated her.

"They are so different," she remarked thoughtfully, as if she had known them a long time. "Dason is handsome and happy, confident and innocent, obviously having lived a life full of praise and encouragement. Gerand has known challenge and disappointment. No doubt he is burdened with the weight of living up to the reputation of a famous older brother."

She removed Gerand's portrait from the wall to study it more closely. "But look at his eyes! There is such determination and goodness there. He lives without the praise but doesn't need it. There is a fire within him, a deep will to be the best of men as he sees it in his own mind. And, as he is Tolnorian and a gentleman, even if he weren't generous—which I think he is—he would act it anyway."

"When was the wedding arranged?" Gen inquired.

"It hasn't been. Father says he will give me to Gerand when he has conquered Tolnor."

145

Gen's eyes widened. *Give* a prince to his daughter?

"What is wrong?" Mena asked, brows furrowed.

"Gerand isn't likely to accept, even if ordered to do so," Gen told her, not wanting to think about a Tolnor under Aughmerian rule. "The war will put him in great peril, as well." She frowned, eyes nearly tearing, and Gen wished he could retract his comment. She steeled herself quickly.

"Gerand is to try for the Dark Guard next spring. Father has already let his Warlords know to leave him unharmed and not to hinder his travel to Rhugoth." Gen's mind reeled. Mena was indeed favored. She said, "But tell me, am I so undesirable that he would have nothing to do with me? I am not a stupid slave girl, and I have studied court manners!" Her vehemence caught Gen off guard.

"Listen, Mena, I meant no offense," Gen said, hoping the Shadan wouldn't show up and find that he had upset his dearest treasure. "You are beautiful, and I am sure you would make a wonderful wife, even in Tolnorian society. But you must understand that for a Tolnorian noble, weddings are about aligning yourself with another family. It may be hard for you to grasp, but by marrying you, Gerand would be allying himself with the family that overthrew his nation. He would lose his honor in the sight of his peers."

This information struck her hard, her hand going to her heart as if Gen had just inserted a dagger there. Again, she composed herself, turning away. Gen had the unpleasant feeling of one who has murdered the dream of another.

"But if I can make him love me. . ." she countered. "If he loves me, then there can be no objections."

Gen nodded, not wanting to reveal the problem with her reasoning. In Tolnor honor and duty superseded love, from King to peasant. An uncomfortable silence ensued. Mena crossed to the window, and Gen busied himself studying portraits, seeing for the first time the nobility of his homeland.

Putting faces to names proved entertaining, though

146

Mena brooding nearby kept him edgy. The Shadan might return any moment to find his daughter upset, and if she was upset, Gen could only imagine what brutality the Shadan would deal to him as punishment.

A thought struck him. "Mena, do the paintings work with something like hair?"

"Yes," she said, turning around, face still downcast. Gen reached into his pocket and removed the braided lock of hair that Regina had given him.

A smile returned to Mena's face. "Is that Regina's? Come, I would like to see her."

She took down the portrait of Duke Sothbranne again and he touched the braid to the canvas. The painting swirled, revealing Regina's beautiful face framed by curly blonde locks. Gen smiled to see it, as did Mena, though Regina's soft blue eyes were tainted by fear and sadness.

"She is lovely," Mena commented, "though she doesn't carry the typical marks of Tolnorian peasantry, either."

"Her father is a freeman and her mother is the daughter of a minor baron."

"You are perfect for her, then. Similar in looks, and I can tell by her eyes that she must be intelligent. I am sorry that she was betrothed to another."

"I don't think it will matter," Gen added sadly. "I doubt she or I will survive past winter."

Shadan Khairn's voice behind them surprised them both. "Such a pathetic tale, Gen," Torbrand mocked.

"Please don't kill her, father," Mena said, stepping toward him. "And spare Gen, as well. Please."

Torbrand laughed. With a tender smile he reached out and stroked her hair. "I see Gen has won your pity, which I should have expected. I will not kill the girl. As for Gen, I have something special in store. I cannot say he will not die, but I will promise that he will have a better chance than most of surviving." Mena frowned but nodded her acceptance. Torbrand continued, "Follow me, both of you.

There is food waiting for us."

They took dinner on one of the balconies facing the sea. There Gen learned another Aughmerian custom—the women did not eat until after the men and then not in their presence. Mena, however, sitting uncomfortably to Gen's left, was an exception. Several girls and one woman saw to their needs, refilling plates and cups the instant they neared empty.

"The woman is the Shadan's first wife, Joselin," Mena whispered to Gen as they sat. First wives managed the running of the mundane affairs of the estate. Despite her veil, Gen could feel the contempt the older woman and the other young women held for Mena.

Two of Khairn's sons, Lodan and Horan, joined them. Gen guessed they were a little older than he was. They dressed as their father, all in black, and came armed with swords even to dinner. Lodan was fair-complected, Hodan dark, and both carried themselves with a confident air, swaggering to their seats. The meal proceeded in silence, Torbrand deep in some thought of his own.

The sun set on the opposite side of the house, and the slosh of the waves on the beach and the caressing breezes of the water relaxed Gen as he engaged in small talk with Mena. She impressed him with her poise and knowledge. Lodan and Horan standing to leave distracted them.

"Lodan, come here," the Shadan said. "Horan, you may go."

Mena closed her eyes and shook her head.

Lodan turned toward his father, face composed. "Your will, father."

"Mena, come." Mena rose and crossed to Torbrand. "Now turn, dear." Mena's back faced Lodan. The Shadan lifted her hair, revealing deep bruises on the back of her neck.

"How did these get here, Lodan?" the Shadan demanded, face angry.

"Mena and I were just sporting with each other, father." Lodan explained, fear overspreading his words. "I did not mean to harm her."

"It was an accident, father," Mena pleaded.

"You are kind to defend him, Mena, but you must understand that I know something of injuries." The Shadan concentrated and the bruises faded. "I know what happened, Lodan. You tried to force her to eat a meal from the floor to amuse your sisters while I was gone. That you would try to cover it up only reveals your cowardice. You have harmed property that is not rightfully your own and I invoke the Challenge of Justice and demand you duel with me to first blood over the matter. If I win, you will become a slave and I will sell you into the care of another master."

"You have no one to second! The testimony of women doesn't count!" Lodan yelled anxiously.

"You are right. What you did was in the presence of women only, a further evidence of your weakness. But you seem to forget that I am the Shadan of Aughmere. I'll just kill you because I am angry."

Lodan dove away from his father and leaped over the side of the balcony. The Shadan's sword flashed out and sliced Lodan across his legs before he fell two stories, flattening one of the many thick bushes surrounding the house. Mena ran to the balustrade and Gen followed. Lodan pulled himself from the tangle of branches and struggled to his feet, limping off in the direction of the high hill.

"I'll catch him later," Torbrand stated unconcernedly. "There aren't many places to hide here." He turned to a pale, shocked Mena. "Mena, dear, do not conceal these things from me. I will not take you to Tolnor with me, and I will not leave you in danger. I am sending you to Ironkeep for the rest of the winter. The soldiers there will have better sense than your own family, it seems."

"Your will, father," Mena acquiesced, though the idea

was clearly distasteful to her.

"Now go pack your things. You leave at first light." Mena left, and Torbrand ordered everyone else away after a slave lit a lantern against the dark.

Gen fidgeted nervously as the Shadan stared out at the calm sea, lost in thought. After several minutes, Torbrand's eyes cleared and he stood up.

"Come here, Gen." Gen crossed to where the Shadan stood near the balcony. "Eyes up, boy." Khairn ordered. Gen stared over the Shadan's shoulder. Khairn stood and took his sword from the mantle above the fireplace. Gen braced himself.

"Have you ever held a sword in your hands?" Khairn asked, fingers running along the ornate scabbard. "I know peasants in Tolnor are forbidden them."

"Just an old sword Rafael has."

"Did you like it?"

"I guess so."

Khairn smacked him across the cheek with his open palm. Gen managed to keep his balance, but his face stung and he fought hard to keep the tears out of his eyes.

"Never answer me with 'I guess so' or 'maybe' or 'perhaps.' Those are words of the weak-willed and weak-minded. Did you like the feel of the sword?"

"Yes, I did, sir."

"Good. Have you ever wanted to learn to use one?"

"Yes, sir."

"Is there anyone you want to kill? That buffoon that's betrothed to Regina, perhaps?"

Gen was silent for a time, but Torbrand's look warned him he was taking too long to respond.

"No, sir."

This time the blow came with a fist, and it sent Gen to the floor, mouth bleeding. Tears stung his eyes, but he managed to stand again despite his reeling vision.

"Don't lie to me again or I'll kill you where you stand. Is

150

there anyone you want to kill?"

"Yes, sir," Gen replied, blood dripping off his lip and onto the floor.

Khairn returned to his seat. "Excellent." For several moments he sat, running his finger affectionately along the blade. "Then learn to kill, you will. I wanted to teach my son the sword, but he being the 'Blessed One', the 'Savior of the World', somehow exempted him from my training. The crotchety old Churchmen and Magicians took him from me and decreed he should never touch a blade for fear he might hurt himself with it!" The range and insanity rose in the Shadan's eyes. "So *they* raised him! How can a man be a Shadan and not know the sword? Can you imagine a King in your country not knowing the sword? It would be a disgrace! No one would even consider him a man. Now my son is a pathetic, spoiled peacock and I can hardly stand the sight of him! All he wants is to eat and dally and sleep. If he wants anyone killed, he orders Cormith to do it so he won't soil his clothes! Damn Churchmen, Magicians, and scholars all!"

Khairn slapped the table, half-coming out of his seat. Gen stood still and silent, trying to rein in knees that wanted to knock against each other.

"Well," Torbrand continued after calming himself, "you will keep me from spending this winter clawing the furniture and hearing the same songs over and over until I know them better than you."

Gen wondered what he meant. He couldn't quite believe that Shadan Khairn would actually expend the effort to teach him swordplay, but he soon found it to be true. The Shadan excused himself from the room for a few minutes and returned holding three necklaces, each with a transparent crystal. One was tinged white, one black, and the third blue. They were cut into pyramid shapes, and each had a hole drilled in the top through which a thin piece of leather had been strung.

"These are old, Gen," the Shadan said, fingering them thoughtfully. "I used them to train Cormith and Omar. They were used to train me. In times long past, before the face of Trys was fully hidden, there were years of war and bloodshed the likes of which Ki'Hal has never known nor should hope to know again. It was during the first war with the creatures of Mikkik that the prophecy of the Blessed One was given. Pontiff Ethelion the Second, like many at the time, thought the advent of the Blessed One was to come soon, in a matter of years, and thus he sought zealously for the child among women. He also searched out the best warriors to serve to protect the Holy Child once he arrived.

"But the years stretched on and the Blessed One never came. In an act of unsurpassed devotion, during the Middle Peace, three of the most renowned warriors allowed the Pontiff to encase their minds and souls into these stones so that the knowledge these fighters possessed could be passed on to generations after. The Second Mikkikian War began not long after, and many soldiers were trained by the masters within these stones.

"You will find the language they speak to be foreign, but, despite not understanding their words, you will learn a great deal from them, often more than you'd care to."

Khairn came forward and placed the necklaces around Gen's neck.

"Usually only one is worn at a time, but we've no time for that. It won't be easy for you at night. The stones awaken when you rest and will change you. Tonight I only have time to teach you two important lessons."

He unsheathed his sword and handed it to a disbelieving Gen. Thoughts of killing Shadan Khairn flashed through his mind, though he knew he had little chance of even laying a scratch on the man.

"Attack me, Gen. I know you want to. Try it."

Gen jumped at the invitation, and he thought he could

muster up a swing both quick and strong. But even as the thought of harming Torbrand came to him, he found he couldn't move his arms. They felt as numb as they had during his trip through the Whitewind shard.

Torbrand retrieved the sword. "That is the first lesson. The virtue of the magic in the stones prevents the apprentice from harming the master during the lessons, though if you are a good pupil, I promise I will remove the stones and give you the chance."

This last was said with a twinkle of anticipation in the Shadan's eye. Now Gen understood what the Shadan was about. *I'm to be the Torbrand's little bit of fun before he gets around to slaughtering more hapless peasants.*

"Now for lesson two. Run away. Get as far from this room as you think you can."

Gen obeyed, though he recognized this would be another lesson in futility. He went into the hall, several of the young women there moving aside as he approached. With every step his legs grew weaker until he could hardly stand up without support. The women giggled, and only as he turned around and headed back toward Shadan Khairn did his strength trickle back into him.

"I can let you go as far as I wish," Torbrand explained. "It's not really a matter of distance but of whether I want to incapacitate you or not. We start back for your desolate town early tomorrow. Enjoy the comfort and the warmth while you can."

Torbrand left Gen alone the rest of the night. He hoped to encounter Mena to ask her more questions about Ironkeep—the capital of Aughmere—before retiring but had no luck. Although it seemed the Shadan had given him the run of the place, Gen didn't venture far, fearing he would do something wrong and incur his new master's wrath. The room appointed for his use was sumptuously furnished with a large, comfortable bed, rugs woven in warm tones, and cushions everywhere.

Despite these luxurious arrangements, Gen had difficulty falling asleep, feeling an uneasy anticipation about the lessons Torbrand said the stones were to teach. As all boys did, he had fancied learning the sword, wielding sticks in pitched battles with youthful friends in the woods. Peasants weren't allowed the weapons of nobility, however, and Rafael's rapier was the only experience he had with swords—which was more than most in Tell. If a deadly encounter didn't await the end of his training, he supposed learning from Torbrand Khairn, acknowledged as the finest swordsman anywhere, would be an opportunity beyond his imagining.

Weariness finally mastered worry, and he slid into sleep and dream. Before him were three men, strong in body and wise in demeanor, warriors all. They stood before the altar of a grand Church, grander than any Gen had ever seen. The whole edifice was built with white marble swirled with gray. The highly polished floor reflected sunlight streaming in through clear glass panes high on the walls of the long Chapel. Carved marble statues of holy men stood solemnly in recesses beneath each window. The ceiling arced high above, terminating in a round stained glass window depicting Eldaloth with his arms extended to embrace the world. Sunlight streamed through the glass, coloring the light that fell upon the altar and choir loft. Gen approached where the men stood, passing dark wooden benches and thin, ornate columns as he traversed the center aisle.

The three soldiers before him regarded him for a few moments. Two were human and one an elf, all dressed in black save for silver moons embroidered on their tabards. Though stern and grave, nobleness and kindness showed in their eyes. Kingly they seemed, though modest in dress and adornment. All wore swords at their sides, and the elf and one of the humans also had longbows. Gen wondered if this were a memory or if he had been pulled into their time somehow. Or perhaps neither.

"Another comes before us. The youngest yet." This came from the man with a bow. He had short brown hair and was clean-shaven. He was thinner than his human companion, giving the impression of speed. Of the three, his brown eyes were the most kind.

"I don't suppose he understands us. No one has for a long time. I wonder how the ancient tongue was lost so easily."

They did not speak the common language, but Gen could understand them nonetheless.

"I understand you," Gen said, though he was surprised to hear a different language come from his mouth. The three soldiers raised their eyebrows.

"Well, this is unexpected," said the first human who spoke, "though a welcome change, indeed. I am Samian Birchwood, Captain under Lord Tolgorth of Audrien." Samian bowed and returned to lean on his massive longbow.

"And I am Telmerran Fourtower, General to the Lady Aisbeth of Thorwane." Telmerran was bald, having thick arms and legs and standing a head taller than Gen. His eyes were the color of the sky, and a long black beard hung from his chin. Gen thought the sight of this man on the battlefield would set any intelligent enemy to running.

"I am Elberen Wis'wei," the elf said. He was thin and tall with a sharp face, gray eyes, and long silver hair. "I am Commander of Ewena's Third House of Wind Marchers. It is a pleasure to again be able to speak to one of our pupils. What is your name and your house?"

"Gen. Of no house of note."

"Welcome," Elberen said. "Before we begin, we have some questions for you. First, why are we all together? It should not be so until the end of the training."

"I do not know," Gen replied, "other than my . . . teacher . . . said there wasn't enough time."

Samian's eyebrows raised and he spoke excitedly. "The

155

marriage approaches, then? Has the Ilch been seen?"

"The marriage is supposed to happen in a little less than two years. As for the Ilch, I haven't heard anything." The three warriors seemed pleased.

"Then our service is nearly at an end," Elberen said, face happy. "I have longed to be released. You, Gen, will likely be the last we train, though there is time for another, if pinched. Is your master the Blessed One's father?"

"Yes."

"And are you to protect the Ha'Ulrich or the Chalaine?"

"I don't think I am to protect anyone."

The three were stunned, and Gen explained how he had come to the training and what Khairn's purpose was. All were angry, but Telmerran was livid.

"I did not let myself be imprisoned in these stones to provide fodder for some mad Shadan's sport!" He swore and raged for several minutes before Samian and Elberen could calm him down.

"What are we to do, Telmerran? Teach him nothing and let him be butchered?" Samian argued.

"He'll be butchered either way!" Telmerran countered. "It's unlikely the Shadan will let him get skilled enough to be a threat to him! I wish I could jump out of this rock and throttle that. . ."

"Calm yourself," Elberen commanded. "If you're going to jump out of these stones, there is only one way, and that is through him. He can understand us, which means he will learn faster and better than his predecessors. If he can mask his knowledge, he might just slay Torbrand and perhaps we can find a new master, or release, soon."

Telmerran considered this for a moment and then relented with a nod. Samian stepped forward and put his hands on Gen's shoulders, eyes sympathetic.

"Gen, each of us left behind those who were very dear to us to enter these stones and commit ourselves to the service of the Chalaine and the Ha'Ulrich. It grieves us that our knowledge should be put to such perversion, but we will not leave you a helpless victim.

"I am sure you understand that this will not be easy. You should learn from each of us one at a time, but our hand has been forced and what we will show you will not be pleasant. We can offer you little comfort, other than the hope for your freedom and the freedom of those you love. May Eldaloth help you."

Samian stepped back and joined his companions, each standing with displeased but resolved faces.

Elberen locked his gray elven eyes on Gen's. "Open your mind. Let us begin."

CHAPTER 10 - BATTLE WITHIN BATTLE WITHOUT

The return trip to Tell proved a little less difficult for Gen. Going through the Portals upset his stomach less than it had when they came, and he dealt with the cold with more control. Climbing from the dog sled up the ladder to the Portal room at the top of the wooden tower was the hardest. The going was slow, and he nearly fell as numb hands gripped the last rungs of the ladder. Floating up through the murky, freezing water proved easier than trying to sink into it had, and, as they dried themselves by the fire and changed clothes, Gen felt his excitement build. He would see Rafael and Regina again, and he was fit to burst with things to tell them.

Near dark they left a grumpy Udan at his cold camp and headed into the woods with the aid of a lantern the Shadan had Gen carry from the forest pool Portal. The night was chill, but the wind spared them as they trudged along in a halo of yellow light that cast tree trunks into long shadows. The Shadan led him a different way back, and Gen wondered if Torbrand was trying to prevent him from remembering where the Portal was.

At last Tell came into view, a clump of lifeless buildings squatting in the dark. Due to the late hour, all lights had been extinguished, and only thin wisps of smoke rose from the chimneys, the pleasant smell something he associated with home. Patrolling guards acknowledged the Shadan expressionlessly.

The Shadan opened the door to the Showles's home. "Get to bed. We start early tomorrow."

Gen wanted to see Regina and Rafael but didn't wish to cross the Shadan. He went to his room and slept but got none of the benefit of it. As soon as his eyes closed, a torrent of images and instructions flowed by, and the lessons were far from comforting.

It started with a catalog of weapons, monsters, and armor. Each item was accompanied by bloody and brutal memories that wrenched Gen from sleep and sickened him to the point of retching into his chamber pot. The stories of war he had learned as a bard hadn't prepared him for corpse-strewn battlefields where orphans wandered in search of fallen parents, or helped him understand the clenching fear of facing down a demon dragged up from the underworld. The songs he knew did not truly reflect of the actual ache of seeing friends torn limb from limb, or the deep sadness of watching as hated enemies trampled beloved people and beautiful places.

Before first light, Khairn woke his disturbed and exhausted pupil. Gen was surprised to see the Shadan happy and relaxed, but he stood quickly anyway, not wanting to test the Shadan's patience.

"How did you sleep, Gen?" he inquired with a sardonic grin.

"Poorly," Gen replied tersely. Torbrand laughed and led him into the great room. Regina was there preparing the morning meal. Her presence comforted Gen. Something about her seemed different, though he couldn't say what. She gave him a questioning look from behind her veil as she set hot rolls and sliced apples before him, and Gen just smiled a reply, not wanting to talk in the Shadan's presence.

Torbrand let him eat as much as he wanted and then led him out into the chill, gray morning. A snowstorm blown in during the late hours of the night had stopped, but heavy clouds still obscured the sky. The guards they met in town snapped to attention as their Shadan passed, and Gen noticed the hint of questioning in their eyes as the Shadan led him into the woods after collecting a lantern from the street. The snow was deep, up to Gen's knees, and the bare branches of the trees were heavily enshrouded in white. Gen wondered what Khairn was up to but didn't have the courage to ask.

After an hour of walking they came to a forest pool that Gen had swum in on many a summer day. It was frozen over and buried with snow.

"Clean the snow off a section and knock a hole in it."

Gen obeyed, though the snow and ice were thick and it took him almost half an hour to accomplish it with rocks and sticks. Afterward his hands were bruised and numb. He shivered in his wet cloak, desperately hoping Torbrand didn't expect him to get in the water.

"There are few people who really know much of what they look like besides murky reflections they glimpse in the water. Even fewer know what they look like when they laugh, or cry, or scream out in pain. But we know others' looks well, even to the point where we can tell when they are lying or hiding something they don't wish to tell. Today I will teach you that you must master the way you look. An intelligent enemy can learn a lot from the face of his opponent, so those that fight must learn absolute control of how they appear. In a fight you must be faceless. Every expression is information that aids the enemy. In a face, an opponent can see fear, arrogance, diffidence, cleverness, and dissembling. And if an opponent knows how you feel, he can exploit your emotion and kill you with it.

160

"So look at yourself, Gen, and tell me what you see. What can you tell from your face?"

The water was a poor mirror, but there in the wavering pool was a face framed by brown hair, punctuated by two green eyes. It was an ordinary face—a face most wouldn't remember well or look at twice. A face that made people he'd never seen ask if they had met him before. Above all, though, he saw sadness and weariness, every bit of how he felt etched into his features.

"I see someone who is tired," Gen replied.

"Good, but easy enough to tell. Before she left for Iron Keep, I asked my daughter Mena what she could divine about you from her brief time with you. She is a perceptive girl. Would you like to know what she told me?"

"Yes, sir," Gen said, turning away from the pool and sitting on the ice. His master brushed the snow off a nearby stump and sat, hands on his knees.

"She said you are someone used to laughter and smiling. You are polite. You are witty. You have had a good life. You were well fed, cared for, and loved. She knew you were learned before she heard you speak. You will find that those who have been taught to read and think have a different look to their eyes than those that haven't. She claims that your intelligence has bred some arrogance into you. You leap to defend the weak but cannot suffer a fool with equanimity—regardless of station—which is odd in your country where people are forced to fawn on those of rank, even if they are idiots. I applaud the trait, however, and would thank Bernard for teaching it to you.

"Now I will tell you some things I know. You care for Rafael more than anyone, even the girl. You see her as a young man would, with longing, anticipation, and a little fear. Since I have come, you have indeed grown tired, a sadness and desperation have settled in you as you have realized that no one is coming to deliver you or your village. You have wisely learned to fear me and know, usually,

161

when to hold your tongue. Mostly, however, there is a cold recognition creeping into your soul and sapping your strength—you are coming to accept your death. How do I hit my mark, Gen?"

"Squarely, sir." Gen felt more depressed than ever. He felt violated.

"And so, by now, you have likely figured out how each thing I have learned about you could be used to control or destroy you. Take Rafael and Regina, for instance. If I wanted to keep you from escaping, even if I hadn't laid the stones upon you, all I would have to do is keep the old man alive and hang his safety over your head. Perhaps if I wanted you to do something, I could promise you that I would free Regina or not kill her. Without intending to, you have made those you love tools for accomplishing my purposes, chains with which I can enslave you.

"So what must you do to prevent this from ever happening again? You must be the master of your words and feelings and the master of body and face. Every slump of the shoulder, every creasing of the brow, every flippant comment, every wide-eyed glance at a passing girl is an arrow in the enemy's quiver. Do you understand this?"

"I do. But how. . ."

"Quiet, Gen. The lesson is just beginning. Look into the pool and watch your face." Gen turned back and stared at his countenance wavering in the makeshift mirror, wondering what to expect. He barely caught the flash of the Shadan's blade before pain erupted from a shallow cut along his back.

"Your face! Look at it! Do you see? Nose scrunched, eyes squinting, mouth drawn back. When I see that look on an opponent's face, I know I have won."

Gen slumped to the ice in agony, barely hearing the words. In a moment, the pain faded, replaced by comfortable warmth. The Shadan had healed him and only bright red stains on the snow and the rent in his shirt and cloak remained.

The Shadan sheathed his blade. "So today you will learn
control of your expressions, how you stand, how you sit,
how you eat. The stones will help you train your mind and
your body more quickly than normal, but it will not be easy.
Your face shows emotion more than most, part of being a
good bard, I suspect. But now you must put that training
behind you. A bard seeks to be the center of attention.
Now, you must find how to be anonymous. The deadliest
snake lies under the rock, unseen and unnoticed, until it
strikes. Let's begin."

The rest of that day was spent doing things Gen took
for granted, the Shadan pointing out things Gen had never
suspected he was communicating with acts as mundane as
walking. Khairn would correct him sharply, explaining how
walking too fast or too slow meant something and that a
nice even gait attracted no attention. From time to time
during the day, Khairn would unexpectedly cut him and
then chide him for the way he reacted to it. After letting
him bleed, Khairn would heal him and then have him do
something else, like fetch firewood, stand on the side of the
road, or drink water.

That night, the Shadan left him, Regina, and Rafael
alone as he inspected his troops, and Gen told them
everything about his trip, his friends amazed at the tale.
Regina's mood was muted, though she asked many
questions as Gen told his story. As he explained the stones
to them, including the limitations they placed upon him,
Rafael frowned.

"We were going to come to you in secret tonight and tell
you," Rafael whispered, inviting him to draw closer. "While
you were gone we discovered the general schedule and
rotation of the guards. This house is guarded by two guards
at the front door. There are none at the back during the
night, though a brace of soldiers circles the town every half
an hour, passing about fifty yards back. We have been

greasing the back door, and, if we time it right, we can be gone a little after dark and no one may know of our passing until morning. But those stones complicate things."

Ruined them, Gen thought, feeling disappointment and fear; he was disappointed that the stones had undone their plan and he feared that they would leave without him. Rafael noticed his distress.

"Don't fret, Gen. We'll figure something out. There has to be a way to get those stones off your neck!"

They tried to lift them, first singly then together, but they simply wouldn't budge, as if they weighed more than Gen himself. The Shadan's return sent them scrambling back to their rooms, though Gen suspected that Torbrand had wanted them to talk.

That night the lessons he learned during the day were reinforced in his mind by Samian, Elberen, and Telmerran. The next day, he had difficulty focusing as the Shadan set him to a variety of exercises meant to increase his stamina and speed, still slicing him at random intervals and healing him later.

If the lessons had stayed as they were, even with the cuts, Gen figured he could have survived and kept up hope. But each day grew steadily more brutal. Once Torbrand was satisfied he could do mundane things without giving away anything, and once he saw Gen could take a cut or two without flinching, he began to teach him the sword.

The thought of learning the sword from Khairn, a renowned master, excited him, but little did he know how the half-mad Shadan would school his student. Along with the expected training on how to stand, move, defend, and attack, Khairn would maim him and show him how to fight while injured. Although the injuries were always painful, at first they were at least comparatively tame. A broken finger, a bleeding gash on the forehead, a turned ankle. Khairn would always heal him in the end, but the daily pain and restless nights slowly sapped Gen of his will.

And it only got worse.

Soon came fighting with a shattered arm, then a shattered leg. One day Khairn had one of his soldiers smash his pelvis with a war hammer. Gen spent the whole day writhing in the snow as Khairn taught him how to attack and defend from the ground should such an eventuality occur.

The dreams at night were little better. Samian taught where to aim arrows to quickly butcher every kind of creature that walked Ki'Hal. Telmerran's lessons on quickly overtaking a village in the dark were made even more poignant by the memories of Tell's own fall. Elberen's memories of ruthlessly destroying Uyumaak camps and infantry lines had Gen's mind swimming with gore for a week.

How to fight on horse and off. How to fight enemies who were quicker, stronger, or magical. How to fight alone and how to command an army. How to attack a tower. How to invade a keep. What to do against demons, evil Puremen, and massive Gagons. Everything seemed a jumble, and just when Gen thought there could be nothing left for them to teach, they showed him more.

Every morning he awoke to a splitting headache, and, in an attempt to get just one good night's rest, he tried for a solid hour to remove the stones. No trickery of his succeeded. Any attempt to do so was met with numbness that prevented him from raising his arms above his head. He even tried standing on his head to let them slide off, but to no avail. He had no doubt Khairn could hear him banging to the floor with each attempt and was giggling madly. In the end, Gen had no choice but to sleep, but he found he could only grab snatches before waking again from the constant nightmare.

One cloudy afternoon Khairn blinded him and took to throwing rocks at him and swinging his sword around him from every angle so he could hear what it sounded like.

Then the Shadan set his chuckling soldiers to firing arrows around and then at his student. Gen tried to dodge out of the way by sensing the path of the arrows from the sound. The only reason the lesson stopped, Gen supposed, was that Khairn had tired of healing him, for Gen knew the Shadan had limits on what he could do without rest. Getting the arrows out of his body without killing him taxed Torbrand to exhaustion.

After being healed at the end of the lesson, Gen entered through the front door of the Showles's old residence feeling a great emptiness. His clothes were permanently stained a dried-blood brown, no matter what Regina tried when she cleaned and mended them. Gen walked as Torbrand trained him, showing nothing of his tiredness, but he didn't even see the food before him. When Regina and Rafael tried to talk to him, faces grave, he didn't respond, going to his room and closing the door behind him. They hadn't talked about escape for weeks. Rafael and Regina pitied and feared him, and seeing them at the table every evening only tortured him more.

He heard Torbrand come in just after him and order food and music, yelling at his friends as if they were nothing more than cattle, but for some reason, Gen could not find the heart to care about them or even himself. As he slept, the voices of the disembodied warriors continued to instruct him with scene after scene of death and slaughter, each analyzed in cold, dispassionate voices.

He awoke in the deep night. It was quiet, and he found himself weeping, but not because of the pain or for fear of the coming day, but because he finally saw the monster that he was becoming. He knew exactly how to invade any home in Tell and kill its inhabitants so quickly that there would likely not even be a scream. When he saw his friends and neighbors chopping wood or hanging clothes or talking in groups, he instantly knew the best way to kill them all.

And while his mind constantly dwelt on fighting, the

stones changed his body, tightening and growing muscles, increasing his reflexes and speed, limbering his sinews and ligaments, sharpening his hearing and sight, enhancing his voice. But all for a purpose, all to make him deadly. While the stones' lessons were meant to help him protect the Chalaine and the Ha'Ulrich, the Shadan's were not. Torbrand Khairn took sick pleasure in hurting his student, in molding him into an opponent he could have some fun with before killing him and the rest of Tell's inhabitants.

Gen lay in the dark, thinking how his whole life revolved around killing. Those things he liked most about himself, the same things he hoped others liked about him, gradually slipped away. His mirth, his art, his courage were all alien memories to him now. He hadn't sung or even talked to anyone meaningfully in weeks. These realizations sent him spiraling down into a despair he didn't want to feel but could not control. And in these depths, and in the dark, alone, he made an attempt to end his life, to stop the constant suffering and abort the birth of the Shadan's monster.

Tying his bed sheet into a convenient noose, he secured one end around his neck and another to a rafter and stepped off of his bed. The Shadan was there almost before his feet could leave the bed frame to dangle free in the air. With a flick of the wrist, he sliced the sheet in two, sending Gen crashing to the floor a sobbing wreck. Torbrand stared at him for some time and then ordered a soldier to take everything from his student's room. He had Omar fetch a rope and bind Gen so he couldn't move.

"If you try to kill yourself again, I will kill Rafael," Torbrand growled.

Gen slept little that night, and if the Shadan felt any sympathy for him the next morning, he didn't show it, bashing in one side of his ribs and making him fight. As further punishment, Torbrand beat Rafael with Gen as the lone audience. Gen felt strangely distant, and even Rafael's bruises and grunts of pain couldn't break him from his cocoon of misery. Every day dawned more pointless than the next. Gen longed for death. At least in dying he would deny Khairn his pleasure.

CHAPTER 11 - FAILURE

Rough weather always accompanied the late fall and early winters on the Rhugothian shard cluster. The scholars attributed the disturbances to several shards that passed close overhead during those seasons, stirring up the air and casting large shadows across the land. Flooding of low-lying cities and fields was not unusual in autumn, and in winter snowy tornadoes descended from solid gray clouds like demon fingers to tear apart whatever they touched.

Snow fell heavily and early in Rhugoth the winter after the First Mother returned from Aughmere, and since that time the Chalaine had noticed a change in her mother that disturbed her. Her eyes were tighter, her manner more stiff, and—the most telltale of all—she bit her lip more often, a sure sign that something uncomfortable was churning in her mind.

While the Chalaine had no inkling of what might be distressing the First Mother, she felt certain it concerned herself. Getting her mother to admit as much proved impossible. Disasters fomented by the weather provided the First Mother with plenty of reasons to be busy and to flippantly push aside her daughter's questions about what she might be feeling.

The Chalaine didn't doubt that many issues in Rhugoth troubled her mother. She asked about the source of her uneasiness, but she only smiled and said that being the First Mother always carried a weight with it and that the Chalaine should not be concerned.

Then the Chalaine pressed the issue, and her mother was not one to be pressed. As gently but firmly as possible, First Mother Mirelle told her that nothing was the matter and that she should not ask about it again. The Chalaine was crestfallen. She felt close to her mother, but since Mirelle had returned from Aughmere, a certain distance crept into their relationship and the Chalaine felt keenly the want of support and affection her mother had always generously shared with her. Fenna was a good friend but one who could not bear heavy burdens, and everyone else she knew would not accept weakness in "The Holy Chalaine."

She left her mother's quarters fuming, Dason trailing behind as she negotiated the maze at the quickest pace possible while still maintaining decorum. What she wanted now was to go into her room and read a book that would transport her out of the Chambers of the Chalaine and into some other place more suited for lighter spirits and laughter—items that had been in short supply since the winter began. The Dark Guard snapped to attention as she entered the Antechamber of the Chalaines and turned toward her own quarters.

As the Chalaine and Dason left the maze and crossed into the hallway where the door to her private chambers stood, Dason circled around her quickly. The Chalaine was startled by the forlorn expression on his face, and she put her hand to her heart as he knelt on both knees before her, clasping his hands as if in prayer.

"Please, Holy Chalaine, forgive me!" he supplicated. "Please let me back into your good graces again! I only wish to serve!"

His handsome face set the Chalaine's heart to pounding.

"Get up, Dason," she commanded softly. "Why should you think that you have done anything that offends me or that you have fallen from my good graces? You have done your duty well and I have nothing with which I could ever fault you."

Dason remained on his knees. "I thank you for saying thus much, but you cannot expect my heart to fully take hold of such an assertion when such a wall stands between us! I mean no disrespect, and I know that I may not be the cleverest of men, but it is not the same between us as it was but a few months ago. You must reveal to me in what way I have wronged you, that I may make proper amends and win back your good opinion!"

"You have not lost my good opinion, Dason!" She knelt before him, concerned. "From what actions of mine do you base this claim? Perhaps it is I who have wronged you."

Dason's eyes widened. "No! Never, Chalaine. You are perfection, and it is I, weak and vile, on which the blame must be placed. If you would but tell me what I must do so that you can feel to speak easily and happily with me again, to dispel the darkness I feel between us, I will exact whatever penance and go to whatever lengths necessary to win back your favor."

The Chalaine wrinkled her brow. It saddened her to see him so indisposed and terrified, and she wracked her mind, searching for some slight she might have made or some word misspoken that would cause him such agony of spirit, but she came up empty. Tolnorians worried a great deal about propriety and honor, but she could not recollect any occasion where she had behaved poorly, save that she was taken to brooding more often of late. She reached out to him and lifted his head.

"I swear to you, Dason, that I think as highly of you now as I ever have and hold you in the highest esteem. If you sense some darkness, then I am sorry. How can I prove my regard to you other than my word that it is, indeed, as

171

intact as it ever was?"

"A holy kiss, First Daughter," he said, eyes penetrating the veil. "Only then will I feel at peace."

The Chalaine was taken off guard by his request and stood.

He stood with her, eyes tortured. "Forgive me, Highness," he bowed. "It is improper for me to ask it from you. I withdraw my request."

The Chalaine thought hard, a strange and unfamiliar thrill building inside her. She had never kissed a man nor had ever been asked to. Dason was the kindest, best man in her acquaintance, and she considered him as much a friend as a Protector. She preferred his company to almost anyone else's, and to see him wracked with such misery drew out the healer within her, and he needed her healing—at least that is what she convinced herself of.

Lifting his head again, her arm trembling, she stepped close and kissed him lightly on the mouth through her veil. The kiss lingered longer than she intended, his lips warm and inviting on hers despite the barrier between them. She closed her eyes, thoughts addled, and an alarm rang out in her mind. She stepped backward, placing a hand on her lips. Dason remained where he stood, face registering sweet rapture. The Chalaine composed herself before he finally opened his eyes again. His countenance had changed to delighted and self-assured.

"I thank you, Chalaine," he intoned reverentially. "I shall never doubt your regard again. I am most relieved and thankful for your solicitude!"

"You are welcome," she responded convincingly enough to elicit a smile from her Protector. "Now if you would let me in, I have some reading I need to do."

"At once, Chalaine," he said enthusiastically, crossing to and opening the dark wooden door engraved with a golden rose. The Chalaine went in quickly and he shut the door behind her. Guilt instantly pressed in upon her at every side, and she placed her veil on her desk and paced about the room wringing her hands. She had kissed a man that wasn't the Ha'Ulrich and had enjoyed it enough to almost let it go too far.

It did go too far! She scolded herself. *It should have never happened! I have endangered this world and everyone in it because I am a silly girl.*

She knew the right thing to do would be to confess to her mother and the Prelate, but she dared not do it. As guilty as she felt, she would not let her own stupidity hurt Dason, for they would remove him from his post immediately and bring down a shame and dishonor on him and his family that would last forever. They might even kill Dason for what he had done.

She knelt at her bed immediately and asked Eldaloth his forgiveness, although the prayer, she felt, did not travel much beyond the confines of her room. Such a transgression would require severe repentance on her part, and she mentally resolved to focus her thoughts on the Ha'Ulrich more firmly, only wishing that she knew more of him so she had a more solid foundation from which to proceed.

Turning to the tapestry above her bed she stared at the man there, bold and handsome, holding aloft a sword in one hand and holding hers in the other. If she had nothing but a caricature to latch onto, then that would have to do. As penance, she resolved to stare at the tapestry for an hour each day before dawn while the winter lasted.

While her efforts let her guilt dim, her enjoyment of Dason's company in the following days always allowed it to flame anew. As the winter deepened, she set every hope on the day her Ha'Ulrich would walk off of his ship on Kingsblood Lake and into her life. Then, she felt, she could truly make restitution for her mistake. But every time she saw Dason standing in the hallway, that blessed day seemed long in coming.

Weeks of weariness, torture, and training added to Gen's burgeoning store of skills and toned his body, but while he learned to ignore physical pain, the unrelenting anguish muddled his discordant mind. Gradually, even that sensation was denied him and he became a mindless shell, scraping by from one day to the next. He no longer cared for anyone or anything. There was training. There was eating. There was sleep with its dreams of fighting, strategy, and war. He felt he had lived through the Mikkikian wars, and the images, blood-soaked and gory, no longer sickened or shocked him.

The Shadan's exercises tuned Gen's muscles to the point of breaking. Gen pulled carts full of rocks, held buckets of water extended in his hands, and ran great distances at all times of day and in any weather. Thanks to hours of fighting blinded and the enhancing effect of the stones, Gen's hearing and reflexes had sharpened to where he could hear a pebble moving through the air in his direction.

While always centered on the sword, his lessons at times deviated to fighting with other weapons or with no weapons at all. His body continued to change, gathering strength, speed, and awareness. His voice widened in range and intensity, a gift to help him be heard in the thick of battle, the Voice of Command, as Telmerran called it.

He saw Rafael and Regina little. At first he avoided them because it pained them to see him. Now the neglect of his friends was routine, and his deep apathy prevented him from wondering what they thought or felt. Even hearing Regina crying in the next room out of loneliness or fear failed to stir him.

A few weeks later, Gen awoke late, the sun already shining outside. Torbrand had always roused him before dawn. Gen thought nothing of it, stretching his muscles and rubbing the grit from his eyes. During the night, Telmerran had instructed him on advanced mounted warfare—he was the only one who fought on horseback of his three masters—while Samian and Elberen combined to instruct him more thoroughly on the bow. The instruction that had burned into the very muscles of his body made him feel as if he had done it a hundred times before, despite relatively scant practice.

Gen left his room, passing into the hall. Torbrand Khairn hummed to himself in the front room, Gen finding him as he often was with feet on the table, drinking a steaming mug of ale. Rafael was gagged and bound in a corner of the room. The old bard grunted furiously as if trying to signal something to his former pupil.

Gen knew he should feel shock, pain, and anger at his former master's plight, but an extinguished spirit and a mind crammed with violence cast even the most depraved sights into an inconsequential light. Death and pain were his constant friends. Seeing them near was no more surprising than finding breakfast on the table.

Torbrand smiled mischievously. "There you are. I wondered when you would drag yourself out of that bed of yours. Sit. Eat. There is plenty, and I think you will find the fare rather better than usual."

Gen knew the Shadan was up to something, but he was beyond caring. Rafael continued to grunt, eventually settling into a quiet sobbing. Gen ignored him and started to eat. The food was of a finer quality—a sumptuous apple pie and moist dark bread with butter. As his master seemed in no hurry, Gen wasn't either.

"You may wonder at the sudden improvement of our victuals. I must confess that I am upset with you a little on this score, for why did you not tell me that Laraen Fairweather was ten times the cook that Regina is? I can scarce forgive you for forcing me to eat Regina's parade of the overcooked and under-seasoned for more than two months."

Gen stopped eating. Something pushed its way through the smothering emptiness within him. Where was Regina?

"And there it is!" Torbrand exclaimed, standing. "A spark! So far I have taught you the banishment of emotion, broken you down and burned your soul to ash. But I left a little ember burning from which to kindle a fire, for the fiercest of fighters are not those who are devoid of passion but those who are filled with it. You are wondering where Regina is, yes?"

"Yes, Shadan," Gen answered, striving to keep the urgency out of his voice. He wouldn't give Torbrand the satisfaction.

"Very well, see how this feels. Last night after you were abed, I dragged Regina and Hubert into the Chapel and there had the Pureman marry them. I know it is a bit out of season for your country but not unheard-of. For their wedding gift, I let them leave town a bit before dawn this morning to go wherever they wished. What do you think of that?"

Gen was confused. Why would Torbrand free her? For Mena's sake?

Torbrand stroked his beard. "It seems that I am forgetting something about the whole affair, though. Hmm, now what was it? I just can't remember. I think Rafael may know. Let's ask him, shall we?"

With a precise sword strike, the Shadan cut Rafael's gag near where it wrapped around his ear. Rafael, still bound, spit the gag out. "He sent Captain Omar to bring them back, boy, just before breakfast! He'll kill them, he will!"

"Oh, that's right!" the Shadan mocked. "I sent Omar to fetch them, but you know Omar! He'll have a hard time keeping his sword in his scabbard when it comes to Hubert. He wasn't very kind to Regina, either, when you and I were away at Ellenais, was he, Rafael?"

Gen stared expectantly at Rafael, who hung his head to

hide his emotion. Anger stirred in Gen's stagnant heart.

"What did he do to her, Rafael?" Gen demanded.

Rafael turned his gaze on Gen. "He . . . he *hurt* her, Gen."

Gen's eyes widened involuntarily—she had never said a word. Rafael had never mentioned it. Anger turned to rage and desperation.

"Here, Gen," Torbrand said. "Take my sword. Don't worry about the stones holding you back. I can let you wander as far as I will. I think they went in the direction of Sipton."

Gen didn't bother to buckle the sword. He sprinted out the door and ran down the road at a dead run for as long as his lungs could take it. The air was bitter chill, and the trees dusted over with dry snow that swirled with the slightest breeze. Thin gray clouds denied the sun its full strength, the world below cold and lifeless in the weak light. These details barely registered to Gen, who scanned the ground in front of him. The trail was easy to find on the untraveled, snowy road. Regina and Hubert walked slowly, Regina slightly behind him. Omar followed the trail jogging, and Gen set off again at the best pace he could manage.

He cursed himself for not taking Rafael's cue, cursed himself for lingering at breakfast. He pushed aside the guilt. It would serve him no purpose. Trees whipped by as Gen did his calculations. If Rafael and Regina left a little before dawn, then by the time Omar left they would have had an hour's head start and on the poor road had likely gone little more than a mile. At a jog, Omar would have caught them just about the time Gen finished his bread. Redoubling his efforts, Gen pressed on, taking advantage of a trail blazed through the drifts and difficult spots by those ahead, affording him a small advantage.

He reined in his imagination of what Omar would do to his victims when he caught them, concentrating on jogging as efficiently as he could, cutting any corners at every opportunity. Abruptly, the trail turned off the road and into the wood. Gen walked over quickly, examining the surrounding area. Here Hubert and Regina rested, and here they discovered their pursuer. They had risen in a rush, and the distance between footfalls widened as the pair had sprinted into the forest. In contrast, Omar's narrowed; he had found his prey and relaxed his pace.

Gen charged forward, the way easy to find though difficult to negotiate. Deadfall and underbrush concealed beneath the snow conspired to trip him almost as if purposefully barring his way. But his training made him nimble and strong, and he pressed forward with fervent haste. The tracks he followed indicated that Omar still had not increased his pace, but Regina and Hubert had slowed, surely exhausted from the labor of so difficult an escape.

Gen stopped and listened. He had to be close. He took the time to buckle the Shadan's sword about his waist to free up his arms as the trail slanted up the side of a difficult hill. Gen wondered why Hubert or Regina would choose to go upward where they would be more exposed. A snapping branch to his left turned his head upward. Above him, some fifty yards, he could just see Omar heading straight up the hill away from Hubert and Regina's path. He wanted to cut them off and meet them at the top.

The sight of Shadan Khairn's Captain rekindled fire in Gen's heart, and knowing that he had hurt Regina during his absence infuriated him. Gen turned and clawed up the hill directly after him, crashing through brittle low-hanging branches and twigs, using the boles of the trees to propel himself upward.

"C'mon, boy!" Omar taunted, twisting to yell down the hill. "I'll kill you, too, and rid us all of Khairn's stupid project. Hubert and the girl go first, though. Come stop me!"

Omar resumed his climb, redoubling his efforts. His squat legs made quick work of the remaining distance to the top. By the time Gen crested the hill, he couldn't see Omar through the thick grove of thin pine trees. Sprinting forward, lungs afire, Gen finally caught a glimpse of his opponent as he cleared the hilltop and started down the other side.

"Hubert!" Regina yelled. "He is coming."

In a moment he saw them through the branches of a dead pine. They were resting in a small clearing, wearing fur cloaks against the cold. Both had stood up from where they were sitting on a log. Hubert held a stout stick, a club for defense, but upon seeing Captain Omar charging down the hill, sword drawn and snow exploding away from the thrashing of his legs, the Showles's oldest son abandoned Regina and ran, leaping over the banks of a small frozen creek. Regina ran to Gen's left into the forest. Thankfully, Omar pursued Hubert first, and Gen altered his course, intercepting Regina, who screamed at his unexpected appearance.

Gen grabbed her hand. "Up the hill and over. Quickly, Regina."

She did not wear her veil, and the weight of her fear and desperation landed heavily on Gen's heart, resurrecting it from its lifeless despair. Hoping Hubert was faster than he looked, Gen half-dragged Regina up the littered slope, heedless of the clawing branches that ripped clothes and flesh. A horrified yell signaled Hubert's end. Time was short. Gen cast about, searching for any way to hide their tracks, but the snow rendered it impossible.

"Where are you, boy?" Omar yelled from behind. One hundred yards. They couldn't escape him. He only had one idea left. Finding a large mature pine with easily climbable branches, he led Regina around its far side.

"Climb as high as you can, Regina," Gen ordered.

She regarded him briefly, eyes pained, conveying all the hurt and anger his inattention had caused her. She had been humiliated and scared, and he had done nothing to comfort or help her in her distress. He had left her to the cruelty of Omar and the Shadan, wrapped himself in his own hurt, and hadn't been a friend or lover to her when she needed his affection the most.

Guilt poisoned Gen's heart, mixing with his rage as he watched her climb, snow falling about him as she dislodged it. There was only one redemption: to save her now. As quietly as he could, he pulled the Shadan's blade from its sheath, laying the scabbard on the ground. Their footprints would lead Omar to where they were.

"You're sending her up a tree, then?" Omar mocked, still obscured by the branches, but close. "I'll beat ya' for that. I'm tired of this chase!"

The cocky captain took no pains to be silent or careful as each footstep brought him inexorably closer to his prey. A wind in the pines blew snow from the branches in a fine dust, and for a moment Omar stopped. Gen could just see his boots on the other side of the trunk.

Gen leapt out and swung his sword at Omar's square head. The Captain blocked, a mighty clang ringing through the forest, startling the winter birds. Omar pushed the blade aside and riposted, forcing Gen to leap aside, the snow hampering his ability to move. Omar's thrust tore through Gen's cloak, narrowly missing his belly. Gen slapped Omar's blade to the ground and swung left, gashing the Captain's arm. Omar, employing his training, didn't grimace or grunt, but, after squaring off, he approached Gen more carefully.

To help his defense, Gen backed around the thin bole of a tall pine with no branches lower than his head. They circled slowly, Gen keeping the tree between him and his attacker. Omar lunged forward, forcing Gen away from the tree, and charged. Gen backed down carefully from the assault, wanting to move farther downhill and away from Regina's sanctuary in the tree, but Omar herded him toward it at every opportunity. Sword strokes came fiercely but sporadically. Branches, underbrush, and slippery footing kept the pace of the fight irregular. Wide swings were virtually impossible, and they had to settle for quick flicks and lunges at each other, neither able to gain advantage. Sweat ran down both of their faces.

As they moved horizontally, staring at each other intently, they found themselves in a small break in the trees. Both charged and blows rained down. Gen's fury powered him forward, Omar inching backward. Once the more seasoned warrior had weathered Gen's angry attack, he pushed back with his own.

Omar was powerful and fast, and he beat at Gen with every ounce of strength his burly arm could deliver. Gen was more than equal to the speed, but Omar's power wore him down, driving him back into a tangle of fallen trees. Omar, seeing his opponent trapped, lunged forward. Gen dodged away and knocked the blade aside, but in the process he stepped into some branches and his right boot got caught under the tangle.

In the momentary distraction, Omar rushed. Gen chopped at him, blade slicing the Captain's ribs, but Omar was inside his guard now. Omar pinned Gen's sword arm against his side with his muscular biceps and kicked at Gen's trapped knee, breaking it with a sickening crack. Pain flooded over Gen, but as he had been taught, he ignored it, remaining standing on his good leg.

"Got ya now, boy," Omar grinned. Gen head-butted him, forehead ramming into the Captain's mouth. Omar's head snapped back, but he held Gen's arm fast. With a bloodied snarl, Omar broke Gen's other knee and the boy crumpled to the ground.

"Time to climb a tree," Omar jeered, wiping the blood from his lips on his sleeve. "Don't worry. You get to see her die."

Omar walked away and noisily started his ascent up the tree. Gen extricated his foot from the bramble and dragged himself along the ground hand-over-hand toward the tree, sword left behind. Regina was whimpering and yelling "no" over and over again. Gen looked up just as Omar grabbed her foot and she kicked at his head. He yanked hard and she tumbled, bones breaking as she slammed into one branch after another, falling near Gen in a shower of pine needles and twigs. Gen crawled to her, fingers raw and numb. Blonde hair spilled over a pale face, blood running from her nose as she breathed in ragged gasps. Her eyes were unfocused and vacant, and she mumbled 'Gen' as if searching for him in the dark.

Tears ran down his face. "I am sorry, Regina. I am sorry."

He went to reach for her face, to reassure her that he was there, but Omar crushed his hand with a heavy boot. An instant later he beheaded her, her lifeblood melting the snow around her. Gen yelled a curse and rolled onto his back, wracking sobs overcoming him. He barely heard Omar say, "And now, for you."

"Leave him, Omar!" Shadan Khairn jogged over the hill and Omar held up, face disappointed and a little fearful.

"I did not give you leave to kill anyone but Hubert!" the Shadan yelled. "I told you that she was not to be harmed and Gen left alive! What have you done? Answer me!"

"She climbed a tree. I went to fetch her and she fell. I killed her out of mercy. She was nearly dead already."

"Liar!" Gen spat in agony, vision too blurry to see either of them. "He wanted to kill her in front of me."

"And I see the boy marked you, Omar! How many times?"

"Three. He should be killed, Shadan! He is too good for one so young in his training. He is too dangerous."

"Ha!" the Shadan laughed. "Dangerous to you. You lied. You killed her out of spite and there will be consequences. The first is that I will not heal you. The second is that you must carry her back to Tell and dig a grave for her, and a deep one so that no animal can disturb it. This respect you must pay."

"But the ground is frozen, Shadan!" Omar protested. The Shadan slapped him.

"Trust me, these are the least of your punishments. I promised my daughter that this girl would not be killed. Now I will have to explain to her that she is dead, and that displeases me, Captain Omar. Now shut your ignorant mouth and get her back to Tell."

The Shadan healed Gen and retrieved his sword and belt from him. Gen was despondent, barely registering their return trip to town. As he walked, he found the only escape from the pain was to seek the dark void the Shadan had fashioned within him with brutality, but even then something was different. His heart burned with purpose. He would have revenge. He wanted it now more than health, happiness, or escape.

Once in Tell, the Shadan sent him to his room for the balance of the day. When night fell, Rafael brought him food, his eyes swollen and face gaunt. He promised to come see him when he could and left. Gen didn't touch the food but sat, arms around his knees, in a corner of the room as emotion drained out of him, leaving him even deader than he felt before. The calm, dispassionate void locked itself into place, for he could no longer bear his pain, and the only way to avoid pain was to feel nothing at all.

And so Rafael found him in the middle of the night, having sneaked from his room against all caution.

"Gen," he whispered as he sat beside him. "Are you awake?"

"You should go. He'll kill you if you he finds you here." The coldness of his voice no longer surprised him. Even in the dark he could sense Rafael's hurt.

"Listen, boy," he said, voice firm as when he used to school Gen in lore or singing. "I had to see you. I'm sorry about Regina. I loved her, too. But you cannot let him have the victory! I'm as angry as you are, but he's killing you, Gen. I don't know to what end, but he is making you his. Fight it, Gen. Find your heart again."

Rafael crouched and put his arm on Gen's shoulder. Gen flinched away and stood.

"You should go, Rafael."

Rafael also came to his feet. After muffling a fit of coughing, the old man started toward the door, head bent in weariness. Several moments of silence passed.

Rafael finally said, "I love you, Gen, and I'm sorry," and slipped out the door. Gen returned to his corner and sat numbly. All night long, Omar labored outside his window, cursing as he chopped over and over at the frozen earth in his attempts to excavate a grave the Shadan would find satisfactory. His every stroke reminded Gen of the fatal blow to Regina, and he fixed her face in his mind as he saw it when they danced on the day before the Aughmerian invasion. That was what Omar had taken from him and what he would pay for.

Hours passed. The dawn broke through his window. Gen hadn't noticed when Omar had stopped digging, but Gen stood and opened the shutters, finding a fresh mound of earth free of snow. Gen stared at it until the Shadan opened the door, crossing to where he stood in front of the window.

"You've been holding back when we sparred," he began. "That was obvious from your ability to even mark Omar, much less three times. A nice little trick, hiding your abilities. You might think that I would be mad about that, but I am not. You are a quick learner and a clever one, and that pleases me. I had no idea what would happen when I placed all three stones upon you at once. I thought you would go mad. Instead, you have learned more quickly than any other student I have taught. In another month, you will likely be as good as Captain Omar.

"And so my dilemma. The Captain was right about one thing: you should not be as good as you are. He would have me kill you before you get too dangerous, but to be quite honest, I am enjoying myself a little too much to let that happen. Besides, I assured the good Captain that as long as I had Rafael, you would be quite tame. In fact, I'm planning to let you visit the old man more often now."

Torbrand leaned in close. "I liked the fire I saw smoldering in your eyes yesterday. Rafael will be your little reminder to keep that alive. When a passion to fight for something consumes you and you can yet feel calm, empty, and in control, then you will be truly formidable. I anticipate standing toe-to-toe with *that* Gen come spring."

Torbrand left, closing the door quietly. Gen's mind played Regina's death over and over again. The Shadan used his friends to trap him, and the only way out was to kill his master, something he could not do. In the cold stillness, he realized that ending Torbrand's life or dying in the attempt was the only way to end the torture, avenge Regina, and possibly secure Rafael's life. The only way he had a chance was to endure a little more, to learn all that the cruel Shadan could teach him, and then attack when given the opportunity. At last he had what he needed to survive—a purpose.

CHAPTER 12 - FAREWELL AND FREEDOM

"We think we can help you, Gen." It was Samian. Gen wondered at the offer. After the first day the three warriors had not once expressed that they knew about his circumstances or feelings.

"Yes," Elberen continued. "With your help we can free you from the bondage of the stones and you can flee. We can no longer tolerate the use to which we have been put. We long to be free."

"Not yet," Gen said. "Teach me everything. Never stop. I must know it all."

"What we propose to do will do that, Gen. You need suffer no longer." Telmerran sounded more compassionate than Gen had ever heard him. From the scenes they showed him, Gen could not see how any of them had a grain of tender feeling left.

"It is not time," Gen continued. "I must learn all I can from the Shadan, and while it is winter, I cannot escape with Rafael. The cold would kill him. And I cannot leave while Torbrand and Omar still draw breath."

"Revenge must not govern your actions, Gen," Samian

counseled gravely.

"Then what should govern my actions? My days are filled with hate and killing! And so far, the killing I've seen has been of the innocent and undeserving. Killing the Shadan and Omar, whether out of revenge or justice, is warranted by everything good and decent. And if goodness and decency are served then I care little what feeling motivates it!"

Silence followed.

"Very well," Samian said, voice resigned. "Our lessons are nearly done. Let's begin."

Torbrand kept to his word, allowing Gen time alone with Rafael every morning to talk, though Gen rarely found anything to say. Rafael's paled skin clung to his bones, face wracked with worry and a hacking cough wearing the old bard down. But valiantly, Rafael ignored his discomfort and doted upon his apprentice. Gen appreciated his attempts to rekindle his interest in music, but no matter how much Rafael prodded, Gen could not fathom ever plucking the lute strings again, much less singing. Music required some depth of feeling from which to be born, and revenge was all he could find in an otherwise vacant heart.

In the following weeks, Gen wholly embraced his training, thirsty for knowledge, and the Shadan took delight in Gen's enthusiasm. Within two weeks, Gen could catch and deflect arrows, fight blinded, and take on multiple opponents with ease. The stones continued their work, refining his senses and advancing his technique.

The lessons of the stones gradually turned to defense, which, unfortunately, increasingly featured the killing of innocent people. Gen never told the Shadan that he could understand the language spoken by his teachers in the stones, for they taught him that, "If you must tell your enemy something, tell him nothing. If you can't tell him nothing, tell him a lie." He could sense that he was now surpassing Torbrand's expectations, and the Shadan took pleasure in sparring with his student, his mood magnanimous and light as the snow began to melt, dripping from trees and rooftops.

Rafael's health continued to deteriorate, and he slept for long chunks of the day. The Shadan took no notice of the old bard's distress and never acknowledged his presence or pressed him to perform further. Gen could hear Rafael coughing whenever his training took him near the house, and at the end of each day Gen found that Rafael was invariably by the fire, hunched in a chair, pale and spent.

One evening after facing down ten of the Shadan's soldiers in a scenario designed to teach him how to detect and defend against an urban ambush, Gen entered the Showles's front room, and his old master smiled at him, face waxy and pallid.

"Let's get you to bed," Gen entreated him gently, taking his arm.

"Thank you, my boy," he said, face kind and sad. "You are truly the best apprentice I ever had, Gen. When you're done training, if you escape, remember you are a musician. You were meant to gladden people's hearts, not stop them. Remember it."

"Don't worry," Gen said, helping him into his room. "You'll have time to remind me later. This winter is almost over. We'll find our way out of here together."

Rafael patted him feebly on the shoulder. "Sleep well, Gen. I am very tired."

Gen left and went to his own room. Since resolving upon his plan, he could relax more easily and he approached the dream lessons with an appetite equal to those he lived through during the day. As consciousness faded, he found himself back in the enormous Cathedral

188

for the first time since beginning. His masters stood before him unchanged but solemn.

"We have taught you all we have to teach," Samian said. "It should not have been taught in this manner. For apprentices past, we at this point would recommend you to service against Mikkik and his Ilch, but you seem resolved upon another plan."

"I think killing Torbrand Khairn will be service against Mikkik."

Samian held Gen's eyes with a sympathetic but firm look. "Then you do not understand. You told us some nights ago that the motive behind your actions did not matter as long as good came of it. We warn you that it is not so.

"We are inspired to act by many things, but if what inspires our actions be evil, then what apparent good they accomplish will rot and come to evil purpose. It may not be readily apparent, but the law of Eldaloth is that pure good can only proceed from pure motive."

Gen knew this teaching. Pureman Millerhsim preached it. To hear Samian say it—a man who killed more than Gen could fathom—was either egregious hypocrisy or some wisdom Gen could not grasp.

"You know much now, Gen," said Telmerran. "But you lack experience. Facing the Shadan and Omar will see you dead. We sacrificed everything we loved ages before you were born to raise up warriors to serve the Ha'Ulrich and the Chalaine. Only in the world they bring will there be an end to senseless misery and woe at the hands of Mikkik and the world he corrupted. Put Shadan Khairn from your mind. Escape."

"We have nothing more to offer you," Elberen concluded. "We will not speak to you again until you seek us." The voices faded, and for the first time in months, Gen slept deeply and without dreaming.

When the first light of dawn woke him, he felt refreshed

and fit. As he stood, his foot kicked something on the floor. A letter, loosely folded, lay upon the ground close to where someone had shoved it under the door. Gen recognized the writing as Rafael's.

Dear Gen,

I've little time to write and deliver this. May I start by saying that I love you as my son and because of this love I have watched every day in agony as you were tortured and destroyed, body and spirit, at the hands of Torbrand Khairn. I know he uses me as leverage against you, to manipulate you to his will just as he did Regina.

I will not be used in this way. I am old. I have lived a life without regret, a happy life, until recent events. I cannot live knowing I am his tool against you. I have cheated Tolnorian winters so many times that I feel I owe them a debt. When you read this, you will be free to act without fear for anyone else.

It is my dying wish that you escape at the first opportunity. I know the stones bind you to him. If you can ever escape or if Khairn ever releases you, do not spend your strength fighting him. Run. Find yourself again. Live again. That is what Regina would want and that is what I want. If you ever loved me, then obey me now. Escape.

Ever your affectionate master,

Rafael DeBellamaine

PS
Do not think ill of my choice. It chose me before I chose it.

Gen bolted through his bedroom door, letting the letter drop behind him, and sprinted through the house. Torbrand was at the room already, shaking his head.

"The old fool left his window open and threw his blankets off. Froze to death."

Rafael lay dead, hands crossed over his chest. His

favorite lute lay beside him on the bed as did an empty bottle of wine. On his desk an open ink bottle sat next to a spent candle.

"Killed himself, then, so I couldn't use him anymore," Torbrand commented, voice flat. "I suppose this is what you Tolnorians consider 'noble.' I assume by the ink bottle that he wrote you a note, or did you sense his death? Well, no matter."

Numbness deadened Gen's heart. Somehow, in the death of his most beloved friend, he found true, abiding emptiness. Calm settled over him, and, as Rafael wished, he felt free. The world was stripped of those he loved, and nothing existed except battle and the sword.

Gen sat, back against the wall of his room, arms resting on his knees. Shadan Khairn left him alone for the rest of the day, and Gen heard him come in twice, and then only for short periods of time. Gen read Rafael's note over and over until he memorized it. As empty minutes turned into empty hours, a remorse leaked into the emptiness that possessed him that morning, a remorse deep and viscous, a regret that—however unintentionally—he was partly the cause of the death of the two people he loved best. If only he'd fought harder, learned faster, treated them with more concern. If only he'd tried to help them escape even though he couldn't go with them.

Dropping the letter, he shut his eyes and pushed away the feelings, using discipline to stifle emotion and plan his next move. Rafael's entreaty to escape touched him, and he wanted to obey, but he also wanted another chance at Omar, and just one chance at Torbrand. Reason, however, told him that the latter course would likely end in his death. Were he to face Torbrand and win, Omar would order every soldier in the camp to hunt him down. Gen knew his prowess at arms surpassed any single soldier in the camp, but one inferior opponent with hundreds to help compensated for any disparity in skill. They would overwhelm him and end a life with but one single claim to glory—killing the Shadan.

He watched the shaft of light from the sun stretch across the floor toward the door. His decision rested on which he wanted more: a chance to create a new life with the skills he had learned or risk death avenging his friends. Near evening, he decided. Escape was his best chance at fulfilling both desires. Above all, he wished to please Rafael, to find some way to be useful in the world. If Samian, Telmerran, and Elberen could somehow release the hold of the stones upon him, he was sure he could sneak out of town and to safety.

The best course was to ride to Sipton as quickly as possible to see if any preparations were being made against Aughmere. If so, he could provide valuable intelligence and with his skill be allowed to fight Torbrand come spring. If the nobility were yet unapprised or unconvinced, then he would try to succeed where Gant and the Morewolds had failed. Shadan Khairn would expect this, and Gen knew he had the road patrolled unceasingly and in numbers. But Gen knew several back ways to Sipton that might keep him away from the Shadan's men.

Gen heard his master enter, thundering to Laeren that he would take dinner momentarily. Gen lifted his head as Torbrand stepped through his door and regarded him with satisfaction.

"The time has come! Spring nears, and I shall have scouts to send, battle plans to draw up, and a fresh contingent of soldiers to prepare. Your training is at an end, so tomorrow I will remove the stones and you will face me. You cannot understand the eagerness with which I wait for the morrow. I will kill you, make no mistake, but it will be a fight the likes of which I will not enjoy again for some time. Prepare yourself, then. I will send the Pureman to you, if you wish. His time, too, is coming to an end and I'm sure he will have many wonderful views of Erelinda to share with you. So farewell. Sleep well."

The Shadan left without waiting for a reply, and Gen didn't give him one. At Khairn's order, Laeren, brown eyes fearful, brought him a double helping of stewed lamb and bread, and Gen gulped every bit down. Food might be scarce in the coming days. She collected the bowl some time later, and Gen waited, unmoving, while the light in his window dimmed from blue to orange to black. When at last full dark came, he lay on his back, fingering the stones at his chest. He didn't know how to summon the three masters, so he kept them fixed in his mind. When sleep came, they stood before him in the Chapel, grave but expectant.

"You have changed your mind, then?" Samian said.

"I have," Gen replied.

Elberen smiled. "Then wisdom claims the victory, and we will at last be free."

Samian and Telmerran embraced each other and then Elberen, faces joyful. Gen couldn't help but be touched. The sacrifice they had made to protect a woman and man they would never know revealed a true nobility of character and an unwavering faith. As to Rafael, Gen felt he owed them a debt. For their sake, he could not squander his life or misspend his strength and skill.

"But how can it be?" Gen asked. "I have tried to remove the stones to no avail. No one can do it. My friends tried many times."

"To be truthful, Gen," Samian confessed, "we do not know if what we intend to do will succeed. The unveiling of Trys was to trigger our release, but long ago, in another day when our training was abused, we devised a way that we might free ourselves. While the stones would still bind master to student and refine the body, we would be gone, rendering the stones worthless for the teaching of war. Accomplishing this, however, will not be easy on you but could also be of great benefit."

Gen felt uneasy. "How? What do you propose we try?"

Elberen stepped forward. "Let me explain. The stones allow us to teach you so quickly by linking us directly to your mind. We will use that link, one by one, to enter your mind, to take your body as our own. The magic binding of the stone prevents anyone save your master from removing them. We, too, Gen are your masters. If we inhabit your body, we think we can remove the stones. You need not fear. Since our spirits are not yours, we will, in time, find ourselves expelled and released to Erelinda, leaving you to you. At least we believe so. Some part of us may ever be trapped here."

"In time you'll be expelled?" Gen asked

"Yes. Perhaps the magic no longer exists, but in our time evil and good Magicians alike would leave their bodies and enter those of others. They could not permanently do so, however. The body will reject any spirit not its own. The less willing the victim, the quicker. We must ask you, however, to be willing so we can remain long enough to remove the stones and let you escape. It is also possible that you will remember a great deal of our lives besides what we shared with you. Passage through the link to your mind should be quick, but we cannot be sure of the outcome. Do you wish us to try?"

Gen swallowed hard. Before sleeping, he had believed that his masters' plan was guaranteed to work. Learning that they couldn't promise its success dimmed his enthusiasm, and to find that it involved opening himself to possession soured his opinion even further. Father Millershim condemned possessions in the darkest of tones, relating tales of good men turned without provocation to murderers and thieves by the manipulations of one of Mikkik's disembodied servants. Gen wavered, wondering if his chances wouldn't be improved by fighting Khairn after all. The prospect of being free, however, eventually won out over his concerns.

"Let's be quick. The sooner I can leave, the better."

"Very well. You will naturally want to resist, but you must fight it," Elberen instructed him. "Samian, you go first. I will come second, and Telmerran last."

Gen breathed in, relaxing himself. Samian, smiling, walked toward him and then *into* him. At once, Gen felt his presence at the borders of his mind, and every instinct within him told him to push it away. He could feel the walls of defense building within him, and it required many moments of rigorous concentration to break them down, to open the door, and to let Samian in.

And when he entered, Gen's inner vision exploded into a riot of images, feelings, and memories accumulated over a lifetime. Samian was a woodsman before a warrior, and he knew every plant and animal that walked through mountain and wood. He spoke fluent Elvish and held a great compassion for all things innocent. Most dear, the clearest of all his memories, were times spent with his elven wife, who he had known would outlive him. Selva'hel was her name, and every memory of her was a joy.

By her, Samian had a daughter, dark-haired and beautiful. He loved her to distraction and taught her everything of nature. Her name was Quaena, his Leaf Daughter. The day he left them, in secret and in the dark, was the saddest of his recollections.

Samian wondered if his wife and daughter still lived. He wanted to know if they remembered him, if Selva'hel married another, and what Quaena chose to do with her life. He had a thousand stories to tell, a hundred things he forgot to say. He longed to return to a place not seen since the Shattering, the Ashwood. Beautiful. Peaceful. Warm. He wondered if Erelinda could be half so wonderful and who of those he loved awaited him there.

Next came Elberen, and the memories of his austere and proper elven master taught him what it was to be noble. Elberen lived many human lifetimes before the wars started, and, even in good times when opportunities to sacrifice and serve were few, he sought them out. He never took credit, never vaunted himself, never sought his own need or aggrandizement. When war came, he was counted the best of warriors, not only because of his skill, but also because of his capacity for compassion. His elven subordinates followed him out of love for the elf, not out of reverence for his rank. Elberen, too, longed for the peaceful confines of Ashwood.

Lastly, Telmerran entered his mind, a sharp contrast to Elberen and Samian. Telmerran was born to command and had confidence—almost to a fault—in his abilities. When decisions needed to be made, he raised his voice first and put down dissident views without regard to the feelings of those who forwarded them. He was brash, and whatever he did, he did completely and without remorse. He loved many women, but loved war more, and, of the three warriors, Gen marveled the most at his prowess. Samian and Elberen earned the respect of their enemies for their character and skill; Telmerran terrified his foes with sheer power, his name a curse on their lips.

Gen opened his eyes and came awake, but not as himself. He could see, hear, and feel, but someone else moved him, all three personalities struggling for the mastery of his mind. The moons shone through the window, and in their light Gen saw the three stones upon the ground. He was free in one fashion, but not another, and Gen feared Torbrand would find him standing stupidly mumbling in the middle of his room while three men fought over him.

Telmerran won the struggle, and Gen watched as a spectator as the warrior used his body to gather the stones and slip out the window. The moonlight was both a blessing and a curse. Telmerran worried about being seen, but he felt grateful for the visibility it provided in territory not familiar to him. Ever the soldier, Telmerran sneaked up on a sentry, broke his neck, and took his sword before sprinting out of town.

To Gen's consternation, Telmerran wanted to go north. He was from Lal'Manar, the greatest of all the former ancient human kingdoms. Telmerran had learned of its fall and its people's migrations west to Rhugoth, and Gen could sense the he wanted to go to the Portal on Emerald Lake. Gen wondered if he realized the distance or Tolnor's need of help against Aughmere. Frustrated, Gen attempted to regain control of himself, finding Elberen and Samian competing against him. But none could breach Telmerran's mastery of Gen's mind, a mastery maintained by his natural will and passion.

When morning came, Telmerran hid in one of the increasingly infrequent stands of trees. Forest gave way to open plain east of Tell, poor land for anyone trying to avoid capture. Sure enough, a scout on fast horse rode by at some distance, and they saw him both coming and going. Telmerran did not allow movement until nightfall, though everyone within Gen's mind agreed on that point.

Over the next few days they saw nothing of scouts or human company, making good time across the flat, even ground, gradually turning north toward the Rede Steppes and the harsh Red Wind Breaks beyond. Telmerran relinquished control to Samian for brief stints so the experienced huntsman could scavenge for food, if it could be called that. Hibernating beetles, roots, and dead grass—and not in great supply—were all they could find. Muddy pools of melting snow provided ample water, but his belly growled at its constant emptiness and discomfort.

As the days wore on, the distinction between the personalities struggling within him started to blur. At times, Gen found he couldn't separate his memories from those of his companions. What they had done, he had done. What they felt, he felt. Gen fought to maintain his identity, force his dominance, and recapture control of himself, but Telmerran and his desires were becoming his own, though more frequently the desires of Elberen and Samian imprinted themselves more strongly upon his mind.

A fortnight gone, they traveled south, east, and west as much as north. The raging conflict of four personalities trying to merge and the lack of nourishment often dropped Gen to the ground unconscious and twitching. The sword they'd carried for untold miles came up missing after one such episode. Gen could not gather enough order or volition in his mind to search for food, and finally, after three weeks of wandering, his mind was such a riot of conflicting memories, vivid images, and powerful yearnings that he fell, only dimly recognizing that the dirt under his hand was a road before he closed his eyes and gave up the fight.

Chapter 13 - The Damned Quarter

Errin, an acolyte of the Church of the One, crinkled his nose. "Pureman Salem, he stinks, and badly."

"That he does, Errin. That he does."

The grizzled Salem rubbed his scraggly black and gray beard, a beard that paid no compliment to the puffy face and thinning hair of a man whose rough, pockmarked skin had been sculpted by the sun, wind, and rain.

Salem glanced back at the young man in the cart. "Reminds me of the time we was laid up deep in the Kingsblood Sea. Hot as the Blacksand Waste in the summer and about as much wind as comes out of either side of a dead man. Didn't matter whether you was above decks or below decks, ya sweat so much you could scrape the salt off yer skin with a knife. That was stinkin', lad. 'Course, everyone stank, though some more than others, ye understand. You could kill fish with yer stench just by jumpin' in the water."

Errin sighed. "That was a delightful story, Puremen Salem. How fortunate that the Prelate chose me to be your acolyte. I may not be able to heal anyone by the time you're done with me, but I'll have an excellent collection of sea stories with which to sicken the heart of the already ill. 'Either end of a dead man.' Did you have to say that?"

"Farging piece of shmite!" Salem erupted. He held little respect for his highborn companion and his milky white skin, wavy brown hair, and unmanly aversion to everything not scrubbed by a servant. "You'd best be grateful you got any appointment at all after the circumstances of you coming into the brotherhood and all."

"'Farging?' 'Shmite?' You made those up, didn't you? With your background you should have better curses at your command."

"Look here, *acolyte*," Salem chastised. "Eldaloth himself taught that we shouldn't swear or profane. Men in my former profession swear as much as they possibly can, whenever they can. I've worked long and hard to overcome me poor speech. You respect it or I'll put one hand on yer collar and one foot up yer, um . . . or I'll kick you right off this wagon and you'll be walkin' the rest of the way to Rhugoth!"

"I would think," Errin opined, "that 'farging' is pretty much the same as saying that 'other' word. The feeling behind it is certainly the same. After all, if I straight out tell a woman she isn't pretty, isn't it just the same as if I had said she were ugly? Same feeling, same intent, same sadness caused, same sin."

"Who is the acolyte here?" Salem asked, dander up. "I'll be doin' the teachin' about sin. Now, as to the young man in the back there. If you think he stinks so bad, you can bathe him once we get to a river wider than a horse trough."

"Then you'll have two sick and crazy people to take care of. Do we have to take him all the way to Rhugoth? The Church runs a fine sanatorium in Khyrum, not two days from here."

Salem snorted. "You noble types. Always scared of dirt

and bodily fluids. Ya wouldn'ta lasted a minute on *The Raven*, not a one."

"I'll take that as a compliment. But really, Salem. We can leave him in Khyrum, right? Tell me we can."

"No!" Salem objected. "He's not sanatorium sick, Errin. He's Mikkik sick! He's possessed. It's the Damned Quarter for him, if he can't be dispossessed."

Salem and Errin both glanced back at the stray they had found lying prone on the side of the road that morning. Days, maybe weeks, of wandering had ruined his clothes, his pants and cloak a mess of rips and dark stains, some of blood. He was covered from head to toe in mud and he constantly muttered in what they figured were three different languages, Common the only familiar one. As they watched, he thrashed about and started yelling in one of the strange tongues.

"Demon possession, all right. He's talking the tongue of the Mikkik, or I'm no Pureman at all!"

"The speech doesn't sound foul. Quite elegant, actually. Well, it would be if he weren't yelling it."

"Ah, but there's the thorn!" Salem gesticulated, taking one hand off the reins. "The words of evil are cloaked in beautiful guise to deceive us, like an ugly street prostitute who wears pretty. . ."

"Please!" Errin plead. "No more analogies!"

"As ya wish, lad," Salem acquiesced.

"You'll never get your own congregation if you can't file the rough edges of your sermons."

"True enough, but who needs a congregation when we've got so much good and kindness to do? Take this poor, wretched lad. Doesn't need words. He needs food and lookin' after. Some of those uppity Prelates and Puremen might think preachin' best, but I ain't yet met a man who liked the word of God on an empty stomach.

"Well, we'll take this one direct to Prelate Shefston. If he can't exorcise him, then I suppose he'll be set loose with

201

the rest of them. Damned Quarter certainly doesn't need another crazy. Ya know the Church has it out for ye when they send ye there. A real black-eye on Mikmir, the Damned Quarter. A fine city, otherwise."

"He keeps saying that word, 'quaena', over and over again," Errin observed after a long lull in the conversation. "What do you suppose it means?"

"It's another name for the Evil One," Salem answered firmly.

"It is not. I've never heard of that one. You're making things up again."

A quick shove from Salem expelled Errin unceremoniously from the cart and onto the side of the road, sending him rolling in the dirt.

"Hey, Salem," Errin yelled, standing and jogging to catch up. "That really hurt, you . . . farging bass turd!"

"Now that was real swearin', brother Errin. You need to repent."

"No, I don't. I was talking about fish shmite."

"What?"

"Never mind, Salem. Can I get back in the cart?"

"If you can catch it, you can ride it," Salem said, whipping the reins to spur the horse forward.

Several hours and a long walk later, Errin lay to the side of the road wishing they could light a fire. Unfortunately, there wasn't enough wood in the Red Wind Breaks to fill a cart half as big as theirs. The long journey bored him, and, as much as he complained about Salem's salty stories, they at least provided a modicum of entertainment. Fortunately, Errin prodded Salem away from his putrid sea stories and onto the more fantastic—and sometimes just as brutal—stories about a General Harband from Rhugoth. Errin couldn't believe half of them, outrageous as they were, but the story about Harband setting squirrels on fire and letting them loose in his commander's tent provided a welcome laugh, true or not.

Errin rolled to his side. As usual, Salem had already drifted to sleep, mumbling real obscenities in his dreams. After tossing and turning for nearly an hour, Errin stood and went to the cart, finding the possessed young man standing behind it, back straight and hands behind him as if at attention. Scars covered him from one end to the other, and Errin wondered how many were concealed beneath layers of dirt. He plugged his nose and stood in front of the poor fellow, looking him in the eyes to see if the young man would acknowledge his presence. He didn't, face devoid of expression and eyes vapid.

"What is your name?" Errin repeated the question several times.

"Telmerran. Samian. Gen. Elberren. Regina. Why couldn't I save her? Rafael! Do you see her? Quaena, do you live? Will I meet you? Where are the trees? We are going the wrong way, curse Telmerran! Always has to have his way. We must warn the Duke! Khairn is coming! Fly! He will fly before us!"

Errin shook his head. Clearly insane. Only one name of many meant anything. Errin surmised the young man was from some poor family in the south of Tolnor who had kicked him out the door because of his ailment, no longer able to care for him. By the scars, he'd had a rough life, probably on some cruel street.

Salem's "ministry" was to travel Tolnor and care for the downtrodden, and the boy was their first find of the season. They had found no weapon with him upon the road where they encountered him, but Errin thought that even a soldier should not have so many scars upon him. If Salem hadn't thought him possessed, they would have traveled to Khyrum and been done with it, but in Mikmir, the Church

203

kept the possessed and others touched by Mikkik in a separate place, not wanting to kill them, but wanting them kept together, nonetheless.

As they traveled north in the following days, the Wardwall mountains slowly peeked up over the horizon, snowy tips difficult to see against the bright blue sky. They passed the turn off to Khyrum, picking up supplies from Gribb, a small trading post at the crossroads between the Lonewall and Khyrum Duchies.

The boy took to sleeping a lot in the day, rising in the evening and standing guard in a soldierly stance. Errin noted his regimental behavior, though the material of his clothes was clearly that of a peasant. They tried to coax him into bathing in the Wind River and Mirror Lake as they traveled by, but the young man resisted stubbornly and was too strong to force.

Three more days passed, and they descended the north side of the Wardwall Mountains into the beautiful Emerald Valley. Despite his indisposition, the young man stood in the wagon and gazed at the long lake, green grass, and newly bloomed wildflowers for nearly an hour, eyes bright with wonder.

As they passed through a pine stand charred from a lightning fire, their charge moved quickly to one side of the wagon bed and stared intently at something in the brush. Not until the deer concealed there sprinted away did Errin see it, and he surmised that the boy had excellent vision. He still kept his rigid vigil every night, and Errin took some time to listen to the language he spoke to himself, finding it enchanting and even inspiring at times despite his inability to understand it.

In stark contrast, Salem sang, fake-swore, and told more disgusting sea stories than Errin thought possible for one man to accumulate, and he got even louder as they neared populated areas. Salem possessed a kind heart and a willingness to help anyone despite their station, and Errin would admire him for that, if for nothing else. Salem always saw to everyone else's needs first.

Fortunately, the brief spates of bad weather as they descended slowly down the rough road on the north side of the mountains provided something to talk about other than the time Salem's entire crew ate a bad batch of fish, or when they came upon a giant, vomiting sea monster who retched onto the deck of their ship (a story Errin didn't quite believe).

The Portal to Rhugoth sat on a small island in the middle of the Emerald Lake. Several small towns clumped around the pristine body of water created a living for the lords and peasants who charged fees to take travelers by barge to the Portal. As Errin, Salem, and the boy neared one such city, Mirrorvale, they found themselves behind a long caravan waiting to be taken to the island Portal.

The ever-gregarious Salem had ample opportunity to serve and disgust everyone. Errin did his best to smooth over Salem's total lack of regard for good manners, though as an acolyte, he could only correct Salem indirectly for fear the man would grab him and do something horrible to him that he'd learned during his seafaring days—like the time he found a crewman cheating at cards, tied him to the deck, and dumped a crate full of angry lobsters on him. Errin hated that story, wondering exactly what they had done to anger the lobsters. Salem would never say exactly what had happened to the victim, always ending the story with a sad shake of his head.

The people of the caravan paid the strange boy no mind, used to the sight of the less fortunate and infirm along the road. Instead, they took their time frequenting the taverns and shops that lined the street. Half-naked boys carrying buckets of water charged a pittance to administer a drink to those who didn't want to go into a tavern for fear of losing their place in the line. Errin had seen such jockeying for position end in brutal fights. As the line got longer, several city guards appeared from a side street, split up, and started patrolling the file.

"This is going to take for-farging-ever," Salem complained grumpily as he climbed back into the driver's seat and picked up the reins. "If that boy would act a little more crazy, we could probably convince the town guard to push us to the front of the line. But," he said, casting his eyes backward to where their charge sat serenely observing the scene, "he seems to have calmed down a great deal of late."

"I think he's getting better," Errin observed.

"'Course he is!" Salem crowed proudly. "Bein' with two Churchmen interferes with the demon's power to use 'im. Gives me hope he can be cured, God willin'."

"I don't think he's possessed. The two different languages he's speaking are beautiful. From what I've read, demon speech is coarse."

"We done talked of this afore! The deceiver uses pretty speech to trick us. Sounds fair, but there's a barb on every shiny, silver hook."

"I think," Errin said, "that when The Writ talks of 'fair' or 'pretty' speech, it's talking about using flattery or being eloquent, not speaking in another language."

And for the next two hours, Errin found himself subjected to a long argument about the methods and signs of possession, though Salem's memory was such that the examples he gave were typically conglomerates of several different stories broken apart and refashioned to his purpose. Fortunately, the discussion—interspersed with diatribe—lasted long enough to pass the time until it was their turn.

Ropes, pulleys, and horses pulled two barges back and forth to the Portal Island. Salem told Errin to put blinders on the horse. Once done, they watched as the long and flat barge glided to abut against the pier. A weathered, shirtless bargemaster signaled the next three wagons forward, of which Salem's wagon was last.

The two wagons in front of them were piled high with straw that had been kept through the winter to be sold in Rhugoth for higher prices than they could get in Tolnor. The bargemaster, voice raspy, ordered someone from each wagon to take the reins of each horse to master it in case it got the jitters on the water. With effort, he lifted a rear gate and placed thick planks behind each cart's rear wheels to prevent them from rolling backward.

Errin found himself standing and stroking the horse soothingly as the barge got underway. It was early evening, and a beautiful blue sky reflected on the calm water. Errin breathed in the clean air, relishing the view. Behind him the Wardwall Mountains of Tolnor drifted away and in front of him the tall, ragged Ironheart Mountains of Aughmere jutted forbiddingly skyward. Errin could just make out the wall running against the opposite shore that marked the boundary of Aughmere, homeland of the Ha'Ulrich.

The Portal Island drawing steadily closer was flat and green with short grass, two large oak trees spreading their branches over the pier. While a major Portal for commerce between Tolnor and Rhugoth, the island's size only permitted a single wooden structure, the home of the Portal Mages that administered the critical location. Due to the excessive amount of traffic to the island, Rhugoth had funded paving the road up to the Portal in white granite stones.

Movement in the corner of his vision prompted Errin to turn. His eyes widened. The boy stood on the edge of the wagon, and it appeared he meant to jump off into the water.

"Salem!" Errin exclaimed. Salem turned about and reached backward to try to catch the boy's cloak, but before he could grab it, the lad jumped from the wagon side to the barge railing in an incredible display of agility. As casually as if strolling down a wide avenue, he walked the length of the barge rail, which was no thicker than the length of a man's finger. The bargemaster yelled at him to get down, but the young man continued until he stood at the front, arms crossed and staring at the island approaching before him

Salem, muttering fake curses, climbed down from the wagon and ambled forward as quickly as he could to soothe the bargemaster, explaining the boy's condition. From the way the bargemaster backed away, Errin figured Salem let drop the word "possessed," and from that point on the bargemaster stood as far from the boy as possible. Despite Salem's entreaties, the young man remained perched on the rail until the barge neared the pier on the opposite side. Thankfully, he walked calmly back down the rail and jumped back into their wagon.

"Mikkik's trick, that," Salem judged darkly, frowning.

"I've seen acrobats who can do as much," Errin countered.

"You think e's an acrobat, do ye?" Salem replied.

"No, but extraordinary agility is hardly demonic!"

Fortunately for Errin, the need to debark and pay the bargemaster precluded another argument. Unlike their experience waiting for the barge, trips through the Portals took little time. The Portal to Rughoth was large, framed in an arch made of the same pale stone as the road, now blushing a warm yellow in the late sun.

At its base, Errin guessed the Portal spanned nearly thirty feet. They watched as the clerk took the names of the company of the wagons ahead of them, finally coming to their wagon and recording their names in a large book for that purpose. Once done, the Portal Mage, dressed in a brilliant blue robe, walked out of the solitary building and stood near the Portal base, concentrating. The Portal flashed into existence, a brilliant metallic blue, the same color as the Mage's robe. The clerk waved all three wagons forward.

Errin closed his eyes as they rolled through the Portal.

Since both he and Salem had passed through Portals many times before, they were able to control the brief sensation of nausea and dizziness. They turned to their charge to see how he fared, finding him placid as usual in the weak light of the Rhugothian morning.

"We know one thing about him," Errin said. "He's been through a Portal before. If he were a Tolnorian peasant, that would be unlikely."

Salem grunted noncommittally.

The Rhugothian side of the Portal was situated not one hundred feet from the edge of the immense Kingsblood Sea. Errin knew from his studies that before the Shattering there had been immense oceans one could sail on for months and never glimpse land. Since the Shattering, the Kingsblood Sea was the largest body of water yet discovered, though he'd heard rumors of one to rival it on the recently discovered Shroud Lake shard.

Around the Portal, the aptly named city of Portal Gate still slept, the sun's light barely a stain on the horizon. For several minutes Salem stared longingly at the large ships anchored on the lake, their hulls and masts shrouded in mist.

"We'd best be goin'," he finally said, as if trying to convince himself. "Five days to Mikmir." They set off, taking the road west around the lake. The pine-framed road was beautiful to nose and eye, and the cool breeze of the sea refreshed tired eyes, but the time difference between Portals always proved difficult, and Errin found himself slapped roughly awake by Salem more than once.

"You sleep now, you won't sleep t'night."

Perhaps due to the time change, the boy stayed awake more frequently in the daytime, sitting erect and watching his surroundings carefully. Still, he said little, and when he did, it was in one of the mysterious languages. His eyes often unfocused into emptiness for long stretches, and—more than once—Errin made out the names 'Gen,'

'Samian,' 'Telmerran,' and 'Elberen.' Still, while his impoverished, filthy condition cast a pitiable light upon him, from time to time Errin sensed an intelligence and self-command in their charge that scared him. If there were anything demonic about the young man, it was the cold, utterly controlled countenance that he wore with increasing frequency.

Errin asked Salem who he thought the names the boy repeated might be, and Salem, of course, speculated the worst possible thing, names of the creatures of the underworld currently inhabiting the soul of their passenger. Whatever training Salem had received to become a Pureman, Errin speculated that it didn't involve a lot of reading or perhaps remembering. All in all, Salem cared little for doctrine or ritual but was quite fond of baseless speculation. If Salem had a motto, Errin thought it would have to be "service before sermons" or "love before learning."

Three days after the Portal and two days from Mikmir, they crossed the immense West Bridge that spanned the gap between two of the many shards that collectively formed Rhugoth. Again, the boy stood on the edge of the wagon, staring down into the abyss between shards with absolute calm. Errin hated the bridges and locked his eyes straight forward. The young man standing so casually caused the acolyte to feel the vertigo his ward apparently did not. Salem guided the wagon back toward the center of the bridge, and the boy hopped back into the wagon.

As they exited on the other side, their charge shocked them both by leaning forward and asking, "How long until we arrive at Mikmir?" in clear Common. Salem brought the wagon to a dead halt.

"What did you say, boy?" he inquired gruffly.

"Elemerean iownea se Mikmir?"

"Bah! Mikkik-speak again!" Salem turned away, whipping the horse into a trot. "Best get him off our hands as soon as possible!"

"We will be there in two days," Errin said slowly, holding up two fingers. "What is your name?" Errin watched as he struggled with the question, eyes narrowing and jaw clenching.

"My name is Gen," he said, emphasizing each word as if to convince himself he was correct. Again, however, his eyes unfocused and he slipped into another stupor for a couple of hours before sleeping until evening.

As the road led through several sizable towns near Mikmir, they lodged in the outbuildings of two large churches for the next two nights. Gen, as Errin believed his real name to be, became the focus of much observation. Puremen and acolytes alike stopped to see the real case of possession that Salem loudly advertised everywhere they went. Unfortunately for them, Gen no longer mumbled, each day his eyes clearing and his stupors afflicting him with decreasing regularity.

By their last night on the road, Errin would swear the boy was fully cognizant. He still stood guard from time to time, but intelligence and keen awareness completely replaced the void in his gaze, and when a group of acolytes stopped to see him, he regarded them so intently with his cold stare that they ran off. Errin tried asking Gen questions, but he answered nothing, and Errin wondered if he couldn't or wouldn't respond. He still rejected every entreaty to take a bath, and, after their earlier failed attempts, they gave up trying. They had long since accustomed themselves to his stench.

As they neared Mikmir the next morning, traffic on the road swelled, slowing their pace. The avenue broadened and ran along a river between the Kingsblood Sea and the Kingsblood Lake. Mikmir surrounded the small lake, and, even at a distance, the city seemed to glow in the mounting sunshine.

Once they drove into Mikmir proper, Errin stared wide-eyed at Rhugoth's sprawling capital, noticing several different architectural styles as they rode along. More recent structures rose several stories in the sky and had an intricate feel to them, leaves chiseled into the stone or decorative artwork painted onto pale plaster. Some buildings even reached the level of art to Errin's eye, testaments to Rhugoth's prosperity and thriving culture. Glass windows, a luxurious, expensive rarity everywhere else, were in abundance in Rhugoth, glinting in the sun.

The clean, orderly streets, the performers, merchants, and people inspired Errin to declare Mikmir the finest city he'd ever traveled to—until they neared what Salem told him was the Damned Quarter. New buildings faded to old, and beggars and refuse lined the lane in equal proportions. Buildings here sat squat, crude, and misshapen from long years of abuse from the weather and from half-hearted, under-funded attempts to fix them.

Salem explained how the Damned Quarter divided Mikmir into two, richer parts of the city bracketing the impoverished strip in the middle. The shortest route from one prosperous section to the other was the lane they traveled on. The rich often took ships across the lake to avoid the carriage ride through the slums.

As they trundled along, a fine carriage pulled by four horses sped past them, bouncing about on the cobblestones, heedless of man, woman, or child upon the street.

"Lot's o' folks get hit every year on this lane. Rich folks race by like Uyumaak Hunters when they come through here. You haven't seen the worst of it, yet, tho'."

Errin didn't see how worse was possible until Salem turned the cart left off of the main road, heading into the heart of the old, dilapidated city. Errin guessed the first refugees from Lal'Manar had built the quick buildings as a temporary solution until finer buildings like those they left behind could be constructed. Now, the ramshackle homes served as places to discard the poor. It seemed the poverty, illness, and ignorance so evident all about them actually dimmed the sun, casting everything into a hazy, brown shadow.

Heavily tanned men and women dressed in rags shuffled about or sprawled, drunken and insensate, in the street near the most dismal taverns Errin had ever laid eyes on. Yelling, drunken mumbling, and the sounds of all manner of animals coalesced into a steady morass of cacophony that filled Errin with anxiety and even set the more experienced Salem on edge.

Children, bellies protruding unnaturally forward, stared dumbly at them as they passed, some yelling for food or money. Sickness. Disease. Garbage. Errin felt outraged and ill. How could it be that the richest city in the world could permit such a blemish to fester upon its otherwise lovely face?

At last, Bainburrow Cathedral, old and sturdy, slid into view, and beyond it the street dead-ended at a gate built against a wall of rubble. Soldiers, though not sharp or particularly fit-looking ones, stood guard at the gate.

"What is through there?" Errin asked.

"That, my boy, is where our young friend here will go if the Prelate can do nothing for him. An evil place, that one, full of the possessed, diseased, deformed, and marked that could not be healed. I went in once and never wish to enter again. They say the Chalaine enters it from time to time to see what she can heal."

"The Chalaine comes here?" Errin exclaimed. "Unbelievable! It would be beneath civility to bring an aristocrat here, not to mention dangerous!"

"She's kinder than any of us, boy," Salem said as he brought the wagon to a halt outside the Church. "Something ye have ta' learn, eh Errin? Let's get 'im inside to Prelate Shefston."

Errin hoped Gen would be spared whatever life—if it

could be called that—went on behind those gates, but as he rounded the back of the wagon, he found that Gen had fallen into another stupor, though different, his eyes darting about wildly. From time to time he convulsed or yelled something in his strange language.

"Looks like e's havin' a fit now," Salem rumbled. "Likely the demons inside 'im can't stand the holy ground of the Church."

Errin cursed the ill timing. If only they had arrived when he was lucid. Errin prayed that the fit would end before they found the Prelate. Hefting Gen inside the Church took a great deal of effort, and they settled for laying him on the dusty floor at the entrance. The Church, like the neighborhood around it, was rundown and brown, dust lying thick on every flat surface. Only the smell of incense and fragrant oil in the air distinguished it from the wrack of its environs.

"Where's the Prelate?" Errin asked as they laid Gen down.

"I am here, acolyte."

Errin looked up. A corpulent man, quite out of character in the midst of so much emaciation, strode down the hall, kerchief to his nose and mouth.

"What did you drag in for me this time, Salem?"

Salem related how they had found him and his opinions of the boy's condition. Errin tried to contradict his master's opinions, but a dark look from the Prelate's deep eyes cut him off in midsentence. Errin could only observe as the Prelate performed a perfunctory and cursory attempt at healing Gen's mind with an exorcism.

"He's beyond our reach," the Prelate concluded. "Conduct him inside the gates and be done with it."

"Yes, Prelate," Salem answered sadly.

"But he was getting better with each day!" Errin protested. "I am sure that with a little more time and care, he. . ."

A sharp look from the Prelate brought him up short. "Salem," he said, face stern, "you teach this acolyte who I am and how to respect his betters. I trust you capable of teaching the lesson?"

"Yes, yer Grace," Salem said, not meeting the Prelate's eyes.

The Prelate left the way he had come, leaving them to haul Gen back into the cart. A crowd of wretched poor gathered as they worked, commenting in low voices about Gen, most agape at the scars all over his body—the miserable gawking at those more miserable than themselves.

Perhaps they find some comfort in knowing someone is worse off than they are, Errin thought.

"Prepare yourself, Errin," Salem said once they climbed back to the cart. "What comes next will be hard for ye."

They had to stop at the gates for a moment while reinforcements from somewhere nearby were called up to help. As the gates swung inward, Errin saw why. No sooner had daylight peeked between the two doors of the gate than a mad rush of the insane, sickly, and half-clothed nearly overcame the resistance set against them. Only determined, well-placed violence sent them howling back into streets and alleys littered with feces and garbage.

Errin swooned with the smell and horror of it all. Truly, the underworld stood agape before them, and Errin turned to look behind him to make sure the way out still existed. What houses still stood here, sagged, cracked, and mutilated, threatened to collapse with every breeze. Only stronger structures of stone stood firm, though spattered and stained with mud, blood, and fecal matter. But more discomfiting than the smells, the screeches and screams, and the dilapidation of the buildings were the children of every age, most with only a scant rag separating them from nakedness, standing dumbly about the streets.

"We can't leave him here!" Errin protested, grateful for

the guards who marched warily beside them. "Who will feed him? What if he comes out of it?"

"They toss food o'er the walls every night," Salem explained, face disgusted. "They have water here, though I'd sooner drink lamp oil. Get him out, Captain."

Salem turned the cart around, and the soldiers roughly dumped Gen onto the ground. Salem wasted no time, driving out quickly as the soldiers again scuffled at the gate with the wretched denizens at the heart of the Damned Quarter. Errin glanced behind him as the gates swung shut. Gen had stood, regarding them coldly as they left. Errin saw sanity dawning there.

"Try not to think of it, boy," Salem said, clapping him on the back. "I don't like it, but there's nothing for it. We did our best. That's all we can do."

Errin folded his arms in disgust. "The Prelate certainly didn't do his best," the acolyte grumbled, mostly to himself.

CHAPTER 14 - BROWN AND WHITE

Gen watched as the soldiers shut the gates behind them, noting the strength of men and the defenses built to keep him in. In vain he swatted at his pants and cloak to get the dust and mud off them. He struggled to remember when he lost his shirt, but couldn't. The last few days, staring at the sun from the back of the cart, the torrent of memories and voices had subsided, his own mind and will returning to him for increasing amounts of time. He could remember each of the men's memories, probably better than they remembered them when they had lived, and, while he thought he had them sorted out, he didn't always feel sure.

The lifetimes of information imprinted upon him made him feel old. Part of the fight for ownership of his mind involved extricating his own memories from the others, a difficult task. Even now, when he remembered Samian kissing his elven wife for the last time, he didn't remember Samian doing it—Gen experienced it as if he were in Samian's place. And when he dreamed, he often had nightmares he knew sprang from the fears and desires of the others. But while he dreamed, those nightmares and desires were his own.

Looking outside of himself with his own perception and

his own senses awakened him to his predicament. Groups of the insane and sickly eyed him carefully as if looking for anything they might steal. Gen took stock of himself. His shirt, boots, sword, and the Training Stones had all gone missing, and what clothes he had—a shredded cloak and tattered pants—set him equal to the poverty and squalor all around him. Memories of the horrors of war lessened the shock of such depravity, but the faces of the sick, the elderly, and the children, all deeply tanned and completely destitute, still sorrowed him.

The emotion slipped away as Shadan Khairn's training took hold. The growling of his stomach and his thirst reminded him of his first duty. Survival. The heart of the Damned Quarter was walled away from the rest of the city, though some of the barriers consisted of the steep, jagged ruins of buildings. These provided the easiest apparent exit, though the loose rubble could prove treacherous and noisy to climb. The city guard obviously had several stations and guards around the perimeter, and silence would be the key to escaping without confrontation.

"She is coming," a nearby child said, coming forward. "Please don't hurt her. She is the only nice one to come to this place."

Gen turned his gaze downward. A boy, ten or eleven years old by his height, looked up at him, one eye brilliant blue, the other a milky white. He wore scraps of a shirt and hole-riddled pants. The face, gaunt from undernourishment, was kind, the boy's demeanor sane and intelligent.

"What is your name, boy?"

"Thepeth."

"Who is coming, and why would I hurt her?"

"Why, the Chalaine is coming, of course. Can't you feel her? I thought you, of all people, would be able to feel her coming. I can."

"The Chalaine coming here? I think you are mistaken. I

218

can't imagine her guard would take the chance."

"It is dangerous," Thepeth replied, "especially with you here. But no one fights when she comes. Please don't fight when she comes."

"I certainly would not fight against the Chalaine and her guard. But tell me, Thepeth, why are you here? You don't seem insane."

"The orphanmaster sent me here. He said I was touched by Mikkik, that Mikkik gave me this eye to speak his lies. I see the things people want to hide. No one likes me around. But I like the Chalaine. She has nothing to hide, at least nothing important."

"She has been here before?" Gen asked incredulously.

"Twice since I have been here. You won't hurt her, will you?"

"Of course not. Why do you think I will?"

"You don't want to hurt her?"

"Certainly not."

"That is strange." Thepeth scratched his head. "I thought you had come to kill her. That's what you're supposed to do, isn't it?"

"If you think I am here to kill the Chalaine, then perhaps you are crazy, little one."

"Is she here yet, Thep?" A little girl, dirty beyond description, poked her head out of a littered alley.

"Almost, Halwen. Get the others."

"What's wrong with her?" Gen asked.

"She has fits. Her Pureman said they were caused by. . ."

"Mikkik," Gen finished for him. After the first war ended and Mikkik slunk away into hiding, his terror still ran through town and city, scores upon scores of people killed by those who wrongly supposed Mikkik to be the author of all irregularities of body and mind.

Gen turned to his young companion. "How do you know she is coming?"

Thepeth shrugged. "I just do. You'd best get away from

us," the boy warned him as a sizable group of children emerged from alley, building, and ruin. "The Dark Guard don't take kindly to anyone being close to the Chalaine except the children. I imagine they would be even madder to see you. You really can't feel her coming?"

"No. Thank you for the warning, Thepeth."

Gen secreted himself inside a half-destroyed house near where the children gathered together. It had a window facing the street and had enough of a roof to be dark, providing a perfect place to watch and not be seen. He leaned against the wall and looked out. Pitiful men and women gathered around the gate, standing away from it and not in the attitude of attack. As Thepeth said, the crowd did not surge forward when the gates swung open. A heavily fortified carriage, black in color and etched with a silver rose, rumbled slowly through the gates. Four strong horses, as black as the carriage, pulled the heavy load, and a formidable column of fifty soldiers marched through the gates with it.

Nearest the carriage were the unmistakable Dark Guard, intimidating in their black uniforms, swords drawn. When Thepeth mentioned that no one fought when the Chalaine came, Gen had thought it out of respect for the Chalaine. He revised that conclusion. They didn't fight because a couple of the Chalaine's visits had taught them that any aggression near the First Daughter resulted in quick death.

The Chalaine's guards stared menacingly at everyone and did a thorough check of the area before forming a wide perimeter and opening the door of the carriage. The first to emerge was a handsome young man, also uniformed as a Dark Guard. Gen recognized him from the Shadan's picture of him—Dason Kildan. He extended his hand, and Gen saw the Chalaine for the first time as she stepped down into the street. She was tall for a woman, nearly as tall as the guard who helped her from the carriage. Everything about her appearance lay hidden behind her pure white cowl, veil, and robe that rippled in the breeze, shining in contrast with the dull browns and grays all around her. Several of the children approached her, and she stooped to hug them all.

Gen could just make out her voice as she asked the names of the children she did not already know and talked with them. Musical. By her mannerisms, Gen could tell that she felt a little afraid or uncomfortable, but she loved the children enough to put aside her own inconvenience. Soldiers lifted food from the carriage, and the Chalaine distributed the bread, apples, and cheese among her little charges while the adults watched enviously. Thepeth sat near her, and, from time to time, Gen could feel the boy's gaze upon him.

Gen couldn't help but think of the children he knew in Tell on the morning of Shadan Khairn's invasion. Fathers and mothers had clung to them to comfort them in their fear and soothe them with whispers that all would be well. The Chalaine did much the same, sitting on the ground and taking each child onto her lap and into her arms, giving each a daisy from a basket brought forth from the carriage. With a hug and something whispered in the ear, she went from one to the next, often pressing the veil to her eyes to dry them.

To spend a moment with every child took the better part of two hours, and by the time she finished, she needed Dason's help to stand. Dirty hands and faces had stained her dress, and, despite a quick attempt to shake and swat away the dirt, she would leave the Damned Quarter with a dress dyed brown in its dust. She didn't seem to mind, however, and she hugged them again, singing a little song to them as they filed past one by one. Before ascending into her carriage, she waved and promised to return soon.

The driver worked to turn the unwieldy carriage about in the cramped street as the soldiers formed up by the carriage and distributed what remained of the food to the most unfortunate, protecting them as long as they could from those who would steal it. The Chalaine opened a window in the door of the carriage and waved to the children as she left, the gates of the Damned Quarter swinging open and closing quickly once she was through.

Gen emerged from his hiding place and out into the street. Thepeth approached, twirling his daisy in his hand.

"You see now why I didn't want you to kill her. Isn't she wonderful?"

"She is everything I imagined. I doubt you could understand what her condescension says about her. I never wanted to kill her, though, Thepeth. I want to do quite the opposite, actually."

"You want to be a Dark Guard?"

"Yes, I do."

"So do I, mister. But she told me that I wouldn't get to because she would be the last Chalaine. After tomorrow, there will never be another Trials. Once Eldaloth returns, they won't need the Dark Guard anymore."

Every boy on any shard of note knew of the Trials, a great contest of warriors where a few were selected to apprentice to the Dark Guard. He, Gant, and the other local boys had staged many a fake Trials in Tell's town square, though in play everyone won the honor of entering the Dark Guard to avoid real fighting.

"They're holding the Trials tomorrow?"

"That's what she said."

Gen thanked Thepeth and walked away. This was a sign, a chance to put his training to the use it was intended. He needed to get a good look at the walls before the sun went down.

CHAPTER 15 - THE TRIALS

Miss Fenna Fairedale, handmaiden to the Chalaine, undid her bonnet, leaning around the First Mother to gain a better vantage point. The First Mother, too, surveyed the tournament field where young men by the dozens awaited their opportunity to demonstrate their skill at arms in hopes of earning an apprenticeship with the prestigious Dark Guard, the formidable protectors of the Chalaine.

Nearly all assembled were the sons of Rhugothian aristocracy, Tolnorian nobles, and Aughmerian Warlords. Others, Fenna thought, must be the sons of men in military ranks since she couldn't recall them attending court the day before. Most of the hopefuls clumped together with fighters from their own nations, attempting levity to dispel nervousness. Some few stood alone in deep concentration, stretching muscles and reviewing proper technique.

As Fenna watched, the morning sun finally crested some of the taller buildings that surrounded the field, promising a pleasant, warm day as the sweltering months of summer proper were at least a month off. The tournament area was a large, circular field covered with close-cropped grass. The nobles and the rich sat on covered wooden benches that formed a semi-circle around the field. A guardhouse stood directly opposite the seating, and a low wooden fence stretched away from either side of it. Along this fence the commoners and peasants gathered to watch the Trials, but others had climbed onto the roofs of nearby buildings for a better view—though more uncomfortable and distant.

As one of the Chalaine's handmaidens and as a daughter of a Regent, Fenna had the right to sit with the members of her class on the benches, but a chance encounter and invitation from the First Mother afforded her the privilege of sitting in "the Box," an area for high aristocracy and dignitaries. Instead of benches there were padded seats, and the First Mother and her advisers sat on the front row, Fenna one row behind. Fenna was supposed to be attending the Chalaine this morning, but she had managed to convince Eldwena to switch shifts with her so she could come and watch. It was a difficult persuasion. Despite the fact that Eldwena was married and had children, she still liked to ogle the young men.

The First Mother turned, and, as she often did, asked about the Chalaine's well-being with several pointed questions. Fenna loved the First Mother as she did her own mother, though her Grace intimidated Fenna more than even her own father. Like the Chalaine, Mirelle possessed a beauty beyond compare, but the First Mother of Rhugoth had a more forceful personality, a penchant for organization, and an air of command that her daughter lacked or held in a lesser degree. The Chalaine, Fenna knew, would not need those qualities as her mother did; she would not rule a nation but would stand in deference to the Ha'Ulrich in all things.

After inquiring after her daughter, the First Mother turned her attention to greeting the regents and nobles as they arrived, many to watch their sons. Due to the war between Tolnor and Aughmere, fewer than usual from those nations made the trip, though more young men than ever entered the contest, Rhugoth supplying the surplus.

Of all nations, Tolnor was the least represented. Fenna noticed Gerand Kildan, son of Duke Tern Kildan, the Lord Protector of Tolnor, huddled with seven other Tolnorians who had made the journey at some expense to the war effort and at some peril. The Aughmerian entries taunted them at every opportunity, but Gerand kept his fellow fighters focused. He was handsome like his brother, Dason, sporting long dark hair and a sliver of a goatee on his chin.

The Trials were held once every ten years in Rhugoth, and the event became a holiday for Rhugothians, the city of Mimkir offering a wide variety of entertainments for those making the trek from other shards. These Trials, however, held more import than any before. While the Chalaines had lived and died in peace for hundreds of years, the current one was *the* Chalaine, the one the Ilch would war against to destroy the God reincarnate that the Blessed One would father within her. Those chosen to protect her would need to be special and skilled young men, indeed.

The First Mother knew this too, though as for that, she fretted excessively over her daughter and would want the best men to protect her, whatever the peace or peril. To this end, she brought her two most trusted advisers, Regent Harrick Ogbith, High Protector of Mikmir, and Cadaen, her longtime bodyguard, to counsel her. Both men were old soldiers and excited to see the crop of young men who wanted to follow them into their honorable profession. They judged the young men like farmers judged livestock at a fair, seeing things—hidden strengths and concealed flaws—that most did not notice. The First Mother would seek their guidance when the time came to choose, and she sat between them, asking them questions about the skills and character of those assembled.

Fenna noticed Regent Ogbith's wife, Serena, approaching the seat next to her husband. While Fenna liked the Regent a great deal, his wife irritated her. Serena assumed the unofficial position of guardian of all matters of propriety—except where they concerned herself. With a shrill voice that penetrated even the noise of the bustling venue, and with unrelenting fastidiousness, she commented without reservation about everyone and everything, uncaring or unaware of the offense that poured from her mouth. The only impropriety Serena would admit to was that she called her husband "Oggie." Regent Ogbith cared little for propriety, though he, ironically, seemed to care for the would-be embodiment of it, smiling at his wife affectionately as she approached.

Fenna shrunk back into her chair, hoping not to attract Serena's notice. With parasol in hand, Serena genuflected perfectly to the First Mother and begged her permission to sit, which she granted with a polite smile.

"Quite the assembly of handsome young men," Serena said haughtily, "except that gaggle of slumping Tolnorians. The climate there must truly be harsh to impart such a weathered complexion. I should never hope to go there." Seeing that no one replied anything, she handed her parasol back to Fenna without looking. "Do take care of this and be useful, dear. You are afforded a great privilege to be so near the First Mother, even if you are a handmaiden to the Chalaine. Oh look, Oggie! There is Kimdan. I do hope he sees me here and behaves himself."

Regent Ogbith's son, Kimdan, was among the hopefuls, and he stood apart from everyone, practicing his sword forms with impressive fluidity and skill. Kimdan was blond, tan, and gorgeous, and Fenna knew many noble daughters in the stands had attended for the mere pleasure of cheering him on and gaining his attention and favor. Fenna fancied herself above all such machinations; she had loved Kimdan since first seeing him at court almost three years before. He was strong, handsome, and smart, and Fenna felt the attraction she imagined most women must feel when near him. Unfortunately, he had done nothing but ignore Fenna in the years since the First Mother invited her to court to become her daughter's handmaiden.

Kimdan was well aware that he pulled the heartstrings of a good portion of Rhugoth's young noblewomen, and his bloated self-confidence often led to an arrogance Fenna disliked. She knew the Trials wouldn't help Kimdan lessen his opinion of himself. Kimdan Ogbith, trained personally by the Lord Protector of Mikmir, was the best sword fighter of any of the young men present. Today was the day Kimdan would get to beat on his peers, play to the crowd, and drive the ladies wild. He had already removed his shirt and collected several sashes from his swooning admirers. A few of the other young men had a sash or two, but the majority had none due to Kimdan's excess. Fenna withheld her own, hoping Kimdan didn't think she would lower herself to such disgusting posturing.

"Well, Harrick," the First Mother remarked, "your son Kimdan is in excellent form. Does he realize that if he wins this he cannot become the Lord Protector of Mikmir in his father's stead?"

"He knows it, Highness," the Regent replied, "though he hasn't the temperament for it. He may one day, but he thinks a bit too highly of himself, I fear, to accept the counsel of others as he ought. My younger son Illin, while not as much the warrior in spirit, is twice the statesman."

The First Mother nodded her head in agreement.

"Illin is such a bore," Serena commented offhandedly. "Married a woman without so much as a spark of liveliness. A woman need be controlled, but not half-dead, for Eldaloth's sake!"

"I think a year of training with the Dark Guard will give Kimdan a new perspective on himself," Cadaen interjected before Serena could go on. "My first year with the Dark Guard was the hardest of my life."

Regent Ogbith chuckled. "I have only heard stories, and I am content not to know the truth," he replied. "I fear Serena here would remove Kimdan from the Trials if even half the stories I've heard are true."

Fenna had heard the stories, too. Going days without food and sleep. Being tortured to learn to resist torture. Forced marches in the winter. Spending weeks blindfolded while learning to defend against unseen attackers. There were rumors that some of the apprentices to the Dark Guard died during the training, and some said that of the six selected during the Trials, only three were expected to actually graduate to the status of Dark Guard.

Studying Kimdan, Fenna felt conflicting emotions. It would be good for his Dark Guard masters to teach him a little humility, but she hoped that his training wouldn't permanently damage him. It would be a travesty the young ladies of Rhugoth would simply not stand for.

A commotion on the field tore Fenna's eyes away from the Regent's son. Silence fell over the crowd as two of the castle guard escorted someone toward the Box where the First Mother presided over the contest. The young man gripped by the soldiers' strong hands wore rags and looked like a beggar straight from the Damned Quarter. With a mud-stained hand he clutched a dark cloak rife with gaping holes. Brown pants were ripped up to the knees, and he didn't even have shoes. As Fenna considered the dirt-caked face and rumpled hair, she couldn't help but feel a stab of pity. Serena gasped and covered her mouth with her pale hand.

Others of the aristocracy and nobility took similar offense at the beggar, perceiving his presence as an affront to the dignity of the field. Kimdan stopped working his forms to watch, a wide grin splitting his face.

"You cannot beg your way into the Chalaine's service, boy!" Kimdan crowed. Many laughed at the jest, but his father and the First Mother frowned in disapproval of the comment. Fenna wasn't sure why the guards had chosen to parade the ragamuffin around in front of the finely appointed assembly, but he didn't struggle and his face seemed calm despite the jeering and mockery. The First Mother stood as the guards approached and the crowd fell silent. Captain Tolbrook of the Dark Guard approached the First Mother.

"Captain!" the First Mother said firmly, "what is the meaning of this?" The young man looked at Tolbrook and waited patiently.

"Forgive this, Milady. Say the word and I shall expel him forthwith."

"Yes, expel him!" Serena cackled, still covering her mouth. "I can smell him from here! Augh!"

"He demanded he be given a chance at the Trials," the Captain continued. "I tried to turn him away, filthy as he was, but he would not be denied."

The First Mother's brow wrinkled and she fixed her gaze on the young man. "Speak, boy. Do you wish to submit your name upon the roll for the Trials?"

"I do." The voice was strong, deep, and clear. Fenna noted his lack of nervousness.

"Do you know anything of the sword?"

"Yes, your Highness." The First Mother's eyes tightened with skepticism as she tried to discern if he were lying. After a moment of silence, she decided.

"Put his name upon the roll, Captain Tolbrook."

"I must protest!" the Captain exclaimed. "His presence dishonors the assembly! He didn't even have the respect to bathe before coming here!"

"Enter his name, Captain. The law says that any man may enter the Trials, no matter what his station—or his cleanliness. What is your name, rank, and nationality, young man?"

"My name is Gen, and I am a serf from Tolnor."

More grumbling from the crowd erupted and the First Mother silenced them with a wave of her hand. "Very well, then. Captain, furnish him with a sword. Gen, I trust I have not made a mistake. The Trials are a very serious matter, doubly so in these times. If you are honorable today, I will see to it that you get a bath and a warm meal, whether you are chosen or not. Understood?"

"Yes, your Grace. I thank you for this kindness," Gen said, bowing his head in deference. Fenna watched as he followed a scowling Tolbrook toward a small booth near the gate where his name would be recorded and where he would be issued a wooden practice sword. The First Mother sat, face thoughtful.

"You are *certainly* merciful, your Highness," Lady Ogbith said. "Much more merciful than I could have been. Disgusting creature!"

"How do you mark him, Cadaen?" the First Mother asked, ignoring Serena's comment.

"It's hard to tell for sure, but I would guess he is a fighter. Look at the way he walks, erect with head held high. He is confident and calm and easily ignores the abuse of the crowd. Whether he is confident, apathetic, or disdainful, it is hard to say. While good posture and confidence do not a warrior make, I am sure that this is no common street beggar. Perhaps he is a deserter from the armies of Tolnor? If a peasant, he would have been pressed into service. Under normal circumstances, peasants in Tolnor are not allowed to wield the blade."

"That is possible," Regent Ogbith returned. "He is young and his inexperience could have made him flee battle, but something tells me that is not the case. His clothes were his and were not the clothes of a soldier, and I wouldn't expect a deserter to want to make himself public by coming to a tournament ground where he would be under scrutiny from some of his own countrymen. If an unskilled peasant, why come and make a fool of yourself?"

Fenna glanced at the Tolnorians, noting their disgust at their unkempt countryman.

The First Mother bit her lip. "While it is hard to tell with all that dirt on him, he is also too tall and too fair to be of

230

Tolnorian peasantry. Keep your eye on him. We shall know more when we see him fight."

"Should he pass Ethris's test," Harrick said. "If he is just some fool or a coward, Ethris's questions will show it."

"Speaking of Ethris, where is he? We can't get this underway without that Magician!"

As if the First Mother's words had summoned him, Ethris strode through the guardhouse gate and across the tournament field. Young men parted for him and gathered their belongings as the Mage's appearance signaled that the Trials would begin. Fenna felt uneasy around Ethris. He was old, intelligent, and always in a somber mood. Even more disturbing, the Mage was by some art completely hairless. She never found out how or why he had become that way, but she always thought there must have been some special reason for it.

Perhaps what made Fenna feel the most discomfort were Ethris's eyes. It was widely known that no one could lie to Ethris, whether he held the Truth Staff or not; today he held that Staff firmly in hand. Anyone who wished to enter the service of the First Mother or the Chalaine had to grasp that Staff and answer Ethris's questions. Well did Fenna remember her turn to face the penetrating glare, the blue eyes without eyebrows and eyelashes, and answer the same two questions all the young men would answer today in front of everyone.

Ethris's bald pate shone in the sun, and his robe was almost impossibly white, the cynosure for the moment. He walked forward without haste, bowed to the First Mother, and then turned to face the assembled hopefuls whom Captain Tolbrook busily tried to form up into regimental lines. Nervous smiles and fidgeting broke out among the would-be apprentices. Kimdan was cool and confident, and Fenna spotted Gen standing in the back. His expression would have been appropriate for one standing alone in a room staring at a blank wall. The First Mother rose and the young soldiers went to a knee and bowed their heads.

"Ladies and gentlemen of the three nations, I welcome you to the Trials. Gathered before us are the finest fighting talents hailing from all human kingdoms. Each has come to demonstrate his skill at arms, his honor, and his wish to serve my daughter, the Chalaine, as a part of the Dark Guard. There are three rounds to the Trials, and with each round a smaller group will be chosen to move on to the next. In the end, six will be chosen and one among them selected to be their Captain.

"Any who fail to achieve the honor of service to the Dark Guard will have the opportunity to enter the First Mother's army, should he so wish it. There shall be no magic or outside help given to any of the candidates today. Any who receive such will be disqualified and barred from further service to the Chalaine or this kingdom. As is required, all must grasp the Truth Staff and answer the questions put to them. I am well aware that two warring nations are represented here. I will look on any petty vengeance with great displeasure. Let us begin."

The crowd applauded and settled in as Captain Tolbrook called names from the roll. One by one, each young man came forward and grasped the Staff with both hands. The nobles from Rhugoth raised a loud shout and applause as Kimdan came forward, grasping the rod and looking Ethris in the eye. Serena blushed at the attention lavished on her son.

"Do you wish to serve the Chalaine for your own personal gain?" Ethris asked, voice cold and serious.

"No," Kimdan answered.

Fenna smirked. Kimdan had already gained plenty of notoriety before the Trials had even started. Perhaps his heart was in the right place even when the rest of him wasn't.

"Are you willing to die for the Chalaine?"

"Yes."

"Rise and take your place."

Only two young men failed the test. Gen, the very last on the roll, passed. Fenna noted that he was one of the only ones besides Kimdan who was able to hold Ethris's gaze throughout the questioning. As if reading her thoughts, Cadaen spoke.

"Did you see, Harrick? He had no fear of Ethris at all! Either he's as cocky and arrogant as your boy, or he's daft! We should have Ethris ask him if he really is a serf. I think not."

"Indeed," Regent Ogbith returned. "If a serf, he is unusually indifferent in the face of Mages and nobles. A bit of a mystery to spice up the event!"

"Hush, Oggie!" Serena grated. "They are announcing the initial assignments."

The first round of the Trials involved pitting one warrior against another in single combat. Five groups of two fought at the same time, one in the center and four in separate corners of the field while one member of the Dark Guard supervised and evaluated each group. While Kimdan wasn't chosen for the first matches, Gen was, and Captain Tolbrook put him and his opponent in the center of the field.

"The Captain wishes to embarrass him," the First Mother observed.

"At least he's given us a good vantage point," Cadaen added.

"Can you mark his opponent, Highness?" the Regent asked.

The First Mother squinted into the morning sunlight. "I'm afraid I can't get a good look at him."

"That is Volney Torunne," Fenna offered, "son of General Torunne."

The First Mother turned with a smile, as did Harrick and Cadaen. "Thank you, Fenna. I should have guessed you would have a good knowledge of the young men." The

First Mother winked and Fenna blushed.

"She's right," Regent Ogbith confirmed. "He has his father's monstrous nose. A good fighter, the General. Haven't seen him in a year or two, but his son should be a solid candidate if he's anything like him."

"Smash the filthy serf a good one, Volney!" Serena commanded. Her husband rolled his eyes up into his head in annoyance.

Fenna surveyed the crowd. All eyes save a few were focused on the match between the serf and General's son, hoping for a few laughs to begin the day. As the Dark Guard gave them instructions, they each began to remove their shirts. The matches, Fenna learned, were always fought bare-chested so that the welts left by the dull wooden swords would stand out. When Gen removed his cloak, he had no shirt underneath. What derision there might have been at this further evidence of Gen's poverty was quashed by the revelation of his form. Every muscle on his torso was firm and rippling. Scars, white against his heavily tanned skin, crisscrossed his chest, back, and arms. Fenna couldn't take her eyes off him.

"Erelinda take me!" the First Mother exclaimed. "Even Jaron in his prime was never that fit!!"

"He's a fighter, all right," Cadaen observed, "and by the scars, one who has seen battle."

Regent Ogbith crinkled his brow. "A warrior, yes, but torture rather than battle gave him most of those scars, I'd wager. Old warriors wouldn't receive half that many scars over a lifetime, if they survived that long. The dirt makes it difficult to guess his age, but he can't be a day over eighteen. Someone tortured him, probably an Aughmerian. We'd best watch this one. It would be easy for him to take revenge."

As with the other groups on the field, Gen and Volney faced each other, and with a drop of the Dark Guard's hand, began to fight. Volney strode forward confidently, striking with energy and precision. Gen blocked every stroke with apparent effort, returning with a series of strokes that at the end landed a large welt on Volney's back. This same scene was repeated every time, Gen narrowly avoiding Volney's swings and then swatting the young noble somewhere on the torso. When Captain Tolbrook finally called an end to the fighting, Volney had several red marks and Gen only one. Gen shook his opponent's hand politely, though Volney's face burned with disappointment.

"Gen didn't seem overly impressive," the First Mother remarked. "Just adequate, if you ask me."

Fenna had to agree. Nothing about the way Gen fought was particularly interesting. Though she couldn't say why, she hoped he would fare better to quiet the rudeness of the crowd and his competition.

"He wasn't trying," Harrick said as Tolbrook began announcing the next pairings. "There is a lot more power and speed in that frame than he showed. It's almost as if he's not trying to draw attention to himself, though that would seem the wrong thing to do during the Trials."

Cadaen nodded in agreement and was about to reply when a cheer went up from the crowd and drowned out any further conversation. Fenna looked up. Tolbrook had just announced that Kimdan was to fight Terrant Brookwater, a Warlord's son from Aughmere.

Kimdan strode out onto the field, hands raised high, taking the center place without being asked. Terrant, a lumbering young man, followed him out and faced him. Kimdan hopped about to warm up, twisting his neck and arms to get limber. This done, he executed another bow for the crowd just before the Dark Guard's arm fell.

"Damned peacock!" Regent Ogbith grumbled, almost coming out of his seat. "Must get it from his mother!" Serena scowled at her husband's remark, and the First Mother stifled a laugh.

"Well, you must forget who you were thirty years ago,

Harrick," the First Mother said as seriously as possible. "I've heard many tales about a man who was loathe to turn away attention when he could get it."

"I was never as bad as that boy is! Tell her, Cadaen!"

"My Lord," Cadaen stammered, "I think I must side with the Lady."

"Traitor."

The conversation was cut short by an "ahh" of approval from the crowd. Terrant was squirming on the ground holding his crotch while Kimdan strutted around and taunted him. Fenna felt torn halfway between the elation of the crowd and a powerful feeling of disgust, a feeling perhaps enlivened by Serena clapping and giggling with pride and glee.

Like Gen, Kimdan was marked but once during the fray, but unlike Gen, Kimdan showed no respect for his opponent, taking steps to paint him the incompetent fool at every opportunity. Each swat on the bottom, face, or groin earned raucous applause from his admirers, and as Kimdan quit the field he received a standing ovation from a good portion of those assembled.

"Maybe he is worse than you were," the First Mother acquiesced. "He's going to complicate some Dark Guard's life for a while, especially if his pride is further bloated by becoming the Captain's apprentice."

Fenna sat during the balance of the long first round to rest her feet. She was a little too short to get a good view when sitting behind Cadaen, Harrick, and the First Mother, all of which were above average height. When the round was over, all three left to consult with the Dark Guard and Captain Tolbrook on who should be cut and who should proceed to the second round. Fenna left quickly, purposely forgetting about Serena's parasol, fearing the woman might request that she attend her during the intermission. Fenna joined the onlookers as they abandoned their seats and moved slowly into the city in search of refreshment.

The sun was full up now, wisps of light clouds stretching from horizon to horizon in the spring-blue sky. As she worked her way by the common folk that lined the railing on the opposite side of the field from the stands, Fenna found voices that described Kimdan in terms quite different from those used by the aristocracy and nobility. They weren't words she could repeat. She heard Gen's name more than once from high-born and commoner alike—to the high-born an offense and to commoners an oddity.

Many of the young fighters sought refreshment in the streets as well, most surrounded by family, friends, and comrades in arms. A flock of young ladies vied for Kimdan's attention, and Fenna felt a stab of jealousy. She desperately wanted to act above the petty flirtations of her peers, but at the same time she wanted Kimdan to notice her and pay her the same courtesy and attention he did the others; being trifled with, she decided, was better than being ignored. She wandered aimlessly for many minutes, lost in thought, trying to plan her next move to entice Kimdan to pay her the attention she was due.

"Excuse me, Miss?" Fenna blinked and found herself staring at Gen's filthy face.

Chapter 16 - Ascension

Startled, Fenna took a step backward. Gen looked dirty and smelly from a distance; up close he was doubly so. Fenna tried to keep revulsion from crossing her face but was unsure if she succeeded. The young man's green eyes seemed to absorb every detail, but his mud-besmeared face betrayed nothing of what he might have thought or felt.

"I am sorry to impose, Miss," he said with a bow, apparently guessing her station. "I have no money with which I might purchase anything to drink, and I do not know where I might find fresh water. If you could direct me toward either, I would be most obliged."

His voice was deep and beautiful with a hint of the country in it.

"You are fair spoken for a serf, Gen."

"Being a serf does not always make one a word-mangling idiot," Gen replied evenly. "But it usually does mean that one is dirty."

Fenna couldn't tell if this was an attempt at humor or not. "Forgive me," she stammered. "Come, let me buy you some cider."

Fenna led Gen along a narrow street that led past Kimdan and his throng. Fenna turned her head away and tried to sneak by without attracting attention, but the observant Kimdan noticed her.

"Where are you taking *that*, Fenna?" he jeered. "You always did have a soft spot for strays!"

Fenna blushed and walked faster, turning to see if Gen would do or say something. Gen appeared uninterested in anything Kimdan said, and if anything he walked more slowly.

"Hey, serf!" Kimdan taunted. "You should leave! You disgrace her Highness! I hope I get the chance to whack some of that dirt off you!"

Fenna feared a fight would break out, but Gen continued casually by as if Kimdan didn't even exist, paying attention to nothing in particular. Hurrying forward, Fenna reached a small hide-covered booth where a thin man filled mugs from a row of barrels behind him. Fenna wanted to run, to get away from Kimdan, Gen, and everyone else. Tossing a penny on the table, she grabbed a mug and turned to find Gen behind her, observing her expressionlessly. His gaze made her drop her eyes.

"Here," she said, thrusting the mug out like a dagger. Gen took it gently.

"I am sorry that I proved an embarrassment, Miss Fenna."

"How did you know my name?" she asked.

"Kimdan said it."

"Oh, right," Fenna replied, color rising in her cheeks. "Yes. I am Miss Fenna Fairedale, daughter of the Regent and Lady Fairedale."

"Well met," he greeted her, bowing again. "I can see that Kimdan's attention is important to you." He took another drink. "I promise there was a time when I was not this unkempt." Fenna met Gen's gaze again. There was something honest about it.

She sighed. "It is I who should be ashamed. My mistress would disapprove of my actions and my feelings. We are all taught that we should not shun the company of the poor, even if it means being ridiculed. She lives that teaching well. Of course, no one would dare ridicule her."

Gen drank deeply and asked the man to refill his mug with water. "Who is your mistress?"

"The Chalaine."

Gen retrieved the mug from the merchant and drank quietly for a few moments.

"She is indeed kind," he said, "as are you. I thank you and hope I can repay you someday. But tell me, what is it about Kimdan that attracts you?"

Fenna was surprised at the forwardness of the question and found it difficult to answer. "I don't know. He's fair to look upon, skilled at arms, and a son of a powerful man." The answer seemed weak, and she realized how little she knew Kimdan. Gen nodded his head as if he understood anyway.

"I wish you luck, then. I just hope he doesn't treat you as shamefully as he did Terrant, should you find your way into his company. I shall make my way back, now. Again, I thank you. Do you wish to have a head start? I'll stay behind until you are well on your way."

"No. No, thank you. I must return as well and it should be with you. You are, after all, a guest in our kingdom and vying for a position of great honor."

Fenna found talking to Gen an easy thing despite his apparent lack of emotion. Maybe it was because of it. "It is true that Kimdan thinks too much of himself. Even his father, Regent Ogbith, says so. Unfortunately, there is no one on the field today that will teach him a lesser vision of himself. His father seems confident that the first year as an apprentice to the Dark Guard will cure his arrogance."

"Perhaps," Gen replied. A trumpet sounded on the field, signaling that the Trials were resuming. "But it is also unfortunate to see that so many of the nobles and aristocracy revel in his behavior. I wonder how they would react were the situation reversed and Kimdan were to receive the same kind of thrashing he gave Terrant?"

"Well, if you think you could do it, then do so with my blessing!" Fenna said, laughing at the thought. Looking around, she saw that Kimdan had already arrived at the field again and was counting his sashes.

"I may just attempt it," Gen said. "Fare thee well, Miss Fairedale. I will be cleaner should we chance to meet again."

The last was said like a promise, and Fenna couldn't help but feel a bit perplexed. By the time she made her way back to the stands, Captain Tolbrook was announcing the cuts. Only seven of the fifty-six had been dismissed. As she sat, Harrick, Cadaen, and the First Mother turned toward her expectantly.

"What?" Fenna said, nervous at their sudden attention.

"What?!" The First Mother smiled. "Dear child, we could not help but notice that you were talking to a certain young man who has captured our interest. What have you learned?"

Fenna's mind spun. In horror she realized that she had spent most of the time talking to him about Kimdan and had failed to ask him something as simple as where he was from.

"I, well, I didn't speak to him long. He asked me to buy him something to drink, or to point him to the water. He speaks as if he were court bred, though there is a bit of the country in his voice. He still claims to be a serf."

"Anything else?" the First Mother asked disappointedly.

"No, I'm afraid not."

"If you should chance . . . no, do not leave it to chance. Speak to him again, and do try to find out a bit more."

"Yes, Highness."

Fenna came to her feet as the second round of the Trials began. In this phase, fighters were placed into groups of five and given sashes of different colors to differentiate them. Captain Tolbrook then ordered one group to fight another. By rule, a combatant struck on the torso or head had to "die" and exit the combat.

As the first fight began, it was immediately obvious to Fenna that fighting in groups required a different ability than fighting one-on-one. Whereas fighting a single opponent involved one point of concentration, fighting multiple opponents with team members could only be done successfully with a broad awareness of everything and everyone nearby.

Fighters who appeared confident and skilled during single combat were dazed and disordered when thrown into a mix of men. Often, the team battles degraded into scattered free-for-alls. Even Kimdan seemed lost with a team and took to fighting by himself, ever in his flashy style, while his team members tried their best to form some sort of order. Harrick and Cadaen shook their heads disappointedly at the proceedings—until Gen took the field for the first time.

"Look at him!" the Regent exclaimed as Gen gathered his team and started issuing instructions.

"Imagine that," Cadaen said sarcastically. "Talking with your team *beforehand*. A novel concept. The serf should be rewarded for his innovation."

"I'm sure Kimdan would have done the same," Serena snorted, "if his teammates were not so far beneath his skill. It would be like commanding a herd of cows."

"The thought of working with his teammates never crossed his mind," her husband contradicted. "I never could get that boy interested in group tactics."

Even more surprising to all assembled was that Gen's high-born teammates listened and obeyed. In his first battle, Gen took command and ordered his men to form a tight wedge and charge quickly, throwing the unprepared opposing team into a discombobulated chaos. The wedge divided them easily. Gen barked orders, voice powerful and clear, and within moments his team had "killed" every one of the defenders. When it was over, Gen congratulated his teammates coolly.

"Now that was impressive," the First Mother remarked admiringly.

"And strange," Cadaen added. "For the first round he was content to underwhelm us all, and now he's out there barking orders like a field general and drawing all kinds of attention to himself."

"I too wonder at his change in strategy. What is his purpose?" Harrick questioned loudly over a crowd alive with comment.

It struck Fenna that she knew what his purpose was. He was going to try to force a confrontation with Kimdan, and the remainder of the battles bore her intuition out. The young men were moved around into different groups and thrown at each other as the Dark Guard sat and judged. Since Gen provided the example, almost all the teams tried some sort of group stratagem. But in the three additional matches in which Gen fought—two more than anyone else—he took command and countered the other teams' ploys with little difficulty, leading to quick victories each time.

Gen stirred up all kinds of speculation in the nobles sitting near Fenna, and the crowd was abuzz with anticipation every time he stepped onto the field. Most vocal were the common folk who came to view Gen as their "man," someone like themselves acquitting himself well in the realm of nobles. By Gen's third match, they raised his name in a chant. Serena very nearly lost her composure at their ebullience, sensing a decline in her son's notoriety.

Kimdan was red-faced and fuming over his inability to match Gen's skill at group combat, and she could tell by the way he stared at Gen that he was itching for a chance to face and beat him. But the Dark Guard never placed the two on the same team or on opposite sides, and by the time the second round ended, Kimdan was visibly furious, crossing his arms and tapping his foot, face indignant. Fenna felt a slight prick of satisfaction.

Again, Harrick, Cadaen, and the First Mother left to consult with the Dark Guard. It was well past noon, and the stands and field emptied as everyone went in search of food and entertainment before the final round began. The next round would not start for two hours to give everyone ample rest before the conclusion and to allow the First Mother and her advisers time to consider deeper cuts.

Fenna tied her bonnet on to protect her face from the sun and went in search of Gen, hoping she could catch him and offer him a meal so she could learn more of him. Much to her disappointment, she could find him nowhere, and the streets were too packed to do a quick or effective search. With a sigh she made her way to an inn and took her midday meal alone, anxious for the next round to start.

She wondered if the Chalaine had been watching using her *Walls*. The Chalaine, of course, was forbidden to come near a place with so many people, but to Fenna, the Chalaine seemed uninterested in the contest. She put all her energy of mind and will into preparing for the arrival of the Blessed One; she wanted everything to be perfect when he and she met, and her preparations in mind, body, and dress consumed her to the point of obsession.

"Who is he?" Kimdan's voice startled her, his eyes devoid of mirth and mockery for the first time she could remember. Strangely, no young ladies attended him.

"Who is who?" Fenna asked as innocently as possible, knowing full well whom he meant.

"Gen, that ragamuffin. I saw you talking to him earlier, remember?"

The acrimony of his tone soured any disposition she might have had to be kind or flirtatious. "I'm afraid I know little," Fenna replied truthfully. "I so wanted to speak with him after his magnificent performance in the second round, but I couldn't find him. I suppose a lot of people want to talk to him now. Did you notice how he defeated every other team easily?"

Fenna knew she was being mean, but couldn't help herself. Kimdan almost growled.

"Let him face me one-on-one and we'll see who wins easily!"

Kimdan strode angrily back out onto the street. Fenna fought down the urge to giggle and finished her lunch quickly. If Kimdan did find Gen, she was sure there would be a fight no matter how calm and collected Gen might be. She paid for her meal and affixed her bonnet, deciding to search a bit more.

After wandering the packed, noisy streets for over an hour, she gave up and threaded her way back to the tournament field to find most of the fighters milling about, anxious for news. She started walking back to the stands when she noticed Gen out of the corner of her eye, sitting on the fence where the common folk gathered and staring into the afternoon sky.

As promised, he was clean and had better clothes on, including a used pair of boots. With a smile she pushed through the crowd toward him. She could see now that his hair was dark brown, not the light brown the caked dirt had colored it. He was nowhere near as beautiful as Kimdan, the scars lending his countenance a disturbing edge, but he wasn't completely repulsive, either.

"I see you managed to get cleaned up before you saw me again, as you said." He turned toward her. The scars on his face showed more plainly now and she wondered what had happened to him.

"Yes, I did, Miss Fairedale. It seems I have a few friends among the common folk."

"You are their champion of the day. Do you intend to face Kimdan, then?"

Gen was silent for a moment before hopping off the fence to stand by her. "I will, should they permit me. He is a skilled fighter but needs to be tempered. It is clear that he will be a part of the Dark Guard. If we are to fight alongside each other, then he must learn to respect me and the other apprentices."

The trumpet sounded and people scrambled toward the stands, filling them quickly.

"Here," Fenna said, quickly removing her light blue sash and handing it to him. "It is not right that one doing so well should fight without the favor of a lady." Fenna hoped it would give her an excuse to talk to him again.

"I thank you, Miss Fairedale" Gen said formally, genuflecting. "I had better go see if I shall have the honor of bearing your favor at all."

"Wait!" Fenna exclaimed, realizing her forgetfulness as Gen hopped the fence. "Where are you from?"

Gen either didn't hear her or ignored her and Fenna cursed. A quick look into the Box revealed that the First Mother and her companions were watching her intently and awaiting her arrival. Fenna walked back slowly.

"I see our boy has been cleaned up a bit," the First Mother commented as Fenna sat down sheepishly. "I can also see by the look on your face that you got little out of him again."

"Forgive me, Highness," Fenna apologized. "I had just found him when the trumpet sounded. I do know that he hopes to face Kimdan and that some commoners bathed and clothed him."

"Well, he will have his chance at Kimdan. Everyone agreed that the two needed to face each other. Gen has the advantage over Kimdan for the captaincy because of his leadership during group combat. However, if I were to name Gen as the Captain's apprentice without him fighting Kimdan, I fear the high-born crowd would have my head."

Fenna nodded in agreement, a quiet thrill building inside

her.

"By Eldaloth!" Serena exclaimed, coming to her seat. "What noblewoman would dare bestow her favor to a serf, from Tolnor no less? I must find out who and have a talk with someone's mother! A shame. A pitiable shame! Perhaps she wished to reward him for the noble accomplishment of finding a bath."

Fenna sat as inconspicuously as possible as Serena produced a fan from her sleeve and worked it furiously. The First Mother turned and gave Fenna a furtive wink that Fenna took as an expression of approval for what she had done.

The second round of cuts were more painful that the first, leaving only twelve from which the six would be chosen. The third round reverted back to single combat. Unlike the first round, however, the combatants were to fight until only one remained standing, a brutal contest of endurance and skill. The First Mother would choose the six and from among them the Captain. Even those defeated could still find themselves in the Dark Guard, as she figured Gen or Kimdan would be despite the fact that one of them would be defeated.

One by one Tolbrook announced the pairings for the combat, and when it became apparent that Gen and Kimdan would fight each other, the crowd on both sides of the field roared in approval. Wagers were laid as the other bouts started and continued almost completely ignored. When the fifth bout ended and Tolbrook tried to announce the last pairing, his voice was submerged in a wave cacophony rolling in from both sides of the field.

"This is getting out of hand!" the First Mother yelled in Harrick's ear.

"My men can handle it," the Regent replied confidently, a glint of anticipation and excitement in his eyes. Serena sat straight-backed, dignified, and confident, only her desperate fanning hinting at her agitation.

The crowd finally settled down as Kimdan and Gen approached each other from opposite sides of the field. Fenna noted her sash tied about his waist, and Kimdan eyed it with disdain. She hoped Kimdan didn't know who it was from.

Captain Tolbrook strode forward to personally oversee the match. Both young men were calm and collected, but as Gen stepped toward the center of the field, he tripped over the heel of his own boot and landed flat on his face, sword skittering across the grass. Kimdan stopped it with his boot as the nobles in the crowd laughed. Serena produced a sound somewhere between cackling and crowing.

"What is this?" Kimdan said grandly, "I have felled him without a single stroke!"

Fenna's enthusiasm drained from her as the high-born crowd jeered. Gen wasn't ready for the noise and wildness of the assembly. Kimdan got his boot under the sword and flicked it high over Gen's head, forcing him to retrieve it like a dog fetching a stick.

"Well, that was inelegant," the First Mother observed. "A case of the nerves, Harrick? He seemed so poised before."

Harrick's face was split in a wide grin, as was Cadaen's. Fenna was confused by the old soldiers' reactions. The First Mother was too.

"No, Highness," Harrick replied mirthfully. "My son is about to get the education he so desperately needs." Serena's eyes darted to her husband briefly and then remained determinedly on her son.

"How so?" the First Mother asked, bewildered. Cadaen provided the answer.

"He faked it. He knows that Kimdan's weakness is his arrogance, so he is feeding him a large portion to fatten him up for the kill."

Fenna raised her eyebrows in unison with the First Mother. "How can you be sure?" Fenna blurted out before the First Mother had a chance.

"Fighters of his skill don't trip on their boots," Harrick replied. "Ever. Watch. This should be most amusing."

Gen recovered his sword and returned to face Kimdan. Captain Tolbrook stood between the men, explaining the rules as he had for each pairing before. The crowd hushed in anticipation, save those still mocking Gen for his clumsiness. Fenna noted that Gen's blunder subdued the ebullient mood of the commoners, their faces grave. Gen was slump-shouldered and beaten, and Kimdan bounced around as cocky and confident as ever.

Tolbrook's arm dropped.

Kimdan raised his sword.

Gen, all feigned defeat aside, sprang into action.

With a quick, precise stroke, Gen hit the wrist-bones on Kimdan's sword arm. Kimdan's face registered agony and he dropped his sword, falling back quickly before Gen could hit him again. Gen didn't press the attack. Instead, he took his own sword in two hands and threw it high into the air. All eyes followed the sword upward, including Kimdan's, and only the sickening crunch of Gen's fist on Kimdan's nose yanked all eyes back to the combatants.

Kimdan flopped backward, trying to retain his balance as blood spurted out of his nostrils. Without looking, Gen caught his falling sword by the hilt. Again, he didn't press the attack but waited while Kimdan collected himself. Harrick and Cadaen laughed, practically the only noise coming from the stands. Several of the Regent's companions, including his wife, stared at him with shock. How could a father enjoy the beating of his son?

"You dishonorable wretch!" Kimdan spat. "Will you attack an unarmed man?" To reply, Gen threw his own sword to Kimdan, who caught it, eyes wide. Gen kept his eyes fixed on Kimdan, making no move toward his opponent's sword, which lay on the ground nearby.

"He can't mean to fight Kimdan unarmed!" the First

Mother exclaimed incredulously, but Kimdan, despite the obvious hypocrisy, rushed Gen without inviting him to retrieve the available sword. In the split second Kimdan took to bring his sword back to strike, Gen moved inside the swing in a blur of motion and caught Kimdan's arm. In one fluid movement, Gen put his hand on Kimdan's chest and used the leverage to drive him hard, back-first, into the ground.

Breath exploded from Kimdan's lungs and gasps erupted from the crowd. Again, Gen did nothing as Kimdan, angry, got back up and rushed him again. This time, Gen pulled Kimdan forward as he thrusted, tripping him and stripping him of his sword at the same time. Before Kimdan could turn over, Gen tossed the sword at him offhandedly, hitting him in the back with it. Kimdan grabbed the sword and stood, and—for the first time that day—took a defensive posture.

In a heartbeat, Gen darted forward and punched Kimdan in the face so quickly that Kimdan couldn't react. Kimdan swung back, missing wildly, and in a blur Gen landed a staccato of blows all over Kimdan's body that came so fast that Fenna couldn't count them. Kimdan staggered backward, disoriented. While Kimdan struggled to focus his eyes, Gen retrieved the sword Kimdan had dropped and proceeded to punish him with it without mercy.

Due to Kimdan's confusion, Gen struck Kimdan at his own convenience, the defense paltry and inadequate. Gen, in an almost artistic fashion, covered Kimdan with welts, kicked him ferociously in the groin, kneed him in the head, and swept his legs out from under him. Kimdan, squirmed on the ground, not having enough hands to grab everywhere he was in pain. To spare Kimdan more shame, Tolbrook raised his hand and declared Gen the winner.

A great cheer erupted from the common folk while the high-born sat stunned. Serena cried at her son's plight.

Harrick and Cadaen, who had laughed heartily at the start of the spectacle, were sobered. Fenna's eyes went to Gen. Pride and gloating were absent from his face, and, in a show of good will, he extended his hand to help Kimdan up. Kimdan refused, struggling and finally standing on his own. Several clapped politely for his efforts, but Kimdan had lost the captaincy and he knew it.

Unlike before, the twelve were led away through the guardhouse gates and into a nearby Church where they were to wait, pray, and be healed as the First Mother and the Regents decided their fates. Six would eventually be called and returned to the field, each proudly bearing on their left breast the Im'Tith, the magical seal of all those who entered the Chalaine's close service, the same seal Fenna had worn since she was twelve.

"Will you please join us, Fenna?" the First Mother asked.

"Yes, your Grace," Fenna answered, surprised at the request.

She followed the First Mother, Cadaen, Captain Tolbrook, and the Regents down the stairway nearest the Box and across the street to a guard station.

A soldier near the door of the squat, gray-stone building snapped to attention while another opened the door. Once inside, they went down a hallway that passed a barracks and an armory, coming to a larger room with a well-weathered wooden oval table in the center. Ethris was there already, sitting in a corner near a narrow window and gazing outward with a pensive expression. There were enough chairs for everyone save Fenna, and, as she waited for one to be brought forward, the Regents chattered excitedly with each other, though some seemed troubled.

After Fenna had been seated, the First Mother called for silence.

"I am sorry to startle you by bringing you here, my dear Fenna, and you shall be released to your duties shortly.

Gentlemen, this young lady has talked to the young man who concerns us, and I have brought her here to ask her a few questions before we deliberate."

The Regents nodded their approval.

"First," Mirelle said to Fenna, "I know that you had little opportunity to converse with him. I want you to tell us everything he said, no matter how trivial it might have seemed."

Fenna did the best that she could, though she wanted to crawl under the table as she related the parts about her feelings for Kimdan, especially since his father was among those assembled. Harrick discomfited her with a lopsided smile. Even worse, Ethris studied her unblinkingly, and by the time she was finished, she felt quite unnerved.

"Thank you, Fenna, and I apologize for this necessity. One last thing. How do you mark his character? Could you tell anything about him from your brief moments with him?"

"He seemed honest, caring, and polite, Majesty. More than that, I cannot say. His face says nothing, though his eyes were kind."

The First Mother seemed satisfied with her answer and turned to the Magician. "Ethris, what could you discern when you subjected him to the test?"

Ethris stood and leaned on his Staff by the window. "He has an iron will, your Grace, almost frighteningly so. I have only known Magicians and Churchmen—and ones long in the tooth, mind you—to have such strength of mind. He also possesses a deep devotion and loyalty to the Chalaine. To be sure, the other candidates possess the same, but Gen's is of a different quality, the type of loyalty you would expect from a friend rather than one inspired by the abstract ideals of religion. It's almost as if he knows her. If you are asking if he is dangerous to her or an impostor, I would say no. He greatly desires to serve the Chalaine.

"My best judgment is that he would be an admirable

Dark Guard, perhaps the best to accept the honor in years. I am concerned, however, about his abilities. No one as young as he is should be so skilled, and no human has ever known the Kuri-tan."

"The what?" the First Mother asked.

"Kuri-Tan. It was an elven martial art. At the threat of Mikkik, the elves, at first, shunned weapons and weapon-making, learning instead an unarmed form of fighting they called Kuri-Tan. While unarmed fighting is known in human kingdoms, elven fighting is elegant and powerful, as we saw today. From the limited display we had, I cannot be certain it is the elven art, but I would wager it is."

"And you say it is unusual that he should know it?"

"Absolutely!" Ethris said. "For one, Maewen the half-elf is all anyone has seen of elves in two hundred and fifty years. Secondly, the elves would never teach a human the art. The humans begged them to teach it to them during the Mikkikian wars and they flatly refused."

"We will simply have to ask him about it," the First Mother said, "but I don't care so much about that as I do his character and his intentions, both of which I am satisfied with at present."

"Hold a moment, your Grace." Regent Julim Magravaine stood. He was old and thin, and he always held his gray-haired head high and dignified. "Doesn't Gen's utter humiliation of Kimdan—no offense, Harrick—show a certain meanness of character? I also noticed that during group combat he tended to hit the Aughmerians in the head and rather harder than others."

"'Tended to hit them in the head' is not correct," Tolbrook interjected. "He did not hit an Aughmerian except he hit him in the head. He was deliberately punishing them and doing his best to cast them in an incompetent light. I was watching carefully there to ensure things didn't get out of hand."

"Gentlemen," the First Mother said, lowering her voice

as if fearing being overheard, "I, for one, cannot and will not reproach him for his treatment of the Aughmerians." Murmurs of assent were heard throughout the room. "As for his treatment of Kimdan, Lady Fairedale gave us the answer; he wanted Kimdan's respect. I daresay he has it, however grudgingly. Kimdan needed humbling, and Gen has done us a service there, if you'll forgive me, Harrick."

"You know I agree with you, your Grace," Regent Ogbith replied. "I shall thank him for the service one day. Cadaen and I share Ethris's curiosity about his skills, but I find no fault in his behavior today."

Regent Magravaine tried to conceal his agitation and sat down.

"Very well, I am satisfied with his fitness then," the First Mother pronounced. "Captain Tolbrook, you have a new apprentice. I'm sure you'll find him quite different from Dason."

"Indeed," Tolbrook replied thoughtfully.

"The real question," Regent Ogbith piped in, smile splitting his face, "is if Tolbrook can teach the boy anything."

At this, Tolbrook took offense, and he, the Regents, and Cadaen all broke out into wild speculation and argument about Gen's experience and abilities. Ethris's comments bolstered Fenna's resolve to find out more about the young man and the root of his devotion to her Mistress.

After a few minutes, an amused First Mother calmed the men. "Gentlemen, we shall all, no doubt, want to be present when the new apprentices undergo their skill tests so we can see just what Gen can do, but now we have eleven—well, ten—other young men up for our consideration and must get to it soon lest the crowd become impatient.

"Fenna, you are free to go. I charge you to say nothing of what was said here. I also command you to speak with Gen when you can and become his friend, for he will be alone when he enters service with the high born."

"Gladly, your highness," Fenna answered, the First Mother smiling at her knowingly. Fenna felt fit to burst with what she had learned, and she had to try hard to say nothing as she returned to the Box and found herself besieged with questions from her court-bred peers, Serena included. But soon, finding they could extract nothing from her, they left her alone.

The sun was sinking, throwing long shadows across the field. The smells of roasted meats, baked breads, and stewed vegetables made Fenna's mouth water, but she hadn't the stomach or inclination to eat until the ceremony was over.

Just at the onset of evening, the First Mother and her councilors returned, all save Ethris who Fenna knew had gone to the Church to perform the magical branding and dismiss those not chosen. The crowd raced back to their seats or to line the fence. Fenna noted that the streets brimmed with even more common folk than before, and their enthusiasm charged the air with excitement.

With great effort, the First Mother managed to silence everyone. A trumpet blew, and the gate to the field was thrown open. A herald rode through on a white horse, bearing a flag with a black rose on a white field, the colors of the Chalaine.

"Hear ye, hear ye, people of Ki'Hal. Six men have recently entered the service of the Chalaine, the blessed future mother of our God. They are released from what former duties were theirs to dedicate their bodies, their hearts, and their minds to protecting the Chalaine from Mikkik, his Ilch, and all other evils. I present them to you now.

"Gen, serf of Tolnor, an orphan of no family, apprenticed to Captain Tolbrook, hereby set apart to be Captain of the Dark Guard."

The commoners cheered and celebrated, much to the

chagrin of the peerage who, while they did not like it, could not fault the decision. Captain Tolbrook, now wearing the half-moon tabard of the Dark Guard, strode onto the field, his apprentice, shirtless so the Im' Tith could be seen, came behind him as calm and emotionless as he was when the Captain's men first dragged him across the field earlier that day. Fenna noted that the First Mother was as shocked as she was at the mention of the Gen's status as an orphan.

As the herald announced the others, the people were almost too abuzz with talk of Gen to applaud when Kimdan's name was read. Volney Torunne and two brothers from Aughmere, Ghent and Pahram Mail, had been chosen. Gerand Kildan of Tolnor rounded out the six, joining Gen to represent his besieged nation among the apprentices. When the herald was finished, the First Mother stood and signaled for the men to come toward her. They knelt, and, after a brief speech of congratulations and gratitude, she released the young men to their masters.

"Tolbrook versus Gen!" someone shouted from the commoner side of the crowd. The aristocracy acted shocked as the commoners laughed at the remark.

"Well," Serena said acidly, "Tolnor is certainly well represented. I shall see you at home, Oggie. Do not stay out too late drinking."

After bowing to the First Mother, Serena departed, Fenna hoping she wouldn't inquire further into the identity of Gen's lady benefactor.

"What do you say, First Mother," Regent Ogbith said mirthfully. "Should we open Gen's skill test to everyone? It would, no doubt, be almost as disorderly as this."

"Certainly not!" the First Mother said, feigning outrage.

While everyone filtered into the city and turned their attention to celebration, the new apprentices were to spend the night in meditation and prayer. Fenna watched Gen—proud that he still wore her sash—as he left in the company of the Captain. She wanted to run and congratulate him, but seeing someone lighting a lantern at the approach of dark reminded her that she needed to hurry back to the Chalaine and relieve Eldwena. She would have plenty of time to track Gen down tomorrow. For now, she wanted to talk to the Chalaine about her newest defender.

CHAPTER 17 - THE NAKED BLADE

Gen left the Church with his fellow apprentices at the break of dawn. Captain Tolbrook collected them and led them by the competition field where they had fought the day before. The streets were empty and quiet, the mass of revelers still sleeping off a night of celebration. What few people milled about stopped to watch the young men pass formidably by, all six apprentices now dressed smartly in the high-collared, black uniform of the Dark Guard. New swords, blessed and given them by the Prelate Obelard of Mikmir, hung at their sides in scabbards made of finely tooled leather embroidered with silver.

Tolbrook set a quick pace. Gen glanced back at his sword-mates. A tense, grueling day at the Trials and a night spent awake in meditation and prayer sapped the liveliness from their step and the brightness from their eyes. Kimdan, while tired, was the most alert and angry of the lot, and Gen needed little experience or training to know that a long time would pass before Kimdan would lose the sting of failing to secure the captaincy. Gen predicted Kimdan would strive at every opportunity to demonstrate his apprentice-captain's weaknesses and flaws.

Tolbrook took them around the back of the practice

fields to the front of a squat gray building nearby. Gen thought Tolbrook remarkably resembled Pureman Millershim—well-built with a ring of graying black hair around his head. Tolbrook's hooked nose and small, beady eyes were the only things that separated him from being Millershim's twin. Gen would have believed it if someone told him they were brothers.

"Apprentices, welcome home," Tolbrook said, indicating the building behind them. "Most of you will find the accommodations sparser than what you're used to. You will share a room with one of your fellow apprentices, and you must be clear on one thing: you have no servants here, only masters. No one will do your laundry, see to your beds, or build your fire. If you have difficulty with these tasks, you will address your concern to your Captain, who will help you."

"No doubt he knows how to do all the women's chores," Kimdan whispered a little too loudly. Tolbrook stopped his speech to stare at the Regent's son. Gen thought Millershim possessed the fiercer eyes, but Tolbrook could wither with a stare quite admirably.

"Well, Kimdan Ogbith," Tolbrook began in a scalding tone. "Still jealous, are we? I thank you for your little outburst, for it will allow me to address another point. When you serve with the Dark Guard, there are no aristocrats, nobles, servants, serfs, merchants, or princes. When you serve with the Dark Guard, you do not endanger, mock, or abuse another member of the Dark Guard—ever.

"If, Kimdan, I hear you say another word against your Captain or any of your sword-mates again, I will have you dismissed, regardless of who your father is. Regent Ogbith informed me himself that you are arrogant and gave me full permission to send you packing home at my convenience. Is that understood?"

"Yes, sir," Kimdan said firmly but not humbly,

straightening to attention.

"Very well. Your meals you will take in the castle commons. In all other matters of schedule and time, you are at the mercy of your masters. Every Sixthday, you have the afternoon and evening to yourselves to take care of personal business and recreate yourselves as you see fit. You will, however, wear the uniform at all times and comport yourself as befits a member of the Dark Guard. You have the rest of this day off so that you can attend to your friends and relations and prepare for the arrival of the Ha'Ulrich.

"You do have an assignment, however. Familiarize yourself with the main areas of the castle if you don't know them. You will be expected to be on duty in the Great Hall promptly at the beginning of sixth watch for the feast. It will be your privilege to be in attendance with the Chalaine and the Ha'Ulrich. Remember, you will be on duty, not there to woo or mingle. If there are no questions, then see the Quartermaster inside for your bunking assignments. Dismissed!"

Gen led the way into the building as Volney Torunne nearly fell over himself in delight about the chance to see the Chalaine and the Ha'Ulrich. Volney was tall and broad at the shoulders, massive arms hinting at the power Gen had felt when crossing swords with him. His face was round and kind, framed by close-cropped brown hair. Large brown eyes shone with excitement.

"Are we not fortunate, indeed?" he effused to Gerand Kildan. "We shall be some of the first ones to see the two of them together in the same place! I cannot help but feel unworthy of such an honor. What will we do if they should speak to us? Surely the Chalaine will want to know who we are!"

"Calm yourself, Volney," Gen interjected. "It is an honor, but we best serve the Chalaine by being alert and attentive. Having both the Chalaine and the Ha'Ulrich in one place is dangerous and an excellent opportunity for the Ilch to prepare some strike against them. Be wary, not overwhelmed."

"Well said," Gerand agreed.

"Yes, yes," Volney stammered. "You are right."

To Gen's satisfaction, the Quartermaster assigned him a room with Gerand Kildan. Seeing his countryman reminded him of the picture he had seen of him at Shadan Khairn's manor house on the Ellenais shard, and the likeness was exact. Gerand's eyes were determined but bore the weight of someone striving to prove himself. From what he saw of Gerand's matches during the Trials, with a little training the Duke's son would be a force to be reckoned with. His demeanor was pleasant but subdued, and Gen found him the most mature of his fellow apprentices.

He wanted to question his countryman about the war and what Shadan Khairn had done since the start of spring, but after a perfunctory conversation about the plainness of the room, Gerand left, saying he was to meet his mother and sister who had left Tolnor before the war spread. Finding himself alone, Gen tested the bed, and, finding it thoroughly unfit for sleeping, left for the castle, thinking food from the First Mother's prosperous larder would do him good.

The sun was full up now, and groggy merchants mechanically set up their booths and shops. Today the Ha'Ulrich would arrive, and potential customers would fill streets and swell profits. At first Gen thought he might brave the crowds for a glimpse of the Ha'Ulrich upon his arrival, but Tolbrook's announcement that the apprentices would be on duty with him that night lessened his enthusiasm. The short time he had spent in Mikmir made him long for empty country lanes, and he found he disliked the noise and press of the city, although, he admitted to himself, he hadn't seen the better parts.

261

The castle Mikmir sat only two miles from the tournament field, situated atop a low hill that commanded a stunning view of the Kingsblood Lake and the river that stretched westward toward the sea. The gates were shut and guarded—though the portcullis was up—and many soldiers patrolled the walls. The Rhugothians took the protection of the Chalaine seriously and always had, even in less portentous times.

Gen wondered if he needed a password, but as he approached, a guard unlocked an inner door built into the gate and opened it for him. The guards congratulated him on his success at the Trials and closed the door behind him.

After passing through the thick walls into the courtyard, Gen found the interior buildings a mix of the old and new. The walls, the Chapel, and the keep were constructed of rough gray granite, a tough but unattractive stone. In contrast, the Great Hall, its attendant outbuildings, and the Chalaine's tower—on a small shard of its own—gleamed in the morning sunlight, all built with highly polished white marble. Trees with plum-colored leaves grew in circular planters set in regular patterns about the courtyard, all pruned into dome shapes and casting broad shadows. Near the trees, benches of the same polished stone provided excellent places for conversation or reading.

Gen stopped. Where was he supposed to go? Walking up to the great doors of the Great Hall and asking entry seemed inappropriate, so he went around toward the back where he guessed the kitchens would be. On the way, he passed the stables, which were alive with the preparations of mighty horses with shining black coats. They were receiving brushings and braidings, no doubt in preparation for the arrival of the Ha'Ulrich. Two white horses were the subject of even more decoration. The farriers, having finished their part of the work, hailed Gen as he passed.

"Good work yesterday, lad!" one said. "Did me good to see Kimdan take a whippin.' Did me good like you could never know!"

"That's double for me," the other chimed in. "You come by and it's a drink on us at a tavern 'a your choosin'."

Gen thanked them and waved, pressing on toward the sound of children playing. He found them chasing each other around in a nicely appointed yard bordered with tall pines. The smells coming from a nearby side door were unmistakable, and Gen entered. Nearly everyone noticed his entrance and all activity stopped instantly.

"I was looking to take the morning meal," he explained to the collection of surprised faces. All of a sudden, a plump woman with short dark curly hair was upon him before he could protest, and Gen found himself the recipient of an enthusiastic hug.

"This is him!" the woman said, releasing him and addressing the others. "This is Gen! Welcome, young master! I'm Marna. You've a room full of friends here. You were magnificent yesterday! Striking low, striking high!"

Marna brandished a rolling pin, and Gen fought down a smile. "I tell you," she went on, "that I've never been treated more rudely by any man than that Kimdan Ogbith. Seeing you kicking 'im in his manhood brought a smile to me face that won't fade any time soon. Oh, but look what I've done to that uniform!"

Gen glanced down to find the black cloth of his uniform mottled with several patches of flour. Marna tried to wipe them off, enlarging the stains, and only after assuring her several times that it was all right and that he would take care of it and that he wasn't angry did she relent.

"Well, I'm sorry all the same," she said. "But, you said you wanted some food. From now on, you can enter the commons from the rear entrance of the Great Hall, not that we would mind you coming to visit us here whenever you like. If that ol' mealworm Captain Tolbrook doesn't let you eat much, well, you just come by here and we'll fix you up proper."

Gen thanked her, quite sure he'd never been so welcome anywhere before.

"But wait!" Marna said as he started to leave. "Mercy me. You're not to eat until you are presented to the First Mother. You're the first to come through this morning and I almost forgot, though the Door Wardens would have told you."

"Where should I enter? Through the commons?"

"Why no, silly," Marna clucked in a motherly fashion. "You march right through that front door. You might not be a noble or an aristocrat, but a Dark Guard is something better. That's what I always say. And you don't let those snobs sneer down at you."

"Thank you again." Gen gave Marna a little bow, and she smiled.

"You come right back here and get your food, if you like!"

Gen took the long way around the back of the Great Hall just to get to know where everything was, all the while working to get the flour off his uniform with only limited success. If he'd had time to let it dry, he thought he would have better luck, but he didn't want to keep the First Mother or his stomach waiting, whatever the condition of his uniform. Once around the front of the building, he ascended the steps, a castle guard standing at rigid attention on each one. As at the castle gate, the doors opened for him as if he were expected.

Gen entered and the doors closed with a deep boom. He found himself in a broad hallway with another set of heavily ornate doors before him, those leading into the Great Hall proper. Two guards stood there, as well as an older man, dressed finely in purple and silver robes. Thin gray hair stuck out in all directions from his head, and he leaned his head on his staff of office. Gen guessed this was the Chamberlain, though the sunshine from high, arching windows showed that his eyes were closed. He was asleep standing up.

"You'll have to wake him," one of the soldiers whispered. "His son does most of the work nowadays, but the First Mother loves old Hurney here and will likely keep him in service until he falls over dead."

Chamberlain Hurney snorted and came awake. "I am not dead!" he protested, poking his staff into the ribs of the guard who had said nothing. "Ah, there's the lad I was hoping to meet. I am the Chamberlain, Chamberlain Hurney Fedrick, at your service." He executed a small bow. "Capital performance, yesterday. Absolutely capital! But, my goodness! What a lot of scars you have! Well, the First Mother will see you shortly. It is a busy day. However, I just want to say that Kimdan deserved every lick you gave him yesterday. Spoiled whelp."

"I'm starting to get the feeling he isn't well liked," Gen commented.

"Oh, he's well-liked by the ladies and probably isn't too bad of a fellow. A little too proud for my taste, though. I have to ask, however, which lady gave you her favor?"

"Lady Fenna Fairedale," Gen answered. "She serves as the Chalaine's handmaiden."

"Ah," the Chamberlain intoned with a sly wink. "She was here loitering around earlier today, waiting for someone, I think. Now there's a pretty girl if I ever did see one. A kind one, too, if she's given her colors to a commoner—not to say that you didn't earn them! You are a serf in Tolnor, correct?"

"Yes, sir."

"Well," Hurney said, patting him on the back, "that's doesn't matter at all now that you're a Dark Guard. Every nobleman you'll meet will know that you can whack his legs off without much effort, and they'll be polite enough."

The inner doors swung open, and Gen watched as several Churchmen, deep in conversation, filed out.

Hurney squeezed his arm. "Looks like it's your turn.

Follow me."

The Chamberlain walked through the doors and, planting his feet, struck the floor three times with his staff. "I present, Gen, recently apprenticed to the Dark Guard, who has come as requested by Her Majesty. He bears no rank or family name of note."

Gen was surprised at the power in his aged voice.

"Let him come before me," the First Mother said brightly. Gen strode forward, taking in the Great Hall and finding it the most magnificent room he had ever set foot in. The marble here was white blushed with red, and sleek, tapered columns rose to an arched roof. Finely worked balustrades lined balconies on either side of him, and the whole room was bathed in sunlight streaming in from a large arched window behind the dais and along the apex of the roof. Tapestries with images of Aldradan Mikmir, legendary king and general of Rhugoth, hung on the walls.

Gen wished he could stop and examine everything more closely, but he kept his head high and turned forward, his face controlled and his steps even and confident. About halfway toward the throne Gen quickly reviewed the lessons Rafael had taught him about presentation to Rhugothian aristocracy, but several other manners of presentation swam about his head from ages past. He strove to keep Rafael's more current instruction in mind. The old bard had played in Rhugothian court before, though not as the main attraction.

The First Mother sat on a burnished wooden throne next to a larger, empty throne of stone and metal, the throne of Aldradan Mikmir, a throne left unoccupied for centuries. Gen remembered from Rafael's history lessons that the people in Rhugoth waited for Aldradan to return, though Rafael said most now accepted that the king was not immortal and lost, but rather long dead and buried. The First Mother was more than the equal to the grandeur of the room, beautiful and commanding. Her youth struck him as it had on the field the day before, and he reasoned that she must have been very young when she gave birth to the Chalaine.

The Magician Ethris stood slightly behind her, face serious, as did the guard Gen saw with her at the Trials. A young, dark-haired scribe sat at a desk nearby, busily writing with a colorful plume. The First Mother smiled as he approached, only increasing the youthful beauty of her face.

Once at the base of the dais, Gen went to genuflect, but instead of bending at the knee as a commoner must do before royalty, something from Telmerran took over. Gen drew his sword and placed it before him, point east, and then went to both knees and placed his head upon the sword. The First Mother's guard loosened his sword in his scabbard and Gen realized that he had made a mistake.

"Resheathe your sword and rise," the First Mother said. "It has been a long time since a naked blade has been seen in this room."

"And even longer," Ethris piped in concernedly, "since anyone has used that manner of genuflection. Do you even know what it means, boy?"

"Forgive me, Milday," Gen apologized as he stood and slid his sword into his scabbard. "This is the first time I've been at Court or near one. I do know what it means, sir."

"Then pray tell us, Gen," the First Mother requested, glancing questioningly at Ethris. "For I do not." The scribe stopped writing, regarding Gen with interest.

"The naked blade," Gen explained, "symbolizes that trouble is near at hand. The point is set against the east, from whence Mikkik first arose. The knees are bent as a mark of fealty and trust for one's Lord or Lady, and the forehead upon the blade signifies that the weapon will be used with forethought and intelligence, not impulse and passion."

"Well, Ethris," the First Mother asked, "is he right?"

"Perfectly," the Mage replied, rubbing his chin

thoughtfully.

"I apologize if I have defiled the hall or worried your protector."

"On the contrary," the First Mother said. "I find it charming and appropriate for the times. As you are Captain of the apprentices, I order you to teach your peers this manner of presentation. I will instruct Tolbrook to learn it from you as well so that all the Dark Guard will use it."

"As you wish, your Grace."

"But we are not offended. Cadaen was only surprised. He is anxious for my health and has served me long and well. In turn, I hope you were not offended by our Chamberlain's introduction. Family and rank are always part of introductions at court."

"If I were offended by the truth, I would have deeper problems than my pedigree," Gen said, painfully aware of Ethris staring at him intently.

"Very well. I welcome you to court and extend my congratulations to you for your fine exhibition at the Trials. I must admit that I am eager to spend some time with you and ask you more questions than you will likely want to answer. I know the rest of the apprentices somewhat by reputation or through association with their families, but you, quite literally, are an unlooked-for—though not unwelcome—surprise. If it were any other day, I would ask you to take a meal with me, but with the arrival of the Blessed One, I am too busy to take the leisure. I will call on you ere long, however."

"I will await your pleasure, Highness" Gen said, bowing to show his gratitude for the First Mother's graciousness.

"But I must ask you a question," she said, a smile coming to her lips. "Did they not launder your uniform before giving it to you?"

Gen had hoped she wouldn't notice. "I am most recently the victim of an eager embrace from a kitchen cook named Marna, whom I knew not before today, but whose favor and affection I have unintentionally earned in overwhelming proportions. It is the unfortunate union of black cloth and white apron that sees me thus arrayed. Again, I apologize to the court."

The First Mother laughed, a sound Gen thought he would like to hear more often. "You take us altogether too seriously, Gen. Marna is well-loved and to bear evidence of her regard is no insult to the court."

"Still, I must beg permission to leave before I commit a third blunder and bring everlasting shame upon myself. I promise to spend some time with the Chamberlain so that he may instruct me more completely in Rhugothian manners."

The First Mother laughed again. "You may have to wake him first. Oh, but you must smile, Gen, or how am I to know if you are joking? But as you are resolved to such a serious demeanor, I will grant you leave, but look for an invitation from me soon. And for a quick lesson, when you depart the room, you must only bow before you turn away from me."

Gen knew this, but he figured feigning ignorance the wiser course. "Thank you, Highness, for your patience. I will be honored to meet with you again. Good day."

Gen bowed and walked out with the same steady gait he entered with. The guards, smirking at the flour-smeared uniform, opened the doors for him, and the Chamberlain, still awake, grabbed him by the arm.

"How'd you do lad? You weren't in there long."

"Poorly, sir." Hurney's yes widened.

"Why yes, yes! I should have thought about that before sending you in there! You're a commoner from another land. How could you know?"

Between introductions, Hurney instructed him on every detail of proper address and presentation to nobility and aristocracy in Rhugoth and wouldn't let him leave before Gen knew the names and standards of all the Regents,

Dukes, and Warlords in the three kingdoms.

By the time he left, breakfast was long over, but it took no effort to coax Marna to scrape up some food for him. Afterward, Gen explored the Great Hall further, finding an exquisite atrium and a well-stocked and well-lit library. Gen could think of nothing he would like to do more than reading, something he'd not been permitted to do under Shadan Khairn's tutelage. Selecting one book from so many fine ones took some time, but he spent the balance of the morning comfortably entrenched in a book of poetry.

Finding himself relaxed for the first time in months, and, owing to his lack of rest from the toil of the day before, he eventually drifted off to sleep, awaking with a start some time later. Judging the angle of the light coming through the high arching windows, he knew he'd missed lunch. Not having the heart to beg another meal from Marna and risk further distress to his uniform, Gen resolved to go without and return to the guardhouse to work sword forms before his duty that evening. But as he rose to go, Gerand and Volney entered the library in a bustle.

"There you are!" Volney said. "We must hurry or we'll miss it. You should be grateful the scullery maids kept good track of you. Probably the first time they'd even *seen* the library."

"You mean miss the Ha'Ulrich?" Gen asked.

"Of course!" Volney said. "What an honor! Let's go. His ship was seen on the lake just minutes ago!"

"We won't be able to see him at all in the throng, I would think," Gen speculated, letting himself be dragged off.

"You forget," Gerand said, pointing at Volney and himself, "that we two are nobles, and nobles get certain privileges. You may not be a noble, but stay with us. You'll have a perfect vantage point, trust me."

The day was warm, the sky clear, and the wind gusting.

As he expected, a great gathering of people constricted the lane that led to the castle to little more than a path, but Gerand and Volney led him away down a different, guarded route where those of the upper class went on carriage and horse to the pier.

When they arrived at the water's edge, Gen found that large covered stands were erected near the platform that extended out into the lake, and as his companions promised, they had a good vantage point some ten rows up. Anyone who could lay claim to the title noble was there, and the general noise made conversation impossible unless mouth and ear were in close proximity.

Close to the pier, a group of nearly one hundred darkly dressed Churchmen stood in formation. Their black robes flapped in the wind, and others huddled with backs against the gale, trying to light incense lamps. Brightly colored flags lined the pier, whipping and snapping, one Rhugothian guard standing at attention at the base of each. The mood around them was an odd mixture of worship and wild celebration, an equal mix of chanting Puremen and singing performers, the reverent and the restless.

Gen turned toward the lake, finding the water choppy and uneven in the wind. A massive ship bedecked in the red colors of Aughmere floated low in the water, sails stowed. The flag of Aughmere, sporting the emblem of the hammer and sword, flew next to the Ha'Ulrich's, the symbol of the veiled Trys, a black flag with a white ring.

"There's a flag I could do without seeing," Gerand commented on seeing Aughmere's colors. Gen nodded in agreement.

Fanfare and a shout farther up the road toward the castle finally silenced to the crowd, and at the same time Gen noticed the sailors lowering the Aughmerian ship's landing boat into the water on the port side. At this sign, the Churchmen launched into a hymn, beautiful and haunting, while eight Puremen swung their lamps slowly back and forth, fragrant, thick smoke swirling in the wind and blowing over the crowd. The song, which neither Gen nor his companions recalled hearing before, subdued the festivity and brought a quiet order to the street.

You rise with the sun,
Savior and King,
To mold us as one
Beneath your wing.
Your praises we sing.

The light of our faith,
Mother and Queen,
For our God the gate
In your womb unseen,
Your praises we sing.

Eldaloth, our God
By evil slain,
Our rule and our rod,
Shout, shout the refrain;
Our God is come again!

From two, the one.
From two, the one.
Holy Mother!
Holy King!
Our God they bring!

Volney shook with excitement, and even the more solemn Gerand wore an anticipatory smile. As they watched the street, those in the crowd below fell to their knees and bowed as a figure in white astride a white horse rode by. The Chalaine, riding sidesaddle, was taller than most women, and, while it might have been trick of the light, she seemed to shine. She rode with grace, back straight, veiled head forward. Beside her was a saddled but empty horse, and around her a wall of soldiers, those nearest her of the Dark Guard, Captain Tolbrook proudly in command.

Jaron and Dason, the Chalaine's personal protectors and the finest sword talents of the Dark Guard, walked on either side of the horse. Jaron, a severe-looking veteran, had a large head—cheeks rough with stubble—atop a powerful neck and shoulders. Close-cropped black hair grayed at the temples, and blue eyes took in everything around them.

Dason was a handsome, courtly-looking man with shoulder length, curly black hair and some of the finest clothes of any in attendance. His face was clean-shaven, perfectly proportioned, and inviting. Jaron scowled as he marched, but Dason smiled grandly, clearly at home in jubilant occasions.

Gen marveled at Dason's position. He was younger than any of the Dark Guard and at such an age was considered a greater swordsman than them all. Gen surmised that his younger brother, Gerand, would someday be just as good.

Gen studied the Chalaine the most, however, and knew he was not alone in that worship. She looked much as she had when he first saw her in the Damned Quarter, shrouded in white and veiled in mystery. Her loose robes whipped about with the wind, and he could just make out a thin circlet of silver set upon her covered head. Chants of "Holy Mother" erupted spontaneously from the crowd. Several worshipers prostrated themselves as she rode by, and the guards found themselves pushing the passionate, surging crowd back on more than one occasion.

Regent Ogbith, the First Mother, and Ethris rode just behind the Chalaine, waving to the crowd, faces strangely somber. On the lake, the landing party approached. Gen felt a surge of excitement. Here, at last, the Ha'Ulrich and the Chalaine would meet and the great prophecy start its march toward fulfillment. He made a note to thank Volney and Gerand for finding him and bringing him along. The nobles and the Warlords in the stands rose and bowed as the Chalaine rode by, Gen following suit. He knew he should kneel, as he was a commoner, but the stands provided no room to do so.

After bowing for some time, the nobles returned to their seats and watched Chertanne, the Ha'Ulrich, Blessed One of Eldaloth, approach. Gen kept his eye on the Chalaine as she dismounted. For reasons he couldn't explain, he felt drawn to her from the moment he saw her kindness and selflessness in her treatment of those far below her station who were inconsequential in importance. The crowd's reaction convinced him his feelings were not unique. In preparation for the Blessed One's landing, she went to one knee, head bowed. Just behind her, the others in the van followed suit.

All attention turned to the pier as the oars were pulled in and the craft secured. The wind had relented enough for the incense smoke to cloud a good view of the Ha'Ulrich as he disembarked. Another fanfare and chorus split the air as the Ha'Ulrich stepped onto the planks shadowed by a massive, bald swordsman—Cormith, Sword-Protector of the Ha'Ulrich, trained by the Shadan to serve his son.

The pier was long, and Gen strained to see the Ha'Ulrich. To his surprise, two greyhounds were lifted from the boat. They dashed quickly up the pier, barking and running along the lakeshore before turning toward the Chalaine. They pawed at her, dark mud from the shore sullying her dress. She bore it graciously, and at last the Ha'Ulrich whistled for them and they heeled.

And then he emerged from the smoke and stood before her, feet planted apart. Gen gazed upon the Blessed One, the Savior of nations, and instead of admiration, he felt shock. Nothing in the young man's appearance evidenced that his father was Torbrand Khairn. Instead, Chertanne—dressed in a red cape, white shirt and breeches, and black boots—reminded Gen of a successful merchant. He was fat and puffy, sweaty—even with the wind—and carried himself with a whimsical, careless air. In stark contrast to his father, Chertanne wore short, almost shorn, blond hair that badly accented a blanched face. With difficulty, Gen could make out the dark circle above his right eye, the birthmark sign of his divine identity.

The Chalaine rose, and Gen wondered if anyone else could see the small mannerisms—the hesitancy, the slightly pulled-in shoulders—that betrayed her surprise. Judging by Volney's and Gerand's faces and by the swooning, chanting crowd, Gen doubted it. Chertanne awkwardly took her hand and pulled her into a smothering embrace, swinging her about like a child. The crowd roared its approval. The Chalaine straightened her robes and veil after Chertanne set her down and watched as he played to the crowd, walking up and down the throng, arms wide in a show of magnificence as the swooning crowd yelled, "Bless me!" The chorus of Churchmen chanted rhythmically, and the whole crowd was caught up in the rhythm, some chanting along.

Unlike everyone around him, Gen sensed that something had gone terribly wrong. The Chalaine stood ignored and slightly bent, working away at the mud stains on her dress while Chertanne reveled with the crowd. He shook hands, embraced people at random without a care for his safety, and even took a drink from a proffered mug. Once he was done, the Ha'Ulrich mounted the provided horse and rode off without acknowledging the Chalaine at all. Jaron quickly stepped forward and assisted the Chalaine back into her saddle, and the Dark Guard had to jog to catch up with the rest of the procession.

The Blessed One's little acts of impropriety toward the Chalaine irritated Gen, though he chose not to show it. He supposed that the irritation stemmed a little from a disappointment. When he set eyes on the Chalaine, she was

275

everything he'd expected her to be and more. Chertanne was far less than what he imagined, though he realized he had carved his idea of Chertanne from what he knew of Torbrand. Expectations, he knew, were dangerous once formed and believed, and he resolved to set aside his feelings about Chertanne until he could better judge his character. Aughmerians treated women differently that Tolnorians and Rhugothians, and he had to give Chertanne some allowance for his nationality. He did seem friendly enough.

"Marvelous!" Volney said ecstatically. "If I were to die tomorrow, my children would say their father lived a fulfilled life."

"You have children?" Gerand asked incredulously as they made their way down the stands.

"No," Volney backtracked, "I mean if I had any, that's what they would say. I can hardly wait until the feast tonight! Our first night on duty! What an honor!"

"If you die tomorrow," Gen deadpanned, "it will likely be from the feeling of too much honor."

Gerand grinned. Volney looked offended for a few moments until his gentler nature took over and a smile crossed his face.

"Gen!"

Fenna raised her hand, working her way through the crowd toward him. She wore her brown hair in a bun against the wind and her green eyes were happy.

"I need an escort back to the castle," she said breathlessly, taking his arm. "The crowd presses so. I fear being trampled."

"Lady Fairedale," Volney said, scraping low. "It is an honor to meet one of the handmaidens of the Chalaine, an honor indeed!"

Gerand shook his head and Fenna smiled.

"Come along, Volney," Gerand said, pulling the young man away. "We've got something to attend to."

"We do?" Volney replied quizzically.

"Yes. We shall catch up with you later, Captain."

"Thank you, Gerand," Fenna said.

Gen nodded as Gerand shot him a smile.

"I suppose you've come for your colors?" Gen asked. "The Chamberlain instructed me that I am to return them to you or I risk offending you."

"Yes," Fenna said. "But you can't now. You must seek me out to return them, not the other way round. Favors are a way a lady may politely lay claim to a man's time and attention."

"I fear Kimdan will miss the entire first year of his training just to complete that courtesy alone."

Gen noted the tenseness around her eyes. Kimdan's lack of attention still stung her.

She forced a smile. "Let's not talk about Kimdan, shall we? I think I said quite enough about him when we first met."

CHAPTER 18 - THE WEDGE

The celebration commenced with the grand entrance of the Blessed One, Savior of Ki'Hal, Mikkiksbane, and the Master and Uniter of the Nations. Trumpets blew, praises were sung, and knees bent in his honor as he strutted slowly to the table at the head of the Hall, waving energetically to the cheering nobles and Warlords.

He wore a white shirt bedecked with lace, tailored to give his ample gut room to hang over his black pants. A red sash accented the ensemble, lending his face a more sanguine appearance than the corpse-white color it had seemed at the docks. His lips were bulbous and curled, affixing his countenance with a permanent, arrogant sneer. Fat rimmed or engorged the fine features of his face, lending normal eyes a beady appearance. In the Chalaine's estimation, he possessed but one kingly attribute—a deep, commanding voice that carried everywhere.

After a short speech about not wanting to delay the proceedings with a speech, he sat down, put his arm around the Chalaine, and tugged her roughly to him to thunderous applause. The Chalaine bore it patiently, grateful for the swarm of servants swooping into the room, distracting Chertanne from his attentions to her with platters laden with steaming pheasant, pork, ripe fruit, and a wide range of breads, cheeses, and wines to satisfy every taste. Steamed and spiced fish, brought in last, accented the head table with the bright colors of purple, blue, and yellow.

After those at the dais were served—and Chertanne was oblivious to everything but food—the servants descended to the main floor and then ascended to the balconies to deliver the meal and satisfy the demands of the jovial crowd.

Once the servants had set every table, the court bard, Shemus, ascended the dais. The middle-aged performer sported long dark hair braided together into a ponytail that dropped halfway down his back. Once skinny, his position in the First Mother's court had puffed him up around the midsection of his festive yellow tunic and green hose. He bowed, a grand smile playing across his tall face. Chertanne appeared genuinely excited to see the bard and stopped eating in anticipation. The Chalaine knew Shemus's pride had recently been stung by the appointment of a Tolnorian bard, Geoff, for the duty of recording her and the Ha'Ulrich's journey to Elde Luri Mora.

"Ladies and Gentlemen," Shemus said loudly, but the noise of the crowd continued on unabated. "Lords and Ladies, your attention please!" Still they ignored him.

"Hey!" Chertanne bellowed, coming to his feet. "Everybody shut up! The bard's trying to do something here!" Immediate silence fell, with several half-said apologies punctuating the silence.

Shemus executed a bow to Chertanne. "Thank you, your Grace. Tonight we have a special treat for your amusement and delight. The Black Quill Playwrights from the free city of Tenswater have agreed to come and perform a little play for you, which, I think you will all agree, is most suited to our little celebration this evening. Without further ado, the Black Quill Playwrights."

Shemus stepped away, and a tall man of medium build

and sandy blond hair walked regally onto the stage. He was dressed in kingly fashion, a purple robe over a deep red tunic and black pants cinched with an ornate belt.

He launched into a song, identifying himself as Chertanne and explaining his role in the prophecy. Next came a woman in a dress and veil. She stood by Chertanne and sang about her role as the Chalaine. Lastly, the Ilch romped into the room, and of all the portrayals the Chalaine had seen of her archenemy—and she had seen many—this one frightened her the most. The costume consisted of what appeared to be the carcass of some enormous black dog or wolf, black glassy eyes punctuated in the center with a red jewel. Fangs streaked with blood clacked as the jaws snapped up and down. The actor, wearing similarly stained claws on his hands, howled, jumped, and cavorted menacingly.

The play proceeded as most of the others the Chalaine had viewed. The counterparts to Chertanne and herself met, courted, fell in love, and were married. The Chalaine had to admit, however, that the singing and dancing were first rate and better than any she had attended previously. Chertanne was so enthralled that the Chalaine wagered she could club him with a drumstick of pheasant and he wouldn't even know it.

"And now," the brightly dressed narrator said after a touching, worshipful melody that the Chalaine had sung to the child in her belly, "the babe has grown large in her womb, and together, hand in hand, the Ha'Ulrich and the Chalaine arrive on the field of battle. Trys shines bright in the sky, the hordes of Mikkik stand before them, but they swallow their fear. The time is come for them to shine forth and bring God into the world!"

He threw something on the ground and a great puff of smoke rose with a loud pop, startling everyone. Chertanne clapped as several actors dressed as scaly Uyumaak with color-changing scales leapt onto the stage, cartwheeling, flipping, and juggling knives, torches, and soldiers' helmets to a pounding rhythm.

At the height of their erratic dance, the actors portraying Chertanne and the Chalaine marched confidently onto the stage and into the middle of the chaos. Chertanne held aloft a sword painted white, and with a powerful song supplicating for divine help, he stepped from Uyumaak to Uyumaak, striking them down. As he finished off the last, the Ilch jumped to the stage, blood dripping from his fur and fangs.

The beat of the drum increased in pace and intensity as the actors danced about in a deadly fight while the actress portraying the Chalaine lay behind in the throes of childbirth. The fight was frenetic and tense, ending as the sword finally penetrated the breast of the shrieking Ilch. At that same moment, the child was born, the actor Chertanne lifting it high above his head and presenting it to the crowd while shouting, "God is born! God is born! God is born!" Thunderous applause filled the hall, and the actors bowed for several minutes before leaving.

Unfortunately for the real Chalaine, their departure left her the center of Chertanne's attention for the rest of the affair. For most of her life, the Chalaine had cursed the need to wear the veil that prevented her from seeing the world as other women did. Meals, especially public ones, were particularly awkward, for her handmaidens had to hold the veil away from her head so that she could scoop food into her mouth or take a drink while every man in the room watched, hoping for the smallest glimpse of her face. The Chalaine relished the time she spent alone in her room, for there she could remove all the trappings and pretenses that separated her from the rest of her sex and her race, making her feel so different and so alone.

But after another hour with Chertanne, she was glad her face remained obscured behind the light mesh, for she would not want anyone to guess the despair or disgust that played plainly across her features. The thought of the Blessed One and her forthcoming marriage to him had filled her childhood and adolescence with many wild and pleasant fantasies and longings, and every minute she spent with Chertanne destroyed them ruthlessly one by one. Instead of handsomeness was unkempt sloppiness; instead of dignity and honor was baseness and crudeness; instead of temperance, there was indulgence and selfishness. There was cunning intelligence, however, and the hint of it in his eyes frightened her.

The aristocrats and nobles before her sometimes ascended the dais to pay their obsequious respects to her and to him, unable to see through years of ingrained deference to them that something was amiss. The Chalaine knew her mother sorrowed for her, though the Chalaine still felt angry that her mother never told her of her husband-to-be's character. She had no doubt that Jaron also seethed to see her treated so.

Anyone who considered her situation with a mind not blinded by station or favor would conclude that the Blessed One regarded her as little more than a tavern wench. Throughout the evening, he pawed her until her white dress—already stained by his dogs—was a smear of grease and crumbs. He leered at her suggestively and told her jokes so bawdy that she imagined—while acknowledging her own inexperience—that even a seasoned soldier would blush to hear them.

In self-defense she stopped eating—not that she possessed much of an appetite to start with—and tried to cover herself and shrink into as small a target as possible. Luckily, when the servants served dessert—an artful white cake decorated with vines of green and blue frosting—the Blessed One left her alone for a few moments. To take her mind off her discomfort and distress, she studied the room and the celebrants.

The great Hall of Mikmir was tiled and columned with a

white marble suffused with a blush of red, quarried and hauled with great toil from the northern tip of the Ironheart Mountains before the Shattering. The light coloration of the rock brightened the room, the candlelight flooding down from the chandeliers, creating a cheery atmosphere.

Above the main floor were arched balconies accessible by elegant, curving stairways. The balconies were usually reserved for dancing and mingling, but due to the great number of nobles and Warlords who came to see the Blessed One and his future bride, a host of servants had earlier hauled heavy tables and chairs up the stairs so those of station insufficient to merit a seat on the floor could still attend. All eyes and all talk focused on the dais at the head of the room where Chertanne and the Chalaine sat in the middle of a long, finely appointed table.

At one end of the table stood Jaron, jaw set and hands behind his back, and because the Chalaine knew him well, she could tell that his calm face masked a gnawing anger. She hoped, for his sake, that he would hold his tongue lest he run afoul of the Blessed One's personal bodyguard, Cormith. Cormith stood opposite Jaron, uninterested in the entire affair and showing every bit of the boredom he felt.

Cormith, Dason had told her earlier, was a perfectly built fighter. He was widely recognized as the second best swordsman in Ki'Hal, second only to Shadan Khairn. Most everyone knew better than to cross the Blessed One in any of his ways, for the one who did would find his head on the floor. Cormith was bald and his body was tattooed with patterns of black dots that some speculated were emblems of a covenant with dark powers. Others said he tattooed one dot on his skin for every person he killed. The Chalaine shuddered as he set his heavy-lidded gaze upon her, and she turned away.

Close by at the left base of the dais, the six young men who recently merited the privilege of training to join her

Dark Guard surveyed the proceedings. Each wore a black, high-collared shirt and a dark coat embroidered with silver moons. The Chalaine knew their masters had awarded them their swords and uniforms in a ceremony earlier that morning, and each wore them proudly. While not yet permitted to eat, they enjoyed the attention they received, and despite being on duty, some talked excitedly to each other or to relatives and friends who passed by. The Chalaine smiled at their budding arrogance and bravado, displayed to good effect to the young ladies, displayed by all—except one.

And when she saw him, she recognized him immediately as Gen, the one Fenna had brimmed about ceaselessly after the Trials. Unlike the others, his copiously scarred face remained an emotionless blank. In fact, he hardly moved. The Chalaine couldn't decide whether he was soaking up every detail as Jaron would do, or if he was lost in thought, oblivious to the celebration around him. Indeed, the longer she watched him, the more his stoicism and discipline fascinated her. Only statues stood so still or looked so poised, and only a dead man could have a face so devoid of expression. A chill pricked her skin, a feeling that he knew she was regarding him, and she quickly turned her gaze elsewhere.

The Dark Guard stood on the opposite end of the dais from their apprentices, and she decided that Gen must be imitating them, as a good apprentice should. They, too, stood still and calm. None could match Gen for sheer control—if that's what it was. Tolbrook shot menacing looks at the young, court-bred ladies that stopped to talk to the new apprentices, though to little effect.

The Blessed One ended her observations.

"Well, Chalaine," he said loudly, wiping frosting from his hand onto her sleeve as he wrapped a puffy hand around her arm, "what do you say we retire a bit early and I get a look under that veil of yours? We can return later, if you wish it."

It wasn't a request, but an expectation. The Chalaine, horrified, found her mouth open but empty of words. Thankfully, the arrival of Dason gave her an excuse to ignore the question.

"Milady," he said, bowing deeply, "I beg your leave to stand by Jaron, if it pleases you."

Dason had dressed as a courtier rather than a soldier this night, handsome in a deep golden coat worn over a blue shirt and hose.

"It pleases me. Take your place, Dason."

"You have two bodyguards, then?" the Blessed One commented derisively. "All I need is Cormith. I swear the man never sleeps a wink, which isn't to say he won't leave us alone when the need presents itself." He gave her thigh a firm squeeze and she fought down the urge to yell. "You know," he joked, "the sooner we get this child born, the better. Should I put it to a vote?"

The last was said through a mouthful of pheasant, and by his expectant gaze to the crowd, the Chalaine thought he might actually stop the proceedings and ask for a raise of hands to validate his wishes.

"I think not!" the Chalaine replied, struggling to control of her voice. Several close to the dais were already staring at them and listening. "We shall be upright as the Church commands lest we spoil the prophecy and bring down the wrath of Eldaloth upon us and the doom of Ki'Hal with it! We are to be married in Elde Luri Mora and the child conceived in the light of the moon Trys. Any other course will lead to ruin!"

The Blessed One laughed. "I'm sure if Eldaloth were going to strike me down for being with a woman, he would have done so long ago! I'm more 'married' to you than I was to any of the others. Besides, prophecy says we will be together. Does it really matter if it's sooner than later? If the child is to be conceived under the light of Trys, then

285

I'm sure it won't be conceived until then. You will come with me."

The Chalaine knew her beauty could pull powerfully on men, but this man had never seen her face. What lust was his came from lewd habits and a lifetime of overindulgence.

"You've obviously thought this through, and I know women are slaves in your country, but I am not your slave and I will not. . ."

The Blessed One cut her off, tightening his grip on her arm and yanking her close to him. "You will!" he whispered intently, coming to his feet. "You will, woman, because I desire it!" He dragged her upward from her chair and pulled her toward the door that led out to the hall to his apartments.

The Chalaine turned toward the crowd, time slowing as if to allow her to take in the scene around her. Her mother bowed her head and closed her eyes in an agony and shame she seemed to have expected. Jaron's knuckles turned white from clenching his sword hilt as he walked forward to follow her. Dason glanced off into the assembly, pretending not to notice. Cormith fell in behind his master, a grin splitting his face. Some of the assembled in the crowd noticed them leaving, but they either did not think anything was wrong or did not care.

She resisted as best she could without causing a scene, but he was strong, and he was the Ha'Ulrich. Slowly the inevitable enveloped her and her resistance eroded to submission and pain. Tears ran freely from her eyes as the Blessed One dragged her out to deliver the unthinkable, final blow to a lifetime of naive anticipation.

Dream after dream of their wedding and their wedding night sprinted through her mind. He was so handsome in the dreams. He was a gentleman. He held her hand lightly as they danced in a hall filled with women jealous of his touch upon her. But his eyes were only for her, and hers for him. Now her eyes darted everywhere before returning to the floor in front of her.

"Let her be!" The voice was loud and the Blessed One faltered but pressed on.

"Let her be!" This time the words cut through the noise of the crowd like thunder and demanded acknowledgment.

All fell silent, and the Blessed One turned, naked rage rising in his face. The Chalaine also turned, wondering who would dare stand for her. Mounting the dais, slowly and calmly, was Gen, face relaxed, even bored. The Blessed One released the Chalaine as if she were no longer important, and she fled to stand hand in hand with her mother. Jaron and Dason quickly flanked the Chalaine, and the rest of the celebrants froze in disbelief.

"Let her be?" the Blessed One said evenly but angrily. "What right have you to order me? I am the Law."

"You are not the Law," Gen returned, not the least bit intimidated. "The prophecy says the Blessed One would 'speak the law', which is far different from inventing laws to satisfy your own lusts. And shame," Gen continued with a sudden fervency, turning his head to include the entire room, "on this company for letting you abuse the Chalaine in this fashion for the entire evening. I will not stand for it any longer."

Rage muted the Blessed One's tongue, and many nobles who had spent the night currying favor with him twitched with outrage and demanded Gen's head. Others, the Chalaine noticed gratefully, sat quietly and considered.

"I have recently accepted the charge to protect the honor and life of the Chalaine," Gen continued, his voice rich and forceful. "The Church includes the chastity of maidens as essential to their honor, even in your country, and you clearly wish to violate that doctrine. I demand honor be satisfied—by combat—as is my right in Rhugoth."

The crowd gasped and whispered frantically. A glint bloomed in Cormith's eye, and he started to stretch and loosen his muscles. A chill ran up the Chalaine's spine. The Great Hall of Mikmir was large, but Gen filled it with an honest presence and power she had never seen anyone project before in her life. He could not be ignored or denied.

"That is Gen," her mother whispered, voice shaking. "The orphan from Tolnor. He came to Court this. . ."

"How dare you come here to parley words with me!" Chertanne's angry retort drowned out her mother's words. "Do you think yourself so well-read and so smart that you can bandy about 'law' and 'principle' like a court scholar? What is your name? What is your rank?"

"My name is Gen. I was a serf from Tolnor and am now apprenticed to become a Dark Guard."

Chertanne laughed maniacally. "A serf! A serf? Since when do Tolnorians put swords into the hands of serfs or let them in the company of high-bred society? You forget your place, peasant. In case you were too daft to understand the point of this assembly, I am Chertanne Khairn, noble born and holy born, and you've no more right to speak to me than a mutt! In a few weeks my father will make you and all your countrymen slaves."

"I am what I am," said Gen, "and the law is what the law is, and I am no slave yet. Seeking to bed the Chalaine before your marriage is an insult to this court and the principles of the Church. Serfs, commoners, and even the male slaves in your country have the right to challenge, and so do I. It would be wrong in the sight of God if I did not."

Some in the crowd demanded the First Mother do something to silence Gen and remove him. The Chalaine felt her mother's hand tighten around hers as she stood tall and ignored them. The Chalaine's heart broke, and the walls of defiance that had so easily crumbled at the Blessed One's insistence rose again, fixed with a stronger mortar. She silently thanked Gen for the return of her dignity, however brief, though she pitied him. As a commoner, he was probably ignorant of the death made flesh that he would face. The Chalaine stared at Gen, hoping to imprint his face in her mind as a reminder to herself of conviction and courage.

"Well," the Blessed One said, silencing the crowd with his hand and a sudden light tone, "combat you shall have. But we will do things as they are done in my country and soon yours. In my country what you are doing now is called a Challenge of Possession. The Chalaine is, I think all would agree, mine and bound to obey me. For you to challenge my possession of her, someone must second your challenge for it to be of any effect. Of course, you're learned enough to know that, right? Is there anyone here who would second the motion of this peon? How about you, Dason? You're the personal guard of her ladyship and this peasant's countryman. Will you second and stand with Gen against the wishes of your Savior?"

"No, your Greatness," Dason said, lowering his eyes and bowing, "I will not oppose the will of the Blessed One."

The Chalaine frowned.

"There's a good man. Anyone else?" He turned to Jaron. "How about you?" Jaron regarded the finger pointing at his chest. He fought a war within himself for but a moment, and then his eyes cleared and he stood erect.

"I will second."

"Very well," the Blessed One accepted flippantly, "The High Protector will act as judge. Where is he? "

"I am here," Regent Ogbith rose from a table near the dais and stepped forward. He walked with a limp but was still every inch the soldier he had been in his youth. Close-cropped gray hair stuck out from an angular head that terminated in a powerful, square jaw.

"You seem to know the rules, boy," the Regent said, and the Chalaine could sense a hint of pride in the older man's eyes. "What are your terms?"

"No, no, no!" Chertanne interrupted. "In a Challenge of

Possession, the rules are quite simple. If he wins, she is his. If I win, she is mine and she must obey."

"But, Milord," the Regent said, face concerned. "If he wins. . ." Chertanne laughed.

"He won't. I name Cormith my champion in this matter."

The Blessed One was extraordinarily pleased with himself and approached Gen, who matched his gaze with an expression of complete disinterestedness.

Chertanne pointed a finger at Gen's chest. "And you ought to know, my dear serf, that Cormith has killed more people than you have hairs on your head! If you're a fighter, you undoubtedly know of Torbrand Khairn, my father?" Gen only inclined his head in the affirmative as a response. "Torbrand trained him. I anticipate seeing your blood on the floor very soon! Let's get this over with!"

Chertanne waved Gen off dismissively and returned to his seat.

"Then let the challenge by combat begin," Ogbith announced solemnly and a little sadly. "By *our* custom each fighter has the right to seek a blessing before the fight starts. Do either of you wish it?"

Cormith declined, but Gen accepted. Prelate Obelard made his way from the back of the assembly, dressed in the white robes of his office. A Pureman in a simple brown habit followed him. Obelard whispered something to Gen and ordered him to kneel. Gen complied as the Pureman pulled a vial from his cloak and anointed Gen's bowed head with oil.

"In the name of the most Holy Eldaloth," he intoned gravely, placing his hand upon Gen's head, "I seal upon you the victory in this matter if your cause be honorable and just. If your cause be in fault, then I seal your doom and prepare your soul against your death."

Obelard extended a hand to help Gen rise.

"Get on with it!" Chertanne yelled impatiently. "You

Rughothians make such a complicated mess of everything!"

"Very well," Regent Ogbith said. "The match is to the death. Prepare yourselves and begin on my signal."

Jaron crossed quickly to Gen, and Regent Ogbith held up. Chertanne threw his hands up at this further delay. The Chalaine could just hear Jaron's words above the fading noise of the crowd.

"Let me face him, Gen! Name me your champion, and I shall do it! You don't have the training to beat Cormith. He is skilled beyond your imagining and has killed men with more experience than you have. Only I have a chance. Let me fight!"

Behind the logic of the plea, the Chalaine could hear the desire for absolution; he felt that he should have raised the challenge.

"You do not know me," Gen replied, removing his coat and shirt and tossing them on the floor. "I will fight. The challenge is mine."

"Then Eldaloth rest your soul! You are a dead man! A foolish dead man!"

Jaron strode away angrily and returned to his post. If the bitter rebuke hurt Gen, he did not show it.

Cormith and Gen, both stripped to the waist, stood at the foot of the dais facing each other. Each was a perfect form of sculpted muscle and flesh, though Cormith the taller and heavier. Servants pushed tables back at Ogbith's instruction to allow room for the fight. So great was Cormith's reputation that no one bothered to place wagers on who the winner might be. Captain Tolbrook, Gen's master, spoke a few words to his apprentice, but Gen's attention was so firmly locked upon his opponent that he gave no sign that he acknowledged Tolbrook's advice.

"Finish him quickly, Cormith. No playing around this time," Chertanne ordered brightly. "I've an engagement with the most beautiful woman that ever lived, after all!" Some laughed at the quip. Cormith just smiled.

"It should not take long, Highness. He's but an apprentice, though he's got some muscle on him! Jaron would have proved a better match. There shall be little sport, I fear."

The Chalaine marveled at Gen's complacency. Perhaps he simply did not understand whom he was facing, for there was no fear, nervousness, or even healthy respect for his opponent in his demeanor. Regent Ogbith stepped back onto the dais and turned to the crowd.

"The challenge is agreed upon. Both parties are bound to honor its terms, as witnessed by me, Harrick Ogbith, Regent and High Protector of Rhugoth. Let no man interfere till the challenge is resolved by death. You may begin."

The Chalaine gripped her mother's hand, and her mother clutched hers tightly in return. As much as the Chalaine wanted to turn from the awful scene that she knew would result in the butchery of the one man who had the courage to stand for her against a prophetic icon, she could not.

Cormith strode forward, playfully swinging his sword at Gen, who easily blocked the strokes. Cormith laughed.

"Well," he said, turning to the audience with a broad grin, "at least he can block a few lazy swings!" The Blessed One laughed and the crowd followed suit. "Let's see," Cormith continued, "if he can land one on me, shall we? C'mon lad! Take a swing! I promise not to hurt you too badly . . . yet."

And then Gen made him pay for his arrogance.

With speed the Chalaine didn't think possible, Gen laid into Cormith with a vicious all-out frontal attack. Cormith's look of teasing mirth dissolved into one of surprise and fear as Gen drove him back in a line, ending a furious series of humming overhand strokes with a crushing kick to the midsection that slammed Cormith's lower back into the edge of a heavy oak table.

Cormith's breath exploded from his chest and he grunted in pain, barely recovering enough to duck a wicked slash that would have sent his head skidding across the table. Disbelief registered on every face. Cormith, all hauteur aside, smoothed his features into the same emotionless calm as Gen's; then the battle began in earnest.

Blades were blurs of reflected light as stroke and counter-stroke made a quick, irregular beat to which the fighters danced. Inches determined the difference between life and death, sharp edges dodged by less than the breadth of a finger. Cormith sought to use his greater mass to good advantage by wearing Gen down with heavy, powerful strokes. Gen countered with inhuman quickness, seeking to gain advantage of Cormith's injury by forcing him to twist his body.

The entire hall went silent as it became clear that the fight was not going to be won easily by either side. The Blessed One watched with rapt attention, and the Chalaine saw that Jaron's anger had faded, replaced by hope. She barely noticed that Fenna had come to her side, face aglow with girlish admiration.

"Did I not tell you, Chalaine?" Fenna whispered as the men strove with each other. "There is no one like him."

The Chalaine could only agree. What the Chalaine had thought was exaggeration from an enamored girl proved instead to be the truth. Gen fought masterfully, facing down an experienced killer in a way that could only be described as violently beautiful.

They strove intensely for several minutes, neither tiring nor backing away. As time wore on, the Chalaine could tell that each was starting to take chances in hopes of catching the other off guard for the split second it would take to kill. The pace slackened as strategy—rather than pure physical might or speed—came into play. And it was here, the Chalaine surmised, that Cormith had the advantage, for Gen was young and surely less experienced. Still, the youth held his own until Cormith managed to slice him across his upper chest. Fenna's face fell, and the Chalaine trembled. Her mother's grip tightened painfully.

Cormith offered no gloating remark, and Gen showed no sign of discomfort, though the Chalaine knew a wound so severe had to weaken him. The Blessed One half-rose up from his seat, a smile coming to his lips, while Jaron bowed his head momentarily, perhaps in prayer. Gen appeared to tire, his parries coming slower, Cormith's blade inching ever closer. Blood ran down Gen's chest as Cormith drove him backward. The Blessed One stood, sensing victory.

But as Cormith came down with a heavy overhand blow, Gen's speed suddenly returned as he threw aside his feigned exhaustion and pain. Cormith tried to hold his stroke up as Gen dodged away, but before he could rein in his errant swing, Gen hammered him in the side of the head with his sword hilt, cracking the left side of his skull. Cormith crumpled to the ground, landing on all fours and dropping his sword. Gen waited as the dazed, injured man scooted about, wheezing and feeling around for his sword. As soon as Cormith laid his hand on the blade, Gen beheaded him. The Blessed One yelled in rage, slamming his fists down upon the table.

Gen turned, bleeding but calm. Extending his sword toward the Chalaine, he bowed. After wiping his blade clean with Cormith's discarded shirt, he resheathed his weapon and returned to stand at attention with the other apprentices as if nothing had happened.

Regent Ogbith stepped onto the dais with a face that barely checked the glee that threatened to flood from it. "Let it be published abroad that Gen has won the challenge. According to Aughmerian custom, the Chalaine is now in Gen's possession and his right to her cannot be challenged for at least one year from this day. Is that correct, Highness?" Chertanne was too incensed to reply. "I shall take it then that that is correct. The matter is

294

concluded."

No one dared applaud. The Dark Guard in charge of Gen's training gaped at him with a mixture of admiration and wonder, as did his fellow apprentices. The Chalaine wept silently, her mother and Fenna sharing her joy. Jaron smiled grandly, while Dason shook his head in amazement. Moving away from her companions, the Chalaine walked across the dais to stand in front of her defender, collecting the shirt and coat he had cast aside before the fight. Now she wished that her veil could be torn away so that he could see how she felt, for no words could describe it. She felt reborn.

"You shall not heal him!" the Blessed One thundered at her. "Give Cormith that much respect! I forbid you to heal him."

Ignoring the order, the Chalaine extended her hand and laid it upon the wound. His blood wet her fingers and stained the cuff of her sleeve as she concentrated. After several moments, the cut healed so completely that only the blood drying upon Gen's chest and the Chalaine's hand and sleeve suggested that a wound had ever been there. The Chalaine tried to read Gen's face, but as before, it was indecipherable.

"Thank you," she said, leaning close to give him his clothing, whispering so that none could hear but him. A slight smile in his eyes was all he answered, and it was enough.

"This is not the end of this!" the Blessed One yelled. "You will regret what you've done, serf. This I swear!"

Chertanne departed rapidly, leaving a chattering throng in his wake. Arguments erupted, and the hall crescendoed instantly from silence to chaos. The Dark Guard hurried to their apprentices as Jaron, Fenna, and the First Mother joined their daughter in front of Gen.

"We need to remove the Chalaine from the hall, your Highness," Jaron remarked, nodding toward the unruly crowd.

"Yes. Take the Chalaine to her apartments immediately. Accompany them, Fenna, and see to her comfort. Gen, you will come with me in a few moments. I must do what I can here before I speak with you. Be wary. You are in more danger than you know."

The First Mother hasted away, ordering the removal of Cormith's body and trying to soothe the assembly.

"Well done, Gen," Volney said, coming near. "It is an honor to serve with you." The other apprentices, excepting the Aughmerians, congratulated him quietly as the First Mother dismissed the assembly. Tolbrook approached Gen, face disquieted, signaling for him to follow.

"No, Captain," the First Mother spoke up, walking over quickly. "I need to talk to this one. Now."

CHAPTER 19 - MIRELLE

Gen's mind raced as he followed the First Mother and her guard Cadaen through ornate halls fashioned from the same marble used in the Great Hall. Towering arches of stone, thirty feet high, rose into the darkness above him. The hall sloped downward, and they came to a heavy iron gate that opened to a spiral ramp descending deep below the ground. The ramp terminated onto a landing where two of the Dark Guard stood at attention before an ornate bridge that spanned the distance between the shard where theGreat Hall was built and the small shard where the Chalaine lived in her tower. The guards eyed Gen speculatively as he passed, and Gen knew that word of his deed had already spread.

Gen guessed the bridge measured a hundred and fifty feet long. It was made of the same blushing marble, and seeing it hooked between the two shards gave him a real sense of its fragility. If one shard were to move a few feet, the bridge would crumble and send them tumbling into the nothingness between shards.

"There is magic on the bridge," the First Mother explained as they traversed the span. "At the first sign of trouble, it can be destroyed with ease. An additional magic has been placed around the Chalaine's complex to counter creatures that can fly. A most unpleasant end awaits anyone or anything that tries to fly across."

At the other end of the bridge, a short hallway ended in wide steps that spilled into a beautiful underground room with a fountain gurgling pleasantly at the center. The domed roof was painted with a very lifelike representation of the sky which magically emanated light. All about the circular room grew hearty green plants and vibrant flowers. Finely crafted statues of animals, men, elves, and fairies accented the walls from carved recesses. Three ornate doors, one on each extremity of the room, were guarded by two members of the Dark Guard each. They bowed to the First Mother and then regarded Gen with curiosity.

Gen worried that slaying Cormith might have ruined his chances at becoming a Dark Guard for the Chalaine. Perhaps the First Mother, fearing for his life, would send him away. While he had waited for the First Mother to finish mollifying the nobles in the Great Hall, he had seen many murderous glares directed at him from those loyal to the Blessed One. And if any of the stories he used to tell others about nobles were true, he'd have to watch every dark corner and be careful of everything he drank.

"Gen," the First Mother said, stopping and turning toward him. "This is the Antechamber of the Chalaine. If you did not have the branding placed upon you, you would have died before crossing into this room. There are many secrets here, and in time you will know them all. The first secret, as you now know, is that the tower and buildings above us are not where the Chalaine lives. A decoy lives there, and the tower is an excellent perch for observation should we ever come under attack. The Chalaines, past and present, live here, underground.

Straight ahead of you is the door to the Chambers of the Chalaine. It is there that she has spent most of her life, as I did before her. Passing through that door requires an additional brand that you do not have. To the right is the entrance to the tomb of Chalaines, a place of honor for thirteen women bred through the years for beauty and other qualities.

"The door to the left is where the Chalaines of the past live. Where I live. I and all the Chalaines before me have lived there after giving birth to their first daughter. Come."

The Dark Guard opened the door for the First Mother, and, to Gen's surprise, he found himself in a maze.

"There is a similar maze behind the Chalaine's door," the First Mother explained, "though it is larger and more complicated than this one. Their purpose is obvious to you, I'm sure. Follow closely. A misstep in the maze is deadly."

As they negotiated a confusing series of twists and turns, Gen spotted a variety of nasty traps scattered about—pits, spikes, and other machinations of death. Runes ran along the walls, hinting at unseen magical protections. The maze terminated in a short, well-appointed hallway with red carpets and marble walls that arched to a point. Gold ran along the edges of the arches' ribs, a thread bursting forth to filigree the white walls with patterns of leaves and flowers. A polished oak door waited at the end, a smaller door to the right.

"Cadaen, remain at my door while I talk with this young man. You can sleep when we are done."

Cadaen furrowed his eyebrows. "I am sorry, Milady. I cannot leave you alone with a man, especially an armed one."

The First Mother smiled, obviously expecting this. "Are you afraid I might seduce Gen, Cadaen?" she teased, grinning mischievously.

"No!" Cadaen stammered. "But he is a trained killer and not well known! I could not bear it if you should come to harm because of my negligence."

"Cadaen," the First Mother entreated affectionately, touching his arm, "be at peace. I know my business. Gen has saved the honor of this house tonight and I will speak with him alone if I wish it. There is no death for me in his eyes or upon his sword. Now come, Gen, in we go."

Cadaen started to object as the First Mother opened the door and ushered Gen in, but the old soldier bit back his words and turned to the vigil he had kept for many long years.

The First Mother's chamber was immense, and Gen took a moment to absorb it all. Only the finest appointments were deemed worthy enough for the First Mother, and the amount of wealth in gems and precious metals present in the room would have fed Tell for years. There were golden chalices, gem-encrusted chairs, gold trimming along the walls and floors creating elegant patterns, and artworks of silver embedded into the mantel of the fireplace. Brightly colored tapestries depicting the lives of the rich and poor lined the walls while thick, woven carpets lay about the marble floor under the couches, the desk, and in front of the fireplace. Several closed doors hinted at even more rooms beyond.

Only the fire illuminated the room, casting wild shadows and throwing off an orange light that was bent and reflected by the jewels and metals. Gen thought the First Mother would light candles, but instead she motioned him over to the rug in front of the fire and indicated he should sit upon it. Gen unbuckled his hilt and placed his sword upon the mantel. He sat cross-legged on the rug, which proved to be quite soft under his hand.

The First Mother entered another room for a few minutes, and when she returned she was wearing a loose-fitting gown. While Gen watched, she took several pins out of her blonde hair, letting it fall loosely about her shoulders. In the light of the Great Hall, Gen had thought that the First Mother must have been a woman of surpassing beauty in her youth. In the firelight, he knew it. Desire rose within him, for the First Mother was not old and he speculated that many men, Cadaen included, held a secret passion for her. But because of his training, the feelings rising within him simply slid off into nothingness, leaving him empty and in control. He wondered at her purpose.

"What are you thinking?" she asked as she sat down in front of him, legs crossed like his. "Is this a bit less formal than you were expecting?"

"Yes," Gen replied, "but I was thinking that if the Chalaine is your daughter then she must be beautiful indeed."

The First Mother's face grew grave at the compliment. "Beautiful to the point of being dangerous, I fear. Many generations ago, after the prophecy came, the Church sought a beautiful man and woman that they might have a daughter of surpassing beauty so that when the time came she might bear a son without flaw to be the temple of Eldaloth on his return. For generations this has continued, each Chalaine bearing a daughter who, on her seventeenth birthday, was then coupled with the fairest man that could be found.

"Each new Chalaine was more beautiful, more alluring, and more enchanted. To be frank, Gen, my daughter's beauty would drive any man who saw it into a mad passion. I doubt there is a man on Ki'Hal powerful enough to look upon her naked face and resist his impulses to take her for his own."

"Is her beauty natural or enchanted?" Gen asked.

"Both," the First Mother answered, pleased with the question. "The Chalaines were never bred or trained for magical talent. From the eighth Chalaine onward, something unexpected happened and every Chalaine thereafter was irresistible to all but those of the strongest will. Some Magicians and Church scholars say that the beauty simply elevated to a divine, god-like in nature, and this was considered a sign that the advent of the Blessed One was near. I think that if my daughter were to bear a female child, that not even the cloak and veil would be enough to hide her beauty; it would radiate from her and touch all who came near."

"But what of you?" Gen asked. "I mean no offense, but you are a Chalaine and you walk unveiled. Does the allure fail at a certain age?"

"Not at an age. At the birth of a Chalaine's first child, some of the allurement is dimmed. Make no mistake, though. I wore the veil for many years after my daughter's birth because men would start into a frenzy at the sight of me. You have probably noticed that I do not look my age, another quality bred into the Chalaines. Do you doubt that I could seduce you as the good Cadaen fears, despite our difference in age?"

The look she gave Gen was enticing and teasing, but there was only emptiness within him. "I would not have that tested or I fear Cadaen would have my head, even if it were your fault."

The First Mother smiled and relaxed her gaze. "You indeed are a marvel, Gen. I can read men easily, but you are a mystery! Does that noncommittal, uninterested face of yours ever change?"

Gen could hear Torbrand Khairn's counsel in the back of his head: *In a fight you must be faceless. Every expression is information that aids the enemy. In a face, an opponent can see fear, arrogance, diffidence, cleverness, and dissembling. And if an opponent knows how you feel, he can exploit your emotion and kill you with it.*

"Forgive me, your Grace. It is my training that makes me so."

"And that is more to the point of our visit, Gen. You mentioned that Cadaen would have your head when the simple truth is that there isn't one man that walks and breathes air, save maybe Torbrand Khairn himself, that could beat you in a duel. It is obvious to me now that you did not fight to the fullest of your abilities in the Trials, and perhaps wisely so.

302

"Before we came here, I spoke briefly with Regent Ogbith and Cadaen. According to them, you are unbelievably good. How you became so is no doubt one question that you will be asked a great deal, but not now. What I really want to know is why? Why did you confront the Blessed One for my daughter's honor? You've placed yourself in a great deal of danger."

"He does not honor her, as I said in the Hall. He was wrong to attempt what he did."

"Men have been killed for saying less. Yes, what he was trying to do was wrong, even in Aughmere, but that still doesn't explain why you acted. Jaron loves the Chalaine like his own daughter, and he knew it was wrong yet said and did nothing until after you raised your challenge. Dason is an honorable man. He knew it was wrong too, and instead he acquiesced to the will of the Blessed One. There were aristocrats and nobles in the assembly sworn to protect the honor of this house, and some of them are now howling for your blood!

"So, why you, Gen? Here in Rhugoth you are a foreigner, and in your own land a commoner of the lowest station. You owe my House and my honor nothing. And then there is me, Gen." The First Mother's voice wavered. "She is my daughter, the most beloved of my heart, and I stood there and watched her be manhandled away and did nothing. So why, Gen, did you stand when all others— when I—failed?"

"Because I thought I had the means to do so and she is worth the attempt," Gen said gently, discerning the First Mother's love for her daughter. "I was raised, as you were, to believe the Blessed One was to be revered and obeyed above all. At the dawn of each day I chant my thanks to Eldaloth for the Ha'Ulrich's coming and pledge my soul to his service. But I ask you this: what was his coming to bring? What was the Blessed One to manifest? Love, justice, honor, sacrifice, and benevolence. When I saw him

303

debark this afternoon, I suspected he lacked every one of those qualities. Watching tonight, I knew it. Do you agree?"

"I do," the First Mother answered. Gen fell silent, watching her face, and the First Mother considered what he said thoughtfully. "Are you saying the Blessed One is not the Blessed One?"

Gen shrugged. "That is not for me to say. I must trust that he is since he bears the sign."

"Then I am at a loss. Why defy him then? Chertanne will be your King one day, and I do not think he will forget the sting you gave him tonight. You say she is worth your efforts, but how do you know? You cannot know my daughter and have not seen her unveiled, so I do not believe you defended her out of love or passion. Though I do recall that Ethris said he sensed you had a devotion to her that was different than the others. Why?"

"First Mother, I may not know her intimately as you do, but I have witnessed her care for those most wouldn't waste a glance upon. She has the qualities I always thought she would. What is honorable must be defended, regardless of where it is found. Baseness must be despised—and fought—wherever it is found, even if in the Blessed One."

"Do you condemn me, indeed, condemn all of us who work to protect the Chalaine, for our failure?"

The question was asked with such earnestness that Gen knew his answer was important to her. "I am in no position to judge and have no right to condemn anyone. . ."

The first Mother laughed sardonically. "Forgive me, Gen, but you must see that it is ridiculous for you to say so! You judged the most powerful man alive this evening, found him wanting, and shamed him in front of the better part of the ruling class from two nations!" Her face turned serious and her voice filled with intensity. "From the moment you issued your challenge, I have been burned with a guilt and self-loathing you cannot understand. I love her more than anyone! I am her mother! And a stranger from another land has to do what I should have done because I was too weak to do it! I could have raised the challenge. Jaron would have supported me just as he supported you, and he would have fought for her! But I did nothing! Tonight, you proved yourself my better, and in sitting above me, you have the position and the right to judge!"

"Please, your Grace," Gen soothed, "you make too much of what I have done. There is only one thing that matters and one thing on which you and I should fix our hopes: that after tonight there is no one that truly loves the Chalaine or who cherishes honor that will allow the shame that almost came upon your House to ever happen again. I know you will not. Do I miss my mark?"

"You do not," the First Mother replied resolutely. She stared at Gen for several moments in silence, and Gen looked her in the eye, not sure what to expect. There was a fire and resolve in her countenance, and Gen knew he had acquired an ally.

"Such wisdom and skill for one so young," she said, finally. "I would keep you around as my own Protector just for the conversation if I didn't have other plans for you."

"No doubt the Blessed One would take great offense if you named me your Protector."

The First Mother grinned. "And no doubt he will take even greater offense when I name you the Chalaine's Protector, replacing Dason."

Gen's mind reeled. Great offense indeed!

"Ahh!" the First Mother said mirthfully. "I believe I have figured out how to read one of your emotions. Whereas most men raise their eyebrows or exclaim or stammer when surprised, you simply remain silent for a short period of time."

"What will become of Dason?" Gen inquired, noting the First Mother's observation.

"After tonight Dason will no longer have the honor of

305

the Protectorship, though he will continue to serve with the Dark Guard. While it would mean my death were Chertanne to find out, I want the men who guard my daughter to hold her in higher honor than Him, and I know you to be one of them, as Jaron is now.

"The Chalaine will not like losing Dason, for he is a court-bred man who is very gregarious and entertaining, but it must be done. I can see that Dason has passion for her, and, while the brand would keep him from ever hurting her, it would still be dangerous if he were to win her heart, for I can see she is fond of him, as well. I have purposefully tempted you this night in subtle ways that would have at least interested most men, and you have not faltered. I think you will not let your passions get the better of you under any circumstance."

Gen realized he was being silent and spoke up quickly. "It would be my honor to serve her, but is it not a risk? You said I am in danger, and from the looks directed at me this evening, I believe you. The Chalaine may be placed in danger if I am near her."

"That is true, but I also want to protect you. There is no place on Ki'Hal safer than this shard and the Chambers of the Chalaine. I will make you her night Protector. That way, Jaron will most likely accompany her when she is called to perform duties outside the Chambers. I know there are risks. You have put yourself between the Ha'Ulrich and his bride, but if any man in this kingdom can protect my daughter, it is the man who chopped down Cormith in my Hall this night. If you are the target of Chertanne's ire, then your plight will be the plight of many ere long."

Though Gen didn't show it, a brief surge of excitement at his good fortune surged through him.

The First Mother continued. "I trust that you will disregard the idiotic Aughmerian notion that the Chalaine is now in your possession?"

"Of course I will. It is ridiculous."

"Good, though I will not rule out using it to our advantage if need be. There is one thing, however, that I hope you are intelligent enough to realize," the First Mother continued. "Twice I have seen you use the arrogance and ignorance of your opponent to defeat him. You must know that you will no longer have this advantage. As we speak, tales of your deeds and your description are being carried from Mikmir and throughout Rhugoth. From Rhugoth it will go to all nations. In two days time you have become a legend in your own right, and by the time the tales reach Aughmere and your homeland, you will be ten feet tall and breathing fire. The next opponent you face will know to fear and respect you, and as your own fame grows, you too will have to fight against arrogance."

"I thank you for your wisdom, your Grace. Being in the presence of the Chalaine will no doubt keep me humble."

"Perhaps, Gen," the First Mother answered, "but do not forget that under that veil is a young woman who, for all her beauty and importance, is flawed and now fearful. Her future marriage to the Blessed One brings her no joy as it once did, and, as much as you need protect her from evils of flesh and blood, you must also inspire in her the strength to face the unwanted in the name of duty. Will you swear to me, as one who honors her as I do, that you will do this?"

"I swear it. I will be the Chalaine's Protector, if she will have me." It was more than Gen could have hoped for when he first set foot, dirty and ragged, on the tournament field.

The First Mother smiled. "She has no choice. By tradition, the First Mother chooses who will be her daughter's closest guards. You must pass through another ceremony and receive an additional branding. We will take care of it quietly tomorrow morning so that you may begin your duties in the evening. Tonight you will sleep in spare quarters next to Cadaen's. Tomorrow you will have your own quarters in the Chamber of the Chalaine."

"I thank you, First Mother."

"You are most deservedly welcome. And call me Mirelle when we are outside of court. It is the name I took after birthing the Chalaine, for only one may have the title."

The First Mother shifted and reclined upon her side on the rug, resting her head upon her hand and gazing into the fire. A strand of blonde hair fell over her now pensive face, and Gen was surprised at the sudden shift in mood. It was as if by disclosing her name to him, she suddenly changed from the First Mother to a longtime friend.

"You know, Gen," she said thoughtfully, "it is somewhat ironic that we come to this position tonight. Do you even know why Shadan Khairn attacked your homeland?"

"I do not. I have heard rumors that King Filingrail broke the Fidelium. I've been meaning to ask Gerand Kildan more closely about it."

"He did break the Fidelium. Let me enlighten you so that, perhaps, you can take greater satisfaction in your actions this evening. Last summer, the leaders of the three nations met together in Aughmere for their first glimpse of the Blessed One and to arrange for the eventual transfer of power into his hands after his marriage to my daughter. We arrived expecting Chertanne to be well bred, intelligent, and the very definition of noble, even if after an Aughmerian fashion. At the very least, as the son of Torbrand Khairn, we thought he would be a fine swordsman.

"Imagine our horror when a pudgy, spoiled brat made his appearance and treated us worse than his hounds. At first we thought it a joke, but with some subtle investigation we learned that Chertanne's caretakers had pampered him and deferred to him his entire life. His father had not even been permitted any part in raising him—though that isn't necessarily undesirable either.

"You must understand, however, that while it frightened

me to think Chertanne should ever hold the power that he will in a short time, my first thoughts were for my Chalaine, the one who would be forced to marry him. While all young ladies dream of marrying someone powerful, noble, and brave, the Chalaines have long thought that they were guaranteed it by prophetic dictum. Since first meeting my future son-in-law, I felt sick in my heart.

"As we stayed in Aughmere, we learned that Chertanne was lecherous, and the primary victim of his lechery, I am sorry to say, was your kingdom. Your young King Omric Filingrail brought along his lovely wife, Kerenne, to meet the Blessed One. Chertanne's lust for her was immediately obvious. While Omric is not a strong man or a gifted leader, he loves his Kerenne dearly, and when Chertanne made a play for his wife, he stormed out of the country, vowing he would never turn his kingdom over to Chertanne. The rest you may guess. Torbrand, as we speak, is taking Tolnor by force, something he revels in."

"I know it well," Gen said, a flood of unwanted memories dampening his mood.

"I am sorry to remind you of it," Mirelle continued, "but it seems more than just coincidence to me that you were driven out of your land by a war started over the honor of a woman, and from there you come and save the honor of another from the very person who started the war in the first place. Though you may not see it, you could consider your victory tonight a small one for your homeland, though I doubt such a thought will dull the pain of your losses."

"No, it wouldn't. What I did tonight, I did for the Chalaine alone. What I have lost I can never truly avenge, though this service has given me hope that I can do some good with my life, which is no small comfort. Again, I thank you for it."

The First Mother smiled warmly at him, and again Gen fought away the inevitable attraction. She pulled an errant strand of hair behind her ear. "If you ever need an ear,

Gen, your voice will always be a welcome one to me. I owe you a meal, and I intend to keep my promise of an invitation."

A thought sprang to Gen's mind. "You never told her about Chertanne's character after you returned, did you?"

"You are perceptive," the First Mother said. "How did you know?"

"The way she acted at the pier."

"I am surprised you could deduce that from such a short encounter. I did not tell her. I wanted to allow the Chalaine as much happiness as I could before Chertanne tore her hopes apart. I know you will have little opportunity, but if you can, get to know my daughter. The next few weeks will be difficult for her despite—and partly because of—your help tonight, and she could use your strength."

"It will be my pleasure to know you both."

"And we you. Now, I think you should get some rest. I have no doubt Cadaen is more than a little worried at the length of our conversation and will barge through the door any second."

The First Mother rose and Gen followed suit. He retrieved his sword from the mantle, feeling the warm hilt before buckling it on. Mirelle drew near and embraced him.

"Thank you, Gen," she said, kissing his cheek, "for everything."

Gen inclined his head to the First Mother. Leading him to the door, she said, "We must teach you to smile or I fear you will drive my daughter mad! Oh yes, and don't expect to be a commoner or a citizen of Tolnor much longer. Cadaen!" The door opened. Cadaen raised his eyebrows upon seeing the First Mother's informal attire.

"Open the spare quarters for him, Cadaen. And get that stupid look off your face. We just had a nice little talk."

CHAPTER 20 - CHANGE OF THE GUARD

The Chaline fumed. "I cannot believe you have done it, mother! What will Chertanne think? He will think we hate him!"

Her fervent protest did not change Mirelle's determined face. The Walls showed sunrise over the Kingsblood Lake the morning after Gen's defense of the Chalaine's honor. Her mother knocked on the door before dawn and ordered Eldwena to leave before the handmaiden could finish brushing the Chalaine's hair. Mirelle resumed the task herself, and the Chalaine was speechless with surprise at the announcement of Gen's elevation to the Protectorship and said nothing until her mother put the comb down on the vanity. "And Dason will think we despise him!"

"My daughter," Mirelle said firmly, "I desire one thing above all others—to keep you safe. I interviewed Gen last night. This morning I spoke with Harrick and Captain Tolbrook. They agree that Gen is the best swordsman standing on Rhugothian soil. But more compelling than that is something Ethris told me the day of the Trials. He said that Gen feels a powerful devotion and loyalty to you,

Chalaine, as he proved beyond any doubt last night. So what Chertanne or what Dason thinks be damned. If I know Dason, he realized he committed an error when he deferred to Chertanne and will expect dismissal from the Protectorship. As for Chertanne, I find it hard to believe he will find a way to behave *less* civilly to you, regardless of what he may think we feel for him."

"I must marry him, Mother," the Chalaine said. "He will think you his enemy if you award Gen the Protectorship for defying him!"

"So you think Gen should have withheld his challenge, then?"

"No, of course not," the Chalaine replied, tone softening with the remembrance of the feelings her deliverance had awakened within her. "He is noble and courageous and deserves whatever honor we can give."

"Exactly. And I tell you this. If Chertanne continues to treat you like one of his no-account concubines, I will be his enemy. *'What is honorable must be revered and defended, regardless of where it is found. Baseness must be despised—and fought—wherever it is found.'"*

"You're quoting. Who said that?" the Chalaine asked.

"Gen did, last night. The man who lives that creed is the man who will guard my daughter. No other. Not anymore."

"It will hurt you politically in some quarters. You know that, don't you?"

"Most decisions I make do, but I am not making a political decision; I am making a personal and moral one. Chertanne will rise to our standard. We will not tolerate his. It is principle over expediency, dear. Chertanne acts like he does because no one taught him better, or—if they did teach him—never enforced the instruction. Gen, I think, is Chertanne's first true instructor, and with Gen as your protector, Chertanne will have no chance to forget the lesson. We can only hope he understood what was taught."

"But poor Dason," the Chalaine lamented forlornly.

"He is such a fine man. Courteous, noble. . ."

". . . handsome, intelligent, charming. Yes, I know you are infatuated with him."

"I am not!"

"Deny all you want, Chalaine, but a mother knows. I've watched you two for some time now. You were hoping that someone very like him would march off that pier yesterday."

"You would have hoped the same were you in my place! I think I comported myself rather well, considering the colossal distance between my fanciful expectations and the disheartening reality. But you could have helped there, I think. Any hint of Chertanne's character beforehand might have spared me being shocked into open-mouthed silence in front of the better part of the aristocracy and nobility."

"Be that as it may," Mirelle replied, dodging the accusation. "You don't have to like Chertanne. In fact, I would be surprised if you could. But beware your feelings toward other men! Truthfully, I wish Gen were at least my age or Jaron's. The last thing you need right now is another young man as your guard! But Gen is disciplined beyond my imagining and anxious to do his duty. I did not choose him because you will like him less than Dason, but if you do, then that is just as well."

"I think Fenna has laid claim to him already," the Chalaine said. "Very well, then. I will accept your will and pretend that I had a choice. I hope you do not think I dislike Gen or undervalue what he did for me—for us. I owe him my honor and my dignity and will give him every respect. Have we learned more about him?"

"A little," Mirelle answered, turning toward the mirror to adjust her hair. "The main curiosity, obviously, is how he is so skilled so young."

"And?"

"And after watching them fight, Regent Ogbith had the answer. The same smith that forged Cormith forged Gen as well."

The Chalaine's mouth gaped. "Torbrand Khairn trained Gen? Why would the Shadan of Aughmere bother training a peasant of a nation he is now overrunning? It's daft!"

"Shadan Khairn is known for swordsmanship, not good sense," Mirelle quipped. "He is not always a rational man. I will try to find out why he did it and how, though I hesitate to ask Gen, as the memory of his training—or Shadan Khairn's presence in his homeland—will not be pleasant. I believe the scars Gen suffered originated from that training or some other cruelty of the Shadan's. I am to take a meal with Gen when time permits, and I'll be sure to pass along anything interesting. But we should go. Ethris and Gen will be waiting for us. Is Fenna coming?"

"Yes. She will meet us there."

After retrieving one of the Chalaine's hairs from the brush, Mirelle opened the door. Jaron bowed deeply to the First Mother and the Chalaine, falling in behind them as they navigated the long passages underneath the Tower, emerging into the main corridor of the Great Hall and arriving at the double doors. Hurney stood there fast asleep. The First Mother motioned for silence from the guards, and they opened the doors to the outside without disturbing the old Chamberlain, who remained asleep despite the daylight that flooded over him through the doorway.

The Chalained whispered, "How much longer do you think Fedrick can keep up his post, Mother?"

"His family is long-lived, so I hope he can keep at it for some time to come."

Once down the stairs, they turned toward the old Chapel. Rather than go in the Chapel proper, they circled around to the back toward a small building where the acolytes gathered in small groups for meditation and prayer. Fenna had already arrived, leaning against the building near the door, absentmindedly twirling a spring rose between her fingers.

"A gift from Gen?" the Chalaine whispered as she greeted her beloved handmaiden with an embrace.

"No. It is from Kimdan. He gave it to me this morning." Fenna sounded confused, and the Chalaine grabbed her arm and pulled her inside after her mother entered.

"We'll talk about it later," the Chalaine said, surmising that Kimdan's sudden demonstration of affection toward Fenna was no doubt tied up with her recent interest in Gen.

The room where Ethris performed the branding for protectors was square and ascetically appointed, a room for instruction and meditation. Rough wooden benches faced a modest table upon which Ethris had placed the implements of branding, an ornate silver knife, a variety of dyes, and a wooden cup with some sour-smelling draught that deadened pain. Gen stood at attention by the rough-stone hearth, hands behind his back, and Ethris stoked the fire. Both turned and bowed as the First Mother and the Chalaine entered.

It was the first time the Chalaine had seen Gen in daylight, and upon seeing him again, a chill ran down her spine. Something about his presence invited her to bow to him instead of the other way around. Though a commoner, he commanded a regality, intelligence of eye, and apparent self-control to match any noble she had ever met. Now that she knew what he could do—both in terms of sword-skill and courage—she couldn't help but feel awed and even a little fearful. Such a man as Gen would brook no weakness, accept no quarter, and never compromise his principles. The Chalaine passed and he nodded his head to her in deference. She returned the courtesy, feeling his inferior in everything that mattered.

Mirelle and Fenna, the Chalaine noted, did not suffer from the same discomfort, approaching and addressing Gen very familiarly, her mother—surprisingly—even kissing him on the cheek. Jaron closed the door and stood by it, Cadaen at his side, as the ladies took a seat on the bench nearest the table. Despite feeling intimidated by her new protector, the Chalaine couldn't help staring at his face, noticing the tanned skin and white scars that crisscrossed everywhere. Fenna looked at him too, rose clutched in her hands, and with eyes that indicated a mind preoccupied.

"Welcome, Ladies and protectors," Ethris greeted them. He wore his white ceremonial robe as he had the day before. "We gather at the request of the First Mother to induct Gen into the Chalaine's personal Protectorship. Since the first Chalaine, the best of men were sought to guard her against the day of the accomplishment of her purpose. Now that the moment is close at hand, Gen, you must realize that you will have a unique place in history and an honor that few in that history can lay claim to. You should know that it is the unanimous agreement of all those employed in the protection of the Chalaine that you are most worthy and fit to serve her in mind, body, and purpose. We thank you for what you have done thus far for the Chalaine and have full confidence that you will do many more great things in her service."

"Thank you, Ethris and First Mother, for this opportunity to serve," Gen replied.

"Let's begin. Just do as I instructed you, Gen," Ethris said. "I know it is a lot to remember on short notice, so ask me for any help, should you need it. Most inductees have some time to prepare, but you are a special case, so there is no shame if you forget some of it."

Gen nodded, and the Chalaine sat up straight as Gen approached her and knelt, unsheathing his sword to lay it on her knees. The Chalaine swallowed hard. His green eyes seemed to penetrate the veil, and she was grateful when he bowed his head.

"Most Holy Mother, bearer of the hope of nations, I

offer my sword to you and ask that you accept me into your service. I declare myself fit for that service and proclaim my unswerving desire to protect you against any you should call enemy. Will you have me?"

"I will," the Chalaine returned weakly, clearing her throat to speak more forcefully, "if you swear, under Eldaloth's watchful eye, to obey the will of the crown of Rhugoth, to be willing to brave any trial that my protection and the protection of the holy babe will require of you, and to never betray me, my house, or the will of Eldaloth."

"This I swear."

"Do you swear to fight every device of Mikkik and his Ilch that are laid against the path of my duty, even unto the laying down of your life?"

"This I swear."

"Do you swear to behave with honor, dignity, and compassion, as is befitting one who represents and protects me?"

"This I swear."

"Then rise and take your sword. May such peace attend us that you never need draw it in my service, but should such days come, wield it well."

Gen lifted the sword carefully, resheathing it. "My sword and my life are yours. Command and I will obey."

He bowed again, the Chalaine inclining her head in return as he returned to stand by the table. The whole ritual made the Chalaine feel awkward, but what came next she could scarce bear to watch.

"First Mother," Ethris said, "do you have one of the Chalaine's hairs?"

"I do."

She unclenched her fist, and Ethris squinted to find the blonde strand. Taking it between his thumb and finger, he moved it to the table, trapping it under a bottle of dye.

Ethris picked up the drink and offered it to Gen. "Swallow this, and I've got a leather strap for you to bite down on, if you would like.

"No thank you," Gen refused. "I prefer to keep my senses sharp."

The Chalaine couldn't say why, but she half-expected this refusal. Ethris raised his eyebrows, and Fenna furrowed hers. Mirelle regarded him thoughtfully.

"Very well, but this will hurt a great deal."

Gen removed his shirt and Ethris stepped forward with his thin-bladed knife. With a steady hand and delicate skill, he cut into Gen's flesh at the center of his chest, carving a tight spiral pattern. The Chalaine focused away from the cutting, settling on Gen's face, astonished at his control. Not a flinch, grimace, or blink. His eyes didn't even water.

"So tell us about where you are from, Gen," Mirelle asked while Ethris worked.

"I am from a small town in Tolnor just southwest of the Rede Steppes. It was called Tell. Simple lumbermen and farmers, mostly. Cold winters. Pleasant summers. It lay in the Dukedom of Murin Norshwal, if you ever had occasion to meet him."

He might be sitting at a picnic in the sunny highlands for all the strain in his voice, and Gen's indifference to pain gave the Chalaine the strange sensation that the body receiving the violence and the man that spoke were disconnected from each other.

"I never have," the First Mother answered as Ethris finished, blotting the blood away from the completed design.

"Now, Gen," said Ethris, "I will work the Chalaine's hair into the wound. It is the binding agent that will allow you to know in which direction she is and to sense whatever physical duress she may be under."

He dipped the hair in a greenish dye and, while incanting, worked nimbly to insert the hair within the spiral cut. When done, he heated the blade and sealed the wound. The smell of burning flesh twisted the Chalaine's stomach.

"You say it *was* named Tell. Was it destroyed?" the First Mother continued as the blade sizzled around the wound.

"Most of the people were killed when it was occupied late last fall."

"You met Torbrand Khairn there?" the First Mother asked, and the Chalaine caught a slight tightening around his eyes. Her mother had scored a mark.

"Yes."

Mirelle nodded. "That would explain recent reports. I will explain more later."

Finished with the brand, Ethris wiped his stained hands on a cloth from the table. "That completes that portion of the branding. It is customary that a black rose be burned into the under part of the protector's forearm as well, though it is not required. Dason refused it. It is merely a tradition that has persisted through the years. Will you receive it?"

"Yes."

Ethris unstoppered the bottle of black dye, coated Gen's forearm with it, and then removed from a pocket in his robe a rose pattern fashioned carefully of a thin metal. Placing the design on the forearm, Ethris incanted again. The metal flashed white-hot for a split-second, the smell of burning filling the room again. Clearing away the pattern brand and the residue of dye revealed the perfect black rose.

"Now, Chalaine," Mirelle said, "if you would perform a little healing on your new Protector so that he doesn't die of infection, we will conclude the ceremony." The Chalaine stepped forward, completely unnerved. He wasn't even sweating.

"Extend your hand," she requested, taking it as he offered it and concentrating to heal the damage caused by the burning and cutting. His skin, coarse and calloused, was abrasive to hers, and just from his light grip she knew he could crush her hand in an instant. Once finished, she

319

opened her eyes to find him regarding her, and she stepped away from the power of his stare. Couldn't anyone else see it? Did it not discomfit anyone else?

"That concludes my work," Ethris said, hands on the table. "Do the First Mother or the Chalaine have anything to add?"

"Just a welcome into the close society of the Chalaine's service," Mirelle said brightly. "I believe Gen already knows our regard for him. Do you wish to say anything, daughter? Fenna or Jaron?"

Jaron spoke unexpectedly, and all on the bench had to shift to see him by the door. "I, too, welcome him and thank him for teaching me my duty. Since you raised the challenge against the Ha'Ulrich, Gen, I have been your man. I regard you as better than a brother and could ask for no better companion to serve with me."

"I thank you, sir," Gen returned. "I owe you a great debt for supporting me in the matter. You have served long and well. I hope to do the same."

"Report to your post at the start of the sixth watch, Gen," the First Mother instructed him as he replaced his shirt. "If you have any questions about your living arrangements or other mundane matters, ask the Chamberlain."

They filed out, leaving Gen behind with Ethris. The Chalaine just caught the Mage asking him something about pain before they emerged into the bright morning. The acolytes walked about the gardens surrounding the Chapel, plucking out weeds and pulling dead petals off the flowers. The smell of the flowers calmed her nerves, and she took a deep breath.

"How can he do that?" Fenna asked, voice subdued. "Utterly amazing. It's as if he feels nothing he chooses not to."

"Amazing? Unnerving was the word I would choose!" the Chalaine said. "Or unnatural! I have seen four such

320

ceremonies, and believe me, the leather strap was well chewed in each one of them, cup of grog notwithstanding."

"I think, my daughter," the First Mother interjected, catching up from behind, "that you may find all those scars have something to do with it. He has obviously been cut on a great deal more than anyone I've ever had in my company. What was done to him was inhuman, unnatural, though he is not so."

"Unless being treated so unnaturally made him so," the Chalaine returned, anxious to talk of something else. "Tell us about the rose, Fenna."

"I don't know what I'm supposed to think," Fenna said some time later. They hadn't been able to talk much after the ceremony, as a reception with the nobles took up most of the morning. Chertanne, drunk before things got too far underway, raved continually about Cormith's defeat and death, keeping company mostly with the Aughmerian Warlords. The Chalaine, in kind, mingled with Rhugothians, though the few Tolnorian nobles in attendance seemed anxious to meet her and inquire about Gen. Word of Gen's nationality had spread quickly after the Trials, doubly so after the duel with Cormith. The Chalaine was surprised to find that most Tolnorians knew little to nothing about Tell, either.

The reception broke up after Chertanne threw up his lunch and was escorted away from the hall to receive ministrations from the Puremen. The Chalaine didn't know if hangovers could be healed, as she had never been asked to perform a healing on someone thus indisposed. A few bitter herbs, she knew, could do the trick. The Chalaine searched the room, finding Fenna bidding farewell to her parents who were returning to their estate in the south until the betrothal. Once finished, her handmaiden crossed the room to where the Chalaine stood with her mother. They left at once so they could talk.

The Chalaine leaned in close to Fenna so that Jaron following behind couldn't hear. "I find it rather coincidental that Kimdan should at a last pay due attention to you after you take an interest in another man. I suppose recovering the captaincy of the apprentices from Gen isn't conquest enough, then?"

"Do you think Kimdan knows I've been interested in him?"

"Is he an idiot?" the Chalaine asked with smirk.

"No!"

"Then he knows."

"What am I to do?" Fenna pleaded. "Gen thrills me. Kimdan spins my head around. Neither has done anything—well, until today—to return my interest. Gen hasn't even returned my favor."

"He's been busy."

"True."

"But perhaps," the Chalaine said, "there is something we can do after all. You know every detail and fact about Kimdan, his family, his disposition, his birthday. How much do you know about Gen?"

"I know he's from Tell and that he would be the person to see should I want to get someone killed. Other than that, little. Every time I talk to him, I find I'm answering more questions than I'm asking. He always turns our conversations away from himself."

"Well," the Chalaine said, resolved, "let's go to the library and see where this Tell is. It's a start. Maybe we can find out something about the Duke and Duchess Norshwal, as well."

They came in through the rear entrance of the library, knowing that Pureman Obard would be there in his small, book-littered office.

"Good afternoon, ladies," he said, standing after they startled him out of his reading. Obard bowed, straightening his long brown robe. He was tall, thin, and gaunt, skin evidencing his lack of outdoor activity. The flesh around his eyes seemed to have receded to give his eyeballs more room to soak up words. "How may I serve you?"

"We are looking for information on a town in the Tolnorian Kingdom named Tell and wondered if you might point us toward a likely place to find it," the Chalaine requested.

Obard had several places to search readily in memory and ran off into the stacks, mumbling titles to himself. He returned with a remarkable pile of scrolls and books, but after nearly an hour of searching through them, they gave up. No cartographer, it seemed, deemed Tell worthy enough of mention in any official map or census.

"It is quite possible," Obard explained, "that it is a newer town or perhaps one so small or out of the way that no one bothered to record its position on the map. The newest map of Tolnor we have is dated fifty-five years ago."

"Thank you, Pureman Obard," the Chalaine said, feeling tired. "I'm going to go find something to read this evening. I'll let you know what it is before I leave."

"Very well, Holiness. I'll keep searching for more information. I've several ideas on where else to look. May I ask what your interest is in this town?"

"It is where Gen is from," Fenna answered.

"Oh! Well!" Obard stood, a smile coming to his face. "You should have said so. Gen is in the foyer now. He came in this morning. We can just ask him."

Obard followed behind Jaron as the Chalaine and Fenna walked out into the library proper, Fenna squinting as they emerged into the fully sunlit room. The Chalaine noted her handmaiden's nervous look. She had worried the rose in her hand so much that the petals now drooped and bent off

323

at weird angles. The Chalaine busied herself by skimming the titles as they walked by.

"Look," Fenna whispered. "There he is, asleep on the couch."

The Chalaine peeked between the books. Sure enough, Gen lay aslant on the couch, cradling his sheathed sword on his chest, hilt near his ear. A pile of three books sat on the floor nearby. Even in sleep he looked dangerous.

"See how he embraces his sword in rest," Fenna observed, grinning, "like a long-absent lover."

"He fell asleep in the same place and same fashion yesterday," Obard informed them. "The scullery maids saw him so and declared him in 'desperate need of a woman' before I shooed them off. I think I shall have to embroider his name on that couch. Quite an avid reader for a peasant, if these last two days tell anything of his habits."

The Chalaine couldn't help but feel curious about what books a man like Gen might read.

"Should we wake him and ask him to point out where he's from on the map?" Obard offered. "I could record it."

"No!" Fenna declined, suddenly coy. "I don't want him to feel like we're prying."

"Speaking as a man, though not as a Pureman, I think he would feel flattered that two such ladies took enough interest to discover more about him. Let's wake him. I must admit that I, too, am curious about his origins."

"No. He needs his rest," Fenna protested. "He's to start his duties with the Chalaine this very evening."

And then Chertanne was there, and, even more oddly, Dason trailed behind him along the row of books. Jaron scowled at both of them. Obard bowed and Fenna and the Chalaine curtsied to the Ha'Ulrich. The Chalaine met Dason's eyes, finding them on her. She fought back the sense of longing and turned her attention toward her future husband.

He held a large apple in his hand. His 'sickness' required

a change of clothing, and he wore blue pants with a white shirt, a golden sash running from shoulder to hip. Why Chertanne chose to wear tight-fitting clothing that emphasized his protruding gut, the Chalaine could not fathom, though she doubted anyone still living—excepting Gen—possessed the nerve to inform him of his atrocious wardrobe. The Puremen, thankfully, had somehow managed to sober him up.

"Well," said Chertanne, "Chalaine and, um, Miss Fern?"

"Miss Fenna Fairedale, your Grace," the Chalaine corrected.

"Right. Fenna. They told me you two came here and so I thought I would find you and deliver the news myself. Forgive me, Chalaine, if I do not stand closer. I fear I should accidentally touch you and that awful peasant your mother just named your protector should come for me with the sword." He took a bite of his apple, spraying juice everywhere. "Good apple, if a little out of season."

"Said protector is nearby, your Grace," the Chalaine informed him, attempting to deter Chertanne from further comments that might incense Gen.

"Oh, is he?" Chertanne stepped forward to get a better look. "Oh," he whispered, "and he is sleeping. Well, he should hear what I have to say, too, since he is author of the circumstance that necessitated it."

Chertanne pulled a book from the shelf and lobbed it at Gen. The Chalaine, surprised and appalled at this disrespect, opened her mouth to give warning, but took a step back as Gen sprung from sleep, drew his sword, and dodged the missile in a heartbeat. The book bounced harmlessly on the cushions while Gen fixed his stare on Chertanne. Fenna moved around Chertanne and hurried toward a confused Gen, greeting him affectionately. The Chalaine found a lump in her throat and swallowed hard to dismiss it; Gen was ever the adder, even in rest coiled to strike.

"Chalaine, Ha'Ulrich, Miss Fairedale," Gen said, bowing upon noticing the first. "Did someone throw a book at me?"

The Chalaine moved from behind Chertanne, whose feet were rooted to the carpet, face pale. Gen resheathed his sword, which helped Chertanne's indisposition a little.

"The Ha'Ulrich was sporting with you, Gen," the Chalaine soothed. "Nothing more. He has some announcement to make."

Gen picked up the book and eyed the title. "A fitting and excellent choice, your Grace," he pronounced, returning the volume to the couch. "I would not be offended to have a hundred of such books hurled at me."

"You have tried our patience long enough, Chertanne," the Chalaine cut in. "Do make your announcement."

"Yes, yes." Chertanne collected himself. "The announcement. As Dason, a fine man of name and rank, was recently and most undeservedly wrenched from his post in favor of a man with no name and no rank—and finding that recent events have left a vacancy in the position of my bodyguard—I have asked Dason to replace Cormith at his post and he has accepted. He is my new bodyguard. What say you, peasant? How take you the news?"

"He has served your desire well in at least one matter I can recall. While one act does not a full precedent make, I am convinced from other reports that Dason is a consistent man and a solid fighter."

Dason's face flamed red and he turned away. The Chalaine silently cursed Gen for his barb. Dason's pain hurt her, and she wished everyone else would leave so she could comfort him and convince him that she blamed him for nothing. Still, despite her good opinion of him, she felt disappointment at his acceptance of the position. As a Tolnorian, however, he was no doubt honor bound to obey his future king.

326

"But Gen!" Chertanne pressed on. "Do you not feel a bit of pity for the poor Chalaine? Dason is a high-bred man of charm and wit, a Prince of Tolnor, and you have stripped him of his post, leaving the Chalaine with you, a commoner, who has in two days time garnered a reputation for having a wooden personality. What was it I heard the servants calling you? The 'Dead-faced Man', I believe it was."

The Chalaine bit her lip. Why was Chertanne baiting him?

"The First Mother appointed me the Chalaine's protector," Gen said, "because she and her counselors judged me the most fit to act in her physical defense. When an Uyumaak is trying to drag your intestines out, all the nobility and pleasant conversation at one's command will only serve to lend you a clever line to utter at your death. They placed me in this office to kill the Chalaine's enemies, not so I could be anyone's charming dinner companion."

While Gen's tone, on the surface, revealed no heat or ill will, the Chalaine's knees shook. What ire, if any, Gen's controlled face masked, Chertanne's did not. Thankfully, the library doors opened, providing a welcome distraction in the form of Chamberlain Hurney.

"Blessed One!" he exclaimed, executing the best bow his old back would permit. "And Holiness! Forgive this intrusion. I have a message for Gen and beg your leave to deliver it."

"By all means, Chamberlain," the Chalaine said. "We are only engaged in idle conversation."

"Very well. Gen, the First Mother requests that you take the evening meal with her before your duties begin this evening. Shall I receive your response now or shall I wait upon it?"

"Tell the First Mother I accept, though you may wish to warn her that I am reported to have a wooden personality."

"As you wish," Hurney said, wrinkling his brow at the

addendum to the reply.

"It is obvious the First Mother favors you overmuch, Gen," Chertanne observed haughtily.

"In matters of being over favored, I will certainly defer to your judgment," Gen returned.

"I certainly judge correctly in this! I am the Savior of the World and her future son-in-law and she has not invited me to a private dinner!"

"Considering that during the last meal she took with you, you tried to drag her daughter off to your bed like a common street whore, I think it's understandable that she needs an ample period of time to invent some good feeling for you before inviting you to dinner."

As always, Gen spoke without emotion, as if every word were plainly true and not the least bit offensive. As before, Chertanne turned red, stunned to silence at Gen's complete disregard for his station, and the Chalaine feared something awful was about to happen.

"Oh yes. Blessed One," Chamberlain Hurney interjected in the tense lull. "I am informed that your concubines are all safely ashore now and comfortably quartered."

"Thank you," Chertanne replied, embarrassment cutting in front of fury on his face at the Chamberlain's ill-timed information. The Chalaine's heart sank. She knew Aughmerians engaged in the practice of taking concubines, but she thought Chertanne, considering his role in prophecy as the Father of God, would not be permitted. Yet one more thing her mother had withheld from her, though the Chalaine remembered her alluding to it earlier that morning. She thought she caught the flash of surprise in Gen's eye as well, but couldn't be sure. Chamberlain Hurney bowed again and left.

"Concubines?" the Chalaine said, a thin film of politeness overspreading her anger and humiliation. "Why, how many do you have?"

"Only fourteen," he said, apparently missing the

Chalaine's emotion. "Father had many more. I suspect I will surpass him, due to my calling."

He bit into the apple again, chewing it enthusiastically. The Chalaine didn't have the words to speak.

"Forgive me, Chertanne," Gen broke in. "Doesn't law in Aughmere state that one can only take concubines after marriage to a wife?"

The Chalaine knew this to be true. It was a concession Aughmerians made to the Church of the One, which frowned upon the Aughmerian custom of wives and concubines.

Chertanne shrugged. "I have no wish to discuss Aughmerian law with a Tolnorian peasant. I must be going now, anyway." He extended the half-eaten apple to the Chalaine. "Do you want the rest?"

She shook her head in response, not trusting her voice, and Chertanne plopped the apple in Obard's hand, instructing him to dispose of it however he wished. Jaron's face twisted in anger. Gen just stared at Chertanne's back until the Blessed One disappeared into the rows of books.

"So, Gen," Pureman Obard spoke, relieving the silence, "I hear you are from Tell in the Tolnorian nation. I have searched and can find no record of it. I wonder if you might help me locate it."

"Some other time, Pureman Obard," Gen said. "I need to get some rest before my appointment with the First Mother this evening. I promise to return and give you all the particulars. A half-hour should prove adequate to relate them all."

"That will be fine."

"Chalaine, Miss Fairedale," Gen said, bowing, "I must take my leave of you."

"You can take a book with you, if you like." Obard offered.

"You know the rules, Obard," Gen said. "I wouldn't want to start breaking them on the very first day of my new position."

"What rule?" Fenna asked.

"Well," Obard explained, "comm . . . er, those not of noble birth cannot remove books from the library."

"That's ridiculous. Surely Gen is an exception!" Fenna protested.

"Don't look at me so, Miss Fairedale!" Obard exclaimed defensively. "I tried to get him to take one!"

"Don't worry, Fenna," Gen placated. "I take no offense. The library is certainly better than any place I have to put a book. You'd best find a better place for that rose, though, or old man winter will not have a change of heart. Good day."

Gen left, and the Chalaine wrinkled her brow.

"Old man winter?" Fenna wondered. "What did he mean by that?"

"I don't know," the Chalaine answered more glumly than she wanted to.

Pureman Obard rubbed his chin. "That phrase reminds me of something. Can't quite recall it now. But I know where to look!" The Pureman disappeared into the stacks again.

"He is right about the rose, though" Fenna said, examining the flower. "Do you think he knows that Kimdan gave it to me? Oh, I hope not!"

"Fenna," the Chalaine returned, trying hard to act the healer while her soul bled. Fenna seemed oblivious to her pain. "When Kimdan found out about your attentions to Gen, he warmed to you considerably. Perhaps it will work in reverse as well?"

Fenna smiled, her gloomy disposition instantly dispelled. "I think you are right!" she answered happily. "Let's take care of this rose."

"Yes, but wait." The Chalaine went to the couch where Gen had slept and picked up the book Chertanne had thrown at him: *His Master's Secret Law*. Pureman Obard was nowhere to be found, so she tucked the book under her arm. "We'll come tell him later. Let's go somewhere Chertanne will not find us."

Chapter 21 - A Dinner With the First Mother

Gen slept in the empty apprentices' quarters in the barracks, not wanting to go to his new room within the Chambers of the Chalaine since he couldn't be sure if Dason had completely vacated it yet. He wasn't in the humor for a meeting with the man he was replacing. No doubt Dason had taken his dismissal as the gravest insult.

Outside on the field, Captain Tolbrook drilled the apprentices, and Gen drifted off to sleep to the sound of Tolbrook's deep voice barking orders. As usual, he slept poorly. Images of Regina's death and the sight of Rafael laying cold upon his bed surfaced in his dreams like corpses popping to the top of a still pool, and when he awoke he felt sad and out of sorts, not the mood in which to dine with the First Mother of Rhugoth.

Evening drew close and he rose, collecting his black coat from the chair, noting the lump in the pocket—Fenna's favor. Gen shook his head. Chamberlain Hurney had instructed him to return it quickly or cause offense. Now that he would be on duty at night and she in the day, he didn't know how he would manage a satisfactory visit.

Returning a favor required more than just returning the object; a man was to do something special. After dreaming about Regina all afternoon, he had no heart to even try. Guilt ate at him, though. Fenna had gone out of her way to help him feel welcome, and she deserved more than what he could give in return.

Gen scrubbed his face in the basin of water on the table at his bedside and rebuckled his sword belt. Conversation in the hall signaled the return of the apprentices, and a surprised Gerand opened the door, followed by Volney. Both were sweaty and bedraggled, more than one bruise decorating bare torsos.

"Gen," Gerand said, bowing. Volney was speechless.

"Gerand. Volney. Forgive my intrusion. I just needed a place to rest this afternoon."

"It is an hon . . . unexpected pleasure to see you, Gen," Volney finally said. "Can we see it?"

"See what?"

"The branding!" Volney said, excitedly. "Did it hurt? What does it look like?"

"Volney!" Gerand interrupted. "What you ask is most improper, and I'm sure you don't think Gen will actually show you."

"Oh," Volney was crestfallen. "I suppose you're right."

Kimdan rounded the corner, confident and happy despite being bruised more than either Gerand or Volney. "Is that Gen?"

"It is!" Volney confirmed.

"Well, what brings you back to us, Gen?" Kimdan inquired, manner cocky. "I thought protectors got quarters in the Chambers of the Chalaine. Were you denied the berth because of your rank?"

"Certainly not," Gen replied evenly. "I smell just fine. Much better than the three of you anyway. I will take my quarters this evening."

Gerand and Volney smiled. Kimdan rolled his eyes up

into his head.

"And have you seen Miss Fairedale today?" Kimdan asked smugly.

"Yes. I had the pleasure of her company for a brief time."

"And how was she?"

"She seemed to be frowning a bit more than usual and kept staring at some miserable excuse for a rose she got from somewhere."

Kimdan somehow turned red even through his sunburn, and Gen successfully determined the source of Fenna's flower.

"Will you take dinner with us in the commons?" Gerand asked.

"I would like to eat with you, but I am taking dinner with the First Mother this evening and must be on my way."

"With the First Mother herself?!" Volney said. "What an honor!" Kimdan smirked and turned away.

Gen started toward the door. "Yes, with the First Mother herself. Take care. I will try to see you soon. Maybe Tolbrook will let me spar with you some time."

"We'll be ready for you," Kimdan affirmed, he and Volney stepping aside.

"I doubt it," Gen mumbled mostly to himself, walking out into the cooling night air.

Clouds gathered in the west, hinting at a brilliant sunset in store, but somewhere in the city something burned, a column of dark gray smoke billowing up into sky. A stiff breeze brought the smell of wood smoke with it, tinted with a breath of rain. Several people commented about it as he passed, and as he climbed the castle hill, the column of smoke thickened. Chamberlain Hurney was waiting at the doors when he arrived.

"Good evening, Gen. How are your court manners coming along?"

"I will tell you after I dine with the First Mother."

"Just do what she does and you'll be fine. I'm afraid, however, that she is late on some matter of pressing business. She bids you wait for her in the Main Hall until she can come to you."

"Very well."

The Great Hall was mostly empty when he entered it, orange-red light coming through the clear windows coloring everything in fire. On the west-facing balcony servants scrambled about to prepare the table and the meal. Rather than ascend, Gen took time to study the tapestries he had noticed earlier.

A section of them outlining Aldradan Mikmir's life caught his attention. The first panel showed him as a youth, a strapping farm boy. All around him the artisan depicted wildlife, for it was said that Aldradan was a friend to nature and that the animals talked to him.

The next showed the start of the First Mikkikian war, Uyumaak and other horrors pouring into Lal'Manar, sacking it and filling their arms with its treasures. Men, women, and children lay dead upon the ground, and Uyumaak cut rings from fingers and purses from belts while squabbling over which bodies to cook.

The third showed Aldradan leaving his farm and joining as a soldier even though his rank prohibited him from doing so. An eagle with a sword in its talons descended to him, and thus began the gradual rise of Aldradan Mikmir from farmhand to the King of a new nation, Rhugoth.

Gen turned as the door opened. The First Mother entered, beautiful in a blue dress, but her eyes were tight with worry. Cadaen, coming in behind her, appeared equally disturbed. She managed a smile at him despite her distress.

"Finding someone like yourself on the walls, I see."

"I'm no Aldradan Mikmir, your Grace," Gen returned, bowing. "If half the stories of him are true, then I doubt

335

there will ever be another man quite like him."

"Perhaps not, but what endeared Aldradan to the people was the fact that he was so ordinary and plain, not given to device, dissembling, or maneuvering as most nobles are." The First Mother stood silently for a moment as if waiting for something. "Did Hurney not teach you that it is custom on these occasions for the gentleman to extend his arm and escort the lady to the table?" she finally asked.

"He did, Milady. But I am not a gentleman. One of my station is to follow behind you."

"I told you I would take care of that, and I will. You must practice for when I do. Your arm, *sir*."

He complied and led the First Mother up the stairs, Cadaen shadowing them closely. The meal was laid out on a stone table in the open air, attractively arranged fruits, meats, and slices of dark bread spread on a purple silk cloth. Crystal glasses filled with red wine accented the decorated white plates and silver utensils. Gen had never seen such a finely appointed table save at the reception for Chertanne, and he felt grateful for the simplicity of the fare. By most accounts, aristocracy ate rare things.

The First Mother pulled him past the table and leaned on the balustrade overlooking the city. The steady west wind blew her hair about, and she quickly worked her blonde locks into a bun and secured it with a long silver pin. From their vantage point on the balcony, they could easily see the block of the city below where the fire raged, spreading slowly.

"I'd hoped for a calm evening," she commented. "I have a lot to ask you."

"What happened?"

"Reports are a little strange. This is the third time we've had a fire like this in as many months. Ilch's work, but we can't quite pin down how it is done."

"The circumstances are unusual, then?"

"Yes," the First Mother replied, signaling for him to sit.

336

"I'll tell you while we eat. I'm afraid this incident will curtail the time I allotted to spend with you."

"Perfectly understandable, Milady."

"But before we talk of the fire, I wanted to warn you to exercise a little caution. The Chalaine told me about your repartee with Chertanne this afternoon, including the bit about the 'street whore' and 'wooden personality.' Chertanne will try to bait you into mistakes, and you must not return in kind. Despite how childish he can be, the Ha'Ulrich wields a great deal of power and has many loyal friends. There are several rumors of plots on your life circulating, and at least two seem credible."

"I assure you I was more civil than he warranted. I will try, however, not to tempt fate any further."

"Tempt it? As far as Chertanne is concerned, you've been poking fate with a sharp stick! I cannot ask you to act against your conscience, but realize that exchanging unpleasantries with Chertanne only sours his disposition and can only hurt you. Understood?"

"Yes, Milady, but if Chertanne doesn't warm to the idea of behaving more decently, I'm afraid there will always be winter between us. 'Frost will always hate the song bird and the blossom,' as they say."

"And who says that?"

"It's a poem, actually."

"Recite it for me, if you can."

Gen took a drink and leaned back.

Frost will ever hate the blossom,
Set its hand against the flower,
Seek to choke the songbird,
Tempt snow from raindrops
In the shower.

Fog will ever hate the sunshine,
Set its breath against the light,

Blind the keen-eyed traveler,
Cloud the blue-skied day
Into night.

If such enemies in nature be
As frost and flower, fog and sun,
Then lift your eyes and watch;
Nature makes enemies
For everyone.

Mirelle nodded her appreciation. "Not a very cheering poem, but appropriate, perhaps. You let the Ilch be Chertanne's enemy. It will be impossible to protect the Chalaine from every indignity Chertanne will burden her with. It is enough that you keep her alive. So avoid Chertanne, if you can."

"As you wish."

"Very well."

The First Mother sat quietly for several minutes, eating the meal and staring at the smoke plume. She was obviously upset. Gen noticed she didn't use her silverware, absently tearing away the bread with her fingers. The meat and fruit, already sliced, she also took by hand. He imitated her. The cooks obviously spent more time on the First Mother's food than they did on that served in the commons. The meat was tender and perfectly seasoned, the fruit bruiseless and at the peak of ripeness.

After downing a slice of apple, her eyes fell on him again. "I wanted to tell you some news we just received from your homeland, though it may pain you to hear it. Should I continue?"

"Please. I have been anxious for any word."

"Torbrand Khairn is a clever one, I'm afraid. As you know, in late autumn he secreted a sizable force of men in the center of your country, in your town. By the time anyone found out, winter had struck and nothing could be

338

done save the spreading of news that Aughmere had invaded.

"Come spring, King Filingrail pulled a good portion of men off the northern line and sent them on the long march south to support Duke Norshwal's army. Once the King divided his forces, the Aughmerian army of soldiers, hiding their numbers, struck the northern border, putting your countrymen to flight. The latest news is that the Aughmerian force in the heart of your land simply withdrew—though to where, no one knows—their ruse completed. Tolnor has a long summer ahead of it. I am sorry."

"Thank you for telling me. I suspected as much. Tell me more about the fires."

"Yes. As I said, there have been three of this kind. In each case, witnesses said there was an 'explosion' of fire. This isn't someone lighting a fire with a torch or throwing a lantern into a building. One explosion was in the rafters of a Church, another in the cellar of a popular inn. Today's was in a busy guild house. We suspect magic, but have no clues as to who is behind it. The people are terrified. More than I care to count have died, and the fire today is engulfing neighboring buildings, residences for the poorer classes. You're thinking something. What is it?"

Gen thought a few moments more. Mirelle's description touched off something in what he had of Telmerran's memory. "Were animals found at any of the fires? Dead ones?"

"I haven't heard. Why?"

"During the First Mikkikian War, there were brother Magicians, one of Duammagic, the other of Mynmagic. They would use animals and fire against the Uyumaak. The process is taxing and difficult. The brothers would capture an animal—a bird, for example. They would build an enormous fire, and as it burned, the Duammagician would capture its heat until the last ember winked out and somehow bind the collected heat to the bird. The Mynmagician would then control the bird, guiding it into the middle of an Uyumaak camp. The Duammagician would release the binding, causing an explosion and great devastation.

"The process would exhaust both Magicians for many hours, and during such a weakness, an Uyumaak patrol stumbled upon the brothers and killed them, not knowing they were the perpetrators of the strange attacks. Of course, this kind of fuanurgy requires one Magician from each discipline of magic who is powerful. They would probably work away from people and in the dark to hide the smoke from the bonfire that the spell requires. During the period of weakness afterward, they would be vulnerable and easy to capture."

"I do remember a report from the Church fire of a parishioner saying she saw a raven perched on the rafter, taking it for a bad omen and leaving. Aren't the animals burned with the fire or explosion?"

"No," Gen replied. "The Duammagician has to protect them somehow to withstand the heat focused upon them by the binding. The impact of the blast will usually kill them, but when found, they are unburned, unlike everything around them. It's just a theory but one worth pursuing if none of the others are producing anything."

The First Mother rose. "I must relate this to Regent Ogbith at once. It is somewhere to start, the first place we've had. He may wish to speak to you of it. Ethris as well. Stay and enjoy your dinner. I promise I will invite you again. I am determined to have some conversation with you that doesn't relate to Chertanne, my daughter, or killing."

"Good evening, your Grace," Gen said, rising and bowing as she hurried off, Cadaen in tow. Gen relaxed and ate slowly, watching the orange sky deepen to red and purple. The breeze whipped up as the sun fell, lending potency to the smell of smoke. Thanks to Samian, he knew a heavy storm would pass through an hour or so after dark, a welcome relief to those faced with the flames below, though the initial winds would exacerbate the spreading of the fire.

Guessing it was close to the sixth watch, he passed through the Great Hall and descended into the Antechamber of the Chalaine to relieve Jaron. After his branding, Ethris had told him several interesting things about the Antechamber and the Chalaine's Chambers. The most interesting was about the Walls in the Chalaine's room.

"This secret is held even from the Chalaine until her majority," Ethris had explained, "and for good reason, as you will no doubt deduce. The Walls not only show locations within and around Rhugoth, but they can act as a Portal to them as well. The brand upon you is the key you need. But touch the Walls and speak the location and a Portal will be opened. If a foe makes it past the outer guards and into the Chalaine's inner sanctum, it is not your duty to fight. Anything that can win its way past the myriad of protections, both magical and mundane, and navigate that maze will likely be beyond your skill to defeat. In such an eventuality, you are to take her through the Portal. When the lake is not frozen, take her to the Defender. If it is, take her to Renberry Cathedral on the other side of Mikmir. It is the home of the Prelate and has a fighting order of Churchmen—the Eldephaere—attached to it. Once the Portal is passed through, it will be destroyed so that nothing can follow."

Besides this, Gen learned that all of the statues in the Antechamber were Foe Stones, creations from before the Shattering that could detect anyone entering with evil intent and shout warning. Even more impressive, two of them could transform themselves into the image of the enemy and fight. The small pool at the center of the room could heal wounds and cure poison, and behind a plant on either

341

side of the bridge a rune was inscribed that—when touched by someone bearing the protector's brand—would send the bridge crashing into the abyss below.

He entered the Antechamber, finding the number of the Dark Guard there increased by the addition of Kimdan and Gerand. They stood stiffly at attention, one of the other Dark Guard Masters standing opposite them to enforce discipline. Jaron, the Chalaine, and Fenna stood at the entrance to the maze, and Gen crossed to them and genuflected.

"Welcome, Gen" Jaron said.

"Good evening," Gen replied. "Are you to teach me the maze?"

"Yes," the Chalaine answered, "and to say farewell to Miss Fairedale, who is done for the day. Goodbye, Fenna."

"Goodbye, Milady." Fenna curtsied. "It is good to see you again, Gen. I hope you rested well." She turned to Kimdan. "Thank you for the rose, Kimdan! It is beautiful."

And then she left, a little too hurriedly by Gen's reckoning. Kimdan stood silent but grinning, fetching an angry stare from the Dark Guard across the room. The grin disappeared quickly. Inwardly, Gen groaned. Fenna had started a game he did not want to play, and the Chalaine, obviously, had part in staging the first round.

"Let's begin, then," Jaron said, entering the maze. "It's large and tricky, so pay close attention."

Gen figured the size of the Chalaine's maze double that of her mother's, requiring several minutes of confusing turns to get through. Traps, mundane and magical—usually both at the same time—greeted any wrong turn, and Gen's normally good memory was significantly motivated by the desire to avoid them. At the other side, they had him go through by himself while they tagged along to give warning should he choose amiss. Luckily, he learned the maze quickly, and Jaron applied a hearty slap on the back.

"Took Dason four days to get it straight," he disparaged

before leaving. "I'll see you in the morning."

Eldwena, Fenna's nocturnal counterpart, arrived next. Eldwena was older than Fenna and had a round puffy face with short blonde hair. Gen noticed she was pregnant. Her eyes and mouth bespoke a lifetime of fuss and worry.

"Where's Dason?" she inquired, clearly startled.

"My mother dismissed him and named Gen my protector. Gen, this is Lady Eldwena Moores. Eldwena, Gen."

"How do you do?" Gen said. Eldwena gaped in shock and ignored Gen's greeting.

"Your mother dismissed Dason? Was this today? I always miss everything when I go home. How could she dismiss Dason. He was so beautiful!"

"You're married, Eldwena."

"Well you're the Chalaine and you thought he was beautiful, too!"

"Come, Gen," the Chalaine said, turning away. "Your quarters are two down from my door. The first room is Jaron's. He usually doesn't sleep there, however."

"Have you seen Dason, Gen?" Eldwena asked him.

"Yes, of course."

"Gorgeous man, wouldn't you say?"

"I will leave that judgment to you ladies."

"Oh, it is a shame," Eldwena bemoaned. "Dason was a good one, he was. Made me laugh like my poor Robbie never could. Of course, Robbie makes me laugh, just at him, though, not with him. I don't suppose you're any good at cards, are you?"

"Too good for the both of you, I fear." Gen said flatly. The Chalaine stopped with Eldwena, the latter regarding Gen intently for several moments, eyes narrow.

"Is he joking, Milday?" she asked.

"I don't think Gen jokes with anyone, Eldwena. Come, let's go inside and not bore Gen with further talk of Dason. We'll find our own entertainments. Good night, Gen."

"Good night, Chalaine. Lady Moores."

They went inside without further comment, for which Gen was grateful. After such busy days, he felt in great need of several hours of unbroken solitude. If he could get through the rest of the day without hearing the names 'Dason' or 'Kimdan,' he would count himself blessed.

CHAPTER 22 - BETROTHAL

For the Chalaine, the summer, warm and dry, dragged by on lazy, broken legs. Feast after reception after meeting after presentation demanded her attendance, and Chertanne attended every one with her, drunk as often as sober. He jumped at any opportunity to receive the doting and worshipful attentions of his followers while conveniently turning dumb at the mention of any real work to be done or decisions to be made. To be sure, Chertanne was a skilled and charismatic celebrant, and—for all his moaning about Gen's lack of station—he spent almost every night in the poorer quarters of town among common folk, reveling in their adoration and attention.

One day, the Chalaine and Fenna decided to use the Walls to watch him on one of the rare occasions a meeting didn't require his presence. Everywhere Chertanne went, Dason trudging unhappily behind, the people thronged him. He loved it and played to their enthusiasm. But soon, the Chalaine had to will the Walls to fade; Chertanne was not a moral man. Three of the noble born daughters of Rhugoth had joined his harem of concubines since his arrival, raising his "tally" to seventeen. Between the meetings and his carousal in the town, the Chalaine wondered if he ever had time to visit them. She hoped he didn't.

At first she tried to talk to him, attempting to develop at least a rough politeness between them, if not a formal relationship, but a few days decided her against it and she gave up addressing him altogether if she could help it. For one, she didn't like it. Jaron didn't either, and the Chalaine found Jaron's hand on his blade hilt, fingers white-knuckled, on more than one occasion. If the Blessed One were to ask Fenna to join his harem, the Chalaine thought she might use his sword herself. She wondered if Chertanne would still be alive if Gen were her day protector. At the worst, Gen would raise another challenge, and Chertanne would send Dason to his death at Gen's hand.

And seeing Dason still hurt her. He was miserable, always wearing a face full of pathetic resignation, and he would no longer meet her eye. Better than anyone, he knew Chertanne's character. The Chalaine fancied that Dason felt badly for her and wished he could make amends for failing to stand with Gen for her honor. Of course, all she could do was fancy and guess at his feelings. She never spoke with him anymore. He was visited by the full consequence of his choice, and she could not rescue him. Ruefully, the Chalaine realized she was paying the price for choices she had no hand in making, and the cost continued to mount.

She increasingly leaned on Fenna and her mother to fend off her darker moods. Though not typically in Fenna's character, the young handmaiden perversely chose to throw her energies into winning over the quiet protector just because it was harder rather than be content with the ready attention and affection available from Kimdan. She claimed she could see a great depth in Gen, despite his reluctance to share much about himself. The Chalaine saw no depth. Gen emanated power, but otherwise he was single-minded and empty to her view, especially in contrast to Dason's lively, colorful personality.

Nothing convinced her more powerfully of this than the Testing Day for the Dark Guard's apprentices. The testing allowed the Dark Guard to measure the skill of each apprentice so they could tailor their training to each one's strengths and weaknesses. Rather than test the apprentices themselves as they normally would, the Dark Guard invited Gen to do it for them while they watched and judged. The Chalaine suspected they did it out of curiosity about Gen as much as any real need to better their evaluation of the young men. She and Fenna went to watch, Chertanne blighting them with his presence, although having Dason nearby nearly redeemed the occasion.

The first part of the day consisted of Gen going after each of the apprentices using different styles of fighting, some Dason and Jaron admitted they had never seen. Kimdan, expectedly, fared the best but faltered as Gen did combinations of exotic, unorthodox moves. It ended with Gen punching the Regent's son solidly in the face and giving him a black eye. Kimdan, furious, tried to avenge himself immediately, but Captain Tolbrook pulled him back and sternly lectured him for his absence of control.

The scene was then reversed, each apprentice attacking Gen with every slash, swing, and thrust in his arsenal. Gen barely needed to move, even for Kimdan's ebullient assault. Blessedly, the whole spectacle was so engrossing that Chertanne uttered far fewer unsavory comments than usual. The Chalaine could sense that Gen scared him like no one else ever had. He showed his fear by disparaging Gen when he could, though Gen gave little material for him to work with other than his low station and dull personality.

After the midday meal, they returned to a special treat the Dark Guard had planned. In a loud voice, Captain Tolbrook announced to the apprentices that they were to rush Gen as a group, Kimdan in command. Any apprentice who scored a mark on Gen would earn a day off.

"That's not fair!" Fenna protested. "Five against one!"

347

"Not fair for them," Jaron informed her. "You'll see, Miss."

And he was right. Kimdan, not even bothering to pretend to lead his squad, sprinted at Gen madly and attacked, Tolbrook chiding him loudly. Kimdan, however, had nothing at his disposal that Gen couldn't do four times faster and with twice the force, and before the other apprentices even arrived at the melee, Kimdan had fallen in pain. As the Chalaine watched Gen dismantle the apprentices, fighting with unparalleled fluidity and ferocity, she felt for the first time that she comprehended him. Gen was a tool, good for one thing and useless for all others. Her mother and Fenna might see more, but Gen was pure sword fighter. While courage and loyalty were his allies, personality and charm were superfluous to his purpose.

The fight ended rather sooner than the Dark Guard probably expected, though by their smiles they thought it rousing fun anyway. Kimdan managed to pick himself up to renew his advance only to have Gen smack him down doubly hard. The rest of the apprentices fared the same, though the Chalaine thought Gen laid off Volney and Gerand a bit. No one got a day off.

The Dark Guard availed themselves of the Chalaine's healing talent to mend their charges' broken fingers, collarbones, ribs, and many deep bruises. Gen stood on the field at attention, unmarked and unmoving, until Tolbrook gave him leave to go.

Perhaps Gen's impressive performance in the contest or Kimdan's ungentlemanly fuming afterward was what turned Fenna's romantic purposes entirely toward the former. Unfortunately for all, the succeeding months' brutal schedule provided little opportunity for casual time among friends. The Chalaine even heard her mother mention that she regretted not having an opportunity to sit down at a proper meal with Gen. While the first few weeks of Gen's appointment saw him the topic of much conversation, his night post and limited appearances in public eventually let him fade into the background.

His name surfaced once, briefly. His clue about the fires had helped the city guard turn up evidence of the "faunurgy" in some woods outside of the city. They started to patrol them regularly, and during the whole summer, no other explosions or fires occurred, though no one was apprehended for the deeds. In place of fires, horrible messages scrawled in some animal's blood were found on walls within the Damned Quarter. Each threatened the Chalaine's death in some new way. This curtailed her trips outside the castle walls, and though Chertanne was given warning, he didn't heed it, continuing his nightly revelries whenever and wherever he pleased.

The betrothal loomed closer with each setting of the sun, and the Chalaine couldn't decide whether she wanted it to come quickly or not. On the one hand, she wanted it over. On the other, she would be betrothed to the most repugnant man she had ever had the misfortune of knowing. Since betrothed she must be, she settled on wanting it to come quickly. In her mind, she held a secret hope that Chertanne would change, that the eventual weight of his responsibilities would sober him, both in mind and body, and unshackle an imprisoned nobility. She hoped that when he saw her unveiled, he would dismiss the concubines as inadequate and find a real affection for her that transcended his physical desire.

The more she thought and the closer the betrothal, the more her sorrow eroded all handholds of hope. She rarely cared to leave her room or even get dressed, finding every entertainment empty of enjoyment. With two weeks left before the "blessed day," as everyone else called it, she found it hard to sleep, the frightening double dream plaguing her over and over again as if to compel her to some choice or belief. But still, she couldn't fathom what it meant, and in those sleepless nights she finally found the time and will to read the book Chertanne had hurled at Gen to wake him in the library so many weeks before, *His Master's Secret Law*. And after the first few chapters, she had difficulty setting it aside, though she found the story unsettling in the extreme.

The story, written by one Sarvain Obelanne, told of a servant of an apparently upright and pious Lord. The Lord kept up appearances of goodness to everyone—his wife, his children, his peers, his Pureman—to everyone but his servant. The servant, a wretched, sick man low in the ranks of nobility, oddly commanded his Lord's trust because he seemed so inconsequential to everyone. But his Lord took him everywhere, on the trips that he told his family were to care for certain merchant dealings of his that were, rather, trips of riotous pleasure in far countries. The servant was present as the Lord lied, cheated, and philandered.

But in his own country and in his own house, all believed the Lord good, none suspecting in the least the man's secret law, his own way of living different than the life he professed to everyone else. When his Lord went to bed, the servant nearly blinded himself in the dim candlelight to record every name, every drink, every coin, and every word. As time wore on, some close to the family found evidence of his Lord's other life and questioned the servant threateningly about it, but he would say nothing, ever faithful, ever silent, even in the face of irrefutable evidence.

When the master died, the family asked the servant to perform a eulogy for the master he'd long served. In the last chapter of the book he gave it, long, honest, and damning, naming every bastard that could lay claim on his estate, every man the Lord had cheated and owed, every debt he had run up gambling and drinking. The effect of the servant's careful record keeping was the ruin of his Lord's estate, his wife and children impoverished and left beggars. The servant killed himself by poison afterward, joining his master in death.

When the Chalaine finished the book, she felt perplexed. Why had Gen lauded the book so highly? Merely to irritate Chertanne? For herself, she could not recommend it. It left her depressed and upset, though she couldn't decide which bothered her worse, the Lord's fraud or the servant's final act of betrayal, an act which hurt the innocent family rather than the one who deserved the punishment. The Chalaine had hoped the charming wife and children would escape the devastating knowledge of their husband's and father's depravity, but unlike most stories she liked to read, the ending to this story set her to serious thinking rather than pleasant dreaming.

She returned the book to the library next morning, but the story so possessed her that she turned it over in her mind all day, trying to guess at what it might mean and why Gen apparently thought so highly of it. She had assumed that Gen read books about fighting and war, but this book hadn't one sword stroke in it and was certainly meant to discomfit the reader.

For the first time she could remember, she itched for Gen to come on duty, bursting with questions for him. So anxious was she, that when he did emerge from the maze and dismiss Jaron, she didn't think to greet him properly, instead letting the questions run out all on top of each other.

"Why do you like that book? I could hardly make sense of it! What is Obelanne trying to say with such an awful ending? I suppose it's supposed to be symbolic of something or teach something, and I've had some ideas. What do you think?"

"I suppose you're talking about *His Master's Secret Law*?" Gen asked, calm tone a counterpoint to her own babbling.

"Yes," she said, settling herself.

"Which question do you want me to answer first?"

"The first."

351

"Why do I like it? One reason is that it was one of the first books my master had me read once I learned to read well. He assigned me to read it to teach me an early lesson. The lesson itself is the other reason I cherish it."

"What is the lesson?" the Chalaine asked, wondering why Shadan Khairn would have his student read such a book.

"I will do what my master did to me and reverse the question. What do you think it means?"

"I admit that I've thought a great deal on it today, and I keep thinking back to Chertanne that day in the library. I see him as the Lord of the story and Dason as the servant who follows him around silently everywhere. I suppose I thought you were saying to Chertanne that Dason would reveal his secrets one day to his detriment. But now that I say it, it sounds rather inadequate for an explanation."

"If that's what it means to you, then that's a good enough lesson."

"But not the right lesson."

"Obelanne did not leave behind anything explaining what he wanted learned from the story. For all we know, he wasn't trying to teach anything at all."

"But there is something to be learned, or it wouldn't bother me so much," the Chalaine pressed, feeling exasperated. "What was the lesson your master wanted you to learn from it? Surely he told you something."

"Yes, he did."

"Then what!?" The Chalaine would swear he was teasing her.

"I will tell you, Holiness, but I must first explain that I do not see the story as symbolizing Chertanne, at least not in the way you were thinking. My master taught me that the servant, the Lord, and his family are really parts of one person. The servant is the conscience, sickly and silent from his master's abuse, though still faithful. He is always there, recording every deed and misdeed. The family is what is good about a person. The servant's exposition of his Lord's deeds at the end merely represents the inevitable time when the curtains over our memories and deeds are thrown aside and the dark volume of secrets is opened to the light. . ."

"Destroying whatever was good about ourselves," the Chalaine said, understanding the tack of Gen's explanation.

"Or perhaps differently said, degrading what was good to ourselves, or what good we leave behind, by enslaving it to the debt incurred by our dishonorable actions," Gen added.

"What is the Secret Law, then?"

"Whatever law you invent for yourself, the law you really judge yourself by. The law that makes you feel bad for doing something, not because someone else knows you did it, but because you know it was wrong. Or conversely, the law that lets you feel good about doing things a public law says you shouldn't."

"Now you are referring to Chertanne, I think."

"I assure you I am not. The lesson applies to everyone, though some fit my master's explanation of the story more snugly than others."

"One more question," the Chalaine continued after thinking for several moments. "Why would Shadan Khairn have you read such a book? What does all this talk of conscience and law have to do with training someone to be a killer?"

"I do not consider myself a killer, and I never said the Shadan had me read it."

"He was your master, wasn't he?"

"In the slave and master sense, yes."

"If it wasn't him that had you read it, who was the other master?" The Chalaine's curiosity was piqued, and she felt ashamed; she had not thought of the life Gen must have lived before Aughmere invaded his country. But just as Fenna had told her would happen, an immediate wall went up between her and Gen.

"Perhaps we should talk of it some other time, Holiness. I should concentrate on my duty. These are perilous times, and no doubt the Ilch is working against the betrothal. I beg leave to focus on the task at hand. You should probably enter your chambers—for safety."

The Chalaine had half a mind to force the matter, but Gen still intimidated her, and she backed down.

As the next two weeks limped by, the story remained with her, as did her conversation with Gen, which impelled her to rethink her earlier assessment of his nature. The frequency of public appearances in the Great Hall increased steadily, and she spent more time with Chertanne, taking his arm, talking superficially with him, curtseying to him, laughing at his jokes, at least the ones she could laugh at without offending her conscience. Listening to him and watching him convinced her that he had slit the throat of his conscience-servant and buried the body and the record books in the cellar a long time ago.

The day of the betrothal finally came, and she rose that morning with a knot in her stomach and a headache that started in her shoulders and throbbed up through her neck and skull. Eldwena, Fenna, and her mother told her over and over again that most women felt nervous on their betrothal day, but the Chalaine thought that only some few felt so for the same reasons as she.

She had nothing to do for the entire day until the afternoon when she would be primped and dressed for the evening ceremony. They wouldn't allow her outside the Great Hall today until the trip to the Chapel, which meant the whole of her entertainments had to be found in either her room, the indoor gardens, or the library. Out of kindness to Fenna, the Chalaine agreed to go with her to the library to see if they could encounter Gen so her handmaiden could work at him a little more. Jaron trailed along behind, face bemused. He was well aware of Fenna's quest for Gen's attention and enjoyed their plotting from a distance.

But when they arrived, Gen had already fallen asleep on "Gen's couch," as Obard called it, embracing his sword in his usual fashion. The lack of books on the floor showed he had gone straight to sleep rather than reading first, and Fenna was a little disappointed. Two scullery maids skulked around the shelves of books, whispering and giggling, minds on anything but reading. Jaron scowled at them, and they scampered off, leaving the library empty save for the four of them and Pureman Obard.

"Perhaps we should read a little," the Chalaine suggested. "I need something to take my mind off . . . things."

After getting some recommendations from Obard, they both settled in on the couch opposite Gen, and despite the calm and quiet, the Chalaine had difficulty concentrating. If only Chertanne had some redeeming quality she could hang on to. She fancied herself spoiled by years of association with men of quality, only the best, chosen to guard her. She wondered if regular women leading normal lives had many good choices of men or were forced to accept the hand of men who only sought to please themselves.

A quiet groan from Gen ended any pretense at reading altogether. Everyone turned their attention to him, faces concerned and curious. Gen gripped the hilt of his sword so intensely that his knuckles whitened, and on his face smooth calm was replaced with sadness. A tear ran down a jagged line of scars on his cheek, and he calmed, grip relaxing.

"We should wake him," the Chalaine suggested, feeling pity. "He's obviously in some nightmare."

Fenna put her book down and walked toward him.

"Don't get too close, Lady Fairedale," Jaron warned. "He is quick with the blade. Do not startle him from sleep."

The Chalaine couldn't be sure her handmaiden even

heard the suggestion. Her concentration stayed on Gen. Kneeling by him, she placed her hand gently on his, and at her touch, his eyes snapped open and his face went back to its usual expressionless state. He looked at Fenna, then raised his hand to his face to feel the wetness.

"Are you feeling well, Gen?" Fenna asked softly. "I think you were dreaming."

Gen pushed himself to a sitting position, concentrating for a moment before standing and buckling his sword belt. "I am well, Lady Fairedale. I thank you for your concern." The Chalaine couldn't believe how quickly he could shed emotion. "I should take my rest in my quarters rather than the library. I'm sorry to have disturbed you. I will see you both this evening. Chalaine, Miss Fairedale, Jaron." He bowed and left quickly. Fenna watched him go, and the Chalaine saw frustration dawn on her face.

"He will tell me nothing," she complained quietly. "How can I love such a mystery?"

The Chalaine came to her handmaiden and lifted her by the hand, hugging her gently. The Chalaine wanted to tell her to forget Gen, to love Kimdan as she always had, and be happy, but she couldn't. Instead, she shared Fenna's curiosity. Gen kept a lot of himself locked away, and the Chalaine realized she had judged her quiet protector too harshly and in the wrong light.

"Don't worry too much, Miss," Jaron soothed, oddly affectionate. "We all know Gen suffered much pain at Shadan Khairn's hand in his homeland. The pain is yet too near for him to say much. Time will soften the edge and loosen his tongue. Before you know it, you won't be able to shut him up."

Fenna smiled and wiped her eyes, giving Jaron a thankful hug. The Chalaine could see he felt awkward, and she couldn't help but smile. Jaron, a veteran soldier, would have preferred a room full of Uyumaak than the overt gratitude of a young woman.

The rest of the day, the Chalaine spent walking and conversing with Fenna in the gardens and the hallways. They saw Chertanne once, evading him before he noticed their presence. Just seeing him again put the Chalaine in poor spirits, and after taking lunch on the balcony in the Great Hall with her mother, she retired to her chambers and napped before starting preparations for the betrothal.

Later, after two hours of grooming and dressing, the Chalaine willed the Walls to show her the courtyard. Two thick lines of people gathered from the Great Hall to the Chapel with candles and lanterns, forming a broad avenue of light down which she and Chertanne would ride on a white horse. It was the first night of autumn, and those gathered bundled themselves in cloaks and hats against the chill. A wind would gust from time to time, blowing leaves from the castle gardens about and extinguishing any flame not protected by some device. In spite of these inconveniences, the people smiled and laughed, festive and anxious.

The Chalaine wished she could feel the same. While not the formal bond of marriage, the betrothal was as binding as the marriage vow, and her bond to Chertanne, her duty, gave her no happiness. Now that the time had come, she barely felt alive, an emotional rigor deadening her spirit. From somewhere, she knew, she would need to call forth the vitality to survive the week of joint feasting and joint appearances that would follow the betrothal, but now, with Chertanne waiting, that source of strength was distant and unseen.

Fenna's presence comforted her, the young handmaiden humming to herself as she pushed and prodded wayward curls in the Chalaine's hair, hair that no one would see because of the all-covering shroud she wore. Fortunately, that same veil would hide the unhappy face that stared back at her when she looked in the mirror. The betrothal dress was a formless, loose fitting white gown sown from a silky material that would do her little good against the cold; for that, a heavier cloak, also bleached white, had been provided for her warmth.

"There," Fenna said, putting the brush on the table, "all done. Let's get you veiled and wrapped and you'll be ready."

Ready indeed, the Chalaine thought, feeling sick. She said nothing as Fenna placed the veil on her head and helped her into the cloak. Her handmaiden often acted oblivious to the fact that she couldn't stand her fiancé, though she was certain Fenna knew better. Looking one last time in the mirror, the Chalaine couldn't help but feel like a big snowball.

She willed the Walls off, and the picture of the courtyard faded. "Let's go."

Fenna hugged her, encouraging her, and the Chalaine fought off depression as best she could so she would appear resolute and vibrant for the people to whom she was an example. It would be difficult to fool anyone who knew her, but her act, she thought, would be enough for the commoners and nobles who knew her not at all save the legends and stories they had heard or imagined for themselves.

She was to be the Holy Mother. She would bear the child. The child would save the world. She had to go through with it. Even if she found the man repugnant, she must put her life and her future in his plump hands and embrace a future of loneliness and misery.

It was her duty.

And it was time.

CHAPTER 23 - DEMON

"Hello, Gen!" Fenna exclaimed brightly as she opened the door. "Are you ready to accompany the two most ravishing ladies in Rhugoth?"

For the first time in hours, the Chalaine grinned, though briefly. Fenna's attempts to get Gen to notice her always cheered her up, although she couldn't fathom why they should. Gen bowed at the waist. He was handsomely dressed in a formal coat made for the occasion, all black save for silver trimming and a silver pin on his collar in the shape of a sword covering the eclipsed moon of Trys.

"Chalaine. Lady Fairedale. I am ready to serve."

As always, Gen's face and tone were unreadable, but after the incident in the library, Fenna tried to act as happy as she could with Gen's niggardly approach to nonverbal information.

"I do, however, have some concerns," Gen continued as the Chalaine led them toward the maze.

"And what might those be, Gen?" the Chalaine asked, voice distant.

"First," Gen outlined, "I do not like this business of you riding on the horse." *That makes two of us,* the Chalaine thought. Gen continued, "You are the only ones that will be a-horse in this procession, putting you higher than those who defend you and trapping us in the middle of the mob. Secondly, riding exposed at night in the middle of a well-lit courtyard is doubly worse, since you will be easy to see, and any archers some distance away will be practically invisible to us."

The Chalaine didn't look at him, eyes forward as they negotiated the maze. "Gen, if you can somehow undo decades of planning in the next few minutes, then do so with my blessing." She regretted her tone, but had no other to offer.

"Very well," Gen accepted flatly. "I will be walking at your left side. At the first hint of trouble, I will push the Ha'Ulrich off the horse and ride you away from the crowd and to safety."

Fenna laughed, though Gen's tone was absolutely serious. The Chalaine pictured Gen dumping Chertanne unceremoniously onto the ground and galloping off with her and had to admit it made her feel better, whether he meant it to or not.

As they exited the maze into the Antechamber, the rest of the Dark Guard, Captain Tolbrook proudly in command, filled in around her in a protective circle. Jaron and her mother were there as well. Jaron took his place with Gen in the Chalaine's inner circle, while her mother and Fenna were forced to walk behind. Cadaen walked behind them. After entering the castle proper, her protective ranks were again swelled by the apprentices to the Dark Guard, Kimdan proudly ordering them into formation with a wink to Fenna.

Such a large entourage was difficult to manage in some of the narrower halls, but soon the smaller passageways gave way to the wide, sweeping halls that went around the Great Hall and ended in the ornate double doors that opened into the courtyard. The halls were filled with servants preparing food for the betrothal feast afterward, though they scrambled out of the way at the sight of so many imposing warriors. Last to join them was Ethris, who stood, Staff in hand, at the doors with the Chamberlain. He was, as on the day of the Trials, dressed in clothing white enough to rival that of the Chalaine.

She waited as the guard fell off to the side, forming a path to the door, all save Gen, who remained, as he ever was, just behind and to the right of her.

The Chamberlain tapped his staff on the floor loudly three times. "Open the door for the Chalaine, the most Holy, the Mother of God."

The doors swung inward slowly and silently. A chill gust of wind blew brightly colored leaves about the floor, ruffling her veil and giving her goosebumps despite her cloak.

A great cheer went up, and the Chalaine walked forward stiffly, Gen following close behind. Before her was the great corridor of light spanning the long courtyard all the way to the Chapel on the other side. In the distance, visible on the steps to the Chapel, was Chertanne astride a tall black horse. He, too, was dressed in white, and at the opening of the doors he rode forward slowly, a protective ring of his own guard forming about him. Chants of "save us" and "bless me" rose in swells from the crowd, and Chertanne waved and smiled, soaking up the adoration.

The Chalaine felt her stomach wrench as he approached, taking his time as if to make her wait. But all too soon he was there before her, smiling grandly. He dismounted and bowed as deeply as his gut would comfortably permit, extending a white-gloved hand.

"Come Chalaine!" he invited enthusiastically. "The people and our betrothal await. I'm afraid your zealous guard will have to let me touch you just a little lest I be accused of letting you fall from the horse. It is rather spirited."

The Chalaine took the proffered hand, and Chertanne

helped her to sit sidesaddle. Gen approached and Chertanne's guards stiffened. No one took Gen lightly any more. At last the Blessed One mounted, placing his arm around the Chalaine's waist. To everyone's surprise, he galloped away, leaving all protection and ceremony behind, thundering across the courtyard to raucous applause from the crowd and a number of oaths from the Dark Guard.

Chertanne rode back and forth, circling around to wave to the crowd before galloping forward again. From her unsteady perch, all the guards trying to catch up, Gen sprinting to lead the charge. But before they could get close, Chertanne would spur just ahead again. By the time he reined in the horse at the steps of the Chapel, the Chalaine felt ill-used and didn't wait to be helped down. The Pontiff was there along with several Puremen, and they bowed deeply as Chertanne dismounted and handed the reins to an acolyte.

"I hope you enjoyed the ride, Milady," Chertanne joked sarcastically.

"I don't think I've seen a horse handled more poorly, if I must be honest; and I suppose I should, in the presence of so many holy men. The ride's only virtue was its brevity."

"As I hope this ceremony is," Chertanne whispered, coming close. "The night is young and too full of promise to spend in an old Church."

The Chalaine remained silent as everyone waited for the rest of the assembly. Gen arrived first, expressionless, though staring at the Blessed One so intently that the latter turned away and pretended to oversee the care of the horse. It took several minutes for the entire entourage to gather on the steps and regain their composure.

Not many were allowed into the ceremony. The Dark Guard and Chertanne's soldiers were placed around the entrances and exits, bolstered by Rhugoth's own soldiers. Gen was permitted to enter with the Chalaine, as Dason was for Chertanne. The Chalaine invited Fenna to come with her, and a modestly sized group of nobles and Churchmen from all three of the human kingdoms had entered previously. The most notable absence, the Chalaine knew, was Chertanne's father. She had learned that Torbrand had never really been close to his son. Even if he were, he was terribly busy trying to battle his way through the heart of Tolnor before another winter hit.

The Pontiff signaled everyone to enter the narthex. The heavy oaken doors to the Chapel were shut behind them, and Puremen led guests through side hallways and entrances to be seated. The Chalaine and Chertanne, each with their protector, were told to stay with the Pontiff for the procession. Fenna squeezed the Chalaine's arm as she left, whispering, "Good luck. I'll be waiting for you up front."

The Chalaine watched over her shoulder as the Puremen chanted, warding the doors against evil and assault. Gen stared into the back of Chertanne's head as if trying to determine the best way to whack it off.

"It inspires and gratifies me to see you together," the Pontiff said, grasping the Chalaine and Chertanne by the hand. The Pontiff was an old man, wrinkled, gray, and gaunt, but he possessed a kind aspect. He would undertake the long, treacherous journey to the Hall of Three Moons with them in the spring for the marriage, though the Chalaine didn't know how one as old as he would survive it. The expeditions sent to find the Hall in the abandoned city of Elde Luri Mora had all taken casualties and suffered much privation. She wasn't even sure if she could withstand the trip.

"I thank you, Holy Father," the Chalaine said, curtsying. "It as honor to see you again after all these years."

Chertanne inclined his head briefly but said nothing.

The Pontiff straightened, leaning on his staff. "I shall lead you both forward. After my sermon, I will ask both of you to come before the altar and I will recite the oath of betrothal. I'm sure you know it well. Remember that the only answer you need give is 'Under Eldaloth's watchful eye, I swear' and everything will be well. And most of all, be at ease. You are in a house of God doing God's work."

The Chalaine imagined he gave much the same speech to every nervous couple he betrothed. She wondered if he'd had any report of the difficulty between her and Chertanne—or if he cared.

The Pontiff turned, rapping on the dark wooden doors with his staff. At once they swung open and all talk inside died down. The Chapel was one of the first structures built after the people who fled westward from Lal'Manar settled Mikmir. Unlike the fine white marble interiors of other buildings inside the castle walls, the Chapel was made of rough, dark gray stones and heavy pillars hewn from quarries in the Cathedral Mountains to the north. The roof arched high, supported by heavy wooden rafters from which hung three sets of chandeliers. More light was provided by lanterns that hung from the walls and pillars, casting a bright yellow glow about the room.

Everyone rose as the Pontiff led the couple and their guards down the center aisle that split thin rows of oaken pews. Flower petals, preserved fresh against the season, were strewn thickly about the floor, and as the Chalaine walked, she could smell their fragrance rise as their footsteps crushed them. Everyone watched reverentially, heads bowed.

The aisle terminated at the foot of a raised dais. From the dais rose a stone altar, now covered with a finely embroidered cloth made of red silk. The Pontiff signaled that the Chalaine and Chertanne should sit together, the Chalaine to the right of her fiancé. The First Mother sat to the Chalaine's right, and Fenna after. Gen stood at attention at the end of the row, Dason on the opposite side. The Chalaine gripped her mother's hand and leaned on her as the Pontiff struggled up the short stairs to the dais with the help of an acolyte. Once he managed to get to the altar, he signaled for all to be seated.

"My brothers and sisters in Eldaloth," the Pontiff began, his powerful voice belying his age, "I welcome you to this most blessed event. I welcome nobles from all three kingdoms here this night, a sight not often seen in Ki'hal. I would ask that you put aside grudges and hatreds tonight, especially between countries that are warring, that we might be unrestrained in feeling of Eldaloth's presence."

The Chalaine's mind wandered as the Pontiff delivered a long discourse outlining the history and prophecy that she had known—and recited—since she could speak. Her mother also seemed lost in thought, and after one look at Fenna, the Chalaine doubted her handmaiden's mind dwelt much on the holy. Instead, she seemed preoccupied with finding ways to provoke a glance from Gen. Gen's studied disinterest could not be broken, and Fenna whispered that wooing Gen was like trying to woo a rock.

While the Chalaine figured she should be irritated by Fenna's obsession and nonstop conversation about the young man, she instead found them a rather pleasant diversion from her own concerns and whispered in return a promise to help Fenna find devious ways to spark Gen's attention. Unfortunately, the Chalaine had even less experience than Fenna in such matters and doubted she would tender much useful assistance. At the very least, the attempts would prove amusing, and getting Gen to show some shred of emotion—even if utter disgust instead of swooning love—would be a victory.

"All rise," the Pontiff commanded, and the Chalaine shook herself out of her musings and decided she should pay better attention. Chertanne also rose slowly, and he took time to tuck his shirt back into his pants while the Pontiff began the familiar ritual of praise.

"It is by faith, my dear children," the Pontiff said, "that

we have arrived at this point in history where the great events preceding the return of our God Eldaloth are before us. Chant with me now our praise:

> *"Praise be to Eldaloth, God of all,*
> *Creator of all,*
> *Protector of all,*
> *Father of all.*
>
> *Praise be to the Ha'Ulrich of Eldaloth,*
> *Ilch's bane,*
> *Gatherer of the Nations,*
> *Father of the Return.*
>
> *Praise be to the Chalaine of Eldaloth,*
> *Healer of mind, body, and soul,*
> *Divine beauty incarnate,*
> *Mother of God."*

The congregation chanted with the Pontiff. The Chalaine always felt strange when praising herself, and over time, it became harder to envision herself as the woman in the prophecies. That woman was holy and powerful while the Chalaine felt increasingly like a stranger to choice and dignity.

The Pontiff waved them down. "You may be seated. It is an honor for all of us to be here in the presence of the instruments of Eldaloth for the working of his will. It was by the treachery of Mikkik that our God was taken from us. It was through Eldaloth's will that Trys was darkened that we might be protected from the power of the Evil One, and it was through his mysterious means that these two were born to bring forth a tabernacle worthy for his return. May we never be weary in our watch against evil, against the machinations of the Ilch. All rise."

Once again the congregation rose and repeated the

chant, and again they were seated as the Pontiff continued.

"We must remember that Eldaloth's murder and the murder of the Gods that served him came about through the wickedness of one who should have been faithful and grateful to his master and was not. We must also obey all the commands of Eldaloth, lest we too become servants of evil and partake of the bitter pains of the Underworld."

The Chalaine couldn't tell for sure, but it seemed as if the Pontiff stared directly at Chertanne, who studied floor with his head in his hands. "But God's purposes cannot be frustrated. For there are always those willing to serve him at great cost, and through great faith they put down the forces of darkness. All rise."

A third time, the congregation rose and chanted, but as "Mother of God" sounded to end the chant, a deep rumble shook the building, and the air turned instantly and bitterly chill. Exclamations of fear came from those who could find a voice. The Chalaine found Gen at her side immediately, pulling her off the bench and toward a doorway to their right as the building continued to shudder and heave. Her mother, Fenna, Chertanne, and many others followed close behind them as the shaking sent showers of stones and debris raining down from the roof.

Before she could think to be afraid, Gen pushed her to on the ground and under a pew. Fenna came soon after, also helped by Gen, and the Chalaine clung to her as stones shattered around them and slammed into the bench above their heads. Screams of pain mingled with the cacophony as the deep rumble continued, the air filling with dust and the floor with debris. Abruptly, the rumbling stopped, though the cold remained. A thin mist gathered on the floor, mixing with the cloud of dust.

The Chalaine pushed Fenna out and scrambled from underneath the bench. She found that the combination of her veil and the dust and darkness practically blinded her. All three of the chandeliers had fallen, and all but two of the lanterns lay smashed and smoldering. She floundered, feeling unbalanced, and tried find something to steady herself with. Gen grabbed her with one arm and she took Fenna by the hand. Cries and howls of pain echoed unnaturally in the murky gloom.

"Is my mother alive? Where is she?"

"I am here, my daughter. I am well, as is the Blessed One. We must get out! This doorway has collapsed. I cannot see the others clearly."

"I must stay and help the wounded, mother," the Chalaine protested.

"You will not," Gen stated. "There is something wrong here. We must leave immediately."

"Gen is right, my child," her mother agreed. "You must go!"

Gen guided the Chalaine back toward the center aisle, trying to help her over the wreckage and the bodies on the floor. As they neared the altar, the Chalaine heard Ethris chanting. A globe of blinding light appeared in the center of the rafters, illuminating the scene below and dispelling the shadows.

Chunks of the stone and woodwork that made up the ceiling had fallen to the floor with enough force to shatter some of the heavy oaken pews. Peculiarly, however, the bright light revealed that all exits to the Chapel had collapsed, trapping the congregation inside. Those who were able frantically lifted stone and wood to extricate the wounded from the rubble, while others worked at removing stones from the doorways.

"Something is not right. Something is coming," Gen muttered, mostly to himself, his head darting about, searching for some enemy or some explanation. Her defender's left arm was broken and bleeding, hanging lifelessly at his side. Fenna noticed the same.

"Gen! You're hurt!" she exclaimed. Gen raised a finger on his good hand to silence her, uncaring of the injury he'd sustained. The Chalaine moved forward to heal him, but he gently pushed her back, his concentration fixed upon the floor. He had come to some realization.

"Save your strength, Chalaine. Get to the dais. Heal the Pontiff if he lives and do it quickly. It is the only way we will survive."

In the blink of an eye, Gen's sword was in his good hand. "May Eldaloth help us," he said, breaking from his usual flat tone, which frightened her; anything that Gen feared must be dreadful, indeed.

The Chalaine turned toward the raised dais where the altar was and where the Pontiff had stood. A pile of rubble was there now, a frantic Ethris digging through it.

"What is it, Gen?" she asked.

"Go!" Gen commanded.

His urgency propelled her forward, Fenna and her mother helping. As she neared the dais, a painful buzzing sound filled her ears, and a strange circular pattern, appearing from etched grooves in the tiles of the Chapel, sprang to life, glowing with the color of flame. An otherworldly dread gripped her heart and she stopped, paralyzed by fear and unable to move. Everyone in the room froze—everyone except Ethris and Gen.

"You must go! It is our only chance," Gen ordered again, turning and forcing her eyes to meet his. His powerful voice cut through the buzzing, and she felt herself freed, though still numb and trembling. Fenna, her mother, and the Blessed One remained rooted where they stood, transfixed upon the swirling pattern. The Chalaine tore her eyes away from it, and, after mounting the dais, she knelt on the floor next to Ethris, grabbing and pulling at rock and wood with all the speed she could manage.

"We must be quick, child," Ethris said, laboring. "The Pontiff is our only escape."

"I know," the Chalaine replied. "Gen told me." Ethris's eyes met hers her briefly, face dirty and grave.

"Did he, now?"

As they dug, the buzzing grew louder and then died, replaced by a wail so full of hate that the Chalaine fell to the ground and wrapped herself into a ball.

"Be strong, girl," Ethris said forcefully. "Stay with me. Fight it!" Gritting her teeth, the Chalaine fought back her fear, and she rose to her knees and surveyed the room. Only Gen remained standing, sword at the ready. Everyone else had fallen to the floor, some unconscious, others writhing in terror. In the center of the room the swirling pattern faded, replaced by a circular hole into an abyss so black that it sucked in all the light coming from Ethris's globe. With renewed energy, the Chalaine set to the task of uncovering the Pontiff, hoping that something of life remained in him to be healed.

Abruptly, all noise stopped and the chill left, but the sense of dread doubled. The Chalaine turned again, feeling compelled against her will to acknowledge the presence of what had arrived. In the middle of the Chapel it stood, as black as the hole it had come from. Dull metallic bands reflected what illumination was left from Ethris's light.

The demon loomed a full twelve feet tall, a mass of spikes and blades covering its body, arms, and legs. A rank, oily substance dripped from it and onto the floor, and within the depths of the over-sized helmet was darkness. It seemed dead and unmoving while emanating a silent but palpable command to fear and fall.

Gen stood directly in front of it, surrounded by rubble and crushed bodies, dwarfed and alone. His broken arm bled at his side, and, as she watched, he turned toward her. For the first time since she had known him, she understood the expression on his face, even in the poor light. He knew he was going to die. He had turned to her to remember the reason why.

The Chalaine held his gaze for the brief moment he offered it, and as he turned away, two ember-orange eyes sparked to flame within the monster, an evil force aborning inside the steel encasement. Metal scales whined as it straightened itself, and an oily, black smoke from some internal fire issued from the joints of its armor, half-obscuring it in a dark fog.

"Help me, child! I have found him!" Ethris yelled urgently. With effort, the Chalaine turned away from Gen and the demon to see that Ethris had uncovered one arm. She began pulling debris from where she surmised the Pontiff's face would be.

"Eriss urma iggott shant daiyo!" The voice was otherworldly, deep, and full of wrath. The language, while unknown to the Chalaine, felt ancient.

"Umiel! Umiel owa' lien shura Elde joleia ho!" The voice was Gen's, confident and forceful. The language he spoke was different from his enemy's—fair, though foreign.

Ethris perked up at Gen's words. "That boy has a lot of explaining to do," he grumbled as at last the Pontiff's bruised and bleeding face was revealed in the weak light. "Quickly. Does he live, Chalaine?"

The Chalaine placed her hand on the wrinkled forehead.

"Torka bilex ur madda Ilch! Ilch-madda fen-gur enea ko! Chak Diggat, chak Ilch Murmit Cho!" The creature said this, and Ethris was so shocked by what he heard that he turned toward the demon.

The Chalaine followed his gaze. Gen waited, feet planted, as the creature took its first step forward toward him. The heavy footfall sent a shiver through the building. More rock tumbled from the ceiling as Gen sprang forward, hacking uselessly at the demon, which did nothing to defend itself. Gen's sword skipped off the oil slick spikes and plating, and, as he tried to thrust it into a gap in the armor, the sword altogether shattered.

"Hurry, child! Gen knows he cannot win," Ethris urged, though distracted. "It cannot be."

The last was said to no one in particular and with a note

of amazement. The Chalaine laid her hand upon the Pontiff's head and tried to shut out the rest of the world, which proved difficult. With concentrated effort, what was happening on the outside gradually faded away and she searched for what remained of life in the man before her.

"He lives!" she exclaimed, coming out of her trance. "But barely." Ethris, however, was no longer listening or near the Pontiff; he had moved to the foot of the altar rubble, chanting desperately. Thunderous footsteps boomed ever closer. Gen lay face down on a pile of rubble, bleeding profusely, arms and legs broken and bent at wild angles.

"Gen!" the Chalaine screamed.

By Ethris's art, a translucent globe of hardened air surrounded her, Ethris, and the fallen Pontiff. The dust inside the packed air swirled, outlining the barrier's shape in the light.

Ethris turned his head to her. "Work quickly, Chalaine. This ward will only hold it for a few moments."

His voice was barely controlled. Sweat ran in rivulets through the dirt on his face. The Chalaine again laid her hands upon the Pontiff, letting the booming footsteps, the howls of rage, and the impact of the creature's fury on the protective globe fade away. The Pontiff's life ebbed low, and she knew that healing him would exhaust her strength, leaving her nothing with which she might heal Gen or—at the very least—keep him from death.

And she hesitated. Some part of her still felt she owed a debt to her young protector, and she couldn't bear the thought of Fenna's pain at his loss. In her mind's eye she tried to remember his condition, trying to determine if he would live without her healing or if he were dead already. Indecision gripped her, but in her mind she pictured Gen as he was the night when he had defeated Cormith, a gash bleeding across his chest. He'd risked his life for her honor. He would do it now for her life. Doubt fled.

The Chalaine reached deep within herself and poured her life energy into the Pontiff until there was nothing left to give. Dizziness overtook her, and she fell hard against a pile of stone and wood.

She came to herself moments later, weak, drained of energy and unable to move. Before her the creature raged, a giant, spiked fist slamming down over and over as Ethris chanted and exerted his power to maintain the warding globe.

The Pontiff, dazed and surprised at what he saw before him, extricated himself from the rubble and stood just as the monster broke the shield. Ethris leapt forward as the Pontiff frantically started his ritual, and the Magician paid for his attempt at distraction with a puncturing hit to the midsection that sent him across the room and into a wall. He fell and did not move.

The creature stood so close now that the Chalaine could smell it, foul and sulfurous. It fixed its gaze upon her and started to step forward when a swirling pattern formed under its feet.

"Bosh! Humikk, Bosh!"

Its angry yells shook the walls, and as the Pontiff continued to chant, the chill returned to the air and the black hole opened. The Pontiff was gesturing quickly now, eyes closed and arms extended. The demon strove to escape the swirling hole beneath it, pushing forward with its might. The Pontiff chanted louder, arms shaking.

His eyes flew open. "You are finished!" The hole swallowed the abomination, which disappeared with a ground shaking rumble. The hole closed, and the Pontiff fell to his knees. All at once, cries and exclamations filled the Chapel as the creature's hold upon its victims ended.

"Are you all right, child?" the Pontiff asked as he crawled to her side. The Chalaine could hardly think, mind in a chaos born from terror and sadness.

"Help Gen," she cried. "Help him."

"Your protector? Where is he?" The Chalaine could barely manage to move her arm to point where his body lay, Fenna there already, distraught and crying for help. The Pontiff struggled to his feet and left as Mirelle, Regent Ogbith, and Cadaen hurried to her side and knelt around her. Chertanne stood behind them, face pale and pants soiled with urine and dirt. Questions came at her from all sides and her vision blurred. She clutched her mother, and everything went black.

Be sure to catch the entire Trysmoon Saga!

Trysmoon Book One: Ascension
Trysmoon Book Two: Duty
Trysmoon Book Three: Hunted
Trysmoon Book Four: Sacrifice

Get more information at briankfullerbooks.com

22020502R00212

Made in the USA
San Bernardino, CA
16 June 2015